FRAGMENTED SOULS

KASHA ROSS

Fragmented Souls
Copyright ©2021 Kasha Ross

Edited by Nancy Tamblyn

All rights reserved. This book or any portion thereof may not be reproduced or used in any manner whatsoever without the express written permission of the publisher except for the use of brief quotations in a book review.

ISBN: 978-1-66780-800-0 (print)

ISBN: 978-1-66780-801-7 (eBook)

PROLOGUE
(20 YEARS AGO)

Icy sheets of rain soak through Noah's only sweater and pair of jeans. Puddles form in seconds, turning to quicksand-like mud that fills his hole-ridden shoes. Today, Noah turns seventeen, an age that has at times seemed unlikely for him to reach. Usually, he'd be with the two people he loves most, sharing a piece of chocolate cake on the roof of the tall, less-guarded glass building. Instead, he's forced to stand amongst a claustrophobic crowd of a million people who smell of rot and onions, kept in place by Hunters: so-called law enforcers, who are the eyes and ears for the leaders. The Hunters arrest the innocent, team up with criminals, steal, beat and kill anyone in sight because to them, it is fun, as if it were a game.

Noah keeps his elbows pointed out, and his feet cemented to the ground as bodies push against him, each person either fighting for room or fighting to hide behind those bigger than themselves. The citizens drawn toward this gathering occupy the streets and empty places, pressing close to the glistening glass buildings, anxiously awaiting new laws to be announced.

A nimble hand slips into Noah's as his girlfriend reaches him through the crowd. She's always able to find Noah, even when he tries so hard to keep her away from these situations. The stress in Noah's chest grows thicker along with the air as he pulls Ophelia closer, kissing the top of her head, her hair pressed flat and made darker by the rain. She draws circles on the back of his hand, knowing that this time, it won't calm him down.

Three floating billboards move in front of the buildings, positioned to display three men in a way that forces the citizens' eyes toward them, even those who cower behind drawn curtains.

The most powerful leader of the three sits in the middle, the other two shying away, allowing him to hold the crowd with his presence. He smiles, his demeanor rehearsed and manipulated to make him seem pleasant, though, even if he wore a mask, it wouldn't stop his cruelty from showing. Eyes always give away a person's true nature.

No one cheers when they appear. A collective breath is drawn in as people try to stay silent and invisible. Before the leaders address the crowd, all eyes obediently move to watch as two Hunters drag a hooded man to the front of the crowd, placing him on a wooden pedestal for all to see.

The leader in the center, Boris, opens his mouth, the slightly amused smile hiding at the corner of his lips, only hinting at his cruelty. "As we all know just two days ago, one hundred people were banished into the trees for — threatening us, your beloved leaders..."

Everyone stares blankly at the hooded man whose hands are tied behind his back. His shirt is torn and bloody, chest shaking as he openly sobs in front of the crowd. It is true that one hundred people were banished into the trees, but everyone knows it was only for beginning to talk of voting new leaders into power — and although a change in leadership is necessary to the people's survival, they bite their tongues and pinch their lips, too scared to say anything.

"...Therefore he must accept the fate he brought upon himself," Boris says, his voice lost in the echo of a gunshot and the man's body splashing into a deep mud puddle. Ophelia turns into Noah as a woman screams, everyone in proximity begging her to stay quiet, to keep from running to her loved one. "What a shame," Boris clicks his tongue, acting as if he watched the man die. No one turns away, not even when a Hunter steps onto the pedestal where the man's blood is still fresh, his body not yet cold as they drag him away. The Hunter holds something — someone bundled in wet blankets.

"As we have done before every gathering, we shall take in an orphan who lost his mother at birth. Two-year-old Aron is to be brought up in the towers, raised in comfort and wealth," the leader to Boris's right explains.

The crowd forces applause, feeling only lament for the child and the life he will be trained for. However, Noah stays still, knowing this adoption is not out of kindness but rather for Boris's benefit. Before every gathering, a person is killed to show how easy it is for the leaders to win and the citizens to be disposed of, and to display their seeming benevolence, a child is adopted. However, in this case, this infant is rumored to be sired from an affair Boris had with a Hunter after his wife passed away. Once word got out about this mistake, the Hunter mysteriously vanished, and Aron was deemed to be the child chosen to be liberated from a life in the city.

Noah holds Ophelia tighter, terrified of what is to come — that he might fail to protect his only family. The leaders are trying to buy obedience with little things that will win the citizens cooperation. However, no one knows how long the leaders can put out small fires when they expect people to live in an overcrowded city where the ghostly hands of death steal you from your front porch. Where citizens starve and turn on the people they once loved. Where people are beginning to think death is better than life.

Boris folds his hands together as the child is taken inside, and the citizens' attention returns to him. "Today marks the tenth year of our survival from the toxic gas released from Mother Earth's soul. The tenth year of our perseverance, despite the loss of cities, our homes, and especially our loved ones who perished. It also marks the day I scoured the earth looking for any survivors, risking my life to save you. I brought people to this forest, cutting down only the trees necessary to build our haven where you made me your leader." Boris pauses, waiting for applause, gratitude — but still, the people remain silent, frozen in place. "We are survivors who have lived among each other in peace. Yet, I am afraid we may turn against one another one day, as all humankind tends to do." A pleased glint sparkles in his eyes. The two other leaders share a wary, sad look before turning back to the citizens, pretending not to be anxious.

"Noah?" Ophelia whispers, pulling on his sleeve, trying to meet his eyes, but Noah shakes his head slightly, knowing that anything they say among this crowd could be overheard and used against them.

"I bring you good news. Over the past couple of months, five towns have been built around the city, all separated from each other and from us by a thick wall of trees to ensure privacy. If people wish to travel to the city or other towns, they may use the one road that connects us all," Boris says.

"Privacy," Noah grunts as quietly as he can into Ophelia's ear, risking being overheard, "More like a way to keep us apart and prevent us from getting together quickly to overthrow the leaders."

"Four thousand chosen people will be sent to each town in five days. You will be informed by tonight," the leader to Boris's left says, addressing his hands rather than the audience.

The crowd erupts into murmurs, expressing their thoughts and concerns, some naive, some angry. Boris raises his hands, asking for silence. Only a small group fails to obey his order.

"The second piece of good news is that you will now have a chance to gain immunity from the unknowns who beat and kill innocent people." Boris purses his lips, blatantly acting as if those unknowns aren't his law enforcers, his Hunters. He's outwardly gloating that no one can or would dare to challenge him, not even his fellow leaders. "We will now have rankings and gangs will be formed. Anyone allowed to create or join. Anyone allowed to be on their own and not participate. Gangs will fight once a week both in the towns and city. Winning gangs will move up in the rankings. The top five gangs in each town and the top ten in the city will receive immunity, and extra food. I will give you one week to form your gangs and after that, the fights will begin. Choose wisely." Boris smiles as the screens fade to nothing and float away.

Noah watches as the Hunters holding shiny batons and large guns surround the crowd, shoving, herding people away from the towers. It reminds him of the way police dealt with protesters before they died from the treacherous gas catastrophe. Noah wasn't even eight yet when It happened. He can barely remember it, but the law enforcers and incompetent leadership lacked the skills to prevent the destruction of the world — to save their people. Today, nothing has changed.

The day death lay waste to the world, Mother earth was angry with the people, for they took everything from her, never caring to give anything in return. She gave them chance after chance to redeem themselves, but of course, they did nothing. In a moment of pure disgust and irritation, Mother Earth spread toxins through the air, sparing only what she had created, such as animals and trees. She suffocated the guilty, stalled engines, sent buildings to the ground and plunged the world into darkness. She killed almost eight billion people, the population dropping to fifty thousand in weeks, leaving the survivors to wish they had died like the rest.

The crowd begins to disperse except for a small group, the same group who failed to fall quiet when everyone else did. Suddenly they surge toward the Hunters, screaming in defiance. Gunshots echo off the buildings. Random people begin to fall.

"Noah!" Ophelia panics as the world erupts into chaos. People push, grab and trample bodies as they slip in the mud, trying to get away, trying to stay alive. Noah grabs Ophelia's arm, holding on for dear life — protecting her from the elbows and hands, keeping their heads down, praying that their shoes keep their grip and hoping their faces don't meet the earth.

As evening replaces the sun and scatters the night with stars, Noah sits atop the roof of the orphanage where both he and Ophelia live. He holds Ophelia as she sleeps, thin twisted wire around both their ring fingers. Footsteps shuffle behind Noah, but he doesn't jump or turn to see who they belong to. He doesn't want to wake her.

"Shh," he tells the boy who settles beside him, sighing as he leans back against the brick ledge.

Maddick, Noah's best friend of ten years asks, "Are you scared?" as he places a piece of rich chocolate cake between the two of them.

"Yes," Noah readily admits. He's never met anyone, besides Ophelia, who he trusts or cares for more than Maddick. For years, the two have protected each other during fights and run-ins with Hunters and have always stuck together. Most importantly, Maddick has never let Noah's most dangerous secret slip from his lips.

"You have to be even more careful now," Maddick whispers, handing Noah a fork, taking the first bite.

"I know," Noah nods, stroking his bride's hair. "Thank you — for being witness to the wedding," Noah sighs, wondering if he and Ophelia will regret their decision. Both knew they were too young to get married, but the only way they would be able to stay together and not be sent to separate towns was to sign a piece of paper binding them by law. That evening after escaping the Hunters' gunshots and the stampeding crowd, they got married. "Maddick, we can't keep living like this; we need a new ruler — we need a soul ruler."

"I know," Maddick sighs, losing his appetite, realizing what Noah means. Maddick slings an arm around Noah, the only person in the world who he sees as family and who doesn't hate him because of who his family is. "Today I was told that in two years my twin brother and I will be trained to replace two of the current leaders. So wait. Wait 'til you're nineteen before doing anything rash. See if things will get better. Let her live with no burdens." He points to Ophelia, watching as Noah pushes a strand of hair from her face. "If you were to start a family, bringing a baby into this world wouldn't be safe, whether it be a girl or boy. Not now, not ever, especially because of who you are. Wait two years and I will be able to get you out of here if need be and into the town I will be given to run. I'll be able to hide you, give you new identities, new names — and if you have a baby, I can make sure the baby remains hidden for as long as possible. I can keep them off the baby's trail until it's ready. Your children will never truly be safe. My brother isn't like me," Maddick mutters, looking up to the stars, wishing life could be different.

Noah pulls Maddick into a hug, careful not to move Ophelia. "Thank you," he chokes out, pretending not to notice the tears rolling down both their faces.

The two boys sit, eating their rich chocolate cake and listening as screams and fights echo below them. They understand nothing will get better. A new leader is necessary, one born from power. One with all the qualities a fair, level-headed leader requires. They need someone to rescue the humanity that is slowly being ripped from their souls as the seconds tick by.

CHAPTER 1

(HARLEY)

I remember what it felt like, to feel his anger, his hurt, his pain, as his knuckles collided with my skin, how my flesh split and warm-blood crawled down my cheek. I remember how his lips curled up when I refused to hit him back. It didn't hurt after the tenth punch. It never does anymore. I've become numb to the pain. My nerves, too overwhelmed with the constant stimulation, have given up on trying to tell me of the damage being caused.

So whenever they happen, the beatings, I start to count, wondering how many it will take or if one punch will knock me out. Isn't that the dream? Having the pain disappear after the first time you're introduced to it?

I remember the feeling of passing out and waking up on the carpet floor, an iron taste in my mouth, gravel-filled laughter feeding into my nauseating headache. I pushed through sweaty bodies and out the door into the streets, voices calling after me, mixing with their thundering party. I was so unaware of the threats lurking in the shadows, easily able to snatch me up on my way to my alley. On these disorienting nights, when I can't make it far, I fall unconscious on my mold-ridden couch. That's what I remember. That's what makes its way into my dreams as I start to regain consciousness.

"Harley — Harley!"

I try to open my eyes, still blurry with sleep. The stale air raises goosebumps on my arms, my skin blanketed by the morning dew. I push myself further into the couch, trying to rid myself of the unsettling chills brought on by last night.

"Harley."

I drift in and out of last-minute dreams before letting my eyes open, but only one does. Groggy, I follow the voice until I see a shadowy figure leaning against the chipped bricks. My heart knocks against my chest when I can't quite make the person out, but then he ruffles his fingers through his hair.

"Jimmy," I sigh, relieved that he isn't a three hundred pound Hunter coming to jump me.

"Parents fighting again?" His voice comes out weak and tired, as if he'd been yelling all night. He probably has. Jimmy Carter, the boy known to egg the shit-talkers on and shut them up with one punch, yet no one has ever seen him start a fight.

I nod, not ready to start my day. He scans my body, looking for anything out of place, and I do the same. His pale blue eyes sparkle as the rising sun stretches across his face, crystal against his golden skin, contrasting with the black hair that lies untidy across his forehead. His left hand is slightly bruised, not as bad as I've seen it, but his right is wrapped in a white t-shirt spotted with blood.

"Another fight!"

"Another win," he huffs.

He sits awkwardly against the brick wall, his lean muscular build fatigued and restless all at once. Dressed in worn jeans and a ratty button-up with the top two buttons missing, the shirt hangs lazily open, showing the thick scar on his chest. He's styled in a way that adds to how insanely handsome he is. It's the kind of handsome you'd whisper about to your best friend as he walks by. Jimmy says he doesn't notice, but I catch him flashing his goofy grin every time it happens.

"Let me check your hand," I offer, pushing myself up so my back presses against the wet cushions, the dew seeping through my shirt.

"Harley, are — are you okay?" Jimmy asks, leaning forward, his eyes shifting to my cheek. Momentarily forgetting his hand, I lift mine gingerly to my face, careful as I run my fingers over a tender bump just below my cheekbone, where dry blood makes the surface rough.

"I'm fine," I say, which is somewhat true. I can barely feel it, though that's probably not a good sign.

"What happened?" He stretches his hand toward me but lets it fall to his side, not sure if touching my face would hurt or help me. I want his hand to rest there because just his touch makes me feel a thousand different things.

"Nothing. Promise." I try to smile, but the movement only makes my cheek throb.

I start to stand and instantly regret it. Every damn muscle in my body screams at me as I strain to make my movements appear fluid, but apparently, they aren't ready to listen to my brain. Jimmy gets to his feet and, without saying anything, he pulls my arm over his shoulders, pressing my body against his and taking all the weight from my legs.

My body loosens as we start the walk to 'The Shed' through dusty streets, past cowering, underfed crowds of lonely people and gangs who start their day dreading the next. Jimmy lets me go, and I pretend not to flinch with every step as he pretends not to notice.

It's not much farther to The Shed, an old rusty abandoned barn on the corner of Brooks and Baker. Jimmy and I came across it when we were eight and on our way to fry worms. It's an ugly-looking thing, but it makes an impenetrable hideout. It's curtained by two willow trees whose branches intertwine with one another, weeping to the overgrown grass and shielded by six-inch thick bushes.

From the outside, it looks small, covered in weather-beaten wood, rusted window panes and missing shingles. Just the look of it couldn't appeal to the hollow imagination of adults. Though, if you are lucky enough to make it past the broken steps and the alarm system of slime and pinecones set by Rey Dezmend, our gang member with a mad scientist's mind who causes more issues than not, you'd think the door led to a different place. The inside is lined with cedar, 'borrowed' from Finn and Rey's job site, complemented by sidewalk furniture, lamps from the Opulent parts of town, two heaters and a Ziegler Mahal carpet that Tequila claims she found in the trash. (Though the mayor reported a missing, fairly expensive Ziegler carpet from his office days later. The security footage was mysteriously wiped and destroyed.) She managed to steal some solar panels to power the TV and lights, too.

If the Hunters actually cared to look into The Shed, we would all be sentenced to death or banishment. It's a good thing they're too busy beating people up to care. If not for The Shed, there would be no refuge for the five most important people in my life.

The walk from my alley to The Shed is an easy twenty minutes on a good day when we don't have to dodge the wrath of Hunters. Today, however, by the time we get there, I'm sweating profusely, my cheek has a heartbeat, and my head is pounding. So I stop, catch my breath, and prepare myself to go inside. I know I will not be blessed with an empty room and no questioning looks on the other side of that door. The Shed is basically Uri's home, and Tequila has probably already brought in stolen goods for everyone.

Jimmy pushes the door open, and I'm greeted with wide eyes and open-jawed stares. I guess the side of my face looks pretty bad.

"You okay? Let me take a look," Finn says, bringing his hands to my face. His sandy blond hair sticks up in weird places, never cared for. His eyes fix intensely on my face, allowing me to notice how the greens of his irises fade into yellow.

"I'm fine!" My voice comes out shakier than I want it to, but Finn doesn't notice. He only notices what needs to be healed.

"You have pretty heavy bruising. Your cheekbone doesn't seem to be fractured, not a deep laceration, so it doesn't need stitches and I don't think there's any damage to your eye, but we'll have to see when it opens up," he says, dropping his hands and moving on to treat Jimmy. "You should clean it, though," Finn says over his shoulder.

"Thank you," I mumble.

"What happened?" Tequila rubs her hand over my shoulder, directing her question more to her brother, Jimmy, than me. Tequila's twenty, the oldest and no more than 5'3", with elbows too pointy, ribs too noticeable and cheeks hollow. She turns from me, hitting me with her crimson hair that stops in a straight line at her shoulder blades, with not a piece longer than the next.

"I swear if someone asks me that one more time, I'm going to punch them!" I try to laugh, but the movement sends irritating pains through my ribs.

"Chill! Chill, champ!" Rey says, pretending to box, only to end up hitting Uri in the face.

"Whatever!" I snort.

Uri flashes me a gentle smile, no pity in his expression. His cropped coal-coloured hair blends with his skin and boldens the whites of his eyes, making his hazel irises appear as tranquil pools, scattered with gold mist. His eyes are my favorite feature. He tosses me a shirt to replace my blood-stained one.

They smile, going back to watching cartoons on our ancient TV and that's the reason I love them. They don't pry.

I walk into the bathroom, cringing when I see my reflection in the broken mirror. The left side of my face is a deep purple with a cut from the top of my cheekbone to my chin. My eye is sealed shut, and when I lift my shirt, dark red bruises line my ribs. I push on them, deciding nothing's broken.

I place my hands on the cold sink, steadying my tired body, my eye trained on my reflection. Brown hair falls in tangled waves across my sweaty, oily skin, and my pupils are still dilated from the adrenaline coursing through me. I always look like this; Uri calls it dysfunctional beauty. I call it a mess. I carelessly scrub my face clean, hoping to rid myself of last night's memories that threaten to crawl to the surface, but Jimmy's presence in the doorway and his steady breaths ease me a bit.

"If you want to know what happened, Eric was drunk, he and my mom were fighting, and I just got in the way. I'm fine. I can't feel anything anyway," I say, pretending to be annoyed. But honestly, telling Jimmy is like releasing all the pressure in my chest and remembering what it feels like not to constantly fight for air.

"I know. I mean, I know you're fine. I know you can take care of yourself. I just want to help if you would let me." His shoulders tense, and he drops his gaze like he's said something wrong. We know each other so well that even the slightest change sends us to one another, making it our sole duty to fix what's broken, even when we can't.

I want to say that he's delirious if he thinks he can do anything. My parents are drunks, and my stepdad Eric is a Lackey, a brainless drug dealer for the Big Three. They're heartless people who feed on your insecurities, convincing you that the only way to live is to escape into a world of drugs, spending all the money you have to survive, on a reality that constantly slips through your fingers. Eric's been a Lackey for so long, ice fills the spot where his heart once was, making him ruthless and easily aggravated. Every time I blink the wrong way, it brings on a fight.

"I know," I sigh as I push a thick slab of cream across my cheek before sliding past Jimmy.

He reaches his arm out, showing his already stitched-up hand, bringing his lips so close to my ear that it tickles. "You're so fucking stubborn," he whispers.

A smile finds its way to my lips. "We're similar in more ways than one," I say as we walk back into the main room.

CHAPTER 2

(HARLEY)

Our group is a good example of what it looks like in the brain of a person with ADHD. It's a perfect storm of chaos. We yell, talk over one another, play-fight and laugh at random ideas until our chests hurt.

Sometimes I'll get caught up in the hyperactive bull sessions, where we throw ideas at each other, waiting for one to stick. But most of the time, I just watch the way they bounce ideas off one another — happiest in each other's light, making time seem irrelevant.

I love how they move with every word, letting their hands fly all over the place, almost nailing each other in the face. Their lips emphasize every syllable, as if they truly believe in what they're saying.

"Guys, don't you have to go to school?" Uri's voice snaps me out of my daze. Morning light seeps through the foggy windows, illuminating the dust particles floating around the room, disrupted by our movements.

"What time is it?" Jimmy asks as he grabs a pillow from under my arm, turning fast, bringing it down hard on Rey's face.

"That's it!" Rey rips the pillow out of Jimmy's hands, trying to take a swing, but Jimmy dodges it effortlessly, too fast for Rey's clumsy moves. Rey's shaggy brown hair falls in front of his acne-spotted face and piercing blue eyes. Rey's fourteen, the youngest in the gang and a head shorter than

Jimmy. He's a kid, really, with the arrogance of a twenty-five-year-old and the maturity of an eight-year-old.

"7:30."

Jimmy slips Rey's punch, tackling his legs and slamming him into the ground, having him in a headlock in seconds, Rey's face starting to turn purple. Jimmy's a much better fighter than Rey for this to be fair.

Uri springs off the couch, sprawling out beside the boys, "1...2...3" he taps his hand on the ground, smiling with all his teeth.

"Just break it up already," Tequila says, sounding almost bored, fidgeting with pieces of wire and machinery while her knee bounces in anticipation.

Uri's 6'9" muscular build towers over Jimmy and Rey as he pulls them apart with ease, which only makes them laugh harder. Finn saunters over and makes them shake hands, holding Jimmy's arm up in the air, showing him to the imaginary audience.

Growing up with boys taught me how to fight and always be on my toes. When I was eleven, I got jumped by a couple of Hunters, hitmen that work for the Big Three. I had to stay in The Shed for 24 hours while Finn worked feverishly to fix me up, though it could have been longer. After that, Jimmy made me practice fighting with him. He taught me how to punch correctly. Finn and Rey taught me how to use my whole body in a fight, and Tequila taught me speed and to move with silence. That went on every day for a week until I got jumped again. Only this time, two Hunters ended up in the hospital for five days.

"Okay, I'd better go, I have to pick up J and change," I say, pointing to Uri's shirt, which may as well be a dress on me. I push against Tequila as I get up and find my body stiffer and more irritated than before. My lungs strain against my ribs, overexerted from the beating and getting myself to my couch, but at least I can see a little out of my eye now.

"We gotta go too, Rey," Finn says, ruffling my hair as he swings the door open.

"You forgot something." Rey points, shaking his head as he follows him.

"Nah, I'll get a shirt from work." Finn smirks, showing off his lanky build as both boys walk to their ten-hour shift cutting wood. I'm almost at the door when Jimmy stands up to follow me.

"T, you coming?" Jimmy asks.

"Nah. I'll meet you there," Tequila says, winking at me with her brown eye. She's blessed with heterochromia, her other eye a light blue, almost green, both always underlined with thick black eyeliner. She nudges Uri, whose smile only grows with the notion. Flinching, I make a poor attempt to roll my eyes. For a couple of years now, they've been doing this every time Jimmy and I go off alone. Sometimes I wish Tequila would just glare at me like everyone else in this town because her bubbly personality is making my headache worse.

"Are you sure you wanna swing by your house? You still have some clothes at mine," Jimmy says under his breath as the door shuts behind us. He always tries to keep my home situation quiet around everyone. I love him for it, but since my family is pretty well known, with Eric being the most hated man alive (most hated by me, at least) and me being a decent fighter and part-time medic, it's kind of hard to keep secret.

"Yeah, Eric's probably at work by now." I hate the way his name pinches at my throat every time it crosses my lips. I shouldn't be scared, but that man was treacherous enough to become head Lackey to the top drug dealers in all three cities.

Eric has been with us since I was eleven, trying to run our lives while maintaining a healthy relationship with the liquor cabinet and the druggies who line up at our door. On top of that, my mom is an alcoholic who is never sober enough to be in reality and feeds Eric's anger with snarky comments. The only reason I stay is for my brother J because, even though it's a shitty situation, by law, Eric has to give us supplies: water and clothes that we couldn't afford otherwise.

I'm honestly surprised that Eric hasn't gotten a bullet through his head or at least been threatened by his boss with something dire to force him to pay back the money he's been skimming from the profits over the years. But as he says, they have 'respect' for him. I've just been waiting for the day when someone puts a bomb in one of his meeting spots or breaks one bone for every payment he's missed.

We crouch behind rose bushes that separate our yard from our neighbour's, being careful not to walk in on a drug deal or my parents.

Houses in our town aren't so easy on the eyes. Most of them are weather-beaten and run-down, like our Shed; others are slightly nicer with new furnishings on the inside. Then there's my house, the ugliest, most run-down pile of crap in town. If I hadn't known Jimmy for this long, I wouldn't let him come close to this place. The rest of the gang definitely hasn't seen it. The outside was once white but now resembles a beige-tinted rust, with rickety stairs and cracked walls. Weeds and yellow grass replace the cement walkway; bushes cover most of the windows, and ivy climbs up the walls, wrapping itself around the front deck. A two-and-a-half-bedroom house with a broken toilet and a roof that never stops leaking. It's the worst kind of place to be when Eric throws a party, believe me.

I feel a weight lift off my shoulders when no yelling or singing seeps from the house. Knowing that no one bothers to lock up, I hurry up the steps and gently push open the door, ensuring there are no leftover drunks. I instantly draw back, my eyes stinging as I try not to gag as the smell of stale beer and clam chowder rushes out the door.

"I'll stay outside," Jimmy mumbles under his shirt, standing on the very edge of the porch, not risking another step.

"Good choice." I copy him and pull my shirt over my nose, knowing that no matter what I do, that smell won't leave me for days.

I avoid empty moonshine bottles and broken glass, stopping in the kitchen to leave water for Bob, the old drunk who never leaves. I pick up scattered money before unlocking my room. Quickly, I change into my jeans and my dad's old hoodie, the only thing I have left of him.

I make my way back through dirty clothes and unknown liquids, remembering to make a quick stop in J's room. When I reach it, I give myself a gold star for locking my door. J's bed is thrown off its metal frame, his mirror smashed, and his chair sticking out of the wall.

I flip the bed back over, my throat tightening when a picture frame lies face down underneath it. Carefully, I pick it up, trying not to cut myself on the splintered glass as I wipe away the dust that lines the face.

"Dad!" His eyes see right through me as I place the frame on the windowsill. "I love you," I whisper, the imaginary smell of his hoodie making my eyes water, threatening tears. When I was ten, my dad was driven out of town and supposedly killed by the Hunters, although he did nothing wrong. I didn't believe it at first, trusting no one from the government or the hospital he worked at to tell me the truth. I waited and waited for him to show up and take us with him, but after eight years of nothing, I couldn't wait anymore. So for now, I tell myself he's dead, for my sake, and my brother's. I can't give in to false hope.

I jump when the sound of shuffling heavy feet on gravel rings in my ears and reminds me where I am. I grab J's backpack, shove in some clothes and sling it across my shoulder.

Taking my time to regroup, I walk slowly back down the hall, watching Jimmy shift nervously back and forth, his fists clenched. I move toward him, placing my hand on his back, seeing Eric stagger in wavy lines toward us, a bottle peeking out of a paper bag.

"Here we go," I whisper.

Eric sees Jimmy first. Confused, he starts to smile until his eyes meet mine, and a sickly grin appears on his lips.

"What the hell are you doing here? You didn't come home last night. I was — worried." He slurs, raising his eyebrows. "You good for nothing little—" He curses at me, saying any word that pops into his head, but I've learned to tune him out.

"I'm here, aren't I?" I cut off his rant, annoyed.

"Don't interrupt me, I'm your father!" he says, voice taunting.

"You're not my father. You're a good for nothing drunken excuse of a person." My voice is steady, but my hands start to shake as his eyes burn into my skin. Every part of me wants to break his jaw and nose, but I remain still because it would only make things worse. It would make me just like him.

"Don't make me give you another black eye," he huffs, stumbling toward us, struggling to stay upright as he trips over his feet.

"Run!" Jimmy shouts, which isn't his first instinct, but he knows that fighting would only bring trouble.

We jump off the porch and break into a run. The sound of his bottle shattering against the wood makes me run faster, though I know he's too disoriented to follow. We don't stop, not even when my lungs start to burn, and my ribs ignite in flames, squeezing my chest. But I don't care. I choose to feel the pain. I invite it. It makes me feel alive, as if I still have a grip on my world. We run for a couple more blocks, then fall to the ground, Jimmy panting, my arms and legs stretched across itchy grass. Laughter rushes through me, coming out more like a strangled gasp, the sound causing Jimmy to look at me like I'm insane. Aren't we all?

"Is everything okay?" I look up to see a small, blond-haired boy with red-rimmed weary blue eyes staring at me, walking out of his best friend's house, where he spent the night.

"Hey J!" Jimmy says, wiping the dirt from his hands, sitting up. J doesn't acknowledge him. He just stares through me, right past my smile. I give him the 'I'm fine' look that we've both mastered so well as I throw him his bag and stand, wrapping him in my arms.

"What's up, little man?" I ask, squishing his cheeks.

"Harley," he says, without a trace of humour on his face, not letting my appearance go unexplained.

"I'm fine!" I pull him tighter into my arms, inhaling the scent of cinnamon and apple that lingers in his hair. "Finally showered, I see!" I say, taking the opportunity to mess up his finely groomed hair. He pinches me, and I let go. "Ouch!" He rolls his eyes, pressing his hair back into place, trying to suppress a smile. "Go get changed," I say, pushing him to the door.

He's thirteen, a year younger than Rey and very small for his age, lean with little muscle from years of never having enough to eat, even with the extra food I give him or Tequila steals for him. His face could scream cuteness — it's slightly round with big features and rosy cheeks — but he never smiles unless he's with the gang, so his face is forever the picture of pain and distrust. The glasses he wears are too big, taped in the middle, and kept on his head by an elastic band. He seems like a regular kid, although genius-smart, but on the inside, he's ten years more mature than his friends. When you look into his eyes, you see a boy who lost a dad he barely knew, at a young age, forced to grow up too fast.

"You good?" Jimmy's hand falls to the small of my back, and I sigh, turning to him, wanting so badly just to fall apart in his arms.

"Surprise attack," J screams, jumping onto my back.

I lose my balance, falling to the ground, bringing Jimmy down with me. J springs to his feet, dressed in fresh clothes that bunch around his ankles and upper body. "Stop playing around you guys, we're gonna be late for school!" he giggles, placing his hands on his hips and marching forward.

As we walk to school, J goes on and on about his night. They went out, and he met a girl. God, he's growing up fast. I remember when he was only five, and I had to start taking care of him. A skinny boy who watched me with hollow eyes, crawling into my bed when Eric and Mom fought, asking me to sing the monsters away when voices filled the halls.

I end up missing the rest of J's story as we get to school right as the bell rings, just in time to see Tequila lift a wallet out of some guy's pocket, taking twenty bucks and putting it back before he can even take a step toward the door. Not only is she insanely clever with computers and machinery, she is also very good at sleight of hand. I've learned not to keep anything of great value in my pockets, not that I have such a thing.

"Gotta go," J says, running off to a group of boys much taller and bigger than him.

"Have fun!" I yell after him. He looks back, blushing, managing to give me a small smile before disappearing into the crowd. "He's embarrassed by me."

"Nah, the other kids just don't have a cool sister like you." Jimmy elbows me, dead serious.

"Oh, I have to go meet up with Luke," I say, watching Jimmy's face turn to concern, a look that always follows Luke's name, no matter the situation. He hasn't liked him ever since Luke became my boyfriend. Never has, never will, at least that's what he always tells me.

At the thought of Luke, tension fills my chest, building and multiplying as the chaos of today subsides, creating space for a forgotten issue. For the rumours that have been drifting from person to person the past two days. Luke, my boyfriend of a year, who I never once thought I could be with forever, might break up with me today. He made the mistake of telling one of his gang members, so unsurprisingly, it made its way around the school pretty quickly. I was going to beat him to the punch, but I had a lot on my plate. "I'm good. I'll see you in class, okay?" I nudge Jimmy's chin, dreading the conversation I'm about to have with Luke. I consider just sticking to Jimmy's side the whole day in hopes of steering clear of Luke, but that would just prolong the inevitable. *Don't be a coward*, I tell myself before we open the doors and go our separate ways.

There's only one school in town, going from age six to twenty-six. It's built for a lot of people, but most kids drop out by the time they turn ten. It's underfunded, named after Markley, a psychopath billionaire. He survived the gas and built the school in his honour before he drowned his three kids, stabbed his wife and shot himself in the head. They only keep the name because of the generous contribution of money he left behind, but they had some fun with the design, thinking it fitting to make the school resemble an insane asylum; dark tiled floors, gray walls, white lockers and steel bars on every second window. Surprisingly though, they spent most of their money on making holographic computers and putting solar panels on the roof. They have pretty decent teachers as well. So once you get past the suicidal energy, it's not that bad, and the best part is anyone older than twelve can attend any grade level, as long as they pass the entry exam. You can study anything you want.

I run my fingertips along the chilled lockers, positioning my hair to shield the side of my face when someone walks past me. As I round the corner, a grey-eyed boy rests against the wall, his dirty blond hair gelled to perfection, a blue and gold jacket covering his thick arms. Luke is a stereotypical Opulent gang leader: straight white teeth, a heart-stopping smile, clean new clothes. We have very different lives, him being an Opulent, always having enough money for new things, and me being a Gutter Rat, with 'new' clothes coming from older girls. As his eyes meet mine, I can't determine whether to feel anxious or relieved about what might happen.

"Hello, handsome," I say in the happiest voice I can muster, standing on my tippy toes to plant a kiss on his cheek. He doesn't move to embrace me, and when I step back, his eyes sweep over my face. As they rest on my swollen black eye, they show a flicker of anger? concern? pity? He laces his fingers in mine, searching for words to fill the silence.

"You okay?" His other hand brushes over my cheek, and when he presses his lips gently, briefly to mine, my chest tightens to the point where I might pass out.

"I'm fine," I reply, my smile fading.

"We have to talk," he whispers as if there are people around to hear him. "I think we need to break up." His lip quivers, which only makes me want to throw up because he's 100% not sincere. He doesn't really have that kind of emotion in him. He uses that lip quiver every time he tries to get out of the stupid shit he does.

"Why?" I ask, trying to keep my face blank, curious what reason he'll give.

"It's hard to keep up with you, your family, your friends. I can't deal with you always being hurt, or you being with Jimmy every single day. It's too much for me—"

"Too much for you?" I interrupt him, attempting to stay calm. I knew him doing this was a sure thing, but that doesn't make hearing it roll from his lips any easier. I can feel anger creeping into my voice, but I know I can't show it.

"Yeah." He trains his eyes on the tiles, his voice almost provoking tears. Almost.

"That's bullshit and you know it." My steady tone catches him off guard. I want to scream at him, tell him I've been abused mentally and physically for seven years, and *it's too much for him to handle?* "You're unbelievable." I can feel my heart beating against my chest wall, building up a lump in my throat. So I turn away.

He grabs my hand, twisting me around, "Harley, you have to understand. It's — It's my reputation I'm protecting!"

My jaw drops. I want to hurt him the way his words dig into my skin, but I can't. I don't love him, but hearing those words out loud floating in the air, buzzing around my head, confirms what I'm most scared of — being seen as weak, as too much to handle.

I pull my hand away from his, and a sensation of calmness rolls over me, allowing my throat to loosen. "Luke, I'm sure no matter what you do, how you act or who you're with, people are always going to know how shallow and empty you really are." I turn away before he can see the tears creeping into my eyes and walk steadily to the bathroom, not even hearing his breaths follow me.

I check the stalls before I start to punch the wall. Over and over and over until red blossoms from my knuckles as my skin cracks. It's not out of anger solely toward him but toward everything. I can keep all of the hurt bottled up and stored away, but eventually, it has to show.

There's no threat of tears now; all my adrenaline has turned my anger to nothingness. I pull myself onto the windowsill, pushing open the glass, hoping the fresh air will clear my mind and bring some sense to what just happened. I didn't think he could have this effect on me, and I don't even know why I care. I shouldn't care because the selfish part of me kept him around as a distraction, a break from my life — but maybe that's just something I've been telling myself, to protect my heart from the pain of losing another person, because I wasn't enough.

I take another long deep breath, letting it burn as I hold it in, before jumping down and moving to the mirror. I give myself twenty seconds, to break, to put the pieces back together, before cleaning the blood off my knuckles, wiping away my tears and walking out the door.

When I show up twenty minutes late to class, stares follow me, along with gasps and loud whispers as I walk down the aisle between the desks. I guess I didn't really think about how the bloody knuckles and the black eye would look together. Every damn time my classmates make a spectacle of me. You'd think they'd be used to it by now, and why should they care? Everyone participates in gang fights. We're all fucking bruised. I keep my eyes on Jimmy, holding my breath to keep my anxiety at bay. If I'm not weak, they can't hurt me.

Even the teacher stares at me, stopping his lesson, waiting for the room to still, then carrying on when I find my seat.

Jimmy's fingers find mine under the table, his eyes staying locked on my bloody knuckles as it takes all his strength not to ask me what's wrong. He knows he has to wait until class is over. It's an unspoken rule that I wish we didn't need to have.

Class drags on for hours, when the bell finally rings, sending people out the door. Jimmy pulls me back, waiting for everyone to leave before making our own way out. He turns and holds my hand to my eyes as if it wasn't attached to me, and I didn't feel the warm blood staining my skin.

"Did Luke hurt you? Because if he did I'm going to kick his ass!" he grunts, starting down the hall.

"No, no." A nervous laugh bubbles from my throat as I step in front of him, pushing on his shoulders. "God, Jimmy, you've been eating your spinach." I push harder to keep him from pressing me forward, my shoes sliding on the dusty floor. "We broke up and I punched a wall, it's okay." He stops suddenly, almost sending me face-first into his chest.

His mouth twitches, a smirk showing for a short breath. "Why?" His gaze drops to my hands as he runs his fingers through his hair. That's his nervous twitch. It's like his stress ball.

"He said I was too much to handle. Basically, I was too much of a mess for him to deal with — I mean it's not like he was doing anything to help me anyway," I manage, finding the words hard to get out.

"Should have punched him!" he huffs, not even pretending to be sympathetic.

"You know it wouldn't help. But I did imagine his face when I went a couple of rounds with the wall." This time he smiles, letting it reach his eyes.

"If you ask me, it's his loss. He doesn't deserve you anyway — he probably couldn't keep up with how brilliant you are and didn't want to admit it!" He wraps his arms around me, resting his chin on my head. He's warm. His heart beats fast, and his skin smells of his favourite homemade cologne that consists of grapefruit and lemongrass, with a trace of black pepper.

"Tell you what, we won't go to our next class. Let's go get the Brightly brothers to scrounge up some ice cream or whatever you want."

"Can J come?" I ask, still wanting Jimmy's arms to stay locked around me so I can feel safe for a second longer.

"Everyone can come. You stay right here. I'll go get Tequila and J, then we can run and get Uri. Finn and Rey are still at work so obviously they can't come — okay?" he says, already sprinting down the hall before I can answer, his jet-black hair flopping as he runs. He's another reason why I stick around because, without him, I'd be lost.

Suddenly goosebumps run up my arms, and a chill falls down my back. Jimmy's been gone ten seconds, and all the other kids have gone to their next class, but I sense I'm no longer alone.

"Behind you," a warning whispers in my mind.

I don't look back. Cautiously I start forward, retreating to the bathroom, but before I can take two steps, solid arms lock around my stomach, and a calloused hand clamps over my mouth as a person effortlessly pushes me up against the wall.

CHAPTER 3
(JIMMY)

Every time I hug that girl, it electrifies my body. Harley's beautiful with her brown hair and seemingly plain brown eyes that, at the right angle, catch the sun and radiate gold. It's like someone waited thousands of years for the perfect pieces to give to her. It sounds cheesy, but when you're in love with someone, nothing about them is ugly, except for the fact that we're 'just friends.' We've always been 'just friends' ever since we were four. That day when I first met her behind the old church where scarlet roses lined the fences, her hair falling wildly over her eyes as she danced with her dad — that was when I fell for her, actually fell! I tripped over a rock, falling face-first into the dirt, introducing myself with a mouth full of mud. She laughed, that cute girlish laugh, helped me up and said, "I like you, we're gonna be best friends — okay?" All I could do was nod because I was busy promising myself that when I married her, I'd marry her right in that very spot.

From that day on, we've never left each other's side. We work effortlessly together, there for each other through the best and the worst. I helped her with her fighting, and she taught me what living felt like. She saved me from destroying myself after the day I watched and ran as my parents were beaten to death by the Hunters on our way home. It's not that uncommon in The Sticks for people to die like that. Half the kids that live here are either raised by their grandparents or live on their own. We could have stayed in The Shed after they died, but my grandmother took us in because she wanted Tequila and me to stay in school and be able to get decent jobs. She thought it would make things easier, but it didn't.

Tequila started stealing more and stopped caring about her grades. I turned to drugs to stop the voices, to stop watching my parents die every time I closed my eyes. I wanted to stop feeling like it was my fault, but it only heightened the pain, and I liked it. For a month, I managed to hide the cocaine and ecstasy from Harley, knowing she would hate me for falling into the world Eric had forced her into. I had no choice because once I started, I couldn't stop. It made me feel something again. I hid the drug use behind my grief, irritation, depression and nightmares, until the day I collapsed on the cool kitchen floor, overcome with hallucinations. I was drenched in sweat, with my knees to my chin, calling for my parents to run when my grandma and Tequila found me.

Confused. Stunned. Ashamed. Tequila ran for Harley, and when she got there and stood over me, she didn't scold me or watch with disgust. Harley lay down beside me, her face inches from mine, her scent wafting gently, making my tears fall harder as she ran her fingers over my hair. She smiled gently, carefully, and whispered to me like my mother used to when I was home with a fever.

"Jimmy, look at me." She lifted my chin, so I was forced to look her in the eyes. "They loved each other, you know how I could tell?" I shook my head, trying not to count all the faces circling around her. "It was the way they looked at one another and how they talked like poets, as though with every word they breathed, oxygen fuelled their love. Theirs will forever be the kind of love I'll always fight to have," she whispered. I stared at her, her steady gaze sobering me up. She didn't cry. Her voice stayed calm, as if she did this every day. "That love they held for each other was only half of what they had for you and Tequila." I let my eyes drift to Tequila, watching her silent tears as she led our grandma from the room. "You shouldn't blame yourself. Never in a million years would they blame you. They would rather die than have to bury their own son." That's when Harley stood up, stretching her hand to mine. I hesitated before I let her pull me to my feet, where she slid a jar of detox pills into my hand, uttering the words that I will never forget. "Jimmy, I can't make you take these, and losing your parents will never get easier. It will always be in the back of your mind, but eventually it becomes almost bearable. They wouldn't want you to live like this, as if you died with them. It's time for you to make them proud, live your life for yourself. They would want that."

"Watch it!" I turn the corner and collide with Tequila, causing her to stumble backwards into a locker.

"Sorry," I say, shaking the memory from my head, trying to suppress a laugh as she hops on one foot, rubbing her knee.

"What the hell are you so happy for?"

"She's single — she's finally single," I say, panting.

"Harley?" she asks, puzzled. She knows I'm talking about Harley. I've only been pining over her for years, and the only person who knows the absolute truth is Tequila.

"No, the girl who lives down the street," I reply, exasperated, ruffling my hair.

"I'm pretty sure she's four."

"Oh shut up," I huff, rolling my eyes. "Anyways, Luke broke up with Harley, quite rudely I'd say, but that's not the point. He broke her heart and now she's single." My breathing starts to steady.

"Well, aren't you sympathetic!" she laughs as I start to pull her down the hall with me.

"Yeah, yeah, whatever, we gotta get J."

J's class is only a few doors down from where I collided with Tequila, so we get there pretty fast. The sound of laughter and voices talking over one another drifts from room 124. They're probably doing arts and crafts or something stupid, so I fling open the door and shove Tequila in. She has a better chance of interrupting the class without getting yelled at. The teacher, Ms. V, hates me. I couldn't tell you why; she just never did like me. Maybe it was the slime in her desk or the chicken that laid eggs on her chair, but we'll never know.

"Oh Tequila!" Ms. V greets her, genuine excitement in her voice.

Tequila tenses up, anticipating Ms. V's suffocating hug. "Hi! I need to steal J from you for the rest of the day. Please," she says with an air of politeness.

I stifle a laugh, and she shoots me a look. "Sorry," I mouth, "it's just so fake."

She swings her foot back, hitting my shin. I cringe as sharp pains shoot up my leg. I step back, holding my tongue when I see Tequila and Ms. V pleased by my pain.

"J, you are dismissed," Ms. V chirps, and a chorus of groans and objections follow J out the door. His grey bag looks ten sizes too big and too heavy for his twiggy shoulders. When his eyes lock on mine, they narrow, conditioned from a young age to expect the worst when two people you love pull you from class for no reason.

"J, wait! I have something for you." Ms. V stops us, walking over to her desk, her big hair and round hips swaying with every step. She rummages around for a bit before pulling out a tin box with flowers neatly painted on the side. She shuffles back over and stops in front of J.

"Here are some extra rations. I thought maybe you and your sister could share." She pinches his cheeks, then shuffles back over to her class. "Now back to work, my loves," she says in her squeaky voice, irritating everyone with the clapping of her hands.

"Yummy treats, hey buddy?" Tequila mocks, pinching his cheeks. He slaps her hand away, sticking his tongue out when she turns, walking back down the hall.

Most of the teachers give J food. Others give him clothes, and they all give him extra help in school. They feel bad that they can't stop what happens to him outside of these walls.

"J, let's go, we have to get back to your sister." I grab his hand, pulling him faster through the halls.

"Why?" he finally asks, his nimble legs rushing to keep up with us.

"Harley and Luke broke up," Tequila smirks, ruffling my hair and lifting my wallet, looking for any spare change. She sighs, throwing it at my chest when she finds only dust because my wallet can only dream of having money to hold.

"Is she okay?" J asks, clearly the only one concerned.

"She will be, once Jimmy swoops in and sweeps her off her feet," Tequila says in her best dream-like voice, making the sweet sound of J's giggles fill the halls.

"Shut up you guys, I can't even tell her I love her yet," I say, a part of me deflating, not wanting to admit what I know is true.

"Why?" they both exclaim, their eyes widening.

"She doesn't feel the same way," I answer, turning into the hallway where I left Harley. My smile fades as I stop in my tracks, J and Tequila colliding into my back.

"What the fu—" Tequila's words catch in her mouth when her eyes follow mine.

In the middle of the hallway, two middle-aged men hold Harley against the lockers. The one holding her shoulders has brown hair and an excessive number of spiked earrings lining his ears. The other, leaning against the wall, has a scorpion tattooed on his bald head. Both have bodyguard builds, guns under their belts, outlined by their tight black shirts, and their features are covered by white masks with a symbol or letters painted in red.

The earringed man moves his hand to pull a knife, his grip so strong on her one side that she can barely move. I start forward. She kicks and flails until the blade finds her neck. Only her eyes move, and they harden when they meet mine, panicked and wild, but her expression remains calm. I've only ever seen that look once, when Eric was on a drunken rampage, and J and I were still in the house.

As I get closer, Harley fights harder to break free, causing the earringed man to press the knife further into her flesh until blood drips from the steel blade. She stills. I want to go to her, but her eyes keep me motionless.

"Can I help you with something?" Her voice is as casual as one could be with gorilla hands so close to their throat. It scares me when she acts like this because she doesn't bow to pain like the rest of us, and if she says one thing wrong, he could slice or crush her windpipe in seconds.

"Where's your dad, sweetheart? He's missed a couple of payments. Boss is starting to get mad," the earringed man says, the tapping of the bald man's metal bat against the lockers making it hard to hear.

Whispers cower behind doors as teachers pull students into classes — the sound of doors locking echoing through the hall. We have no help — she's alone. The only rule teachers have for this situation is not to get involved.

"You think I would know? He's not my dad," she says. He presses harder, hesitating when she doesn't flinch, her eyes staying locked on his. The man turns to his bald friend, who is now humming to the sound of his bat.

"I think she's lying to us, boss." The bald man doesn't even look up, doesn't twitch a muscle. "We think you're lying, sweetheart," the earringed man decides, turning back to Harley.

"Trust me, if I knew where he was, I would tell you. I want him dead as much as you do and your mute friend knows that."

He looks back over at him. The bald man nods and stops humming as he brings his bat to Harley's stomach, leaning into it. She stiffens.

"If we can't find him and we find out you're lying, next time we aren't going to let you off with just a scratch." He taps her stomach gently then pauses, looking around, his eyes landing on J. My heart drops.

"Get him out of here," I hiss, but Tequila already has him at the door.

"Next time..." the bald man presses his lips to her ear.

When he pulls away, she screams, digging her nails into the closest piece of flesh she can find, which happens to be the eye of the man with the earrings. She catches him off guard, almost escaping before the man pulls her back from the wall and slams her head hard against it. She goes limp, sliding to the ground. The bald man turns and winks at me before they disappear into the shadows of the lockers.

The sight of her on the floor makes my legs weak, but I force them to move toward her, slowly at first, then so fast I might fall over.

"Mmm, it doesn't hurt." She tries to lift her head, but she drops back to the floor. "I'm just glad the other guy didn't use his bat," she laughs, running her fingers over the back of her head. Within less than twenty-four hours, she's had two beatings. She now has a black eye, cuts on her face and neck, bloody knuckles and surely a concussion.

"It's okay, I got you," I say, my voice seeming too weak to be my own. I crouch down and lift her into my arms, letting her head rest on my shoulder as I walk down the hall and out the doors.

CHAPTER 4

(HARLEY)

Evening light fills the room, playing with my eyes, making my head spin. It feels like I'm hungover. My lips are cracked and dry, my skin sweaty and itchy. I try to speak, but my throat is bone dry, hurting when I swallow. I stretch my hand out, feeling cotton sheets under my fingertips, a silk pillow pressed against my slightly swollen cheek. I don't remember going to bed.

The covers beside me are wrinkled, a separate imprint pressed into the mattress. Why can't I remember what happened? I bring my hand to my throat, feeling cotton dressing just under my chin. I look around, making sure not to move too fast because my head is pounding.

Light blue paint is covered with pieces of paper scribbled with words, and the unmistakable smell of grapefruit, lemongrass and black pepper clings to the walls. I've been here so many times, yet for some reason, I'm drawing a blank. As if in answer, the door slowly creaks open, revealing Jimmy with a tray of food balanced in one hand. He pauses, squinting at me through the dim light, possibly thinking I'm still asleep. The steaming bowl of oatmeal he holds sends the scent of brown sugar through the air, tickling my nose.

"Why do you always stand at the door like I need to invite you in?" I ask, smiling.

"I'm a gentleman," Jimmy winks.

"Yeah, and I'm a princess."

"I'd believe it," he shrugs, crossing the room. I'm so far from being a princess that the rats on the streets are closer to royalty than I am.

"I don't think I can eat that," I grimace, pushing myself up so my back rests on the wall. Nothing really hurts; I'm just stiff. I have a pretty high pain tolerance from years of repeated injuries, the pain never lasting as long as it should. The injuries hurry to heal before new ones join them. Sometimes it's almost as if I can choose how fast I heal.

"It's not for you." He plops himself on the bed, passes me a small glass of water and scoops a heaping spoonful of oatmeal toward his mouth, leaving residue on his lips.

"You know, you always look so peaceful when you sleep, not so mean," he teases, poking my cheek with his spoon, leaving the spot sticky when he pulls away.

"Hey!" I yelp, slapping his hand away. He laughs, nearly spitting his food out, which makes me hold my sides begging myself not to laugh. "Was someone sleeping beside me last night?" I ask, running my fingertips along the edges of cloth wrapped around my ribs.

"J did for a bit, then he had to go lie on the couch. You were moving too much."

He sets the tray down and moves beside me, crossing his legs over mine and stealing a pillow from under my back to prop his head up.

"I could have slept on the couch or something. I didn't have to take your bed."

"You didn't really give me much of a choice. You were kind of delirious, with blood dripping down your neck and a big bump on the back of your head. I wasn't about to leave you on a hard couch. Anyways, my chair right there is pretty comfy," he smiles, pointing to a lumpy brown armchair with springs hanging out the bottom.

"You slept here all night?" I ask, suddenly wary of how I sleep.

"Don't worry, you don't snore, and someone had to wake you up every couple of hours because of your concussion. Finn would have done it, but he had to go."

"What are the injuries?" Asking this only makes me feel like I'm the one who has to treat them; it's a way of regaining control.

"Badly bruised ribs, no stitches for your neck wound and a concussion. I'm paraphrasing, obviously, because Finn used way fancier words that I truly cannot remember, no matter how many times he repeats them." His voice drops as he turns away from me and runs his fingers roughly through his hair.

My spirits lift and fall all at once when I remember the hallway, the earrings, the rough hands pressed against my shoulders, a cold knife digging into my flesh, and how my heart felt when the bald man's eyes locked on J.

"How's J?" I ask, trying to get up, but Jimmy holds me down, inching closer.

"Don't worry — he's fine. Tequila kept him company this morning. Rey and Finn took him to school on their way to work and Uri's there now, keeping an eye on him and waiting to walk him home," he says, lightly keeping hold of my arm, scared I might try to run, "He's okay. That kid has a whole village behind him. We're not going to let anyone hurt him."

I wish he were right, but his version of a whole village is just six kids who have no idea what the Hunters and the Big Three are truly capable of. I sink back into the bed, pretending that his words put me at ease.

"Rey was pretty mad about what happened to you. He wanted to wake you up and get you to tell him who the guys were so he could go after them. He ran upstairs, came in here, saw you lying there being treated by Finn and he nearly lost it. Uri punched him and that calmed him down a bit." Jimmy looks away, dancing around the events that shadow his face, then he flashes me a playful smile, one that releases the breath I didn't know I was holding.

"Rey has a temper, hey? Reputation of a Doberman, only showing his sweetness to the people he trusts," I say, resting my hand on his rough jeans. He clasps both hands around mine, sending his warmth through my fingers.

"He just loves ya."

Like you love me, I want to joke, but his pursed lips and hooded eyes hold the words in my mouth. He cares about me in a deeper way than I thought. I can tell by the way he holds himself, as though at any minute I could break him. And he'd let me.

"Your neck looks better," he says, changing the subject, a worried tone edging its way in his voice.

"It feels a lot better," I say, my voice gruff, wanting to cut the tension between us, to avoid the question bubbling in his mind and waiting on his tongue. I don't want to tell him what the men said to me. If I say it, then it becomes real.

"Harley," Jimmy says tentatively, anchoring his legs on mine and pulling himself closer to rest his head against the wall.

"Yes?"

"Those men were looking for Eric, right?"

"Yes," I answer slowly, feeling small — broken, almost as if I'm no longer in control of my world, as if all the bits and pieces are shattering, and all I can do is hope I know how to glue them together again.

"What did they say, before, you know..." he trails off, taking a strand of my hair, twirling it around his finger.

I don't want to drag him into the problems that without fail find me on a daily basis, but I know he'd follow me into this one blind if he had to.

"They told me that if they didn't find Eric they wouldn't let me off free like they did this time. They wouldn't come after me like they did this time either." I bite my lip, fighting to hide the words in the back of my throat and bury them deep inside myself.

"They'd come for J," Jimmy nods slowly, closing his eyes as he puts the pieces together, finishing my sentence so I don't have to.

"They'd come for J," I repeat.

We sit in silence, his hands squeezing mine before they retreat to his hair. Finally, he whispers, "They won't get to him. We won't let them. We'll take care of him."

I nod, resting my head on his shoulder, sighing as he wraps a protective arm around me.

Jimmy isn't like other guys; he doesn't see me as hurt or weak. To him, I'm a gang leader, a soldier, able to be pushed past my breaking point. Though, sometimes, when I'm lucky, he realizes I need more than just words to keep me moving.

"Nothing bad will happen to him," he repeats, and I have a feeling it's more to reassure himself than me, "You should try to go back to sleep," he says, getting up to leave me alone again. I let him go, even though I want to pull him back into bed, so he can hold me a little bit longer, just until the nightmares stop finding their way into my dreams.

I let my eyes flicker shut, almost drifting to sleep, when a feather-light body falls over my legs.

"What's up, little man?" I throw him effortlessly off onto the floor. He puts his hands up in surrender, peeking over the bed. "Get up here." I pat a spot beside me, making room for all ninety pounds of him.

"You said you'd stop calling me that," J grumbles, jumping to his feet, scrambling onto the bed and hitting my ribs on his way. I wince.

"Hey, be careful with her, big man, you don't know your own strength," Jimmy says, leaning against the door frame, his arms folded over his chest.

"Sorry," J mumbles. "You're coming to school on Monday, right?" His big doe eyes plead with me, twisting my stomach.

"I'll try," I smile, poking his belly, even though the mere thought of walking through those halls makes me want to curl up in a ball. Though, I could never admit that. Not to him, at least.

"When you aren't there, people talk, they — they pick on me. It's not that I'm not tough enough to handle it, because I am." He straightens, pushing out his chest. "It's just the stuff they say. It — it makes me want to punch everyone in the face." He gets up and starts pacing the room.

"Hey, big man, leave that shit to me," Jimmy says, grabbing the top of J's head, pushing him into the chair.

I know people talk when I'm not there. Most of it is true, the beatings, stealing and Eric, but the endless social gossip that I'm, without a doubt, featured in, is not. I hate that they're dragging J into it. It focuses attention on him, and every Hunter listens for the weak and looks for an easy target. We've all had our fair share of run-ins with the Hunters, but I've always managed to keep J off the grid.

"You don't have to worry about that kid. You just gotta stay in school and get strong. Harley and I will teach you how to fight," Jimmy offers, moving back to the door frame. J nods. But by the way he's bouncing his knee, I know there's something else.

"Spit it out!" I order.

"Those men said something about me, right?" he blurts. I look at Jimmy, not knowing if telling J the whole truth would be worth the worry. "Now don't lie to me. I heard Rey talking." His gaze drops to the floor.

"That fucking loud mouth," Jimmy grunts, storming out of the room.

"Come here," I beckon. J moves to the edge of the bed. It's an instinct of his, to keep his distance from me, as if the space between us will lessen the impact of my words, and It breaks my heart.

"Yes, they did, but we're gonna protect you. Whatever's happening, whatever the Hunters want is between me and Eric. Nothing bad will happen to you, I promise." My throat tightens because what if that's a promise I can't keep.

"Okay." He slides his feet under the blanket, punching the pillow before flopping down. "But I'm not sleeping on the couch this time so try not to kick me so much," he grumbles, rolling away from me. His mind is surely racing as mine does, but before I can say anything more to reassure him, his snores fill the room.

CHAPTER 5
(HARLEY)

Practically stumbling into the shower, I twist the knob, screeching as ice water pelts my skin, the only temperature to ever exist in the town of The Sticks.

"At least I'm awake now," I mutter.

Foaming my hair with shampoo, untangling it with conditioner, I watch as pink water surrounds my feet, swimming down the drain. I let the cold rain slide over my face while images of the two featureless Hunters play in a loop in my mind. I try to absorb every detail. The men both had distinct marks: one with a scorpion tattoo, the other with spiked earrings lining one ear. But those earrings could be clip-on, and the tattoo could be fake. I review them carefully, focusing on the letters JC painted in red on their masks as it burns into my eyelids.

"What does it mean?" I whisper, drying myself off. I slip into the same jeans, smelling of sweat and blood, and pull on Jimmy's t-shirt. Blissful laughter drifts up the stairs. It's Saturday, I think. On Saturdays, we usually all meet at The Shed to go to a house party or the Warehouse, but since I'm here, I guess they're all downstairs, giving Jimmy's grandma a heart attack.

Sometimes I wonder why Jimmy hangs around The Shed so much. His house is beautiful. It's in the Opulent part of town, modern, the inside lined with dark stained wood, furniture with no holes or broken springs, and white marble tables that Finn fawns over every time he comes here. The hardwood floor is cool under my feet, and the banister is so smooth my fingertips glide easily against it.

As my bare foot grazes the first step, a sharp scream cuts through the air, sending me flying down the stairs. *No, no, no, no, no, they couldn't have known I'd be here.* Jimmy catches me at the bottom, grabbing my shoulders.

"Where are you going?" he asks, beaming.

"Someone screamed," I say, confused. Why does he look so calm? Why is he smiling?

Jimmy tosses his thumb over his shoulder, gesturing to a very disoriented Tequila. She's standing on the table, messy bun leaning to one side, mascara smudged under her eyes, and an oversized old cartoon t-shirt stopping just above her knees. Finn and Rey burst into laughter, rolling on the floor, while Uri traps a spider under a cup, tossing it out the window.

"What the hell Tequila?"

"It was really big," she squeals, shivering. They all laugh, and I glare. Jimmy places his hand on my back, his warmth radiating through my thin shirt as he guides me to a chair.

"You didn't have to scream bloody murder," I argue, only to have my annoyance dissipate when I notice her eyes sparkling as tears start to form.

"Harley, I have arachnophobia," she emphasizes, "It's out of my control." She jumps down, redoing her drooping bun.

"How can you be so tough, yet so afraid of something so small?" Uri laughs.

"Just because I am the oldest and clearly the most intimidating out of all of you, doesn't mean I can't be scared of creepy insects that can walk all over you without you knowing." She shivers, shutting the window quickly.

"Oldest by two months," Uri huffs, unable to let her forget that.

Rey springs up, sliding into the chair beside me, his eyes begging.

"Can I help you?" I ask, anticipating a weird or Warehouse-related request.

A smile stretches across his face. Finn and Uri move beside him, resting their heads on his shoulders, smiling even bigger.

"There's a big Warehouse fight tonight," Rey says, changing the subject. He props his head up with his hands and gives me his best smile.

"You really think she can go?" Jimmy exclaims a little too protectively, but that only encourages Rey to lean in closer.

"She's been through worse," Rey shrugs. "Besides, it's not like we're fighting tonight, and she doesn't have to drink. She just has to make an appearance and smile a little," he says, pulling up the sides of my lips. I slap his hands away, making a conscious effort to frown.

"Lame!" Tequila puffs. The only reason anyone goes to these things is to drink and fight. No one in their right mind would go sober.

"I don't know Rey, who's gonna stay with J?" I say, picking at the cracked skin lining my knuckles.

"He could come," Uri offers, and my eyes instantly widen. If I can help it, J will never have to go to the Warehouse or a party.

"Or," Finn jumps in, cautiously, "we get the Brightly brothers to watch him. They owe us a favour."

"I might have to stay home and watch with 'em," Tequila winks, sliding me a bowl of flaky cereal.

"They're a bunch of idiots," Uri says, jostling her side, causing her hair to fall loose around her shoulders. She abandons the elastic altogether, leaving it on the ground and teasing her hair with her fingers.

"Sexy idiots," she responds with a punch to his shoulder, grinning and daydreaming as she slides up onto the counter.

"*Pleeease* Harley, it's the 'big' fight! A Big City gang against Amy's gang — *pleeeeease*," Rey begs. At his words the bloody letters 'JC' flash through my mind again.

"Uri, do you know what JC means? The letters were on the men's — the Hunters' masks." The instant I ask, the atmosphere in the room drops.

"Jackson Clarke," Finn says under his breath, no longer smiling.

"Oh..." I say, my voice trailing off, forgetting the power and threat those two letters carry. Not knowing may have been a little better. "One of the three brothers. I forgot."

"Yeah, he's part of the Big Three, east side. Meanest and most charming bastard out of all of 'em. Harley, if you really saw that on the masks, that's like seeing a death crown," Uri finishes, leaning against the counter.

We call the three cities that sit in the centre of our world the Big Three because they are ruled by three brothers. They rule side by side in glass towers that are so tall you can see the top halves peeking over the tree line that separates us from the towns and Big Three. We also only call the leaders by their initials because no one has enough respect for them to call them by their names.

"Rain check on the party?" Rey offers. Finn smacks him.

"No," I say, watching from the corner of my eye as Jimmy's lips pull down in disapproval. "People probably already know what happened to me and if we're gonna keep our rank we all have to show them we're not scared." They look at each other uncomfortably.

The Sticks only has sixty gangs, which is lucky considering some towns have hundreds, and the cities have even more. Fights are held every day, starting after five and ending at midnight. We're ranked third and have an alliance with Amy's gang that's ranked fourth. The Brightly brothers' gang is ranked second, Ace Beckett's gang is ranked first, and Luke's gang is ranked fifth, but I guess our alliance with him is broken now. Gangs don't have to fight every day, every week or every month if they choose not to, but to improve your rank, you're supposed to challenge the higher-ranked gangs. However, no one has asked us in weeks, and since we are in alliances with most of the gangs, we never ask anyone to fight.

Another way to get a better rank — if you're crazy enough, like the Brightly brothers' gang or Amy's gang — is to challenge the gangs in the Big Three. If you win, you get bragging rights, a couple of extra meals, and you get to move up three places in the rankings. The Brightly brothers' gang has challenged the Big Three four times, and each time they show up at our doorstep with fewer guys and more cuts for Finn and me to stitch up.

Jimmy taps his knuckles on the table, "Well, then, we might need the Brightly brothers' gang and Ace's gang to back us up at the party, especially if JC's gang shows up," he decides, keeping his eyes from me.

"Mikea's gang can watch me," J chimes in, watching from the top of the stairs. "His sister and I went out the other night, he said he'd help us out anytime. I think it's 'cause he has a thing for Harley," he says, trying to joke, but just looking at him, I feel exhausted. With the big bags under his eyes, he seems so small and fragile.

"I don't have to go," I sigh, wishing I could take J away from here. We'd never have to worry about being hunted or killed, but does a place like that even exist?

"We all know that's not an option," Tequila snorts, annoyed, walking up the stairs and folding J into her arms.

I trust Mikea's group. They're ranked seventh and aren't a bad group of kids. They've shown their loyalty many times before, but leaving J doesn't seem like a smart thing to do.

"You trust him?" I ask J, playing with my bowl of cereal.

"I trust his sister, so yes." He watches me, not breaking eye contact. If he does trust him, then I can't say no. It's hard to get that kid's trust.

"Fine."

Rey cheers, jumping up and down, punching my arm.

"Watch it."

"Sorry, gotta get changed, be back in twenty, best be ready when I get back," he yells, sprinting out the door.

"You better get running if you're gonna catch up with him, Finny," Tequila smirks, ruffling J's hair as she gets up to get ready.

"Nah, I'm not gonna talk to anyone anyway, so I don't gotta look good — also Rey isn't coming back. He's too excited; he'll forget. We better just meet him there," he says, shying away, plopping himself on the couch.

"Jimmy, liquor," Uri offers, beckoning to him, grabbing his wallet and opening the door.

"Yep, coming," Jimmy slips his shoes on, following Uri. Liquor is the one thing that this town has plenty of, and it's cheap too, since people make it in their basements.

J moves to the chair, watching old reruns on TV with Finn. I'm about to sit beside Finn when Tequila calls my name; "Harley, it's time to pretty you up."

"Shit," I growl, wondering if I could stay quiet and make her think I left with the boys.

"Good luck!" Finn says, he and J stifling a laugh as I grudgingly get up.

When I step into her room, she has ten outfits laid across her bed, heels scattered on the floor and a table full of makeup.

"What do you think?" she asks, stepping out of the bathroom in six-inch heels, tight black pants and a red long-sleeve crop top, her hair slicked back into a ponytail.

"No makeup?" I ask.

"I'll do it while you try stuff on."

"Dresses?" I gawk, running my finger over soft silks, rough jeans and fuzzy cotton. Clothes like these are extremely expensive. The only silk dress my family owns is my mom's, and she'd never let me touch it.

"You're not fighting tonight," she says, smearing on a thick layer of mascara, "But I think this is more your style." She hands me a pile of clothes with low heels sitting on top and when she turns away I toss them on the bed.

"Red?"

"Hides the blood," she winks.

I roll my eyes and change into red cargo pants and what looks like a very small black shirt.

"This is a bra!" I fold my arms over my stomach, showing way too much skin.

"No my love, *that* is a solid, lace-up back, cami crop top." She flicks a brush toward me.

"Still!" I complain. I tend to stick to jeans and baggy shirts when I go out, unless Tequila guilts me into dressing up.

"Shows off your figure. Now shut up and have a seat," she demands, pointing at the chair in front of her handmade movie star vanity. Tequila now has thick red lipstick on, complemented by highlighted cheeks and dark eyes. It looks great on her, but it would make me look like a clown. She tried that look on me once, and the boys wouldn't stop laughing for weeks.

She sweeps brushes and pencils over my face, and after twenty minutes, she spins me around, "Voila!"

My face is slim, every curve darker, bolder, my bruise almost gone. My eyelashes have a thin layer of mascara, enough to make them longer but seemingly natural, and instead of a bold red, clear lip gloss lines my lips, making them look fuller.

"Wow!" I say, shell-shocked.

"I know, right? The things I am capable of," she chirps, throwing her brush down, as if she's just completed a ten-hour surgery.

"You ready yet?" Finn calls, bursting into the room. "Mikea's—" He stops, his mouth falling open, eyes sweeping over the both of us and the clothes that are strewn across the bed.

"Finn Arnelled, pick your jaw up off the floor," Tequila smirks, cleaning up her mess and showing off her outfit while she does it.

"Wow, Harley you — I mean, Mikea's here, so we can go," he stutters, not knowing where to rest his eyes, not knowing what to do.

"Let's get out of here then," I say, pulling Finn along. I'm glad he stopped himself before a compliment came out; I never know how to respond to them.

"Shoes!" Tequila yells, holding up two pairs of heels, chasing after us.

"Converse!" I yell back, almost making Finn tumble down the stairs as I pull him along faster.

"Uggggh," she complains, following us down the stairs. No chance I'm wearing high heels. I'd like to be able to get to the party without breaking my ankles.

Two athletic men stand at the open door. They appear to be in their mid-thirties, with cropped hair, pale skin and blank features.

"Hey, beautiful." A plump boy appears from the shadows and hurries through the open door. He takes my hand, spinning me into his arms, his face inches from mine.

"Mikea!" I grimace. His full lips and brown eyes make me cringe. If you took a hardened gang leader and mixed him with an Opulent girl who checks her reflection every ten seconds, that would be the spitting image of Mikea. His black hair is heavily gelled, a (fake) gold chain dangling from his neck, and as always, he is dressed in a printed button-up.

"The boys are here, ready to watch your brother," he smiles, poking me in the ribs. "My sister's here to watch him too." I glance over and see J and Mikea's sister curled up on the couch, watching TV.

I yell over to them, "You two, be smart, Jimmy's grandma is upstairs, so you stay down here." I lean over to the boys and whisper the same to them, more lightheartedly. They both smile, taking a seat in the two chairs by the door and whipping out a deck of cards. Finn puts his arms around Tequila and me, dragging us along.

"Wait, I'm coming with you!" Mikea's heavy footsteps thunder behind us.

"Maybe if we run we can lose him," Tequila whispers, quickening the pace.

"Hey, be nice," Finn says, not sure if he actually wants Mikea to join us or not. He has wandering hands and makes jokes everyone finds offensive.

"We'll lose him in the Warehouse." I wink.

Every town fight takes place in old Bob's Warehouse, a job he is meant to host, but he's usually passed out on my kitchen table, leaving me with his job and the responsibility of dealing with hundreds of drunk teenagers. Yet, he always manages to show up for my fights.

As we turn the corner to where the rusted Warehouse stands, heavy metal blares out the open door. Drunken idiots sing and dance, tripping over each other, pretending to all be friends. The Warehouse serves as a kind of white flag, and, by law, Hunters can't come close to it. The official reason is that they would interfere with the fights, but the real reason they don't show up is because they're outnumbered, with plenty of enemies willing to kill them the moment they show their faces. The only fights allowed to happen in the Warehouse are the ones between the two gangs of the night, or else you get kicked out and harassed for the next week. Since I'm the leader of one of the top-ranked gangs and have the hosting job, I have to make sure no one breaks the rules. Sometimes I hand my duties to other people when I don't go to the fights, but all the drama usually piles onto me, and I end up kicking people out. It's mainly boys who try to test me. They tend to end up walking home with a broken nose.

Tequila runs off, finds the three hottest guys and convinces them to give us their drinks. She hands them to us, then runs off to say hello to everyone in the building. Finn chugs the drink, then slowly drifts behind me.

"Not tonight Finny, I want to hide as much as you, but I need you right here." I lock my fingers in his. He gives me a bashful smile, grabbing my drink and chugging that too. Finn is quiet as a mouse, sweet like lemonade and the shyest person I know. He's not one to hold big groups captive with his words or even be in a group of people, but when he feels up to it, he can go up to anyone, strike up a conversation and have them smiling and laughing within seconds. He's the one I take with me to talk angry gangs out of starting unscheduled brawls, and to keep Rey from angering the whole town.

A sea of people overflows out the door. Three guys stand on their cars, grabbing money from outstretched hands, placing their bets on the gang favoured to win. The Warehouse is set up so that there's a big open space in the middle, the ground covered with concrete, enclosed by old boxing rope and screaming kids. An upper floor hangs over the ring, so there's no escaping the boos or the cheers.

As we move through the crowd, Finn ends up behind me so he can lock his hands tightly onto my shoulders, making it very hard to walk properly through the already impenetrable crowd.

In front of us, fifteen girls form a circle around three boys, so Finn and I assume that must be where Jimmy, Rey and Uri are. I push through as hard as I can, using Finn's bony elbows and my sharp nails, but they just push back.

"You guys better move before I decide I need a new punching bag!" I shout, not really meaning it. They pretend not to listen, pushing Finn and me back until one girl turns around and utters my name. A domino effect happens, causing all of them to turn around, rolling their eyes as they disperse.

"Hey, wait! You haven't felt my bicep yet!" Rey calls, chasing after them. Jimmy's eyes meet mine, then drift to Finn's hands, holding me. Finn instantly lets go.

"Never a dull moment with that kid," he laughs nervously, kissing the top of my head, leaving me to chase after Rey. Jimmy brings a big bottle of brown liquor to his lips. He's drunk, his eyes a scratchy red, his movements lighter and careless.

"You clean up nice kid," Uri says, handing me a bottle that looks like water, but I know by the bitter smell that it's not.

"You don't look so bad yourself." I slide past them and pull myself onto a table, allowing my feet to dangle over the edge. He looks better than 'not so bad,' and everyone here would more than agree with me. Uri's handsome, but a different type. He doesn't show off by wearing tight shirts that hug his muscles or by acting like he can get any girl, which he could. He's humble about it, only adding to his attractiveness.

I watch as gangs begin to roll in, showing off, aggravating one another. I spot the Brightly brothers as they stroll in with thirty other guys. They have one of the biggest gangs in the town, picking up misfits and stragglers, which also makes them one of the most unorganized gangs. Watching one of their fights is like watching toddlers have a temper tantrum, but their size and pure strength make up for it. They knock over beer bottles, shove people out of the way and manage to find every single guy and girl in the room. They have the most character, that's for sure.

"Fuck off! She was about to say yes to a date!" Rey yells.

"Yeah right, pipsqueak."

"You buck-toothed, hillbilly piece of—" Finn slings Rey over his shoulder and trudges toward us, dropping him on the ground. Finn grabs my knee and slides into the chair beside me, his head resting on my leg. I feel bad for Finn. He hates this stuff, becoming exhausted within the first few minutes of being here.

Rey springs to his feet, grabs the bottle out of my hand and takes a couple of swigs, then passes it around, leaving me two shots. The bitter liquid burns my chest and hurts my head. The Brightly brothers stumble over to us, with Tequila between them.

"Hello, Miss Harley," Buckey Brightly says, nodding at me while wrapping Tequila tighter in his arms.

Johnny Brightly grabs my hand, spins himself around, leans down and places a sloppy kiss on my scabbed knuckles. "Hello, beautiful," he slurs, spirits sweet on his breath.

I try not to blush. They're pretty attractive guys, their sleeves rolled up to show their veiny, tattoo-covered arms. Johnny's hair is light brown, short on the sides but long enough in the front for it to flop to one side. His eyebrows are dirty blond, making his blue eyes almost look grey. He's shorter than his brother but still has a couple of inches on my 5'8" build. His facial features are close together, which would look weird if he weren't always smiling. For the most part, the brothers share the same body type and same olive skin, but Buckey's muscles are more defined. He's been studying fighting since he was eight. He doesn't drink or do drugs, but his personality makes him seem both high and hammered 24/7. He has buzzed brown hair, thick eyebrows and a bristly beard that makes him look harder and more sophisticated, but his long eyelashes and copper eyes bring light and playfulness into his appearance.

"Boys, you betting tonight?" Jimmy asks, slapping Johnny on the shoulder, not making eye contact with either of them. Already he's halfway through his bottle. Finn reaches across me, shaking Buckey's hand, pretending that they both don't scare the shit out of him.

"Are you kidding? We got most of our money on whatever crew the Big Three sends over," Johnny says, cracking open a moonshine bottle with his teeth, offering it to me and throwing another at Rey's head.

"I don't know, man. Amy's group is pretty good." Uri puts Johnny in a headlock, and he taps out right away, more to keep drinking than to not fight back.

Amy's a big girl, 6'2", with a good amount of muscle on her. She and I are the only two female gang leaders in the top rankings. She is ruthless and sure as hell doesn't get along with most of the gangs, but she has my respect, and I have hers.

"Nah man. Two of her best fighters are in the hospital from getting jumped the other day by five Hunters," Buckey adds, nuzzling Tequila's cheek while ignoring Jimmy pretending to vomit.

"Shitty," Finn whispers, slowly moving me in front of him to shield him from the conversation.

"You got pretty banged up yourself, hey," Johnny says, placing his hand on my knee.

Jimmy sighs, looking at the small gesture and taking a big swig before pushing away from the table and disappearing into the crowd. I ignore Jimmy when he drinks because he shouldn't; his mood bounces all over the place.

I'm about to answer Johnny when a burly boy with curly black hair sprints at me. He has a birthmark across half of his neck, complementing his butterscotch complexion and mischievous eyes. He screams at me, smiling with all his teeth, "Harles, it's time, it's time!" He collides with my knees, nearly knocking me off the table. He greets everyone quickly, then lifts me onto his shoulders, bouncing me to the ring, making my head pound.

"What the hell, Ace?" I laugh as he sets me down, handing me a mic, his amber eyes beaming at me. His laugh brings out the dimples and imprinted smile lines that show even when he has a serious expression, which doesn't appear often. He's the boy next door, well, three houses down. My first and best ex-boyfriend, my other best friend, always in a good mood and always there to put me in one.

"Your turn to announce, Harles." He steadies me on an unstable chair right beside the ring. Everyone's off in their own world, swaying to songs that scream the words, drinking out of paper bags, kissing random people. Ace tugs on my hand, "Here, little lady." He hands me a shot of some brown liquid. It smells like peppermint and spices. "To calm the nerves." He winks, drinking two. I toss the contents into my mouth, trying not to scrunch my nose. It burns so bad. "Plug your ears," he yells over the crowd. He pulls out a blue air horn and leans on it until everyone's eyes are on me. Cheers fill the room, a couple of whistles coming from the crowd.

"You should have worn heels," Tequila yells, raising her cup in the air. Heat rushes to my cheeks, and I do my best to cover them with my hair.

"Did a good job of covering that bruise," someone chuckles. For a second, I'm caught off guard.

"Shut the hell up," Uri growls, cracking his knuckles.

"Well, makeup is a wonderful thing," I reply, and laughter ripples through the crowd. "Anyways, let's get this shit started." My voice booms over the speakers. Loud cheers and clapping mix with it. I'm so nervous I could fall off this chair. I straighten, locking my knees, hoping they won't buckle. If you ask anyone, they'll tell you I'm pretty confident, that I could address the whole town and seem collected and unscathed, but really I'm begging myself not to mess up. "Today we've got one of our own: Amy, her gang ranked fourth in The Sticks!"

Stomping thunders through the room as a gang of sixteen walks into the ring, pumping their fists, getting the crowd to do the same. They're not the biggest group or the most muscular looking, but when they get angry, they're able to gain the strength of ten Uris, and they sure as hell don't hold back. They'll beat the shit out of you until you're unconscious or dead. The only way we were able to beat them was with speed and stamina. Also, when you face a gang from your town with five more members than your own, they can only have two extra people, making it a fair fight. We have the smallest gang, but damn, are we fast, and skill helps too.

Amy walks over to stand beside me. She wears black leggings and an oversized hoodie that I know is covering some kind of protective vest, but I'm not going to say anything.

Ace hands me a small slip of paper. "And their challenger of the night, coming all the way from MC's city, Gang number 91!"

Loud boos replace the cheers as twenty-six hulking men and women walk into the ring, yelling, "Who! Who! Who! Who are we? 91! Who are we? 91!"

A glass bottle lands in the ring right at the feet of their leader. He looks at it for a minute, then picks it up, flinging it back into the crowd. Glass shatters on someone's head, and a couple of people carry an unconscious kid out while a couple more drag out a girl who's laughing hysterically.

"Now that we got that out of the way, gang leaders to me." The gangs walk to opposite sides of the ring as a massive man walks toward me. His hair sits in a tall mohawk, dyed blood red. He's wearing contacts that make his eyes entirely black. At first, I think he's wearing a shirt with different designs scattered all over it, but as he gets closer, I see his body is covered in tattoos, stopping just above his blue jeans where a silver chain with sharp spikes dangles.

I crouch down so I'm at eye level with them but still keep the mic close to my lips. "You guys know the rules; no guns, no knives, no bats, nothing that isn't your own body." My eyes focus on the man's chain. "Including that big boy." He glares at me, sizing me up but decides to hand it over. "In this case, the number of fighters in each gang stays as they are, and you know what the winner gets?" They both nod. "Perfect." I stand up, slinging the chain over the bell. "Shake hands and return to your teams."

The man stretches his hand to Amy, but she just taps it and walks away. He doesn't move, though. He watches me for a minute, points to the letters, 'MC,' stitched on his jeans, then points to me and winks, a soft laugh leaving his lips as he turns back to his gang. Disoriented, I stand there watching his back as I figure out what he means. Ace taps my leg, making the motion to hurry up.

"Make it a fair fight and may the best gang win!" I say numbly. The man keeps his eyes on me until I hit the bell, and all hell breaks loose. Fists start to fly. Faces smash into elbows, and the sound of flesh on flesh rings in my ears. Ace pulls me back onto his shoulders, carrying me over to the table, but I don't laugh or smile this time. I bite down on my lip, my mind spinning from the liquor and the new obstacle that has formed in my path.

Ace sets me down, hugging me tightly before running off, yelling and whooping, pushing through the crowd to get a better view. I glance around for any sign of Hunters or trouble, but there's nothing.

"Harley, you look like you've seen a ghost," Finn says.

CHAPTER 6
(JIMMY)

The car hood bundles me in warmth with the help of the almost empty two-six bottle of moonshine. I'm not supposed to drink, and I don't like it, especially the hard shit. It makes my head fuzzy, slow, and makes it incredibly hard to throw a punch, but tonight I don't care. I pour the rest in my mouth, letting it sit there, burning my tongue and my throat before it swims past my chest and sinks to my stomach. Everyone's squished inside the Warehouse listening to Harley introduce the two gangs, so the only people left outside are too drunk to walk or too interested in the person they're with to pay any attention to me. I'm alone, as always.

    I don't want to listen to people in the crowd talk about Harley, good or bad. It's been getting on my nerves. Ever since she broke up with Luke, the guys and girls talk about her at school, on the streets, and especially when she looks like that at a party — so dominant and beautiful. Every single person fights for her attention, wanting to know the same thing as me — If her kiss makes your head spin like the liquor does. It's hard to watch them flirt with her and to watch her flirt back. It's pathetic. I'm pathetic.

    My head feels heavy, so I lean back, hitting it on the windshield. I wonder if she even notices that I don't treat any other girl even remotely close to the way I treat her. I have never loved another girl. Yes, I've dated many, and yes, they've loved me, but I could never feel the same.

"You're missing a good fight."

I squint, trying to make out the fuzzy figure walking toward me, but all I see is swirling hair and plump lips.

"I'm busy reminiscing," I say, tilting the bottle to my lips, smirking when I realize I finished it already. I fling it to the side, hearing it crack, disrupting the bugs lingering on the dandelions.

She speaks again. "About Harley." I raise my eyebrows. "You've been saying some stuff out loud." She pulls herself onto the car without asking if I want company; I don't. "You know, she literally has every guy falling all over her. The Brightly brothers' gang can't stop fighting about who's gonna marry her. Ace wants her back and it's annoying, considering I've been single for a year and no one's falling all over me."

I wonder why, I think. "Who are you?" I ask, watching the stars spin, dancing with the partly cloudy sky, twirling with the Milky Way and waltzing with the moon — silly, like a bunch of fairies floating around my head, jabbing at my brain.

"Sarah. I'm in your history class." She slides closer, making her features more prominent. Her blonde hair falls in untidy waves just below her chest. She's a typical girl from The Sticks with too much makeup painted across her face, but she's still pretty. It's not natural like Harley, but she still grabs your attention with her flirty lips.

"I'm sorry, I'm a bit drunk," I say, trying not to be rude, but the truth is, even if I were dead sober, I couldn't pick her out of a lineup with only two people in it.

She places her hand on my thigh. I stiffen but don't push her away. I don't want her to try to kiss me. Every girl I've ever kissed leaves a bitter, unsatisfied feeling in my heart.

"You don't have to know me to kiss me," she slurs. Shrugging, I let her lips open mine. It feels rushed and forced, like she's gasping for air, and I'm the only one with oxygen. It doesn't feel right, like in a dream where you feel nothing. Long hair keeps getting in my mouth, and she tastes like cigarettes dipped in moonshine. Her hot breath tickles my skin as she climbs on top of me. A laugh creeps up from my stomach, and it takes all my strength to keep it from reaching the night air as I think about how weird kissing is. How meaningless it can be, when it's not with the person who makes your heart stop and your breath hitch in your throat — though I guess I wouldn't know, I've never kissed her.

I flash back to the time I asked my mom how she knew my dad was the one. She told me that when she kissed him, she felt a switch flip. It woke her up, sent life into her body and love into her heart. He made her feel whole. I've never felt that; out of all the girls I've kissed, and it's been a lot, I've never felt that once.

"I've always wanted to do this," she whispers, in between biting my lip, which hurts. I'm somewhat relieved when I hear footsteps coming toward us. I roll my eyes as a whistle breaks the air.

"Get a room!" Sarcasm sings in Rey's voice.

"Jimmy, we've got to go — now!" Her voice sends a rush of irritation over me. I press harder into Sarah's lips, gently pulling her hair. "Jimmy," Harley hisses. I break the connection with Sarah, looking over her shoulder, too drunk to make out the gang's expressions.

"Harley, can't you see I'm in the middle of something?" My words slur as I push Sarah away, sliding off the hood, nearly falling as my ankles forget how to support my legs.

"It's important—"

I interrupt her, "The world doesn't revolve around you. If you say jump, we don't have to."

Her foot taps in annoyance. When Harley gets mad, she doesn't usually argue or say anything. She watches you, waiting for you to snap, and enraged by her silence, you feel the need to keep digging, and this only makes you confused and careless with your words. On a normal night, I wouldn't give in. I'd hold her stare and wait for our anger to be dulled by silence, but this isn't a normal night. The others watch, inching closer to her like I might do something stupid.

"I think it's best you go home," says Finn. He knows her silence will break me. He knows my words won't be welcome.

"Shut up." My heart beats against my rib cage, wanting her words to come first to stop what I might say.

Harley crosses her arms, scowling at me as I fight the impulse to give in. I know I'm too drunk and out of line, but if she doesn't say anything...

Sarah slides off the car, hurrying away, mumbling under her breath. Tequila snatches a pack of cigarettes out of her pocket on her way by.

"Jimmy," Uri says, grabbing my arm.

"No." I wobble over to Harley, my lips inches from hers, glossy and pink. I bet they taste like strawberries sprinkled with sugar. "You think you're so special, so great! You're not. No one voted for you to be in charge." Her eyes mimic the night, the moon reflected in them, which only angers me further because that's another thing guys will fawn over. "You're nothing, you're just a girl who has no home who gets —" I stop myself before the words that I will surely regret tomorrow leave my lips. But the damage is done. Her eyes narrow, sobering me up instantly. Was I really about to say that? Throw Eric in her face just because people like her. I give my head a shake, pushing my fingers through my hair. We fight like this sometimes because we spend a lot of time together and tend to get irritated, but never have I even thought about using her home life against her. "You just don't get it," I sigh. She makes me crazy. She makes me feel things I can't explain.

"I might not, but while you've been out here drinking the night away, we've just figured out that two of the Big Three leaders are most likely after J. MC and JC, but you're right," she huffs, using her hands to exaggerate the words she is about to throw at me, "the world so clearly revolves around me." She turns and struts away, Finn at her heels. Uri and Rey pull me along, and I don't know if it's the liquor or not, but I swear Tequila's hair and eyes are blazing with fire.

"What does she mean?" I mutter, not having full control over my mind.

"Gang number 91, from MC's city. Harley said the gang leader pointed to the letters MC and then made the 'I'm watching you, they're watching you' gesture while she was announcing," Rey whispers, gripping my arm too hard, his face flushed with boiling anger.

"Shit!" I mutter, more regret and dread swirling in my stomach with the liquor. Harley's hair bounces when she walks, her curves swaying with it. I swear she was sculpted by the hands of a famous artist just so I could watch her leave me behind. "Where are you going?" I call after her.

"To your house, considering I'm just 'that girl with no home.'"

"Walked into that one," Uri mumbles.

She amazes me. How she can be so strong in the most breakable moments. Sometimes I just want to keep pushing, to see how far my words can take her, how much anger I can pull from the damaged parts of her heart. Every inch of me wants to know how much it will take, just to know how to fix her. It's weird, I know. It intrigues me how day after day, year after year, she feels so much pain, so much hurt, yet she never runs. The world doesn't revolve around her. I do. No matter how much I distance myself or how much we hurt each other, if she said jump, I wouldn't even think to ask why. She would do the same. I hope. Finn wraps his arm around her, letting her head rest on his shoulder. I start forward.

"Whoa, man, I think you've hurt her enough tonight," Uri says as Rey grips my arm tighter.

"What's with those two?" I spit, looking at Rey.

Disgust replaces his joking eyes, "Buddy, I think that she's the only person that doesn't know you're in love with her, so chill."

"You didn't answer my question."

"I don't need to," Rey replies. He lets my arm drop, running over to Tequila, whispering something in her ear. She glances over her shoulder, her eyes burning holes into my face, but she doesn't do anything. What did Rey mean by 'I don't need to,' like I should know why Finn's always by her side, supporting her, getting close to her, or I'm just an idiot. It's probably the latter.

Harley stops abruptly as she reaches the front door of my house, bending down, picking up a small slip of paper gleaming with gold flakes. A strangled cry forms in the back of her throat as the paper falls from her hand, drifting like a feather through the air, landing silently in the dirt. She jumps over a box, flinging the door open and hitting one of Mikea's men in the arm.

"J, are you okay?" she yells, frantically looking through the room.

Uri leaves my side, sprinting after her along with everyone else. I wander over to the dirt pile, scooping the paper up, running my fingertips over the gold handwritten letters. *'We're watching you — Love, MC.'* The words jumble around on the paper, my stomach lurching. I crawl over to the bushes, throwing everything up, which burns more than it did on the way down. Harley most likely won't talk to me tomorrow.

I retch over and over again until I'm convinced my organs are the only thing left in me, and for obvious reasons, I hope they stay there.

Crawling on my hands and knees, the cool stones making my skin tingle, I stop at the pearly box. 'MC' is branded on the top, a black bow used as decoration. Hesitantly, I open it, sliding the white lid to the side. White roses spotted with blood lie in neat lines all the way to the bottom. Wafts of iron sting my nose. Another slip of paper resting perfectly on top reads, *'Both of you,'* the letters dripping with red. I stumble to my feet, falling three times before I land on the living room floor, where icy-cold energy fills the room.

"Is he okay?" A small voice asks. I lift my head to see J enclosed in Harley's arms. He tries to push her off, but her arms stay locked around him, not ready to let him go. So instead of sitting with her and waiting for her breaths to even, J pulls her along as he walks his girlfriend over to the men and out the door. Harley kisses the top of J's head and gestures for Tequila to take him to bed.

"I wanna help," J complains, moving toward me, but Tequila shoves him toward the stairs.

"I think it's best they handle this one," Tequila whispers, still looking disgusted.

I move to push myself up, but my hand slips and I smack my face on the floor, blood trickling from my nose. Uri pulls me to my feet, dragging me to the stairs, but Harley steps in front of him, pulling her hair into a messy bun and tilting my head up to stop the flow.

"I got this," she says, her face blank as she pulls my arm over her shoulders.

"You sure?" Rey grunts, basically growling at me.

"Thank you for tonight guys, it was good. Go home — get some sleep."

"I'm staying," Finn decides, pulling out the couch.

"Of course," I huff, rolling my eyes.

She looks over her shoulder, flashing him a smile and mouthing, 'Thank you.' The thought of Harley and Finn walking so close, fitting perfectly together, his clueless freckled face next to hers, plays through my mind in a loop, making me gag. She hurries me up the stairs and into the bathroom, setting me over the toilet. Mostly brown liquid comes up. There's so much pressure in my head that my eyes sting as uninvited tears run down my face. It's like ten thousand hands are all squeezing it at once. The sour smell of spirits and toilet water makes me throw up more. Gentle fingers run in circles on my back, a warm washcloth dabbing at the sides of my mouth as she gives me a small cup of blue liquid.

"Swish it around your mouth, but don't drink it, okay? I don't want you to keep throwing up." A pained smile fills her face. Why is she doing this, helping me even though I was a complete ass to her all night?

Hours go by before she pulls me to my feet, and I lean all my weight on her as we walk to my room. "You're strong," I say, surprised, but why? I know she could probably beat up over half of the guys in our town, probably could even beat me up once or twice. Snores fill the room, so I know J's asleep. "What time is it?" I whisper too loudly, kicking my shoes off.

"7:00 am," she says, her eyes not meeting mine. "Can you stand by yourself?" I nod. She lets me go, and my legs start wobbling like a newborn deer.

"You're mad," I state between hiccups. She doesn't answer, but the drawers opening and closing tells me I'm not far off.

She holds a pair of pyjamas out to me, her eyes locked on the floor. I undo my belt, letting my jeans fall to the ground. Using her arm to support me, I struggle to lift my feet up as I pull on soft shorts. When my eyes meet hers, she looks away, not irritated, simply tired. I lift my arms above my head, knowing if I try to take my shirt off, we'll probably be here for hours. Her hands grab the hem of my shirt, sliding the smooth cotton up, her cool fingers brushing over my bare skin. My breaths quicken, becoming heavy as I lean forward so she can pull the shirt from my arms. Strands of brown hair fall across her eyes, mixing with her lashes. I brush them away, tucking them behind her ear. My fingers move over her jaw, tilting her head up until our breaths collide. A yearning hunger builds up in my stomach, pushing me forward, parting my lips to make room for hers. I pause, feeling the tension, the electricity building between us, my heart pulsing in my ears. I want this. I want this so bad. But at the last minute, she pulls back, my lips brushing softly over her neck instead.

"Harley," I sigh, keeping my hand steady on her cheek.

"Not like this, Jimmy."

She leaves my hand hovering in the air as she walks over to J, tucks him in and places a kiss on his forehead. Her hair leaves trails of vanilla as she walks past me, grabbing the door handle. I panic, grasping for anything that will make her stay, make her want me.

"I love you," I blurt, meaning it in all the ways anyone could ever mean it.

She turns to face me, her hand still on the edge of the door. "I love you too, Jimmy," she says without hesitating, but her words carry no meaning, coming out dull and colourless. She must not understand what I mean.

I've told her I loved her before but as friends. Maybe I'm slurring my words or something.

"No, Harley, *I love you,*" I say again, moving toward her, wanting all the space to disappear between us, making sure all the emphasis is on those last three words.

"Harley, some of Amy's gang are here. We gotta stitch 'em up." Finn's voice carries up the stairs, breaking the atmosphere, sending sharp oxygen-stealing pain through my heart.

"Dammit!" I whisper. He always ruins shit.

Worn down, she closes her eyes, exhaling softly, brushing her fingertips over my outstretched hand. "I know," she says breathlessly, shutting the door behind her, leaving me alone in the dark.

CHAPTER 7

(HARLEY)

Finn's steady hands stitch suture after suture, effortlessly, like a dance performed a thousand times, with every move, every turn perfected, not a step missed. It's interesting how a person's mind can wander in the most demanding of situations, but when it's something important, something they love, it's almost like their mind is held captive by its own brilliance.

We stayed up past eleven in the morning, bandaging and stitching up fourteen members of Amy's gang from the fight. It's pretty obvious they lost. At only eighteen, Finn and I are the docs for our gang and most of the others. In The Sticks, if anyone can help staying out of the hospital, they usually end up at The Shed, Finn's door or Jimmy's house. Hospital equals money, which also means going more broke than you already are and living on the streets where you're an easy target for the Hunters.

Finn sets broken bones, can control some internal bleeds, stitches up the most horrific wounds, treats burns and does other small things like stopping an eye from swelling shut. I can do some of those things too, but I'm mostly there to assist. I sometimes know exactly what to do to treat a person, but other times, I draw a blank. Finn taught me most of my technique when he figured out I had steady hands and knew more than him about healing, but the rest comes from my dad and books. My dad was a surgeon at our neglected hospital, which everyone avoids because, well, no one can afford it. When my dad worked there, however, that wasn't a problem. He would open the clinic after midnight when the hospital was as quiet as it could be, when the Hunters were focused on searching for people to beat up. If there were patients who were turned away throughout the day, he and a couple of other doctors would take them in and work on them for free.

When I got old enough, he took me with him, letting me practice on the equipment and sit in on surgeries. I went on rounds with him. I was basically a mini version of him. He told me I had 'the healer's gift' in my blood and was destined to become a great doctor, even better than he is. He was. When he died, that dream to work beside him died as well.

For a year, I didn't touch or even look at anything to do with healing, but when I was eleven, Finn came along. He convinced me that helping others feel comfortable in their own pain was worth reviving the memories that clouded my mind. Eventually, he was right. Helping others gave me a sense of worth, and after a while, the memories became less frequent. It brought me peace.

"Harley, you okay?" Finn asks, leaning his head against the back of the couch, his eyes shut as he massages his hands. I've never really noticed how boyishly handsome he is, with his goofy manner, shy eyes and sun freckles curving over the bridge of his nose.

"No," I say, packing up the medical tools and ridding the room of bloody cloths, "Everything that's happened in the past two days is overwhelming. Two of the three leaders are after us, and I'm certain the third will make an appearance soon enough."

For once, I don't know what to do. I can't think of anything. On top of everything, Jimmy told me he loved me. Not the way he usually does. Mind you, he was so drunk he threw up for hours, but still. He might not even remember how close our lips were, how our breaths mixed, and how close we were to crossing that line. I don't even know if I want him to remember because, for years, I've been fighting with myself, telling myself that if we crossed that line from friendship to relationship, nothing would ever be the same. It could ruin us. I could lose him.

"Do you want to talk about it?" Finn asks, yawning. He kicks his shoes off, stretching out on the pull-out couch, his stripy sock feet hanging over the edge.

"No," I repeat, curling up beside him, so overcome with sleep that my head finds his chest. I curve my body away from his, lulled by his even breaths and steady heartbeat. His fingers run over my hair, an odd comfort blanketing me.

"Sleep with only good dreams," he whispers, and I drift off.

An aroma of scrambled eggs on crispy toast topped with bacon stirs me from a dreamless sleep. I keep my eyes shut, as I did when I was a child, when my mom made us a special breakfast at the end of each month with all the leftover food, because the next day brought a new shipment. On those days, J would jump into my bed, and we would play a game, where we imagined every flavour of mouth-watering ingredient, guessing what she had made.

"Wakey, wakey, eggs and bakey," a sing-song voice rings out. I scrunch my nose, searching for a face to match the man's voice. It can't be Finn. He doesn't know how to cook. Jimmy is probably too hungover to be that cheerful, and Uri and Rey left, but maybe they came back? *"Harley, my love, get up!"* The voice says again, turning frustrated and high-pitched, inching closer with his hot breaths. *"Get up, little girl, breakfast is ready."*

Fear runs through me, increasing my heart rate. I shouldn't open my eyes. If I pretend I'm sleeping, maybe he'll forget about me, walk the other way and focus on something else, but my curiosity gets the best of me. I open my eyes so just a slit of light comes through, but I see nothing but the room I fell asleep in. I open them wider, and when they adjust, I'm no longer on the couch. Instead, I'm in a chair pushed so close to a wooden table I can't breathe, my ribs poking holes into my lungs. I gasp, willing the chair to move, only to realize that I'm paralyzed, unable to move anything but my eyes that frantically search from side to side.

Relax. Relax. I blink, and a silver platter appears in front of me, covered by a lid so shiny I should be able to see my reflection, but even though my face is inches from it, I see nothing. I blink again. This time, the lid's gone, revealing a head engulfed in flames, with empty eye sockets and mouth so wide its jaw seems to be detached. My nose stings from the scent of burning flesh mixed with spirits and sizzling metal. Tears stream down my face, a scream building up in my throat, only to die just before it reaches my lips. I know this is a dream. I know this isn't real, but every part of me is saying it is.

Wake up, wake up, wake up! I scream to whoever is in my brain, forcing me to watch this happen. I shut my eyes, squeezing them so tight that my face aches. Screams climb into my ears, prying my lips apart and crawling down my throat.

Then the sizzling sound stops. The screams leave a tingling sensation on my lips, and when I open my eyes again, I lie panting on the pull-out, the scent of perfumes and cologne trapped in the air, no eggs, no burning flesh. My hands go to my ribs, the shadow of the table still lingering on my skin, the pressure slowly releasing. The steady breaths of Finn don't move beside me. He's gone; I must have slept through the rest of the day and night, so it's now Monday, and he's at work.

"Another dream?" Jimmy asks, startling me as he stands in the kitchen, eating a bowl of cereal, backpack slung over his shoulders. His eyes are blank, mouth drawn in a perfect line, emotionless to the nightmare I just woke from. He usually would have tried to wake me.

"Yeah," I shiver, pushing my hands through my greasy hair. His appearance is so neutral it unsettles me. It would be better if he were mad or yelling at me; that way I could at least anticipate the conversation we're about to have. No! I should be the one who's mad at him, not the other way around. He moves around the table, taking a seat in front of me.

"Harley, maybe we shouldn't go to school today. Just take a day to think about everything going on."

"Has J gone?" I ask, noticing my sweat-soaked shirt and the goosebumps that line my skin. Maybe he's right, we shouldn't go. Instead, spend the day locked inside, away from the world, away from life. But a part of me knows that no matter where we are, life will always find us.

"Tequila and Uri took him to The Shed to practice fighting, just to get him out of the house before school." Jimmy doesn't move closer; he sits on the corner of the pull-out couch looking over me, his sky blue eyes heavy.

If I were anyone else, I could get lost in those eyes, pulled in by their warmth and comfort — their strength. If I were anyone else, I could fall in love with him and give every part of myself to him with no questions or concerns. We could walk through the halls with our hands locked together, kiss in the back seat of a car we could never afford, and hold each other while we slept. But I'm not anyone else, and we aren't like the others. Every decision I make, every situation I find myself in, could hurt him as much or maybe more than it hurts me. I already see the way he looks at me when I get beat up, get in fights, disappear to The Shed, or my couch in the alley when I'm too broken for people to see. It's unrealistic to let someone all the way in, only to have them get hurt or leave like they always do.

"We should go," I say, "to school, I mean." I drag myself out of bed, my body surprisingly fresh and ready as I start up the stairs.

"But, Harley, you're both an easier target there." He follows me, staying at the bottom of the staircase, resting his hands on the slick, polished cedar.

"We're an easy target anywhere. There's no way to protect us from a bunch of Hunters who have guns and years of experience killing." The words come out harsher than they're meant, as all my frustration from last night comes back to the surface. For the first time in a while, he hurt me in a way that's hard to forget.

"I can try."

"But how? What could you do? At least if we're there, we have a shit ton of witnesses, ways to disappear into the crowd." I walk back down so that my hand rests on his. His are callused and scarred from years of fighting, so powerful, yet so capable of showing kindness.

"Okay," he agrees, his hand slipping from under mine. For a moment, he looks wounded, like I've hurt his pride or something. "You slept with Finn last night," he says in an undertone, telling me, not asking, as though he doesn't want to hear the answer.

He's jealous? I know he gets jealous. He's shown it so many times with Ace and Luke and any other guy who's walked into my life, but toward Finn? I never thought he'd be like that toward any of the guys in the gang.

"We fell asleep because I was exhausted from getting slammed against a wall, being threatened, going to the Warehouse, taking care of you, helping Amy's gang, and I'm confused about what happened last night," I spew in frustration.

"What about it?" He's irritated, oblivious to what I'm referring to, making me want to hold my tongue and end our argument because it sheds light on how completely wasted and out of it he was.

"You don't remember?"

"All I remember is throwing up, you putting me to bed and Finn calling you to come sleep with him," he retorts, walking toward the door.

"Jimmy, we didn't sleep together!"

He puts his hand up, gesturing for me to stop. "It's okay, I get it." He stares at the door, the neck of his shirt wet from dewy hair. "Get ready, we've got to go," he sighs.

"Jimmy," I call after him, but he's done with me, flinging open the door and waiting for me outside. *Well, this is going to be a fun day*, I joke to myself.

We gather into class, the rusted desks filled with deafening teens throwing pencils, talking about who kissed who at the Warehouse and ignoring the daily announcements that blare from the speakers.

Jimmy left me the minute we walked through the front doors of the school. He didn't even talk to me on the way there. So Tequila is the only one who grins at me as she slips into our desk. Around her finger, she swings a smiley face keychain that was previously on the girl's bag in front of us. Loud whispers echo through the room, and I can barely hear myself think; everyone's too loud, too unaware of the chills running down my spine.

"Wasn't Buckey handsome the other night? I mean his face and his hair, and don't even get me started on the muscles!" She looks past me dreamily, thinking of her new boy to crush on.

"Who?" I ask, not paying attention as my thoughts run circles around me.

"Buckey Brightly." Her voice seems far away, lost in the room. "You okay?"

I'm not okay. All I can see and think about is the burning head and its empty eye sockets filling with flames. When I have dreams, most of them come true. Not in the exact way they were dreamt, just the idea of them. I've learned to notice which ones seem logical, predictable, like if certain objects in my room or in The Shed appear randomly in them. This one was different, not logical but not completely false. That high-pitched voice telling me to wake up, I've heard it before in every other dream that has become a reality. I usually talk to Jimmy about it because he helps list situations that it might be predicting, narrowing our ideas down to one or two, but with no second opinion, it's got me stumped.

"Yeah." I rest my head on the cool metal desk, trying to push the heat from my cheeks. We shouldn't be here. We should have stayed home. I should have just listened to Jimmy, let him be right. I was so irritated and hurt that my own indignation got the better of me. Maybe I should go find him now and get everyone out of here. "Tequila," I start, sliding my hands across my jeans, wiping away the sweat, "We should--"

BOOM.

A loud explosion plunges the room into silence. The keychain clatters to the floor as desks shake and dust from the chipped walls blankets us. For a second, no one moves.

Absorbing the sound of the explosion, we stare at the teacher for direction, but even she looks lost. Someone twitches, and all at once, people surge forward, screaming, climbing over tables and pushing others to the ground as they fight to escape the room.

Tequila's eyes lock onto mine, wild, an idea struggling to form in her brain. We come to an unspoken agreement, sprinting forward, pulling people to their feet and into the hall. Hands tug at my clothes and scratch my skin.

Panic is contagious, mainly in the unknown. A person's first instinct is to follow the panic, follow the crowds and become a part of it. I want to fall into stride with the mindless mania, but a magnet beckons me toward the explosion site.

"Tequila!" I yell. Her eyes find mine. I point toward the explosion, bodies trying to knock me to the ground. She frowns, not quite sure what I'm implying, and I'm not too sure myself. But she nods, trusting me, clinging to my side, pushing against the crowd.

"Where do you think you're going?" A loud, obnoxious voice stops us. I roll my eyes as Ms. Perara steps in front of me, her bald head and pointed nose still reflecting light even though the power has gone out.

"To help," I say, not hiding my irritation. I hate that woman; she always shows up in random classes, teaching a stupid lesson that no one gets, forcing us to clap for her when she's done. She marches through the halls yelling, looking to add people to her detention list; I think she likes to hear her own voice.

She sneers at us, pleased when she shoves us out the front door. "Go down to the field," she says disdainfully, directing us with her bony, wrinkled finger to an already packed area.

"What do we do now?" Tequila asks, shoving people away from us and taking little things from their pockets as she tries to remain calm.

"Go to the field and see how we can help down there." We let the crowd carry us to the grass, where students ranging from six to twenty-six stand screaming, yelling and shoving one another.

"Holy shit!" Tequila gasps.

As we turn the corner, the whole school comes into focus. One side of the building is engulfed in flames, ashes falling from the clouds, coating the green in a thick grey. A row of teachers holds back students, pleading with them to stay put, to calm down. Their voices are submerged in the screams as all common sense is lost, instincts driving them to make careless decisions. We stay at the edge of the crowd, not wanting to be trampled, considering our options.

"Thank God," Jimmy yells, hugging me from behind, "I'm so sorry, I'll never get mad at you again," he whispers into my hair.

I smile, hugging his arms because we both know that's not possible. He moves over to Tequila, squeezing her, lifting her off the ground, worry subsiding from both their faces. Seeing his arms around her drops a weight onto my chest.

"Where's J?" Alarm courses through my veins. I sprint into the crowd, grabbing anyone with blonde hair, searching for his blue eyes, yelling his name over and over. I shove people aside, mumbling apologies as I go, but there's nothing.

I push my way to the front of the crowd to feel less claustrophobic, to collect my thoughts, to be able to breathe. My eyes cling to the group of screaming six-year-olds clumped together at the edge of the crowd. Some scream at the top of their lungs calling for their moms, but others stand completely still, staring with wide, curious eyes at the nightmare surrounding them. I place my hands on my head, closing my eyes as I trace J's thought process after the explosion went off. Jimmy and Tequila appear by my side, panting.

"We couldn't find him," they say.

"Neither can I," I breathe, pushing my palms harder against my head, adding more pressure.

J could be anywhere. He's smart, so the only reason he wouldn't be out here, somewhere he knows I would be, is if — my legs suddenly feel numb and unsteady like freshly cooked noodles as my thoughts begin to spiral.

I make myself look at the school to prove I'm wrong, but I'm not wrong. By the look of the smoke billowing from the roof, the explosion was close to his classroom, maybe a couple of doors down. He has to be stuck in there. That's the only conclusion I will let myself come to.

"Harley, don't even think about it," Jimmy says. He knows what I'm about to do before the plan forms in my mind. I turn on my heels, his hand brushing over my arm, but I'm too quick. I shove a teacher to the ground and sprint back toward the school. People yell for me to stop, but my legs keep moving, adrenaline clouding my judgement.

I slip past the open door and am instantly taken aback. My eyes sting, and my lungs begin to burn. I gag, forcing in small breaths and covering my mouth and nose with the inside of my elbow. If I breathe in too deeply, I might pass out. The entire hall is layered with thick, oxygen-destroying smoke. Stumbling around, I slide my other hand across the wall, tricking my brain into thinking that the further I move into the building, the less smoke there'll be. It feels like hours pass before Jimmy taps my shoulder, bearing two clear masks. He pulls one over my face, and I do the same to him.

"Where did you get these?" I gasp. I feel my chest loosen, but I already inhaled too much smoke. My mind is starting to spin, so I hold a hand out to steady myself.

"Fire trucks!"

Good, if the fire trucks are already here, they'll be in to help soon, I think. I look at him, a little stunned, but I'm grateful that he came when he did. Without another word, we start down the hall, jumping over fallen lights, avoiding burning wood, slowly making our way to the class that J was in this morning. There's not as much fire as I expected, so it's easy enough to walk unharmed through the heated hall, but the further we walk, the more screams and cries surround us.

"Help me!" A small whimper comes from my right, so quiet I almost miss it. "I want my mom," the voice cries. I scan the rubble, the fallen lockers and shattered windows, but I don't see anything until a small hand reaches for my shoe.

"Jimmy," I whisper, pointing to the child's bloody, soot-covered hand. Jimmy's eyes follow my finger, a small gasp escaping his mouth. The door of a locker lies over the boy's body, a torn-away strip of metal pointing down at his stomach and the puddle of blood surrounding him. He's small, no older than thirteen, and his pupils are so dilated with fear his green irises have almost disappeared.

"Help me!" His eyes cling to me, pleading with me. I fight with myself to stay or leave him, but I know the right thing to do is hold his hand while he dies.

"Hey, what's your name?" I ask, kneeling, ignoring the smell of burnt iron, and the glass digging into my knees. I take his bloodstained hand between mine, clean and alive.

"Forrest," he says, his voice weak, flinching from the pain.

"That's a cool name," I say, steady and soft, using the voice I reserve for young patients. A hint of a smile twitches across his face. "You're gonna be okay, we've got you. Jimmy's going to lift the metal off of you so I can see how it looks."

Jimmy nods, pulling the locker door away from him, revealing a strip of metal lodged deep in Forrest's stomach, likely slicing through his liver and diaphragm. Nothing can save him, it's a miracle he's still breathing. A scream of pain falls from his lips, and I want to leave. I don't want to be the last thing he sees when he dies.

"How bad is it?" Forrest asks, his eyes wide with hope, tears drawing lines down his ashen face. I don't know what to say. Finn would know what to say. He would tell him exactly what he needs to hear. I don't want the last words he hears to be his death sentence or the phrase we use to send off the dying.

So I do what doctors are forced to do sometimes — I lie. "You'll be okay. You're going to walk right out those doors and your mom will be waiting for you, okay?" I squeeze his hand tight, watching his eyes go blank, peaceful almost, looking up at me with all the trust in the world.

"What's your name?" he squeaks, his body relaxing.

"Harley," I smile, trying to stop the lumps forming in my throat from turning into tears.

"That's a pretty..." His breaths get shorter, and his hand releases mine as every muscle in his body relaxes, eyes staring blankly at me. I shut them.

I read somewhere that when your heart stops beating, your body starts to cool until it reaches room temperature, everything shutting down. But even after a few days, your skin is still alive, and because of this, bacterias have to break it down, which causes a body to decay.

The thought of this boy's decaying body sends me to my feet and moves me forward. I fight back tears as I turn away from his forest green eyes.

With each step we take, more bodies appear, more hands leave shadows on my skin, and for each person we help, two more fill their place. Every second it takes to carry a screaming child out is a second taken away from finding J. Yet I can't bring myself to walk by, indifferent to their suffering, and neither can Jimmy.

On our sixth trip inside, after carrying a seven-year-old girl out to medics who tried to stop us from going back in, an eerie silence makes me miss the cries for help as bones and ash take the place of the wounded. The air is now pungent and smouldering, the smell making its way into the masks, our oxygen gradually depleting. This is the last trip we can make, and the thought of J being one of these piles of dissolving flesh rises up in my mind.

"No," I whisper, "he's too smart."

The head engulfed in flames invades my vision as careful steps turn into careless ones — the thought of J being dead finally hitting me. I snag my foot on a piece of wood, sending me stumbling forward. I try to gain momentum, but there are too many things in my way. A pile of glass cushions my fall, digging into my hands, but of course, the impact doesn't hurt, nor does it distract me from my thoughts. Jimmy's hands wrap around my shoulders, pulling me to a sitting position.

"This is your fault!" The high-pitched voice from my dreams comes from my left, enjoying the scene unravelling around me.

"Did you hear that?" I ask, turning toward the sound.

"No!"

To my left lies a girl with ratty brown hair, red blood bubbling from her burning flesh, her golden eyes dancing with flames and her mouth tugged into a disgusting smile. I reach out, grabbing her hand, confused when her flesh dissolves into mine. Her head rolls back, her mouth releasing a scream so animal-like it pierces my eardrums.

"Look what you've done," she shouts, *"you did this!"*

What does she mean? I didn't do this. I didn't blow up the school. Jimmy helps me to my feet, only fatigue in his eyes, not terrified by the girl.

"You didn't see that?" I ask, pointing down, but when I look again, she's gone, vanished into the tiles.

"Maybe we should go back and let the firefighters do the rest. You've taken in a lot of smoke and you're running out of oxygen," he says, his mask running out as well.

"No!" I say frantically. "They haven't been here; they haven't saved six kids and watched one die. They can't save him — I have to."

The firefighters haven't come into the school yet because the fire isn't under control and the building is unstable; they won't be here for a while. I pull my arm from his alarmingly warm hand and walk on. Disoriented, my arms and legs move in un-rhythmic patterns, and I find myself stumbling more than normal. I can feel a part of me fighting to stay steady, to heal me and keep me going.

We reach door 124, which is charred to a crisp, so brittle it could collapse in a slight breeze. No noises greet us, except for the crackling of burning wood coming from the room.

I'm too late. I should have left the others behind and pushed forward until I knew for a fact J was safe. *I'm too late.* Defeat starts to dilute my adrenaline, and I'm ready to fall apart, walk out those doors, crumple to the ground and stop breathing when a muffled, 'Help,' comes from behind the door.

"Harley, he's in there," Jimmy says, his voice strained, his face drained of blood. I look down to find his jeans are singed near his calf, a deep line of blistering flesh in its place. I don't think I even heard him scream or felt his grip falter from my arm.

"Yes," I agree, not asking him if he's okay because just by looking at him, I know he's not. Jimmy clenches his teeth, steadying himself to kick the door open, stepping back just in time as a gust of smoke bursts past us.

In the room, the flames are alive, devouring every bit of oxygen, leaving us breathless. It's beautiful if you think about it, how they dance with the music of the crackling wood and the slight breeze coming through the window, how the flames are so numerous, they build their own wall. A small cough surfaces from the corner, and my eyes move to Jimmy for help, but he's gone. Out of every moment he had to back out of this poorly planned rescue mission, he chooses now. I search the floor, looking for anything that will help me break through the wall of fire, but when I look up again, I see Jimmy limping toward me with a dripping blanket.

"I thought you left," I say, panic evident in my voice.

"You know me well enough never to think that." He wraps the blanket around us.

"Will this work?"

"Hopefully." He gives me a reassuring smile, but the way he grimaces doesn't make it convincing.

"On three," I nod, "One...two..." We jump through the fire. Slight warmth kisses our skin, then nothing. We check ourselves on the other side, pleasantly surprised when neither of us finds new burns.

"J! J!" I scream. *Where is he?*

"Harley!" he screams back.

I spot him just in time to watch the earringed man and the bald man drag J out the window — the ones who assured me this would happen. I lunge at him, flames lashing at my arms, my legs. I yell as my hands lock around his ankles. Jimmy finds my waist, and we pull, playing tug of war with my baby brother. J screams in pain. He's so close that if I moved quickly enough, I could grab his chest. But the tension breaks — his untied shoe, the only thing remaining in my hand. We fall back, my head slamming hard into Jimmy's chin as J disappears from my sight.

"Harley, we have to leave!" Jimmy's voice is hushed by a scream that sounds as if it's from outside, but when my throat feels hoarse, I realize the scream is mine. The sound of cracking wood increases as the ceiling starts to dip toward us. The incandescent flames wave at me, urging me to come to them, their open arms heavenly, welcoming. They inch closer, licking at my feet, bringing the scent of burning rubber into the room. Their fingertips tickle my skin as they climb up to my knees. Hands drag me back as the flames' long nails push lines into my flesh.

"Harley, get up," Jimmy yells, too close to my ear. I flinch away. Sounds of falling wood and sizzling flesh — my flesh — make me weak. I don't want to get up. I just want to stay here where it's warm.

"Harley, you have to get up," a soft sweet voice whispers, but there's no one else with us. Maybe I'm having more hallucinations. Maybe J was a hallucination, and he's waiting for me outside. I put my arms around Jimmy's neck as he helps me to my feet. I stumble as he drags me along, too slow for his liking, so he ends up carrying me, groaning with each step.

"Harley, I know it hurts, but I need you to wrap the blanket around us." His eyes mirror the pleasant light, but I do as he asks. I swing the blanket over his head, draping it around his body, connecting the two ends in the middle.

"Stay with me," he begs. But I am with him. Darkness tugs at my eyelids not from the pain of the burns but from my mind trying to forget. It wants to shut down. "We're almost there." His careless steps bounce me from side to side. I imagine being on Ace's shoulders, laughing as he sprints through the crowd. *Almost where?* I don't want to go anywhere. I want to stay here in his arms where reality doesn't exist.

"Jimmy, I want to sleep," I mumble, laughing to myself because I didn't mean to say that.

"I know, but you have to stay awake." His voice is sweet, elastic, bending with my vision.

I pull the blanket over my eyes as bright lights start to play tag with the dark spots. Jimmy bumps into doors, and soon wet pavement stings my delicate skin as he sets me down. A sigh of relief drips from my mouth as the cool rain quiets my flesh.

Jimmy pulls the blanket away, and three familiar faces stand over me. My hands play with the itchy grass at the edge of the pavement as someone rubs cream over my legs.

"J," I choke. I want my brother. I want someone to bring him to me, even though I know he's gone. I want to be wrong. I want his kidnapping to be another hallucination from the smoke.

Jimmy strokes my hair, pulling the mask from my face and his own. "He's gone Harley," he whispers as water drips onto my face — not rain, tears.

"You're crying," I lift my fingers to his cheek, wiping under his eyes, noticing the red I leave on his skin and the blood running down my arm, shards of glass poking out of my palm. *Weird, glass shouldn't be there.*

"I think that's the least of your worries right now," he laughs nervously for a quick breath, moving my hand back to my side.

Suddenly something digs into my legs, and I arch my back, gritting my teeth as rough bandages wrap around my skin.

"Stop, please!" I beg. *Why does it hurt?*

"It's okay, it's okay," Finn says, "Just a little more." Tequila must have gotten him when Jimmy and I ran into the school.

"I want J!" I yell, unable to control myself. They watch me with such sad eyes. It feels like a dream. This must be a dream. They've never looked at me like that. It's just another one of my dreams. I have to wake up. J will be here when I wake up, giggling, with bright eyes.

Wake up! I dig my nails into my palms, pushing shards of glass deeper, hoping more pain will pull me from my nightmare. It's not working. "Wake up!" I scream in frustration, "just fucking wake up!" I slam my head hard again and again against the pavement, "Please. Please," I beg.

A hand slips under my head. Jimmy winces as the back of my head slams into his knuckles. Medical workers swarm around me, the gang arguing with them. Then weightlessness overcomes me as I'm lifted into the air, my weak limbs swaying with the world.

"We've gotta take her to the hospital."

"No, she's not covered."

"We can't just fucking take her home."

"My grandma's, we can take her to my grandma's."

"How?"

I drift in and out of the darkness as hands touch my skin.

Trauma hurts the brain more than physical pain. When my dad disappeared, people told me that when you lose someone you experience a kind of trauma that can make you emotionally numb to your thoughts and surroundings. So I shouldn't be worried about my mom shutting us out or forgetting where she is. That's how some people cope when they can no longer tolerate their reality. What they failed to tell me was that when a person loses their ability to connect with reality for an extended period of time, they eventually turn into fragmented souls and lose their footing on earth indefinitely. She never found us again. I don't want to do that. I never want to be like her.

"Luke! He has a car."

"Not him!"

"Jimmy, my grandma lives on the other side of town. We can't carry her all that way, we need a car, so get over yourself and look at her; she needs help."

I want them to shut up. Their voices keep interfering with my thoughts. They keep pulling me away from sleep.

"Fine!"

Someone leaves, making me uneven, causing me to tilt to one side. I don't want to lose my foothold in reality. J's still out there. I can't just leave him to fight for himself. If I leave, no one will care enough to find him. My mom barely even looks at him anymore, people turn a blind eye to kids being taken, and Eric caused all of this. I'm the only one he has in his corner. He's too young for this, too pure, his blue eyes and curved nose, so like my dad's, so unlike mine. He doesn't belong here. He belongs in a world with enough love and compassion to keep him from a burning building. But that world has never existed.

"Use the pain to bring yourself back, to keep you in the present," a different voice in my head whispers, responding to my thoughts.

I listen. I can't let my mind slip away. Two more minutes of nothingness, then I'll bring myself back. I absorb my weightlessness, the empty emotions, the rain moistening my skin, the feeling of almost letting go. Then I let the wind throw knives into my flesh. I try to stay still, but I can't help it. I squirm, wanting to get rid of this feeling. It burns.

"Keep her still."

"Harley, it's okay, Luke's coming."

"Oh, god, is she okay?"

"Open your damn car."

Luke's voice comes closer. Keys jingle; car doors open and hands leave me in the arms of someone who rests me on top of four legs.

"It's okay, just a bit longer."

The fire is following me, burning from the inside out. They can't see the person lighting matches and tossing them down my throat. They must not be able to see it, or they would help me.

"Please go unconscious, please," someone mumbles. I cry out again as Finn lays wet cloths across my legs.

"Where the hell did you get those from?" I groan in agony, black spots replacing all the light.

"I know it seems like it's making it worse, but it's drawing out some of the heat, I promise," Finn says. I don't think he's right, but the sound of his voice calms me.

Jimmy's hands hold my head still, forcing me to watch him. He startles me. His normal eyes now tense, agitated. I've never seen him like that. Even in a fight, he's stable and calm. Even when he's angry, he doesn't look like this. I lift my hand to his cheek, moving his head so his crystal eyes look into mine. His cheeks are soft.

He moves his forehead to mine, "I should have stopped you," he whispers, more of his salty tears falling onto my nose.

"I wouldn't have listened," I croak, trying to move, but he holds me still.

The car squeals to a stop, lurching my body forward. Jimmy straightens, lifting his head, more of my blood on his cheek. The doors fling open. Frantic rounds of arguments on how to get me inside distract them, but I keep my eyes trained on Jimmy. He's beautiful, even when pain and fear are more present than his playful demeanour. I take one last look before resolving their arguments by lifting my upper body painfully and sliding toward an open door, gritting my teeth.

Uri comes out of nowhere, rushing over to me. He slides one arm under my legs and the other around my back, gently, effortlessly lifting me from the seat. Rey must have gotten him. Rey was with Finn at the factory when Tequila came for him, and now he stands scared with the others. We rush into the house, startling a small, older woman sitting at a table. She looks up, her wrinkled face confused for a second before what I can only describe as the look a surgeon gets when faced with a problem takes the place of everything else.

"Set her here," she says, pulling a metal table into the room while sweeping the dust off. "Finn, get me Sleepers Serum and my kit."

"No," I grab her hand, "no sleepers! I can turn the pain off," I say frantically, slowly pulling myself into unconsciousness before she can stick me with a needle. A gentle smile appears on her face. Jimmy and Rey hold me down as I try to move the woman's needle away from me.

"It's okay, it's gonna be okay! It's not bad," Jimmy says, but he's lying. J's gone. He's gone, and I may never get him back, and the last thing I want is to drift into a world of drugs that I could stay in forever. You hear about it all the time. A kid gets painkillers or medication or tries a 'harmless' drug at a party that helps them escape their pain, and then, bam, they're an addict.

"I don't want—" My words get lost with a pinch in my arm that pulls me into nothingness.

CHAPTER 8
(HARLEY)

I wait to be pulled back under by the numbing drug-induced haze I've been drifting in and out of for hours, but when I feel parts of my body pressed against a solid table, I know there's nothing left to pull me back. Sweet smells of chai and fresh bread create a hollow pit in my stomach, triggering sudden hunger. Bright lights bounce off rusty orange walls, lined with strange plants that wrap around lamps, chairs and anything they can reach. The house is warm and old, probably from the 'First Days,' when the towns were created. Only a handful of these aging houses like our Shed remain on the edges of town.

A steady rumble rises from a copper kettle that sits unsteadily on a makeshift stove. Bottles of diluted purples and sickly yellows fill the counters and overflow onto the floor, and white cloths lie so close to the flames under the kettle, I'm surprised they haven't caught fire.

Finn's grandma, a short woman no taller than five feet, hobbles into the room, humming. Her steady, sun-freckled hands move the kettle off the burner, silencing its rumbling.

"Tea dear?" she asks, her voice honeyed and full.

"No, thank you." My voice is so hoarse it takes me a couple of tries to make my words audible.

"I wasn't asking, dear. This tea is for your throat." She places the cup in my hands. The smile she gives me makes her words seem motherly, not rude. The ceramic cup burns my fingers, but I don't pull away, like you'd think a person who'd spent hours in a burning building would. I let it sting, reminding me of how the flames licked at my legs. *My legs.* I lift the purple blanket, revealing light pink skin where charred red should be. If I hadn't witnessed the fire, losing J, and everything, it could have been just another dream.

"Isn't it beautiful?" she says, rubbing a bitter-smelling cream gently across my new skin. The cream is a pale brown in the container, but when she rubs it on, it fades, blending with the pink.

"How did you…?"

"You were pretty bad off, but you heal quicker than the boy! You had third degree burns on your legs, first degree on your arms. Finn did an excellent job of calming the skin down, perfectly executing the treatment plan. All I had to do was apply Stem 47 to your burns and the cuts on your hands and help you sleep so your body could heal without the stress of your mind."

"Stem 47?" I question, puzzled, looking at my palms, where only thin red marks remain. She takes long strips of white cloth, wrapping them around my hands.

"My co-workers and I developed Stem 47 for the purpose of creating a single remedy that could speed up the healing of new cells in any part of the body, but it never went mainstream. We stocked up on the creams for our own personal use and to help those in dire need of a quick fix, and now there's only a little left for emergencies," she pauses, frowning. "Luckily, I still had some, or Jimmy would have been in for a long recovery without it — though I believe you would have been fine, whether I helped you or not." Her hands move like Finn's, quickly and with no hesitation, like a much younger person.

"Did you teach Finn how to heal?" I ask, avoiding her presumption.

Her eyes drift to a picture frame with a smiling man and boy. "Yes and no. His grandfather, late grandfather, was a surgeon, just like your father."

"You knew my father?" I say, hesitant. The feeling that someone knew him and might know of his whereabouts warms me.

"Why yes! Everyone knew him. My husband was his mentor. A brilliant man he was." She presses her lips together.

"Was..." I echo, my small piece of hope deflating.

"He was a good man, dear."

When you lose someone you love, it makes other people tiptoe around you and pretend like you can't hear them whisper behind your back. She's not doing that; she knows saying 'I'm sorry for your loss,' doesn't make anyone feel better.

"My dad told me about his mentor — your husband taught him all he knew. My dad thought very highly of him." An empty smile fills her face. "Where's Jimmy?" I ask, trying to break the silence. She lifts her bony finger, pointing behind me.

I turn to see Jimmy, slumped in a green chair, mouth hanging open, arms crossed over his chest. His jeans are cut just below his knees, revealing deep pink skin, but the smaller burns on his arms have a thick layer of clear cream over blistered red flesh.

"That boy refused to leave your side. He wouldn't even let me treat him before he knew you were okay. Stubborn boy he is."

"Very," I agree, sipping my tea. It stings on the way down, but relief instantly follows. This lady really knows her stuff. She seems so brilliant that she doesn't even have to speak for you to know how intelligent she is. "And the others?"

"Finn stayed with you for a bit before going with Rey for more supplies. Tequila and Uri are off getting some people, some brothers, I think, and a boy who's named after a card. Spade maybe, or something like that, and there's another boy who's sleeping on my couch, he wouldn't leave either."

"Luke?"

She shrugs, "All I know is that Jimmy and him don't agree on much."

Why would Luke be here? He drove me, yes, but he had no obligation to stay. I could even go as far as to say he didn't have a reason to. Maybe he does care about me. A pang of guilt digs into my chest. Why am I sitting here wondering if my ex still cares when my baby brother is either dead or locked up somewhere cold and dark with other prisoners who have done much worse things than being Eric's stepson. I've got to get out of here and start forming a plan to find him because I can't just sit here and wait — for what? For them to find me? To kill everyone else I love?

I start to choke on my tea, my throat becoming so tight I want to cry. *Stop it*, I tell myself, *J's not dead, he's okay*. Finn's grandma takes the cup and assists me to a chair, humming as she starts to leave the room.

"Could you wake Jimmy for me, please?" I call after her. She smiles and shakes his shoulder. Jimmy draws back in panic, but when his eyes settle on mine, he relaxes, rubbing away the sleep. His wild hair falls across his forehead, covering his thick eyebrows. He looks relieved, his crooked smile loosening my throat. He inches his chair forward until our legs are in between one another.

"I'm so sorry," he starts, holding my face in his hands, leaning his forehead to mine. He flinches slightly as I push his hair out of his face. Three neat stitches sit just above his eyebrow, a purple bruise accentuating the cut.

"How did you get that?" I hold his hair back so I can examine it and I can't help but admire the perfect and well-placed stitches. "I didn't even notice."

"When we were leaving the building, and I don't blame you," he smirks for a second, then his lips turn down, tightening. "You scared me, I thought—"

"Hey, it's okay, we don't have to talk about it. There's more important issues right now." A crease forms between his eyebrows as he tries to read my thoughts. "We need to come up with a plan. We can't stay here.

They'll come for us, and J — he's still alive. I know he's still alive. We have to find him."

"Harley," he frowns, pushing his hand through his hair.

"No! Jimmy, J's alive, I know he is, and we can't leave him."

"I know, we already have a plan forming." He places his heavy hand on mine, sighing, looking at me in such a way that I blush, and butterflies move lightly through my stomach.

"He's right." Luke strolls into the kitchen, fidgeting with a switchblade before jamming it into the countertop. His blue and gold jacket seems sooty against his white shirt and blue jeans. He looks calmer than I've ever seen him. Jimmy rolls his eyes, leaning back. "I have a cousin out of town. We're going to stay there for a bit to give us a chance to come up with a better plan to get into one of the three cities," Luke explains, his expression turning serious for a moment, almost like he's reconsidering something before he picks up a purple bottle and slips it into his pocket.

"We?"

"I'm obviously coming with you. My cousin wouldn't let you stay otherwise," he grumbles.

"And you're okay with this?" I ask Jimmy, slightly shocked by the fact that the two of them aren't trying to knock the other's teeth out. Jimmy's features harden, making him look older, meaner.

"No," he huffs, "But he has a way to get you out, to keep you safe. So I had no choice. I asked Ace and the Brightly brothers to come along for support, if that's okay with you?"

Never in my life did I think I would be in the same room with these two, let alone forming a plan to get out of The Sticks. They're very different, in every possible way. Jimmy is harder, more cunning, smarter even, but Luke is cleaner, brought up in a better life, giving him a more optimistic view of the world. It serves him well and makes him less impulsive and reckless.

"Yes, but I need to get some stuff from home."

"Finn and—"

"Finn and the others are going to meet us at The Shed," Luke says, cutting Jimmy off, "and I'll go with you to your house."

"No, I will," Jimmy says, getting to his feet.

"You both can," I sigh, using Jimmy's arm to pull myself up. I still feel weak, and my joints ache. Even though my skin is mostly healed, my lungs and body still need time to get back to normal after all the smoke I took in, but time is one thing I don't have.

"How long was I out?" I ask, trying to break the tension.

"Half a day." Jimmy is passing me my shoes when a bony finger taps my shoulder.

"Take these with you." Finn's grandma passes me two cans that fit easily in my palm, "Use it sparingly dear." Her wrinkled hand brushes over my cheek, her eyes tender.

"I can't take this from you."

"Shh," she lifts a finger, dropping her voice to a whisper. "Protect my grandson, okay? He's all I have left and I know that if I tried to make him stay he would only run off alone, while I sleep, to follow you. So promise you'll keep him safe." She has Finn's eyes, only hers are a lighter green, like leaves in the forest when light hits them.

"I promise." She takes my hand in between hers. "Thank you," I whisper as she leads us out the door.

Once we leave her house, my senses are heightened as I look around every corner, watching every shadow, waiting for the slightest noise to set me off. "What's the plan again?" I ask, searching for a distraction as we drive to my house. I've never had a car. We couldn't afford one, and there's really no use for them, since everything is within walking distance. The only people who have cars and use them are the Opulents, people who have always had enough, like Luke. But even those people aren't really that well off. They can just afford more luxuries like cars, better houses and nicer clothes, but they still have to deal with the Hunters and the same amount of food as the rest of us.

"We'll stop at your house for a few minutes, then meet everyone at The Shed," Jimmy yells from the back seat, sticking his hand out the window, letting it bounce with the rushing wind.

"Then I'll get gas and a couple other things," Luke continues. "We'll stay the night at The Shed and leave at dawn. It's not a great plan, but it's all we've got."

"How are we going to take everyone? There's ten of us now," I frown. Ten is far too many people to go unnoticed. Far too many people to risk their lives for me.

"I'm going to grab the trailer, you know the one that we took camping."

"Yeah, it's small..."

"I know, but it fits four and we only have to fit three."

"and no one can see inside," I whisper, grateful that he's here and that driving around with a trailer isn't uncommon. Luke smiles, taking his eyes from the road for a second to let me see it in full. I think his smile is my favourite part about him, it's easy and natural — the same as Jimmy's.

"Then we'll take the windy road through the trees and make the day's trip to Dead Man's Hill where his cousin is," Jimmy says, pulling himself forward so that his head blocks my view of Luke. "Oh, take a right here."

I tense slightly because Luke has never been to my house. I've always made excuses when he asked to come over, telling him I was somewhere else or that it was easier to just hang at his. I never wanted to show him how bad off I was.

We pull into the empty driveway, that now — from a 'I'm skipping town let's have a ragger,' I suspect Eric threw last night — has garbage strewn across the deck, clothes hastily draped over the railings and what I think is a to torn-apart coach was used in the place of firewood, now is charred along with the grass it sits on, smoke still rolling off the top. "This is where you live?" Luke stares incredulously, his eyes wide.

"Yep. Pretty, hey?" I say, my cheeks flushing with embarrassment. Luke hops out of the car, walking to my side.

Jimmy rests his hand on my shoulder, his warmth seeping into my skin. "Harley, why are we here?" he asks, concern clear in his voice.

We shouldn't be here. In fact, this is probably the worst place to be, I think.

"I don't know," I whisper, almost sad I'm about to leave the home I've dreamt of running from for years.

Luke opens my door and offers me a hand. I push it away and hop out. "We're going with you," he says, hurrying after me.

"You can't."

"Yes," Jimmy says firmly, catching up, "we stick together, okay?" he whispers in my ear firmly.

I nod, avoiding his eyes. I don't know why I had to come back. It wasn't smart to bring them either. Maybe it's for the picture of my dad or the guns, or because the young, overwhelmed eighteen-year-old part of me still needs her mom. I just knew I had to come back.

I don't bother to be quiet when I walk into the house. Eric won't be here; he's not dumb. He's probably in a different town or hiding in one of his Lackey friends' houses by now.

Luke and Jimmy stand guard at the door as I grab some of my things, both keeping their eyes off each other, their egos trying to gain dominance. Out of habit, I leave a glass of water for Bob, who still sits sleeping at the kitchen table. J's room is as I left it, his chair in the wall. No one bothered to clean it up. I grab the picture of my dad first, then shove some of J's clothes in the bag, the scent of apples and cinnamon choking me. I press his shirt to my nose as tears start down my face.

"You shouldn't be here." Her low, rough voice makes my tears crawl back into their ducts.

I whip around to find my mom, her eyes scolding and panicked, a bottle of freshly opened wine in her hand, her yellow housecoat falling off one shoulder. When I was younger, I was told I looked like her, when she was once beautiful with thick hair, flawless skin and lively eyes. But now she looks run down, roots fully grey, hair thinning, her skin spotted with red, her eyes hollow.

"*You shouldn't be here,*" she hisses with more urgency, grabbing my wrist, wrenching me into the hallway.

Out of instinct, I shake my arm free and move away, training my eyes on her fluffy pink slippers. J got them for her birthday when he was nine. He saved up every penny he found on the street for two years so he could make her feel happy. She hasn't stopped wearing them since.

"He's gone," I mutter, feeling weaker in her presence.

"I know Eric's gone, but he'll come back! You can't be here when he does." She grabs me again, pulling me toward the door, digging her nails into my arm, the contents of her bottle sloshing and swirling.

"J's gone," my voice cracks, "he's gone — they took him." My words feel numb against my lips, sounding wrong to my ears. She turns around like she might scold me for lying, but when she sees the painful expression I can no longer hide, the wine bottle falls from her hand, shattering. The crimson liquid pools around her slippers, staining them as she comes to a stop.

"No!" she gasps, her hand moving to her mouth, her eyes becoming glossy as she starts to gravitate to the floor, "No!" she cries.

I grab her arms, keeping her from crumpling to the ground. "You don't get to do that," I hiss, pulling her up.

"What?" She gasps, looking so hurt, so confused, as tears drip from her eyes. I wish she didn't look like me.

"You don't get to pretend like you care." I lift my head so she's forced to look into my eyes. "You don't care. You haven't cared about him since Dad went missing — he's gone because you didn't care."

"That's not—"

"*Shut up,*" I interrupt, "you left us Mom, *you fucking left us.* We had nothing." I try to keep my voice steady, not wanting to show her how much she's hurt me, how much I miss her. "You did nothing — absolutely nothing when Eric, the man who got J into this situation started to beat him, beat *us*. You stood there blocking us out with drugs and liquor, watching like we were someone else's children." I let go of her, not caring if she is too weak to hold herself up. "But I'm not even mad about the fact that you left me, because a part of me understood, felt sympathy for you even. But you left J — who was only five, a little kid who hid in your arms at the slightest hint of trouble. You left him without a dad or a mom. He was raised by me — *me*."

She grabs my hand, pleading with me, "I lost the love of my life — you don't understand." I step back, rubbing my face, trying to figure out how not to scream at her. How not to lose control. "Harley, you — you have to leave, you don't know how bad this all is, how much trouble you're in." Her eyes shift to Bob for only a second, fear playing across her face. "There's so much you don't know. So much you haven't seen."

I hold her hand between mine, attempting to plead with her, lowering my voice to a whisper because that's all my tightening throat can handle, "Then tell me Mom — explain it to me."

She hesitates, weighing the repercussions in her head. "I can't, he said I can't." She shies away, "He'd—"

"You're pathetic," I spit, throwing her hand away from me and walking over to the couch. I pull two guns from between the cushions and a stack of cash taped to the inside of the fireplace. When I pass them to Jimmy, I realize my hands are shaking. I press them to my side, trying to keep them still.

"You can't take those, he'll—" she starts toward Jimmy, stretching out her hands, but I step between them.

"He'll what?" I'm yelling now, the strain scraping at my throat, "Beat me up? Kill me? What the hell do you care? You've done nothing about it before." Luke takes hold of my arm, pulling me backwards. "What the hell do you care?" I shout, tears running down my cheeks and into my mouth.

She presses her index fingers to her temples in agitation, attempting to keep her demons at bay so she can collect her thoughts. "I'm your mother, of course I care. I love you."

Her eyes turn soft, like they used to when she read us bedtime stories and held us as storms rattled the windows. She was my best friend. I used to tell her everything, from losing my first tooth, to meeting Jimmy, to gossiping about the girls at school. But she hasn't told me she loved me since I was ten. This woman standing in front of me — isn't my mom. She's gone.

"No!" I hesitate for a short breath, clearing my throat and making sure she doesn't miss a word. "As far as I'm concerned, my mom died the same day I lost my dad." I turn, hearing a small whimpering sound behind me as her knees hit the floor.

Luke yanks me back, stopping me from saying anything else, but what else could I say? I've shown her the one thing she fears most, that she was successful in pushing all the people meant to always love her away. I knew it would break her. It's the only thing that would break me.

Luke's nails run across my skin as I start toward the car. My mind goes blank for a moment as my brain tries to reset. The strings between my mom and me are severing — the ones I've held on to for years, tying and retying, fighting to keep them together until she came back to me, just like I held on to the hope of my dad coming back.

When I slide into the back seat, I realize I'm pulling Jimmy with me. He sits at my side, concerned and shocked. I don't snap that often. I can usually find peace so that I don't charge into a verbal attack that will only get both our feelings hurt. I can absorb the words thrown at me, store them deep inside until their effect is lost. I can look into someone's eyes and see their pain, what drives them to hate, and understand that a part of them is so damaged, they have nothing left to do but break the people around them, in order to fill the empty spots of their broken hearts. I'll stand there, letting them yell, cry and hit. I let them try to destroy me, knowing that they never will because my silence gives me all the control. When I saw her, though, in those fuzzy slippers, I couldn't find what anchored me to that silence. I only saw the woman who had me when she was eighteen, who grew up when I did. She was my best friend, who I had loved so unconditionally and yet the same woman who left me when I needed her the most.

For six years, I've held all my anger in, and I chose that moment to let it all out, when I was possibly seeing her for the last time.

"That's your mom? Harley, I'm — I'm so sorry, I didn't know," Luke says, sliding into the driver's seat, making the car purr with the turn of his key.

Of course you didn't, I think. "Just go," I yell, burying my face in Jimmy's shirt, trying to hide the tears I expect will come, but they don't. I'm too overwhelmed to feel anything.

Jimmy holds me tight, trying to relieve the pressure in my chest — trying to keep all my pieces in place. *He's too late,* I think.

"I didn't—" I start, but my regret clumps in my throat, blocking my words, forcing me to try and bring in air.

"I know." He pulls me in closer, pressing his cheek to my forehead, "she knows."

"But—"

He shushes me, lifting my chin, "It's okay." His breath is minty; the night of his drunken 'I love you' rushes into my mind, but I push it aside. "She knows you didn't mean it. She knows you love her." In his arms, I feel safe. Like the world beyond him doesn't exist.

He's right. Part of me didn't mean what I said, but the other part ... It hates her, not for leaving me but for leaving J. She gave no warning, no time to adjust. One day she was gone, spaced out in a different world, where her own daughter couldn't reach her. That part of me thought every word I screamed tasted like candy, saying them with every intention to hurt her, more than she hurt J.

"Hey guys, I need directions," Luke breaks in, somewhat annoyed. I push away from Jimmy, letting him do the talking. I have to pull myself together. I can't stay curled up in his arms where he unties and unravels me with his voice. Not now, probably not ever.

We pass Uri and Tequila when we're a couple of blocks from The Shed, the Brightly brothers and Ace smiling by their side. Sometimes I wish they'd never met me, never got dragged into any of this. They'd be happy and safe with one another in other gangs, and I'd be alone, with only J to protect.

We pull up to The Shed, where Finn and Rey sit by the open door, heads in their hands. Rey lifts his head first, his features hardening when he hears the car, while Finn slouches more. Rey jumps to his feet, waving for us to stop.

"What is it?" Jimmy yells from the window, then jumps out of the still-moving car. Rey whispers something to him that makes Jimmy run into The Shed. Finn walks over, helping me from the car, his expression unreadable.

"How're you feeling?" he asks, supporting me with his arm.

"I'm okay, what's going on?"

"My grandma did a good job, hey, with the cream and all." His eyes look at everything but my face. He's avoiding the question.

"Finn!" I turn to look at him. His eyes are red and puffy, either from crying or lack of sleep. Most likely, both.

"It's probably best if you see for yourself," he sighs, leading me inside.

My mouth drops. The Shed is absolutely destroyed. Stuffing is scattered across the floor, the couch torn open and lying in the spot where the TV once was. Glass is everywhere, from the windows and the lamps, along with pieces of wood from the walls and tables. Someone breaking into The Shed and destroying it wouldn't have been so bad if it weren't for what's now on every single wall — the letters 'AC,' spray-painted with a smiley face under them, eyes crossed out alongside the words *'See you soon, love.'*

Laughter from the Brightly brothers quickly dies when everyone files into The Shed.

"Holy shit!"

Holy shit doesn't even describe how much trouble we're in. The third leader of the Big Three has finally joined the party, making it clear to all of us that I have a target bigger than the moon on my back, meaning everyone around me has one on theirs as well.

How did they find The Shed? It's hidden, and the only people who know are in the gangs, but they promised to keep their mouths shut about it in exchange for medical help. But I guess there's always a rat. My heart starts to race. I close my eyes, thinking about how I could be responsible for the deaths of these nine people who have no obligation to be here besides being my friends. I can't make them follow me into a rescue mission that I haven't thought all the way through. It might not even work. But J. I have to save him. I take deep breaths.

"If any of you want to back out, now is your chance. This plan to save J won't be easy. The Big Three are targeting me, as well as the people I'm with. There's a real chance you'll get hurt or be killed and I don't want you to follow me blindly," I bluntly say, expecting to see stunned faces when I open my eyes, but they all just stare at me, taking in my steady voice and calm demeanour. I know how to appear stable in the worst situations from years of lying to people and trying to talk Eric out of a beating.

"I'm with you," Jimmy pipes up, resting his hands on my shoulders. I knew he would say that, but I want him to look me in the eyes and see I'm begging him not to follow me.

"Me too," Tequila says, not hiding the mascara running down her cheeks and the hesitation in her voice.

"Us too." Rey gestures to himself and Finn.

"For the kid," Uri calls.

"I've always wanted to go to the Big Three," says Buckey, nudging Johnny.

"Anything for you, beautiful," Johnny winks. Those two boys, even in the worst moments, can't help but add humour. I love them, and I don't deserve any of them.

"J's like a little brother to me, I can't stay here knowing I could have helped and didn't." Ace moves toward me, wrapping me in his arms, his familiar touch making me grateful and scared for him — for his decision to follow me, his best friend.

Everyone turns to look at Luke, who is leaning against the door frame, picking at his nails. "What?" he says, defensively, "I thought my presence was implied, given I'm providing the ride and place to stay."

"Ass!" Tequila coughs. Stifled laughter starts at the Brightly brothers, then ripples through everyone, and suddenly I'm glad no one left. I know, no matter what I go through, I will always have people I can trust and depend on.

"Whatever! I'm going to get gas," Luke says, leaving.

"Is it a bad idea to stay here tonight?" Tequila asks, picking up a smashed-in heater that sparks when she rubs two wires together.

"I don't see why we can't," says Jimmy, "They probably got some Hunters to do this and they'll expect us to get scared and run, so they won't come back."

"What are we gonna sleep on? The couch is kinda wrecked."

"There's a couple of mattresses in the back," Finn mutters, setting his bags down, beginning to sort his supplies.

"And I saw a couple on the street," Uri adds, already walking to go get them.

"You know what that means, Buckey," Tequila purrs.

"What?"

"We're gonna have to sleep real close," she pokes, causing Buckey to blush and Johnny to break out in laughter.

"Oh go help Uri," Jimmy says in disgust. Tequila skips out the door. Rey follows her, his fist clenched, probably off to punch someone.

We spent most of the afternoon moving the furniture outside, sweeping up glass, and filling the rooms with old mattresses and blankets that Tequila 'found' on the streets, although Uri said she found a couple of unlocked windows and empty houses. At some point, Finn ran off and came back with a proper meal of fresh bread, scraps of chicken, mayonnaise and bananas from god knows where. We feast on more than enough food for ten people, leaving only the bananas for the long road trip tomorrow.

As everyone settles down for bed, I perch on a table with my back to the wall, a gun loaded in my hand. Jimmy argues with Uri to let him keep watch with me. But exhaustion takes over, and Jimmy settles for sleeping right by the table. He makes me promise to wake him if I feel tired, but there's not a chance I'm sleeping tonight. I'm scared that if I let myself fall asleep, someone will sneak in and kill everyone, leaving me alive to wake up to dead bodies. Uri sits beside me, resting his back against the wall, placing his gun on the table close enough to grab if any trouble comes.

"Are you scared to go back to the cities?" I ask, remembering his connection to the Big Three. I want to ask him what he went through, but the distant look he reveals every time the cities are mentioned makes me feel the torment he faces from thinking about it.

He stiffens, his breath catching. "Yes. I have a photographic memory, remember — no matter how far I get from that place, I can never truly leave it." He laughs for a second and looks away. He hasn't been back home for years, and whatever happened to him that day still makes him wake up screaming for someone to run. All he's told me is that he grew up in one of the Big Three cities where crime was a way of life, and if you didn't roll with it, you'd die by it.

He was sixteen when he showed up at The Shed, a bullet in his shoulder and soaked in sweat and blood, his face so bruised he looked nothing like his ID. He scared Finn and me half to death when we found him, barely breathing, begging us to let him die. Of course we couldn't let that happen, so we treated him, and four years later, he hasn't gone a day without showing me he's thankful for us.

"Do you regret leaving?"

"No," he says instantly. "I had to. But every night — every moment when I feel at peace here, the faces, the screams of the people I left behind appear in my dreams and my waking thoughts. As if to remind me, that even though I'm here with you guys, my family, I will never be safe. I will never be truly at peace."

"You don't have to come with us." I swing my legs back and forth, a rush of guilt washing over me because I do want him to come. We have a bigger advantage on the streets with him because he knows them better than any of us.

"Yes I do." He looks at me, his hazel eyes sending chills through my body, "Every time I give in to how scared I am, I remember how scared J is — how many people the Big Three have done this to. I feel the strength of all their families and friends, and that makes my fear become hope — hope that if I am strong I can save people. It makes me brave." We sit in silence, listening to the steady breaths and snores as I let his words sink in.

I never thought about how many people have been taken, tortured and killed by the Big Three for not paying them back, not doing a job or for getting in the way. The Big Three act like they own everyone and everything. They've been disrupting, destroying and terrorizing innocent people for years because they crave power and money. The tightness in my chest loosens, and I no longer feel scared or hopeless. The idea of actually getting J back feels brighter and more promising than I ever thought possible.

CHAPTER 9
(JIMMY)

"I can't be the only one who thinks bringing Luke along is a bad idea," I say, slamming my cards on the table. At 4 am, the earliest any of us, besides Harley, has ever gotten up, we started debating who would be the three to travel in the trailer. Everyone was grumpy and getting on my nerves as soon as the topic came up. We all instantly volunteered to take the day's trip in the old, cramped, rusty trailer that creaks so loudly it sounds as though, at any minute, all its nuts and bolts could pop out and send us into the ground. Although Luke was driving and couldn't volunteer, he wouldn't stop making snarky comments, trying to get Harley to ride shotgun with him. After thirty minutes of debating and arguing, we finally agreed that Harley shouldn't be in the front where she could be seen, but she also couldn't be in the trailer because we needed her eyes and instincts. In the end, Ace, the Brightly brothers and I ended up in the trailer. Although there were only supposed to be three of us, I needed some space from Luke, Ace fell asleep the moment he got in, and the Brightly brothers never separate when traveling, so we all piled in and began the long drive to Dead Man's Hill.

"I don't know man, he doesn't seem so bad," Johnny says, rummaging through cupboards, looking for the jackpot of drugs Luke's rumoured to have hidden in here. When Luke started to date Harley, who is known to unleash her wrath on people who lie to her, no one thought he would dare hide drugs in a place so easily accessible. So the rumours died off.

However, every once in a while, people try to break in, hoping to find the stash that could probably buy them freedom for life. Out of the thirteen people who have tried various ways of breaking in, all have ended up in the hospital with damaged vocal cords from what appeared to be acid reflux. Though, no one believes it. There have been far too many people with that diagnosis known to have tried to break into this unlikely fortress for it to be a coincidence. In the Brightly brothers case, the injured have not dulled their dreams of one day stepping foot in here.

"I agree with Jimmy. And Go Fish, Buckey," Ace laughs.

"Shit," Buckey grunts, sifting through his cards, looking for any pair that can keep him from losing the twenty bucks he bet but doesn't have.

"Luke's a sketchy dude. He seems to belong to all the Opulent gangs, but no one knows where his loyalty lies and he never gets caught or even connected to the shit he does. One time, I saw him beating a little kid with a wrench, and the mayor stopped, nodded his head and kept driving," Ace shivers at the memory.

"You two are biased."

"What?"

"Yeah, you two are biased! You're both in love with her!" Johnny mutters as, becoming reckless with his snooping, he pushes bowls and cups to the floor, not caring if they break.

"Watch it man, you've got to leave the crime scene the same as you found it," Buckey says, smacking Johnny on the back of the head, but he just shrugs, only making more of an effort to knock things over.

"No, I was in love with her. Different thing, we're just friends now." Ace flashes me a timid smile, flitting his gaze to the cards instead of me.

"And I'm not in love with her," I object, running my hands through my hair, pretending not to notice their entertained looks.

I am in love with her, and they know it. Apparently, every god-damn person in the town knows it — even she knows it. I told her I didn't remember what I said to her that night. I was embarrassed she didn't let me kiss her and a little hurt that she only said 'I know' and not, 'I love you too.' I understand why she didn't. I was drunk and wasn't myself, but the thing that hurt the most was walking down the stairs and seeing her wrapped in Finn's arms, so peaceful and perfect. It felt like she stabbed me in the chest with a frozen knife.

I wish no one knew how I felt about her. It would make suppressing my feelings easier. Or I wish I could just find something wrong with her, like how we argue over dumb shit that doesn't matter, how she bites the skin on her lips when she's nervous, how she sings so off pitch it's not even annoying, just funny. How she values everyone's life over her own — treating it like it doesn't matter if she dies. But when I make that list in my head, it always ends with traits that make her unique, that make me want to be with her more. Frankly, it makes things confusing and frustrating.

"Okay buddy," Ace says, patting my shoulder, "keep telling yourself that and maybe it will come true."

I brush him off, truly considering if that could work. Out of all the boyfriends Harley's had, Ace is the only one I can tolerate. I don't like him, but I don't hate him. I respect him for actually being a decent human being. When they were thirteen and first started dating, I would try to avoid him, but somehow, we always ended up together, at fights, parties, even at The Shed whenever Harley was late to meet him. Eventually, he grew on me. Ace treated Harley the same, if not even better than I would. They were together for two years. It was torture, and I couldn't even hate him because he doesn't have a mean cell in his body. But I can't say I wasn't over the moon when they decided to break up. He stuck around because, both fortunately and unfortunately, Harley has a habit of becoming friends with her exs.

"Oh, shut up," I say, struggling to suppress a smile, "When you find the drugs, you're not gonna smoke 'em now, are you Johnny?" I ask, starting to fidget.

"Nope! We're all aware of the sobriety pledge you made to Harley, and even though it would be fun because you are hilarious when you're high, it won't be for smoking purposes. Anyway, I don't really feel like getting beat up by Harley today. Besides there's another rumour that Luke hides expensive liquor like scotch and whiskey from the Big Three in here. None of that moonshine crap. We could sell that shit watered down and still get a good price for it," Johnny grins, starting to tap the ceiling and behind the sink, listening for hollow spots.

The Brightly brothers have always been known for stealing and reselling expensive products for up to double the perceived value, despite the fact that every single Gutter rat and Opulent knows it's not worth it. Johnny and Buckey somehow get people to buy or trade for anything, no matter what the value.

Tequila says it's because Buckey's good-looking and Johnny has loads of charm, but I think it's because they play on everyone's desires, painting a euphoric picture no one can resist, advertising that what they give you will make your worthless life better.

I met the Brightly brothers when I was eleven, before they met the rest of the gang. Johnny was in my Intro to Psychology class, and Buckey was in Math with me until they both dropped out of school to run their dysfunctional gang. I knew the minute they opened their mouths, that they would have my back, and I would have theirs. When the gang met them, they instantly loved them, and we were declared allies on that same day.

"I don't think Luke's trustworthy, though," Buckey adds, sliding a couple of cards from his sleeves.

"I might have to agree with you now," Johnny states, pulling out a matte black piece of plastic that appears to be a cell phone.

"Jeez. What is it?"

"I've only seen those things on old TV shows."

"I didn't know phones still existed," Ace gawks, dumbfounded.

Cell phones haven't existed since the population was above eight billion. Most people only know about them from TV or their parents. I was fortunate to learn about cell phones in my History of Technology class. Thirty years ago, almost eighty percent of the population had a phone, even little kids. It was considered an essential, the sole means of communication, which ultimately taught people how not to communicate in person. It was a useful piece of technology in some sense but very wasteful in others, so straightforward a child in the Big Three could recreate it in minutes.

When the Earth released its poisonous gas out of nowhere, all the infrastructure that made the phones useful was dissolved like most mechanical and man-made objects. After everyone got settled, they could have figured out how to get things up and running again, but I guess funds were needed elsewhere, and phones were the only piece of technology we no longer required. In the Big Three hierarchy, you can get a special ear chip that they permanently implant in your ear so they can contact you anytime they see fit. Mostly the Hunters and government workers require those.

"Does anyone know how it works?" Buckey flips the screen up. I grab it, running my fingers over the smooth black plastic. The buttons are weird with letters and numbers on the same keys, and the screen is foggy. It's an old version and dead like all the rest of them. Why would he want a piece of junk?

"What do you think he needs it for?"

"Selling to stupid people?"

"To pretend he has friends to talk to," Johnny chuckles. We all shoot him daggered looks. "Sorry, not the time."

"I don't know." I'm about to give up and say maybe he just likes antiques when I remember these types of phones have a compartment for a battery. Carefully, I slide a thin piece of hard plastic off its back, revealing a small clear bag with an even smaller green and gold hard drive in it. Hard drives are as common as dust, but why would he have to hide it in a phone? In something so eye-catching?

Suddenly, the trailer screeches to a stop, throwing Johnny off balance. His elbow strikes my head, causing the phone to slide from my hand and the hard drive to fall out of sight.

"Why are we stopping?" Johnny gasps, rubbing the knee that collided with the metal bar of the table.

"Quick, find the hard drive," I order, scrambling toward the phone. We all scour the floor before Ace hollers and passes me the clear bag. Luckily, the hard drive doesn't look damaged. I fumble with it, sliding the plastic back in place, and toss it to Johnny, who jams it in the wall. Ace and I pick up the cups and plates that aren't broken while Buckey sweeps the shattered pieces to the side. Johnny slides the board back in place as Tequila flings the door open, nearly nailing Buckey in the stomach. Out of habit, we stand with our hands raised, ready for the Hunters.

"Calm down, it's just a pee break," she yawns, lines on her red cheek from where she slept.

"Coming," Buckey squeaks, clearing his voice, jumping out and almost smashing into Luke, who scowls, taking in the damage we've caused.

"You could've kept to yourselves and not looked around," he grumbles, staring at the pile of broken plates.

"Wasn't us man, it was your careful driving," Ace chuckles, hitting his shoulder hard against Luke's as he jumps from the trailer. Luke eyes the spot in the wall where the phone sits, the left side of his mouth curling up.

"Gotta get some supplies," Johnny says nervously, quickly leaving me alone with an almost snarling Luke. He cracks his knuckles and flexes his arms. I ready myself, then straighten when Harley appears behind him, rolling her eyes.

"Jimmy, come on," Harley beckons. She has lines on her cheek, too, surrounded by a rosy blush, her bruise appearing faded. I obey, not wanting to get stuck alone with Luke.

I'm not scared of him. I'm quicker than him, stronger than him and have beaten him in most Warehouse fights, but on the streets, he never fights fair. Anyway, if we did fight now, he would play to the fact that Harley would assume I egged him on and got him to throw the first punch.

"Yeah, run after her like you always do," he snorts under his breath. I bite my tongue, focusing on Harley, on her face, the curve of her lips, the point of her nose. "Too bad you'll never get her," he says, loud enough for Harley to hear. Before I can turn around and knock him to the ground, she grabs my arm, guiding me away.

"It's not worth it, Jimmy." Her smile is weak, but I know she's right. He's nothing — a nobody.

She also hates it when I fight, for fun at least. She'll never admit it because everyone does it, but I can tell by the pitiful look that dims her eyes whenever she stitches me up. Maybe some sick, messed up part of me fights for fun just to get time alone with her, where she feels for me — pays attention to me.

The gas station we stop at is discoloured and run down. The once red stripes that wrap around the building almost blend with the dirty white walls and soot-dusted windows. The gas pumps are out of date and barely used anymore. The building is surrounded by a bed of gravel, fading into yellow grass that disappears into oversized pine trees bordering the back. These days, the primary purpose of a gas station is for bathroom breaks, backroom deals, and to hide drugs and people. Durçk, the man who runs this place, is known for his Hawaiian patterned shorts, always carrying around a tabby cat with one eye, and his ability to mislead even the smartest Hunters when hiding runaways. We know him because he had to hide Rey after he rigged a slime bomb to go off when the Hunters opened their car doors. Durçk was able to keep him off the grid for a couple weeks until the Hunters found a new person to chase. Tequila still owes him dance lessons from that one.

"Here to give me my lessons?" he asks playfully, his husky voice rough against the classical music seeping from the speakers. He's in his mid-twenties, but his bushy eyebrows, full beard, and face with scattered tattoos make you think otherwise.

"Nope, decided to let you wait given the promises you've made me and never followed through on," Tequila chirps, running her hands over everything in sight and taking a bit of Durçk's homemade candy we all know she won't pay for.

"It was one time..." he trails off, stiffening when Harley and I come into sight, "you shouldn't be here girl!" His eyebrows come together as his voice hardens.

"What?"

"Not you, Tequila, Harley!" His tone falls, saddening with his eyes.

Harley stops, dropping the flashlight she was inspecting. She walks to the counter where he sits, steadying herself by placing her hands on the cracked surface.

"What do you mean?" Her voice shakes a little but only enough for someone who knows her every tone to notice. Durçk drops his cat and reaches under the counter, pulling out a slip of blue paper.

I watch her, confused for a second before crowding around with the others to see what makes her stiffen.

There are two pictures side by side with writing above and below them. As I get closer, I see the images display Harley's and Eric's mugshots from years ago with the words: 'Wanted Alive. For failure to pay 15 million dollars to the Three Leaders. For resisting arrest and for the murder of Jaylen Hudson aka 'J,' brother of Harley Hudson and stepson of Eric Froning. The reward for turning in these runaways will be one year of guaranteed protection and extra food.'

For a second, I forget to breathe as the word murder becomes bolder on the page.

'Anyone who helps these criminals will be considered an accomplice in their crimes and subject to the same punishments.'

"How could they say that?" Harley whispers as Uri takes the paper, ripping it into pieces. "I didn't kill my brother, Durçk, they took him."

"I believe you. I've seen you two together, but no one is going to see you as a person anymore. They're all going to see you as a way to get full bellies and freedom from the Hunters for a year." His voice is calm, gentle, almost making the situation seem less threatening than it is.

"Can you hide her here?" Finn asks, squeezing Harley's arm, but she only looks at her fingers, drawing lines in the dust.

"Unfortunately, no. The Hunters have been through here three times this week. I had to get rid of my products in the back because someone gave a list of all my hiding spots." He leans closer so that his face is inches from hers, lowering his voice so only the people closest can hear, "Only trust these eight." He nods toward our group, excluding Luke with a glare. Luke looks away, beginning to fidget with the door handle. "No one else." Durçk straightens, changing his expression. "I have something for you." Disappearing for a couple minutes, he comes back with a black duffle bag.

"What is it?" I ask, pushing my way beside Harley. She grabs my arm, leaning into me, all colour drained from her face.

Durçk flashes us a playful smile, unzipping the bag to reveal five walkie talkies, a rifle, six handguns, a couple of knives and three boxes of bullets. "You can take these. Sorry I only have five walkie talkies. Do you guys know how to use guns?"

"Harley and I do," Uri speaks up, zipping the bag and slinging it over his shoulder. "Thank you."

"I do too," Luke offers, stepping forward. The tabby cat jumps out of nowhere, hissing and scratching at Luke until he steps back to the door. The cat paces back and forth in front of him, making sure Luke doesn't get closer. I'm also convinced I heard Durçk hiss at him too, but everyone's too tense to laugh.

"Teach them how to shoot. You'll need all the protection you can get. The Hunters are more armed than ever before and I know for a fact that wherever you're going, people will be packing heat." Durçk frowns, placing his dirt-stained hand on Harley's. "Be careful," he says, flashing his rotten teeth.

"Okay," Harley stutters, pulling her hand from his, thanking him numbly and walking past Luke, who follows her out the door. I press my palms into the table, trying to steady myself as this new information threatens to knock me over.

"Take anything you want — on me." Durçk takes a heavy seat, rubbing his eyes.

Everyone grabs one thing, knowing that we could never repay Durçk for what he did today. Before I can leave, Durçk grabs my arm, holding me back, waiting for everyone else to go.

"Don't trust that boy."

"Who, Luke? What do you know?" I say in anticipation.

"Nothing yet, but I know he's bad news." He hands me a slip of yellow paper with the five towns, a name and address beside each.

"What's this?"

"I don't know where you're going, but these are my contacts in each town. They can give you information on J, but be careful around them. They're good people, but they don't trust easily, and they like to play games," he warns, a slightly amused smirk curling his lips. He drops my arm, nodding toward the door. I barely catch his words as the door shuts behind me, "Take care of her — she's special."

Special? To whom? Special to us? Special to the people trying to get her killed? Why do people keep saying shit that doesn't make sense? I mindlessly climb into the trailer and find Harley and Finn in the place of the Brightly brothers. Ace sits on the floor, sorting through the bag of guns, mumbling as he counts.

"Did I miss something?" I ask, stepping over Ace and taking a seat next to Harley as the car begins to move.

"Uri sent the Brightly brothers to the front because he said I need to stay hidden, and all of us need to talk about what just happened."

"All of us?" I look at Harley, expecting tears to be overflowing from her eyes, but she sits staring blankly at Ace. She's distracted, and I can see the slightest trace of anger glinting in her eyes, an emotion she doesn't often show around others. I try to move toward her, but she pulls away, inching closer to Finn.

"They have a walkie talkie up front," Finn says, letting her leg touch his.

"Goose to Top Gun, Goose to Top Gun, over and out."

"Seaweed to ocean, seaweed to ocean, over and out."

Laughter ripples through the walkie talkies. "Oh! I got one. Peanut to butter, peanut–"

"Johnny, Rey, cut it out."

"Sorry, Harley, go ahead, over," Uri's voice crackles.

"Do we really have to say 'over' every time?" Tequila complains.

"No, guys, just focus," Luke shouts, his voice coming out muffled and far off.

If I'm going to be completely honest, I don't think this will work. I don't think we will be able to save J. I don't want to be the pessimist of the group, but everything is against us. Even if the whole population weren't looking for Harley, I still don't think we'd have a chance.

"Okay," Harley sighs, "We need to find someone who can give us information on where they keep the prisoners, and in which city of the Big Three. Luke, do you have any ideas?"

"Umm—"

"Oh! Durçk gave me his contacts from each town. Here, Dead Man's Hill is at the top," I interrupt, handing her the slip.

"Okay. So we have that covered." She gives me a timid smile, reaching for the paper but not letting our hands touch. What the hell did I do? From the time she left the gas station to when we got in the trailer, she's just been distant ever since — oh right. She's been distant ever since I told her I loved her, then lied about not remembering. "Luke, Uri, do you know Dead Man's Hill well?"

"No," Uri says, "I know a little from researching it but probably don't know where Durçk's contact would be."

"I don't either. I only visit my cousin once in a while, but Emma would most likely know," Luke adds, hitting a pothole, making us bounce.

"We should go tonight then," Harley starts.

"No," I blurt. Her eyes fix on me, sending chills up my arms. "It's just, everyone's tired and hungry. We don't know what waits for us at that place and you and Uri still have to show us how to shoot," I say cautiously. She considers my point for a moment, probably calculating how much sleep a human can function on and still perform well.

"He's right, Harley, Tequila's tired," Uri laughs.

"No I'm not!" she argues, but you can hear her yawn over the walkie talkie as everyone falls silent, waiting for Harley to respond. She looks at me, then at Ace, who still sits counting bullets on the floor and then over at Finn, who gives her a nod.

"Yeah! Okay, we'll go tomorrow night, when fewer people are out," Harley sighs, leaning her head back.

"Yes! We'll shoot pumpkins in the morning so we can blow them up!"

"And have a competition! Whoever hits the most pumpkins won't get shot in the foot!"

"Johnny, Rey, you're giving me more reasons why I shouldn't show you how to shoot," Harley says, shaking her head. Everyone knows that even when she's stern with those two, she really doesn't mean it. To her, they're like puppies who need lots of attention.

"No, no! We promise not to blow up any pumpkins," Rey pleads.

"Or—" Harley furrows her eyebrows.

"Or shoot anyone in the foot," Johnny grumbles.

"Five minutes away."

Ace bounces up, peering out the small window. Harley's face softens as she puts the walkie talkie down, running her fingers over the names on the paper. I want to pull her in — to tell her everything will be okay, but I can't, because I have no idea what will happen to her, J, or any of us. We're walking into unknown territory with landmines and snipers on every corner and no way around them. Me saying that it will all work out wouldn't make a difference anyway. So I turn to the window instead.

I've never had any desire to travel to the other four towns formed around the Big Three because they aren't much different from each other. Having the same layout and being the same size, you're able to walk from one side to another in under thirty-seven minutes. Between each town is a forest with a road going through it. Without a car, it's a two-day trip to get to the next town, discouraging any visiting between them. Mixing town members isn't illegal, but it isn't encouraged.

The roads are worn down asphalt, cracked, with potholes more prominent than smooth patches and lined with houses beaten by weather and time. The townspeople all live the same, eat the same, grow up the same, the only difference is the rules — The Sticks probably has the least of all. There are basic rules: don't steal, don't kill and don't grow or raise your own food, but since each leader has a town to run along with their city, they get to enforce their own cruel ways to punish us.

MC runs The Sticks. He didn't make any extra rules. I guess it's because he doesn't care enough or because it has the smallest population of all the towns.

AC runs Dead Man's Hill, where liquor and all parties are illegal except at the fights. So, when you attend a fight, since you can't drink anywhere else, the entry fee is six shots of alcohol, ensuring that angry kids are drunk upon entry and therefore will try to beat up everyone they see.

Since there aren't six towns to divide evenly among the three of them and since MC and AC are the lesser leaders, they have to run The Back Roads together. The one extra rule is a five o'clock wake-up time and an eight o'clock curfew every night. The Back Roads is the most populated and most challenging town to control. They figured, why not make the people more agitated by enforcing the rule to get up before the birds do. Hell, I'd try to beat up everyone if I had to wake up at five.

Then there's Shadow Cove and Hunter Valley, the worst and strictest towns to live in, ruled by the sociopath JC. Per his authority, all townspeople have to join a gang. The people of Hunter Valley are trained to be Hunters, and the people of Shadow Cove are trained to be doctors, technicians and scientists, all starting when they turn ten. If they pass their training when they are sixteen, they are shipped off to different towns and the Big Three to fill the jobs. If they don't pass, they have a choice to fill the lower level jobs, like construction and garbage duty, or to be banished and sent into No

Man's Land, the place that separates us from the Big Three, where a person must learn to survive or die. Most people choose lower-level jobs. There are more subtleties and details, but that about sums it up.

As we drive through the streets, people don't notice or acknowledge six people in a car with a big trailer. Most don't even look up, and those that do, look away quickly. This makes me feel a little better because maybe they won't notice ten strange kids walking through their streets.

We hop from the trailer, and the pack of guns weighing Ace down make him land on his knees in a pile of mud. I can't see why we're staying here. The house is small, probably smaller than The Shed. I have no idea how Luke's cousin is going to be able to take all of us in, especially eight boys. The door swings open, and a beaming beautiful girl walks out.

"I think I'm in love," Rey whispers, his eyes wide and mouth hanging open as he slaps Finn on the back.

Rey falls in love with everyone, but in this case, it wouldn't surprise me if he did fall in love this fast. She's muscular and stunning. Her caramel skin and dark curly hair make her eyes seem kind and her smile soft. She's beautiful.

"I'm Emma — let's get you all inside before people get suspicious." Her voice is perky and oddly comforting.

She pulls Luke into a hug. "Long time no see," he says.

"You saw me last weekend."

"Still," Luke smiles.

I can tell she's overly happy to take us in by the way she talks and bounces with every step as she leads us inside. Even though I've just met her, Emma seems like she's one of the few people who can maintain a cheerful, sunny expression. It's almost refreshing. The creases around her lips tell me she's just happy to be alive.

"It's just me and my momma here, and she's gone most of the time anyways, so there's plenty of room for all of you." Emma leads us inside and up the stairs to a loft, where mattresses cover half the floor and sheets dangle from the roof.

"What are the sheets for?" Tequila asks. She glares at Emma a little too harshly, probably because the Brightly brothers and everyone else in the gang besides Finn and Luke are drooling over Emma, taking all the attention from her. At the sight of this, a laugh escapes my mouth, causing Tequila to turn her glare on me.

"Well, no one comes up here much, so I figured I'd put them up to make sure the dust and stuff doesn't fall on you while you're sleeping."

"Well—" Tequila starts.

"We're very thankful that you could take all of us in," Harley interrupts a fuming Tequila.

"Oh, it's no problem. After all the kind things Luke's told me about you. I knew the wanted posters weren't real. So it was my humanly duty to keep you safe, for the time being." Emma draws a heart in the air with her fingers, making Harley and Luke blush. Barf. If my stomach weren't grumbling so bad and the aroma of food drifting through the floorboards didn't smell so good, I would think something was a little off about Emma's kindness, but my mind is too overcome by hunger to care.

"Is that chicken, beans, mashed potatoes with gravy, and bread?" Buckey sniffs. All I can say is that boy didn't get so muscular by not knowing his food. I think his muscles grow just by smelling the stuff.

"Wow, that's exactly what it is!" Emma chirps, touching his arm.

"How did you get all of that? Gravy's hard to come by," Harley inquires. She scrunches her nose, biting the inside of her cheek, making it look like she's thinking, but I can tell she's anxious. Something's off with her senses; what could be wrong? Emma's so nice, and the room's so warm, and the food will fill us right up and get us ready for tomorrow.

"Oh, it's my birthday today and in this town, that means a good dinner." She turns, skipping down the stairs, all the boys on her heels, Tequila sulking after them. I grab Harley's hand, holding her back. She doesn't resist, but she doesn't look at me either.

"What's the matter? You're acting weird." I go to push the stray hairs out of her face, but she stops me, pulling away. I swat at the air, pretending there's a fly.

"I'm not! I just found out I'm wanted for the murder of my brother," she snaps. "Sorry, I'm just tired and shaken up from today. I'm not mad at you." Her eyes become glossy, but I don't move to her. She doesn't need me to act like she is weak just to make her feel better, though, as tears continue to well up in her eyes, my muscles flex and relax as it takes all my effort not to move toward her.

I'm not heartless. I know when she needs me and when she doesn't, and right now, all I can do is distract her from focusing on the bigger picture. She needs to focus all her pain on this rescue mission because that's when her best plans are formed. I almost change my mind when her eyes lift to mine. The cut and bruises make her puffy red eyes look so much worse, and the cut on her neck only adds to the effect.

"Harley,. the rest of the gang needs you to appear strong, or they will give up on saving J. You give them hope on a daily basis, so give yourself some for a change, okay? Now go downstairs and eat, tomorrow will be long and you need to be prepared. You'll have your hands full teaching Rey and Johnny to shoot." A smile forms on her face — a genuine one that reaches her eyes.

"Okay," she whispers, turning and walking to the stairs.

I should have told her I remembered what I said that night, drunk on a bottle of basement-made whiskey. That I might have meant it. That I did mean it. What good would it do besides make her life more complicated than it already is? I can't do that to her. My cheeks start to feel hot. I push open the only window in this loft.

"Fuck."

Luke stands at the back of his trailer with a tall cloaked figure. Their hands are over their mouths, making their voices muffled and their lips impossible to read. Not that I can read lips. The man hands Luke a small object that he quickly slips into his pocket. Then Luke holds out the plastic phone — the phone with the hard drive. In all the chaos, I forgot to tell Harley about it.

Luke shows the man the battery compartment in the back. The man takes the phone, nodding, then disappears into the shadows leaving Luke alone, checking to see if anyone saw him. He moves his head up. Quickly I duck, crawling to the stairs, swearing on my way down. I move to the big dining table and slide into a chair beside Tequila, waiting for Luke to burst through the door. But he doesn't.

"What are you doing?" Tequila inquires, eyeing me suspiciously. I look down at her plate, stunned by the pile of potatoes drenched in gravy, with a fatty piece of chicken on top.

"You're allowed that much?" I gawk at the piles on everyone's plates. There are even cupcakes on a different table. Never in my life have I seen this much food in one place.

"Yeah! Apparently every single person in this town gets these big bundles of food on their birthday. Every year. Weird, right? Did you know about that? 'Cause I sure as hell didn't. It's not in the rule book." Tequila scoops heaping spoonfuls into her mouth, not seeming to care as much as she implies.

"No." My palms are sweating, and my stomach is turning. All I can think about is whether Luke saw me. I ducked before he looked all the way up. I think. *What does it matter? He doesn't scare me,* I think, somewhat convincing myself. I sit up straighter, piling as much food as I can on my plate, trying to force it down my throat.

"Emma, do you know where this is?" Harley asks, pushing the paper in front of her. Emma's smile falters, then brightens quickly.

"Yes, love, but it's a speakeasy. It's going to be hard to get all ten of you in there. It's hard enough getting myself in there most of the time," Emma says, nibbling delicately at her bread.

"How many can you take?" Tequila chimes in between shovelling in mouthful after mouthful of potatoes.

"I want to say three, not including myself, but we can try for four." Protests fill the dinner table.

"Hey, we'll decide before bed!" Harley says, quieting everyone. Her voice has this effect where it carries over the loudest rooms, reaching everyone, somehow shutting even the most stubborn person up. Most of the time it's me, but right now, my words are stuck behind my food. I should have told Harley about the hard drive before it was taken. That way, she could have looked further into it, maybe found the truth out. Now I can't tell her; it's too late.

I jump as the door flings open and Luke walks in, holding a crate full of liquor. He doesn't even look my way when he sets it on the table, passing the brown bottles around.

"I thought this was illegal!" Johnny questions, but he doesn't wait for an answer before cracking the beer bottle open with his teeth and downing it, then reaching for Buckey's.

"Well, Emma has contacts," he winks, opening one, setting it in front of Harley, then forcing himself into the space between her and Rey. I'm pleased when disgust registers on her face.

She's the only one whose plate isn't overflowing with food. She merely has a couple spoonfuls of mashed potatoes, a small piece of meat and barely a sliver of bread. I try to catch her attention, but her eyes stay trained on the potatoes she pushes around. Something's wrong. More wrong than being framed for murder. She doesn't show when things bother her, even the worst stuff. She'd never turn down a chance to fill the never-ending pit in her stomach. I understand that she's exhausted; we all are. She's hurting. She never got to take a minute to mourn her brother and to think about the ties she cut with her mom. I guess, right now, when everyone's focused on the food and the liquor, she's allowing herself to unravel and process everything that's happened, knowing that no one but me would notice.

I should have noticed earlier and not focused so much on myself because I can't even pull her aside now. If I did, everyone's attention would turn to her, trying to fix someone who, at this moment in time, is nowhere close to being okay. It's also an unspoken rule of ours, that I don't get involved. I can't ask about what's on her mind when other people are around because she's too selfless to let people help her, support her. It's infuriating, really, having to sit here for so long, unable to reach out to her.

"Jimmy," Tequila nudges my arm.

"What?" I ask, startled, too focused on Harley to notice all the faces on me.

"Luke asked you something." I stiffen like a person would if a venomous snake was inches from them, taunting them with its fangs.

"Are you volunteering to go with Harley?" he repeats, with a look so smug I want to punch *myself* in the face.

"I thought my presence was implied because, well — you know," I smirk.

"Ditto." He leans back, throwing a piece of bread into his mouth.

The first time I ever met him was at a Warehouse fight. He was all over Harley, and she was trying to push him off. I ignored the fact that she was smiling while she was doing it, and I punched him. It wasn't a hard punch. A nice little one that happened to bruise. Then he hit me. We got into a big fight and kicked out. That, on top of us both loving Harley, has made us hate each other ever since.

"We need new clothes," Harley says, still staring at her plate. "Whatever we can get. I can't—"

"I can look around," Emma offers, pushing out her chair. "I'll be right back." She flings her coat on, leaving in a hurry, trusting all of us alone in her home.

"Thank you," Harley whispers, clearing her stuff and disappearing into the kitchen. Finn starts to clear away the rest, following her.

"Look what you did!" Luke surges the minute she's out of sight.

"Yeah, 'cause every damn thing she does is my fault!" I snort. Everyone knows that she'd never do something simply because a man, or anyone for that matter, told her to.

"Well, isn't it?" He picks at his teeth with his switchblade. I keep my mouth shut, knowing that Harley's close enough to hear anything he says. "You were too drunk on the night MC showed his face and she had to take care of you when she needed help. You never stopped her from running into that building. You never helped her when her dad beat her up."

"Luke, shut up," Tequila snaps, starting to get up, but I stop her.

"No, let him talk," I say.

I push away from the table, rolling up my sleeves, but he just sits there. He wants me to hit him. I guess I'll make someone's day after all.

I lift my hand, but Harley steps in front of me, not even flinching. "You're better than this," she says, then she turns to Luke, "You think I need him to make decisions for me?" She inches closer. "You think he can stop me from doing what I want?" Luke tries to stay casual, but you can feel his anxiety. "If anyone should be feeling bad about what they've done it should be you because last time I checked you ended things with me, because it didn't suit your life, your world. And I know the only reason you let us stay here, the only reason you came with us, was to suit your agenda. So grow up and learn to work with him, or don't come with us when we leave." She straightens, turning to the rest of us, her face returning to the way it was before. "Now, since Jimmy and Luke volunteered to come to the speakeasy with me, we need one more person."

Instantly, everyone raises a hand, either too scared or too impressed with her to not step forward. "Uri, you can come. We need your street smarts. Thank you for volunteering, everyone else. I'm going to bed. You guys should do the same," she says, her voice devoid of any emotion, like a teacher addressing students. Then she focuses her glare on me. "Uri and I will teach you all how to shoot tomorrow. Goodnight. And If I hear another word I swear—"

"She should have slapped you," Johnny mutters, slouching in his chair.

"Goodnight Sergeant Major Hudson," Rey salutes her as she disappears up the stairs.

I turn to Luke, lowering my voice and balling my hands into fists, "I have no idea what you're doing here, what you're doing with her, but I promise you when I find out, I'll beat the living shit out of you."

He pockets his knife, his lips curling up. "What's that going to do for you? Make her hate you more?" He drinks the rest of the liquor, throwing the empty bottle into the garbage can, making it shatter. "We aren't so different, you know, we're both liars and we both hurt people. The only difference is, I've been her boyfriend for a year and you've been in love with her for fourteen." He walks forward, stopping at my side, "I know you saw me hand off the hard drive, and you'll never know what's on it — you never had the balls to find out." He moves away before I can take a swing, shutting himself in a room.

"That guy's an ass!" Finn huffs, his fist clenched. I almost start to laugh at his out-of-character statement.

"Wow! Finny, coming from you, that must mean something," Ace laughs.

"Finally joined the dark side, doesn't it feel exhilarating?" Rey claps him on the shoulder.

"Guys, we should go to bed, we don't want Ms. Harley getting mad at us," Buckey says, pulling Tequila up the stairs with him. *They better be sleeping in different beds.*

CHAPTER 10
(HARLEY)

Everything around me has a grim darkness to it, the air thick with cheap perfume and cigarette smoke. I hold my hands out, putting them inches from my face, but I can't see them. My first thought is that I've become blind, but as I move further in, a small dot of light shines at the end of a tunnel. I stretch my hands out farther, trying to use my other senses, but the pungent air and the echo of my shuffling feet on the rock floor leave me with only touch. There's nothing in front of me, beside me, behind me. I can't sense any walls, though something is pushing me forward, yet every time I swing my hand back, there is only darkness — nothing pressing against me.

"Hello," I call unwisely, but it shouldn't make a difference. If I'm the only one in here, this has to be a dream. I'm not stupid. I wouldn't go off on my own unless absolutely necessary.

"Open the door," a voice whispers. I whip my head from side to side, but I think that voice spoke in my mind. I listen, slowly inching forward, brushing my fingers over a chilled metal plate with something engraved on its surface. I push hard, and to my surprise, the door easily squeaks open, blinding me with the light it lets through.

With my sight still gone, I cautiously move forward, waiting for my eyes to adjust. When they do, I'm standing in an empty speakeasy, with streamers and confetti on the floor, from a party that just finished or one that ended abruptly. Blood is streaked across the wooden floor and on the mirrors that don't show my reflection. The bottles behind the bar are smashed, dripping red, and the bartender is unconscious on a bar stool. I move toward him, my hand almost touching his back, when suddenly he dissolves, sinking into the cracks of the bar, leaving behind a small white pin with flames painted on it. I reach for it, only to watch it vanish as well.

"*Go toward the beads*," the voice says again. Unconsciously, my body turns to where a row of sparkling diamond beads dangles in the far corner of the room. My mind starts to fight with the voice, screaming not to go in, but my body doesn't listen.

I walk forward, pushing aside the diamonds, revealing a small dark room with two flaming red couches facing each other. One holds two faceless men and a faceless woman with long blonde hair and a skin-tight leather suit. The other couch holds Jimmy, Luke and Uri, their eyes blank and empty. They don't turn to me when I call their names. I freeze, feeling my feet cement themselves to the floor.

"Hello, Harley," the woman says, lifting her drink to where her mouth would be. Relief rushes over me when her voice comes out monotonic, low. *Maybe this won't be real*, I think.

"How do you know my name?" I ask.

"Who doesn't, my dear? You're wanted by the entire world," she laughs, her men grunting. "Take a seat." She points to the space between Luke and Jimmy. I stay standing, making my face emotionless. "Fair enough," she sighs, gesturing to her men. Out of nowhere, they place three silver plates on a glass table — one with a heart, the next with a lotus flower and the last with a snowflake. "You must pick. And if you choose wisely, your friends may go," she says nonchalantly, as though this were just a meaningless chore in her busy schedule.

"And If I don't?"

She sets down her drink to pick up a gun, raising it to Jimmy's head. The two men do the same, placing their barrels on Luke's and Uri's foreheads. I still don't move, worried that any motion toward them will lead to a bullet in each of their brains.

"It would be such a shame to kill this one," she runs her long fingernails across Jimmy's lips, "He would make such a good plaything."

With her words, I can't help the impulse to move toward him, but I'm paralyzed. "Why can't I ever move in these damn dreams?" I mutter, digging my nails into my legs, trying to get them to feel something. "Fine," I spit.

The heart must mean life and love. I want them to live, and my love for them is stronger than anything else. The lotus flower means rebirth, and the snowflake represents individuality, making no sense in this situation. I bite at the skin on my lips, my heart pounding in my ears.

"Pick!" The woman screams, rotating a white ring on her finger.

"Heart," I blurt. As soon as I do, the lotus flower and the snowflake disappear. Tension fills my chest, anticipating her decision.

"Wrong!" She places her finger on the trigger.

The voice laughing in my head turns high-pitched, *"You will fail, you will fail, killing everyone you love, too slow, too reckless. You aren't strong enough to save them all,"* it sings.

I start to scream for the boys to run as I hear the bullet slide into place. *Bang. Bang. Bang.* I wake, gasping and drenched in sweat.

Pushing myself up, I make sure Jimmy and Uri are still sleeping in the same room. I see Uri first, his chest rising and falling with his breath, but Jimmy, his space is empty. I hurry to my feet and fly down the stairs, stopping at Luke's door to be sure he hasn't disappeared as well. Snores fill his room. Then I run into the living room, where Jimmy sits reading a book.

"Jimmy! What are you doing?" I sigh. He looks up, startled by the harshness in my voice. My heart skips a beat when he looks up at me, his hair silken and messy, eyes puffy with sleep.

"It's six. I woke up and couldn't go back to sleep so I came downstairs, got bored and picked up a book," he explains, shocked, holding up

The Tale of Despereaux. "Did you know the mouse falls in love with the princess and she loves him too — wait. Are you okay? Why are you mad?"

I close my eyes, taking a deep breath, "I'm not mad. It's just, I had a dream and when I woke up you weren't there. I was — I was scared." I pick up a blanket from the couch and drape it across my shoulders, trying to suppress the goosebumps on my arms. He lowers the book, patting the spot beside him. I sit, placing my head in my hands.

"Tell me about it," he lowers his voice, his hand moving up and down on my back. I keep my mouth shut. I don't want to tell him that there's a good chance he might die tonight. "Was the voice in it?" he presses, now leaning his face closer to mine.

"Yes," I whisper. He pries my hands from my face and smiles, making my heart drop. "It was the speakeasy and there was blood everywhere, so much blood." I search for words that could do this dream justice. "There was a back room, two couches facing each other. Two faceless men and a faceless woman with long blonde hair who sat on one couch and you, Uri and Luke sat on the other." My words catch.

"Harley, it's okay," he whispers, taking my hand and running his thumb in circles on mine. But it's not okay.

"She made me choose between a heart, lotus flower and a snowflake. I chose a heart because life and love and whatnot." I start to speak fast, wanting to get the words out and be done with them. "It was the wrong choice, and the high-pitched voice was in my mind this time and he said, 'You will fail, you will fail, killing everyone you love, too slow, too reckless. You aren't strong enough to save them all.' And then the woman..." I trail off. Maybe I shouldn't tell him. Leave this part out — No. No matter what I tell him, he would still go with me. So it's either he walks in knowing or walks in blind. "I woke up to the sound of them shooting all three of you."

"Oh!" He says, pulling away from me.

I turn to him, watching his hands start for his hair. I hold them back. "Jimmy, you shouldn't come with me. It should be only me and Emma who go." He sits staring at our hands laced together, tracing lines over my skin.

"Harley, you're stupid," he snorts.

I look at him. "Stupid," I repeat. I'm not being stupid; I'm trying to save his life. But as I try to move away, an even bigger smile stretches across his face. "You idiot!" I punch his arm, making him laugh.

"Harley, we both know I can't send you off with only Emma as backup. I know you could probably beat up twenty hulking Hunters on your own, but I couldn't live with myself if something happened." He lets go of my hand, brushing his over my cheek.

"I know," I groan, rolling my eyes, ignoring the feeling running down my spine.

Footsteps thump down the stairs. I move from Jimmy, pushing back my hair and tying it in a ponytail. Rey runs into the room, jumping on us, Johnny following his lead. They press into my ribs, but it doesn't hurt anymore.

Ace plops himself on the chair, barely acknowledging us before shutting his eyes, snoring in seconds. Finn and Uri start rummaging through the fridge, throwing random scraps of food at Buckey since he's the only good cook. And last, Tequila stumbles into the kitchen, her hair standing up on one side.

"Get off," I laugh, pushing Rey off me, squeezing his sides and making him howl.

"That's pay back," Rey says, slapping my hands away.

"For what?"

"I'm not sure yet, but I'm sure at some point you'll shoot me," Rey says. Something bites around my heart, my chest starting to burn.

"What?" I say, stunned. He didn't mean that; he didn't just say that.

"'Cause you're not letting us shoot pumpkins. Are you okay?" Johnny asks, pushing himself off Rey, one eyebrow raised. Rey looks at me, then folds me into a long hug.

"Harley, I know you're scared right now, but it will be okay, we'll find him," he says, holding me tighter, his voice small and sweet. He pulls back, smiling, then runs off with Johnny to wake up Luke. Jimmy stares at me, almost as surprised as I am. Sometimes I forget Rey is only fourteen, still a child by some people's standards.

"Told you he had a sweet spot for you," Jimmy says, getting up to help Buckey cook us breakfast.

I know Rey was only trying to reassure me, but all he did was cause a memory of J to surface. One time, Eric was having a really bad night, losing poker games left, right and centre, and he'd gotten a new batch of drugs the Big Three sent for him to test out. They were hallucinogenic drugs, and unsurprisingly, they showed him his father, the man who taught him how to hit. How to live a violent life. Eric was screaming and crying, saying, 'How does it feel?' over and over again.

I knew the drug shipment was coming that day, so I had made arrangements for J to sleep at his friend's house to ensure he didn't get involved in what I knew would happen, but I didn't anticipate Eric testing them so early. When J and I got home from school, Eric and all his friends were sitting around the table smoking and drinking, higher than the sky. I tried to push J out the door, but one of Eric's friends blocked it. So I held him behind me, trying to talk Eric down, trying to pass without a fight, but he took one look at me, stood up and punched me so hard I thought he'd broken my jaw.

I pulled J down the hall with me, stumbling, trying not to pass out. I locked us in my room and dragged him into my arms, doing the best I could to cover his ears, to stop him from listening to Eric tell us how stupid and ungrateful we are as he slammed his body against the door.

Eventually, Eric got bored and gave up, but I never let go of J. He was keeping my world from spiralling out of control. That's when he turned to me, making a fortress around me with his skinny arms, burying his face in my hair. I tried to look at him to make sure he was okay, but all I saw was my blood dripping onto his grey shirt. He said to me in the boldest voice he could muster, "Harley, I know you're scared right now, but it will be okay. It will be over soon. I'll take care of you."

We fell asleep in each other's arms that night. For the first time in that house, I felt okay because I knew that even though he was scared, J was also strong, and I didn't mess him up. He could protect himself.

That sentence has been keeping me from falling apart. Besides my breakdown at school, I haven't been able to take a minute to mourn over J. All of the stress and grief has been bubbling up inside, and I've tried so hard to push it down to anchor it to my peace, but Jimmy was right. Something's wrong with me. I'm losing control, and I have no idea why.

Jimmy places a plate with a couple of spoonfuls of scrambled eggs on my lap and sticks a piece of bread in my mouth when I open it to say thank you.

"So are we going to analyze this dream or are we going to assume it's pretty spot on?" he asks, talking with his mouth full. I glare at him, and he quickly swallows. "Sorry."

"Well, the voice was there, so it is a guarantee something in that dream will come true. But this time there was another voice, softer. I've been hearing it more often." I grimace, hoping he somehow didn't hear that last part. I didn't want to tell him about the voices jumping into my head more often now because then he'd for sure think I'm going crazy.

"Hearing them more often, like not just in your dreams?" he looks up, almost alarmed.

"I was hoping you didn't catch that," I grimace, shovelling some eggs into my mouth, buying myself time before I have to admit I might be losing my mind. He continues to stare at me, so I explain. "It started when the men jumped me at the school. The high-pitched voice is there still, but so is another voice, a woman's voice maybe. It interrupts the other, telling me to stay in control."

"Stay in control of what?" He taps his fork against his mouth.

"I have no idea. That's the one thing I haven't quite figured out."

My train of thought is interrupted by thundering footsteps storming into the room. Johnny and Rey sprint to avoid a soaked Luke and his swinging fist. They jump over things, weaving around us, knocking cups aside. Then Luke makes the mistake of running toward Uri. Uri sticks out his arm, almost flipping Luke and effectively knocking the wind out of him.

"Oddly satisfying way to start the morning," Tequila chirps, taking a sip of steaming coffee.

"By the way guys, how are you going to shoot guns without being noticed?" Finn asks, helping Luke off the floor.

"Maybe we'll get lucky and the sound will bring a couple of Hunters into range and we can get even," Buckey says. Tequila elbows him hard in the stomach, making him cough up chewed eggs. I wrinkle my nose.

"You're not even gonna try to shoot, Finny?" Ace asks, forgetting he shouldn't ask Finn this type of question in a big group because he will draw back and stop talking for the rest of the day.

Finn shakes his head, avoiding the conversation as he always does. He doesn't believe in holding a weapon that could take someone's life with a single shot. When we were fourteen, we witnessed a Hunter shoot a younger man in the head because he stole a loaf of bread. Later that day he explained that he doesn't believe people should have the right to make that type of decision, deciding whether someone should live or die, so he's never touched one. He doesn't even like fighting all that much, but everyone has to fight eventually, even if they run from it for years.

"How do you expect to protect yourself when there's a group of Hunters showering you with bullets?" Luke asks. I know he doesn't mean to be condescending, but it doesn't come across any other way.

"He'll probably be too busy saving your ass when someone shoots you," Rey defends.

"That person will probably be me," Buckey adds.

"Well, sorry to start this, but to answer your question, Finn," Ace says, pulling the duffel bag out from under the couch. "Durçk added two silencers, so we can use them without drawing too much attention."

"Where's Emma?" I ask. If she hasn't already woken up from all this noise, she has a gift.

"She went to work, left a note in my room and clothes for us too," Luke says, taking my plate to the kitchen.

"And she's not going to tell anyone, right?"

"Nah, she wouldn't," says Luke.

I don't know why, but I have a feeling it was more than her humanly duty that drove her to take us in. Luke has never told me about her, not even that he comes out to visit her a lot. He's never even mentioned that he's left town before, but she happens to know loads about me.

"Can we go now?" Rey begs, jumping up and down, punching Tequila's arm. "Please, please, please."

"Yep, come on," Uri says, slinging Tequila over his shoulder. She squeals, resting her elbows on his back. Ace slings the bag over his shoulder.

"Hey," I stop him. "Might only want to take the two out with you and some knives so Johnny and Rey don't get any ideas — Finn, I'll show you how to throw a knife instead, okay?" Finn nods, and Ace loads the guns, screwing the silencers on, following them out the door. As a precaution, I slide a gun into the waist of my jeans.

"We'll talk about the dream more later, okay? Don't think too much of it. There's no point in stressing over something that might not happen," Jimmy says, pulling me out the door with him.

But there is a point in wondering if my best friends will die because I made them dive into this situation head first with me. I have to think of every possible way that dream could come true and every possible way I could change it.

Emma lives on the edge of town, so her backyard is a thick layer of pine trees that curves around her house, making it impossible for anyone to see us. Luke pins a piece of paper to one of the trees, with the tiniest red dot drawn in the center. I'm not even sure I could hit that. He reaches for one of the guns, but Ace quickly passes them to Uri and me. The gun feels heavy, cold in my hand, yet comforting, but I'd say that out of everyone, I lean more toward Finn's side of how he sees guns. Shooting is fun and all until you're face-to-face with another human. Their heart, beating as fast as yours. Their skin, still warm. Wondering if they'll make it home to tell their mom they love them or kiss their child good night. In one split second, panic could pull the trigger, and the one with the best shot gets to live. It's not fair.

"Okay," Uri says, standing in front of our staggered half circle. "You got your clip. You can remove it to add bullets, or remove and add an already loaded one. Next, you're going to pull back the slide with your thumb and four fingers or the palm of your hand if the first option is too hard. To grip, put your dominant hand first, then the other on top and adjust till it feels comfortable. Keep your finger off the trigger until you're ready. Stand however you want and straighten your arms out from your body, with your elbows bent slightly because the recoil is big when you aren't used to it. Don't try to control it, but don't be too flimsy with it." He stops, waiting for any questions, not realizing it all went over their heads.

"Sorry, I would like you to repeat that much slower, in simpler terms, and maybe add some pictures to your slideshow," Rey says, smiling at his bad joke.

"You know what, let's just show you. Harley, care to make this a competition?" He moves beside me.

"There's no other way!"

"Move to the sides where you can see us — No, Johnny, not in front," Uri sighs.

"First one to hit the target?" I ask.

"Yes ma'am."

We set ourselves up, doing precisely as Uri said. I pull the slide, hearing the bullet click into place as I take a deep breath to relax my mind. My finger brushes over the trigger, sending a thrill up my arm. Uri fires first, missing by inches. My eyes focus on the cloth, my muscle memory taking over as I extend my arms. I breathe in ... breathe out ... and fire, hitting the red dot dead centre.

"Lucky shot!" I hear someone say.

"Wait for it," Jimmy replies, admiring me.

Smirking, I fire five more times, every bullet hitting the same spot, the casings bouncing off my bare feet. When I'm done, I turn to Uri, pressing the gun in his other hand. "Well played! Better luck next time," I smirk.

Everyone but Jimmy and Uri gawk at me with wide eyes, the others having never seen me shoot. My dad took me shooting twice when I was ten and took Jimmy too, but he was never very good. However, I took to it, hitting the bullseye after one day. I never forgot the feeling, the firing of my senses.

"Never thought I was gonna win, but I wanted to see you do it," Uri says.

"Yeah, yeah, you teach them how to do it and I'll work with Finn." I pull Finn along with me, still feeling their eyes on my back.

"How did you learn how to shoot like that?" Finn asks incredulously.

"I'm a natural," I joke, passing him a couple of knives and pinning a white cloth to a tree. He looks at the blades, uneasy, rolling them over in his hands, poking his fingertips with the end.

"You don't have to do this," I frown, realizing that throwing knives is almost as bad as shooting someone. It's closer range. Close enough to see the life leave your victim's eyes, and you'd have to retrieve it from their body.

"No, I'm fine. I've got to protect myself, somehow. I know how to fight. A knife will make it end quicker..." he trails off, training his eyes on the cloth.

I don't think I could send him into any type of battle. He's too gentle and good. He'd probably try to come up with a peace agreement while bullets are flying before he'd think about killing someone. No one in this group has ever killed anyone. They don't know the feeling of grief and regret that comes with it. I don't know that feeling, yet I'm expecting them to be ready to do so. I turn and watch Rey and Johnny take turns disrupting the dirt around the tree.

"Harley, they know what they're getting into. They know the consequences and the hurt that will come with it. Don't beat yourself up," Finn reassures me, squeezing my arm.

"Okay, are you ready?" I grip a knife and try not to overthink. "It's like throwing a ball." I swing my arm back and throw, burying the whole blade.

"You make it look too easy," Finn says, trying to copy me. His lands harmlessly in the grass.

"Try to use your front arm to aim. Point to where you want it to go," I say, positioning his body. He throws another one. This time it bounces off the bark. He scowls, narrowing his eyebrows in concentration. "Try again." He tries two more times before the tip of the knife sticks. He looks at me, beaming. "Good, now do it again." He misses, but the second time it sticks, and the third and the fourth.

"Finn, we need some help over here," Uri calls. Finn's concentration breaks, and the knife goes flying too far to the right and into the thicket of trees. He flinches, turning to see blood gushing from Rey's nose.

"I'll get the knives," I offer, pushing him forward.

"Rey, you broke it again," Finn yells, running after him.

I retrieve the knives from the tree, sticking them in my back pocket before searching for the stray, but it's not on the ground or in a neighbouring tree. It's disappeared. Then I hear a branch break. I move slowly around to see a man staggering toward me. My heart panics, but I don't run. Something about him is familiar — the sway in his step, the curl of his mouth.

"Eric!" I pull a knife from my pocket, straightening but keeping my shoulders loose as I twirl it in my hand. "Shouldn't you be with one of your drug dealer friends or selling your soul to the devil?" I say, forcing my voice to stay calmer than my heart. His sore-covered face and yellow teeth come into focus, his clothes torn and soiled.

He smiles, hiccupping through a laugh, "Well, first off, don't have any friends and second, I sold my soul years ago." He tries to come off as cunning, but a series of coughs disrupts that. He sizes me up, inching closer, removing his hands from his pockets to show he's unarmed, but I still creep back with every step he takes.

"Why are you here?" I question, suppressing the fake arrogance I use to talk to strangers. He can see right through it.

"To see you, make sure you aren't putting your life in danger," he says with a slight drawl. He jerks his head to the side, cracking his neck. I grip the end of my knife tighter, moving my other hand to my waistband, the metal grip of the gun cold against my fingertips. "Not for the reason you think, you can stop acting so tough," he grumbles, having to take a seat on a nearby rock. His hands shake. A thick layer of sweat covers his forehead and what I thought was a twitch is really him being paranoid of his surroundings.

"You're in withdrawal," I state, bringing my arm back to my side.

"So you are smart! Your dad always told me you were, that you were the kid to change the world, but I never believed it until you ran into that school — even though you were unsuccessful."

He ponders for a minute, in mock sympathy, making my attempt to save my brother and those people feel meaningless. Now I understand how he found me. Once he got wind of the Hunters attacking me at school, he's been trailing me, watching my every move. He understands I'm smarter than him, and thought I might have a way to avoid the capture of the leaders, up until he figured out I was walking straight into their arms.

"You knew my dad?" I question, almost missing his admission. He couldn't have known him. He always made it seem like he hated him, out of spite but never because my dad was Eric's opponent or enemy.

"More than I've let on." He holds his ribs, kneeling over to vomit.

"Do you have any detox pills?" I ask, distracted by the blood in his vomit. He looks awful, bald spots forming on his head, dark purple bags under his eyes, his skin a sickly yellow.

"No, my hook ups won't give me any, and the people who would are also the people who would hand me over to the Big Three within seconds of seeing me."

"Most people would," I mutter. Eric has no shortage of enemies — drug dealers, Hunters, hospital workers and so on — people who would be ecstatic if they could say they caught him and turned him in.

"You wish you could turn me in, but they'd probably take you over me. You're the one wanted for murder after all," he states, struggling to inhale.

"Did you do what they said?" I ask, feeling around in my back pocket, the weight of a single detox pill heavy on my conscience. I know I must have an extra one. I always try to carry a couple around. I have a constant fear that Jimmy will forget the promise he made to me and go back to doing drugs.

"You have to know, the wanted posters are Big Three propaganda to ensure our arrest. The people of The Sticks know for a fact you would — could — never kill your brother, but since it's on a piece of paper with official signatures at the bottom, they're forced to rethink everything."

I raise my eyebrows. "You didn't answer my question." I find the pill and toss it at his feet. No one should have to be in that much pain, even Eric.

"Not fifteen million *per se*, more like ten, give or take a couple of dollars," he says, trying to resist my kindness, not wanting to owe me anything, even if it would make his suffering stop. He's a selfish man to not want to be in my debt but not caring if he's in everyone else's.

"How did you manage that?"

"Tested the drugs more than I sold them, kept most of what I made. You know, your Jimmy was shaping up to be one of my best customers, maybe could have even made him a Lackey, that is until you got in his head." He scrambles on all fours, rummaging through the leaves for the blue pill, a sigh of relief rushing over him as he finally swallows it.

I clench my jaw, his words hitting me hard in the chest, "Wouldn't have given you that if I knew you were going to throw him in my face."

"Ahh, but you didn't know," he points, "and you're too nice. You would have given it to me anyway," he pauses, his eyes unfocussed as he gathers his memories. "Isn't it crazy how your dad made a single pill that counters the effects of any type of withdrawal — genius, but like you, he was also too nice. That's why I'm here and he's not!"

I honestly couldn't care less about being in control and anchoring myself to my peace. Eric knows every place to hit me and make it hurt, and since he's in withdrawal, there's no chance of him trying to act friendly.

He reaches into his pocket, and without thinking, I throw my knife, aiming for a tree, inches from his head. The thud of the blade makes him cover his ears, lose his balance and fall off the rock, smacking both his elbows on the ground.

"Jesus, Harley, it's a fucking picture!" he scolds, reaching in his pocket again and pulling out a folded, stained photo, handing it to me.

I inch toward him, another knife in my hand. I grab the picture, retreating back to my tree. I unfold it, stunned, sad and confused as to why my dad, with his purest smile, has his arm wrapped willingly around a grimy-looking Eric.

"We were twenty when that was taken. My birthday," Eric grunts as he pulls himself up.

"How did you know him?" I ask, so quietly I'm surprised he heard me.

"We were good friends. He helped me get a job with the government, as a garbage man, not a Lackey. I chose that path myself." He slowly moves closer. "He helped me with school and work. He was kind to me, something I never knew before him. So I stuck around." I hand the picture back. The weight of his words is making my head pound and my throat close. They were friends for years, and it even looked like they were fond of each other. "That's why I'm here, 'cause your dad made me promise to always watch out for you."

"Done a pretty good job," I snort, tracing my finger over the scar on my cheek.

"Considering you haven't gotten in any trouble till now, I think I've done a decent job," he says, mocking my snort. I roll my eyes, turning to leave. "No, wait," he calls after me, trying to follow, only to take two steps and be stopped by loud wheezing. I turn back. "Wait — you don't understand and you probably never will. I didn't do what I did for no reason. I roughed you up to make the Hunters think one of their own had already gotten to you so they'd go for someone else. I said what I said so you'd learn to keep your anger in control -- I knew your dad thought you were special in a way he never told me. So I promised him I would try to keep you safe. I didn't want to, believe me — I owed him a favor, so I had some fun with it." He smiles, moving closer, till his nauseating breath burns my nose. "That's why you can't go after your brother, not now, not ever."

"What?" His words don't make sense to me, not computing correctly.

"You can't put yourself in danger. They're using him as bait so they can get you, for who knows what, but going after him would be like walking straight into their open arms."

"You're delusional if you think I'm leaving him there." I slip past him, retrieving my knife. His hand locks around my arm, his grip weak but still dangerous. I turn, slamming his back against a tree, pressing my arm to the lower part of his neck and bringing my knife to his jugular. Watching him try to fight me makes me feel bad for him, but that quickly fades when he smirks.

"Harley," Finn calls from afar.

"You have no say in anything I do. He's my brother, my only family. If you try to stop me or get in my way, I swear on every person dead or alive that I will beat the living shit out of you." I push him to the ground as Finn's footsteps come closer.

"I've always admired that about you, girl," he coughs, staring at me as he wipes the blood from his nose, "You've got a lot of spunk."

"You disgust me, get out of here and pray I never see you again." I spin around, marching back to Finn before he can get any closer.

"Just think about it," Eric calls after me.

I punch the bark off the nearest tree, letting my knuckles sting. "Jimmy," I call, feeling the blood rush to my cheeks.

Eric says he did what he had to do. He did what he had to do for years to protect me? He bruised my skin and drew the eyes of people at school to make sure I was safe? And now he wants me to leave J to die. No! I wrestle with my thoughts. "Jimmy," I yell watching Finn step back, leaving me alone on my walk of anger. I must look wild.

"Yeah," he cautiously runs over.

"Let's practice." I drop my knives and my gun, rolling up my sleeves, raising my hand and clenching them into fists.

"What's wrong?" His look almost calms me, but the words 'I did it to protect you' flash in my vision.

"Come on." He stares at me, straightening, the rest of the gang circling around us. I don't want to hurt Jimmy; I never would. I'll let him win. All I want is to distract myself. "Come on." I wave him forward, swaying back and forth. He narrows his eyes, crossing his arms. He's never hit me, never practiced full force with me.

"No. You only ask me to fight when something stressful happens," he argues.

"Or when I want to practice," I retort.

"I'll do it," Luke offers, stepping between Jimmy and me, removing his jacket. Jimmy grabs his arm, trying to stop him.

"No, let him," I say.

I would have rather had Jimmy fight me because at least I know he wouldn't actually try, but I have some hate toward Luke that has recently come to the surface with everything else.

Luke steps before he throws the first punch, so I dodge it easily, stepping to the side, feeling the weight of his strike in the air that ruffles my hair. He swings again. This time, I let his fist hit my ribs, the feeling inviting more. I jab, purposefully making it sloppy and slow. He grabs my arm, hitting my stomach, then flips me to the ground, his knee catching my chin on the way down. I smile, wiping the blood from my skin as I look up at him. He hesitates, so I sweep his feet from under him, causing him to land hard on his back, air rushing from his lungs. He moves to get up, but I'm already on top of him, swinging my body around, so I have his wrist in both of mine, my legs over his chest squeezing his arm, my hip pushing up. He tries to move, and even though he's bigger than me, he has no chance, so he taps on my arm, signalling his submission. But I keep moving my hips upward, the words, *'I was protecting you,'* playing over and over in my mind.

"Harley, he tapped," Tequila yells.

"Finish him!" the high-pitched voice yells back, *"You know you want to."*

"Harley, you're going to break his arm, let go."

Luke taps again, starting to groan. *"I did it to protect you. Finish him, finish him."* I grit my teeth holding back a scream, feeling Luke's bone start to give. *"Stay in control,"* the soft, gentle voice says, bringing me back. *"Finish him." "Stay in control."* I release his arm, rolling onto my side, holding my head. He does the same, panting, holding his arm.

"Sorry!" I manage as I turn to see Jimmy, who looks as I feel — disappointed and disgusted. Finn kneels beside me, but I wave him off, moving him in Luke's direction. I know nothing's wrong with me. My ribs aren't any more bruised than they were; my pain tolerance has only increased since the fire. Luke only opened a small cut on my chin. I won't need stitches. I heal, even when I don't want to.

Buckey helps me to my feet. "Someone had to teach him a lesson at some point," he mutters, and the looks on everyone else's faces tell me they feel the same.

Not Jimmy, though. His arms are still folded over his chest, his finger tapping his arm in irritation. I move toward the house, wanting so badly to forget what I just did. But Jimmy steps in front of me, his steady eyes holding me still.

"What's the matter with you?" he asks, his voice hard and strained.

"You fight for fun all the time!" I snort, trying to stay agitated, but the way he talks to me only brings me back to how I was before Eric showed up.

"Yeah, but you don't, and that wasn't for fun. You're better than that."

"Maybe not," I look away. "Something's wrong with me Jimmy." I lower my voice, making sure the others can't hear me. "I can't control them." He looks at me, scared, then curious. "And if Eric can trail us, that means the Hunters already know we're here. We have to make a damn good plan so we don't get caught tonight."

"You saw him?" His arms unfold, his anger instantly dissipating.

I nod, then raise my voice to address the others but don't bother to turn around. They think that what I did to Luke was necessary, that he deserved it, but it was an irresponsible gross use of power, an outlet for my anger. "We're done shooting, everyone back inside, have a shower or whatever and get new clothes. Meet downstairs so we can talk about tonight."

Johnny and Rey grumble, but everyone else starts to pack up, moving inside. Jimmy holds my arm, wiping my blood with his sleeve. I don't flinch, even when it stings.

"What did he say?" he asks, his voice gentle now.

I move past him, not surprised when his footsteps follow me to the house and into Emma's room. Her room is dark even with the light on, everything black or grey, not matching her sunny personality at all. There are no books or keepsakes anywhere, and a pile of mismatched clothes are scattered on her bed. I pass Jimmy a pair of shorts and a hoodie that will either fit him perfectly or not at all.

I have clothes in my bag, but I assume they're already soaked in the scent of cinnamon and apple, and I can't handle that right now. I pick up sweatpants, an oversized T and a rainbow sports bra, cradling them in my arms. I turn back around to see Jimmy already changed, somehow looking better than he did before.

"Eric told me not to go after J, and that, if I do, I'll be handing myself over to the Big Three."

He scratches his cheek, the wheels in his brain working overtime. "So they only want you," he decides.

"I guess so, considering they accused me of murder and Eric of failure to pay." I look at my blood-stained hands, so alien, holding the clean, pressed clothes. "Eric was friends with my dad, for years it seems. My dad trusted him to protect me. My dad knew something was going to happen to him and that I was more important than anyone thought," I say, and suddenly I get the feeling that my dad's disappearance was my fault, that everything is my fault.

"Durçk suggested the same thing at the gas station, and I think your mom said something along those lines too."

"What do you think it means?" I ask, knowing he won't have the answers.

"I don't know, but we'll figure it out, I promise." He takes my hand, but I don't take his back. I want to be alone with my thoughts, with my new findings.

Promise is a very dangerous word, I think as I walk out the door, disappearing into the bathroom, soaking up the newly formed conclusion that my dad may be dead. And I did it to him, and now maybe J too. It's my fault, not Eric's.

CHAPTER 11
(JIMMY)

I stand outside the bathroom, waiting for Harley to emerge, but it seems like hours before she does. She dumped a boatload of information on me, too much for my brain to handle. My potential death, voices in her head, Eric showing up and telling Harley he knew her dad and was trusted to protect her. And that if she goes after J, there's a chance she'll be taken instead. Talk about dropping a bomb.

I wish Eric had never found Harley. He has ways of placing words in her head that she keeps close, overthinking them to the point where they become real.

"We're still going after J?" I ask as she finally opens the door. I know the answer to my question, but I'm hoping she'll say, 'Yes. But I'll stay behind and watch from the sidelines so I don't get taken too.' I wish she were more selfish.

She stares at me, her eyes slightly puffy, the bruise on her cheek almost gone. Her hair is still dripping with water, all the dirt and ash washed off her skin, and now she smells of soap and grapefruit. She's still wearing my shirt.

Then she moves off in a frantic twister of anxiety. "Of course! We simply need to be more careful, trust the right people and think of any possible thing that can go wrong," she says, grabbing a piece of paper and a pen.

She's good at that, finding the little things that can cascade into other mistakes and problems. She obsesses over them, writing them down, counting them in her head, making me check her ideas over and over. At first, I thought it was her being careful and wise with her plans. But I know now, from the handful of times I've seen her like this, it's an unhealthy way for her to feel in control, to feel like she can ensure everyone's safety.

She's not crazy. The voices she hears don't scare me, and the visions never did. She has them so often it's become almost normal to me. I simply don't want her to feel like she's out of control. That's what scares me the most because she's never had trouble with that before. She's the calm one in the group, the level-headed one who makes all the decisions and keeps the gang in check. I'm scared we wouldn't know our right from our left without that part of her personality. She takes a spot by the table on the ground, starting to make a list.

"Harley, wait for the others so they can help." She doesn't stop — she doesn't even look up. "Harley," I say, pulling the pen from her hand.

Her brown eyes shift to mine, narrowing as they consider something, "You're scared I might do something crazy." She tilts her head, gets to her feet, and steps closer. "You're scared I might be losing my mind. I've seen that look on your face before; it's used for the druggies that are too far gone." She gives me the kind of look that tells me not to test her, but I do anyway. I'm the only one who can do it and not get absolutely destroyed by her logic.

"No. I'm scared you're starting to think yourself into insanity. So stop and think of them. Think of the people who are marching into who knows what, without asking you for anything in return," I say, using my hands for emphasis, trying to get her to see a sliver of who she is to them. "You're their leader, and I know it's hard right now. So painful and unbearable for you to be a leader to them when your brother is locked away and you can't get to him. I know it's hard that you're starting to see and hear the voices more, but you have to do what you do best. I'm not telling you to snap out of it because I know it's not that easy. I'm telling you to put yourself aside like you always do and think of them. Be selfless — be their leader."

"I didn't ask for this," she says. Her voice becomes small, showing me the saddest part of her, but then she straightens.

"I know, but that's why you are," I say, pulling her into a hug before she has a chance to push me away. She leaves her arms hanging at her side, but I feel her release a heavy breath. She brings her arms around me half-heartedly. "Sorry," I whisper.

"No. I needed that."

"Good. I'm prepared to keep giving you these lectures until you don't need them anymore." I meant to say that as a joke, but it came out more seriously than I intended. I mainly want her to be okay again, but I'm also scared I might actually lose her. She lets go, sliding into a chair so I can't sit near her.

Harley has so much potential for great things. People follow her, listen to her with unconditional loyalty and little complaint. Her ability to see every angle of anything makes her unbelievably wise for her age. She can go from seething with anger and rage for a fight to calm and grounded in under two seconds. She can heal so fast and is almost better than Finn at fixing people. She can pick up anything and be good at it. Also, she can see the fucking future. What else could you ask for in a perfect leader?

"Why do we need to talk about this again?" Luke mutters, stomping into the room and perching himself on the arm of Harley's chair, shaking his wet hair on her and flexing his shirtless upper body.

"Because we don't want to get caught," Harley says, trying not to push him onto the floor.

"Well, since Uri, Jimmy and Luke were picked for this little operation and I wasn't, I will be taking a beauty nap before I have to use all my energy to give Harley a makeover," Tequila yawns, walking up the stairs.

"You enjoy it!" Harley jokes, smiling at Ace, who mimics Tequila's yawn.

"Well, you aren't wrong." Tequila winks.

"Don't you mean cat nap?" Ace asks.

"Does it look like I want to have the face of a cat when I wake up?" she replies, disgusted by his comment.

"Too late," Rey laughs, nudging Johnny.

"If I were you boys, I'd sleep with one eye open tonight," she calls down in a sing-song voice.

Their smiles instantly fall. Last time she said that to them, they both woke up with Q-tips glued into their nostrils. It took Finn and Harley forever to take them out.

"Anyway," I say, bringing the group back on task. "When we go tonight we need to stick to the shadows and do our best to hide Harley's face."

"Well since it's a speakeasy and no one can drink anywhere else, I'm almost certain people will be too hammered to see properly," Luke chimes in. Even though he's right, I still want to make him look like an idiot for talking, but since Harley gave him a good beating already, I'll let him be.

"And from what I've studied about the underground of Dead Man's Hill, the tunnels are too dark to see one foot in front of you, so we'll have to make sure flashlights don't shine on her face," Uri adds.

"You can take a walkie talkie, in case you need backup," suggests Finn, eyeing Luke suspiciously as he scootches closer to Harley.

"We're only going to find Durçk's contact and leave when we get the information. No partying or socializing, okay?" Harley orders, directing that comment at me, but I am in no mood for a party. Rey groans in objection, flopping to the floor, his arms and legs outstretched.

"Dude! You're not going with them," Buckey reminds Rey, stomping on his stomach.

"So we can party it up here," Ace suggests, poking Rey's nose.

"You guys have to be careful about making too much noise," Harley says sternly. If they draw too much attention to themselves, we're going to have a hard time leaving this place or even staying in the house.

"We are splendidly, sophisticatedly, astronomically, careful human beings — mademoiselle," Johnny reassures, bowing to Harley. She sighs, about to say something, when Emma bursts through the door, holding a bundle of new clothes.

"Outfits — I have your outfits. Everyone must get ready," she puffs, her arms full of clothing bags.

"It's only three!" Luke groans, taking some of the bags from her.

"Yes, but it's 'Roaring Twenties' tonight and you boys have to wear tuxes and I'm guessing none of you have ever worn a suit. You will need lots of time to figure it out." She drops most of the bags on Luke, holding onto two and pulls Harley to her feet. They disappear up the stairs, leaving us boys to our own devices.

CHAPTER 12
(HARLEY)

The dress I'm given is a deep crimson, silky between my fingers, stopping just above my knees. Fringe dangles from the bottom, ruby beads embroidering the rest. I don't belong in such a delicate, beautiful dress.

I haven't been able to sit still for the last hour as the time for my friends' potential death creeps closer. I keep making excuses to leave the chair Tequila forced me into. I run downstairs, my hair half done, the first layer of makeup painted across my face, to fight with Jimmy about tagging along.

He didn't take me seriously at first, joking about how the makeup looked weird, but as I continued to talk, he became cold and stern, trying to convince me that if I prevented him from travelling to the speakeasy with us, he'd find his own way there. Since we are evenly stubborn, we got nowhere. He stormed off, leaving me alone with my thoughts, with no more excuses to get out of Tequila's makeover session.

The night's theme is the 1920s, which, according to my history class, was when flapper girls existed, prohibition struck, and the age of jazz was born. Pretty suitable for a speakeasy, considering that's when they were created. Out of everything, the dress was the only thing I didn't argue about putting on, and despite my many complaints, Tequila managed, with great effort, to get me into a pair of short black heels that squeeze my toes. Emma tried to get me to put on a wig, but even though it would help disguise me, there was no way it was going to happen. So instead, we curled my hair and pinned it back with a shiny rose.

It's weird how Emma can afford all these outfits. She doesn't seem like the wealthiest of people. Something's not right with her situation, the extra food, the outfits, her over-sunny personality. It's a gut feeling I can't get rid of, and the problem with a gut feeling is that it's hard to prove anything. The sooner we get this information, the sooner we get to leave.

Too many things cloud my mind as Tequila shows me her finished product. She has a natural talent for turning people into something they aren't. My skin is clear, unscarred, my eyes bolder, and my lips plump. She might have done her job so well that a stranger could look me dead in the eye and never recognize me from the posters.

That would be too much to ask for.

I make my way down the stairs, already completely exhausted from the events of today. For the first time in my life, I've become the person I buried deep down in the darkest parts of me, chained and locked away, promised by myself to never set free.

"I have never seen you with that much makeup on," Rey notes, releasing me from my thoughts. I look him over, and his polka-dot boxers and striped shirt make me choke back a giggle.

Ace jumps over the couch, hugging me and kissing my cheek. He tells me how beautiful I look and wishes me all the luck in the world, only to be reprimanded by Tequila for potentially messing up her masterpiece. The rest of the gang sits around the TV, a dozen empty bottles already scattered over the table and floor. I don't want to provoke their drunken words, so I walk straight out the door onto the porch.

The cold air wakes my flesh, the moon bright against the stars. I'm starting to miss my home, something I never thought possible. The boys wait for me in full tuxedos, their shoes polished along with their hair.

"Nice top hat!" I chuckle.

Uri turns, beaming at me. He takes his hat off, bows, and takes my hand in his, planting a kiss on my cut knuckles. "You look very handsome tonight, Ms. Hudson."

"And you, Mr. Winston, look very dapper on this fine evening." We giggle at ourselves, forgetting that in a couple of minutes we will be walking the streets where Hunters could so easily spot us. Uri's suit is a tad too short for his tall build. His pants stop above his ankles, but black socks almost hide that fact. You can see the shadow of tattoos covering his arms, peaking out of the too-short sleeves that pinch his armpits. He was born for these types of situations, charmingly handsome, brilliant beyond belief.

"Cut it out!" Luke says, shifting uncomfortably in his tux, which seems too tight and itchy for his liking, but he still manages to look devilishly handsome with his blonde hair pushed back. I'm genuinely sad boys no longer dress this way.

Without warning, my heart does a little skip in my chest as Jimmy turns toward me, his good looks rendering me speechless. His hair is slicked back, giving it the appearance of the night sky as it reflects the moon. Instead of his tuxedo being white and black, it's merely all black, fitting him just right. A stunning red rose pokes out of his breast pocket, pulling the look together.

"Do I look okay? Is the rose too much? Tequila made me wear it. She said it matched your dress. Wow! You look really good!" he exclaims, blushing and nervous. I can tell it's taking all his efforts not to run his fingers through his hair.

"You look marvellous! Went a little heavy with grease, but we'll blame it on Tequila," I wink, straightening his bowtie. I'd say out of all his old-fashioned looks, the way he wears this one is my favourite. As I look into his eyes, the image of him falling limp, blood trickling from a small hole in his forehead, flashes through my mind. I fidget with the rose in my hair, distracting myself with another concern.

I lean forward, "Don't you think it's weird how Emma had all of these expensive clothes on hand, when it's only her and her mom that live here, and she doesn't look like she has a lot of money to spend on frivolous things?" I whisper, worried Luke will hear me and become even grumpier than he already is. Jimmy's smile doesn't falter.

"Yes, but it's a kind of normal thing here — ya know. They probably go to the speakeasies all the time. Stock up on the clothes over the years," Jimmy says.

I sigh, agreeing. Maybe he's right. I'm just on edge from my dream. I don't think it's a good idea for all of them to come, but I feel safer knowing that they will be there.

"I feel like I'm sending my kids off to prom," Rey shouts from the couch, "Except you Luke — if you were my daughter's date, I'd probably knock you out." Finn stifles a laugh as he hands me a purse with a walkie talkie inside that I won't use. If trouble did find us, calling for backup would take too long and put more people at risk, but letting them think I would will keep them calm.

"Protective, how kind," Luke says, his lips curling.

"Only the best for my little duckling," Rey replies, grinning at me. He and Johnny make fists, punching their hands, glaring at Luke.

Emma struts out the door, a long emerald dress hugging her body, a thin diamond band around her head and a white feather scarf hanging off her shoulders. I thought what I was wearing was too much.

"Ready!" she says, shoving something shiny in her purse. I choose to ignore it, readying myself for action.

"Okay, here." Finn hands Jimmy and Uri small flashlights no bigger than their hands and gives the rest of us long grey cloaks to cover our outfits. "Don't turn them on until you get to the tunnels, the battery won't last long enough otherwise. Be careful, we'll see you when you get back." He helps me into the cloak and hugs me before closing the door behind him.

"Does everyone know the plan?" I turn to them, everyone nodding but Luke. "Would you care to elaborate, Luke?" I say, only to make sure he's in the right headspace. He was fine after we fought, almost happy with me, but in between then and now, he's become bitter.

"We stick to the shadows on our way to the school, walk through the tunnels, get to the speakeasy, get the information and get out without getting killed or giving your identity away. It's not that hard," Luke grumbles, the scent of liquor on his breath. He steps off the porch and into the silent darkness.

"And stick together," I mutter. I start toward Jimmy, but Emma slips in front of me, sliding her arm in his, pulling him forward. The nerve this woman has.

"Ms. Hudson." Uri offers his arm to me, relief on his face, probably because he doesn't have to walk with Emma.

"Mr. Winston." I link his arm with mine, using him as a crutch because even though these heels aren't that high, I still find it hard to walk without tripping, my feet aching after a couple of steps. I have no idea why Tequila chooses to wear heels.

On our way to the school, we try to blend in with the others dressed in long cloaks, their hair done up and heels clicking against the cobblestones. I wonder how they manage to get away with this every night and not get caught. Where do the Hunters think these people go, tipsy and dressed for nothing but a party? They could be like the Hunters in The Sticks who don't care what people do or that they're mixed up in illegal business. It'd be hard not to drink when you live in a dirty, unfriendly town like this.

We reach the school in eight minutes, all piling into the tunnels, through the trap door hidden under a sandpit. A group of clearly not sober people stumble in with us. They introduce themselves, giving me a quick embrace, not looking into my eyes. They linger a little too long with Jimmy and Uri before squealing with delight when they see Luke and Emma, catching them up on the latest gang rankings and Hunter beatings.

I weasel my way to the back, behind Jimmy and Uri, so the flashlights don't accidentally cross over my face. I lock my fingers with Jimmy's, his clammy palm uncomfortable against mine, cold and rigid. I can only hope that Luke's right, and by the time we get to the speakeasy, most people will be too hammered to recognize my face.

The tunnel feels the same as it did in my dream, the air perfumed and smoky. The stones surround us, amplifying every sound: dripping water, screeching bats, and loud laughter of the people in front of us. With the flashlight's help, though, the darkness doesn't seem so claustrophobic, so similar to my dream.

"It's a bit creepy down here," Jimmy whispers. His words bounce around us, all the way to the front and the sounds of people agreeing with him make their way back to us.

Creepier than you think. I remember the feeling of something pushing me forward, so I have to make a conscious effort not to swing my arm back because I know there's nothing there. *There's nothing there.*

"*You're wrong!*" the high-pitched voice taunts. I squeeze Jimmy's hand harder, grabbing Uri's arm as well, pulling myself forward, so close to them that I keep stepping on their heels.

"You okay?" they both whisper.

I nod, forgetting they can't see me, "Yeah," I say, my body shivering, praying the speakeasy doesn't look like the one in my dream. The high-pitched voice starts to sing his little song again. I count backwards from one hundred, replacing his voice with my own. In a way, I'm grateful for the darkness because if people saw me at this moment, walking with my eyes squeezed shut, clinging to both Jimmy and Uri like a scared child, they'd think I was crazy.

After what feels like forever, loud music sings all around us, the flashlights revealing a metal door, the word 'Ryker's' engraved in fancy handwriting on the surface.

Three knocks. Pause. Two knocks. Pause. Three knocks. A piece of the door slides open, hooded brown eyes scanning us as bright lights glare in our eyes. I duck my head, Jimmy and Uri shielding me, Luke covering the gaps.

"Code," a deep voice demands.

"Fire breathing rubber duckies," a girl giggles, having trouble with the words.

"Try to get through the password once without laughing, Jenna," the man grunts, rolling his eyes.

"Can't!" she giggles.

He shuts the flap, and two seconds later, the metal door opens. All at once, bright light, music and the smell of liquor mixed with cigars and pretzels hit us. At first, I can barely see anything as I'm guided forward, someone sliding my coat from my shoulders, but when my eyes adjust, the sight completely takes my breath away.

It's nothing like my vision. The wood floors are polished and unscuffed, despite the many heels gliding over them. Brick wraps around the whole room, stopping where it meets the wooden roof and dangling silk fabrics that brush against the ground. Beams supporting the room have fake ivy strung around them, white and purple flowers pinned to the green. The whole place is one big dance floor, people singing and spinning, some being lifted into the air, some squealing when their partners try and fail. Few people occupy the black velvet booths that line the walls, their tables covered with red cloths, and flickering candles placed in the middle. There's not a mirror in sight.

As we turn the corner, there's more. The bar looks exactly as I saw it, dark wood shelves holding loads of liquors, their colours ranging from dark purples to baby blue to black. The only difference is that here there are mirrors, reflecting the gold lights projected to make the bottles glow. If I weren't so skeptical of this place, I might be in awe of everything. I don't want to look for the curtain of diamonds, but it's already facing me. Flaming ruby beads hang over a small doorway and though it's not the diamond curtain from the vision, I still feel a bitter taste on my tongue.

"You guys wait at the bar. I'll look around," Emma offers, leaving us to debate what kind of liquor to try first, our playful banter allowing us to ignore the underlying tension for a moment.

"We might have to build one of these when we get home," Jimmy gawks, sliding onto a black stool rimmed with red.

"Above ground, though," Uri adds, gesturing for the bartender. A weight I didn't know I was carrying lifts from my shoulders when I see the bartender is a middle-aged woman, covered in tattoos, no white flame pin anywhere in sight.

Luke slides onto a stool beside me. His mood is completely changed, now happy and brightened, most likely with the help of coming here buzzed, I suppose. "Can I buy you a drink?" he asks, pulling small bills from his pocket.

"I don't know if I should," I object, not wanting to be drunk when I have to talk to Durçk's contact, who could be holding my brother's whereabouts and his life in her hands.

"Come on, Harley. One won't hurt," he pleads, looking boyish and playful, like the person I met so long ago.

"Fine," I say, giving in a little too quickly, "I'll have the silver one." Luke grins, leaning toward the bartender. I look to Jimmy, who holds a glass of bright yellow liquor in one hand and has a brightly dressed girl brushing against his other. *That was fast. I think.* He has a true gift for attracting pretty girls.

"Harley, I think I owe you an apology." Luke spins me around to face him. He smells sweet, like fresh rain.

There's only one thing he could be referring to because when we were together, he treated me like he'd never hurt me. I heard all the rumours about the drugs, the acid, the innocent people he beat up, but I honestly couldn't see him as that type of person. When he was with me, he was kind and sweet and selfless. He never hurt me physically or mentally. He was a breath of fresh air when my whole world seemed to be underwater. He didn't know every pitiful little detail of my situation, and he never asked, and I loved it. It was like living a completely different life.

"No, it's okay," I say, only so an argument doesn't result from me saying he was a total ass. When he broke up with me, my mind kept bringing up the words he said even after I convinced myself I didn't care. I have very little desire to talk about this right now, with Jimmy behind me and Big Three Hunters potentially in the room. He notices my eyes shifting around, so he moves closer to me, placing his hand on my bare skin where the dress doesn't reach.

"No, I was an ass — I said those things to you because I wanted you to hurt, because I thought you were moving on to Jimmy. I was mad, but I know now that I was being paranoid." He inches closer with every word so that if I were to twitch, my lips would find his.

"You thought what?" I inhale sharply, and I feel an unwanted tension, desire building inside me. I switch between looking at his eyes and his lips, debating which feature I desperately, shamefully, want to stare at. It's felt like a year since I've had his full lips against mine, but really it's only been four days, give or take.

"I never told you before, but when I met you, it changed me. You made me understand what it was like to have someone who made me feel wanted. I still want to have that with you," he gestures to the bartender for another drink, though I haven't even touched my first. He keeps his eyes on mine, not moving back when she slides me another silver drink, and he pays her. "You don't have to say anything about it now. Take your time to think about who actually has the balls to tell you how they feel, and who is hiding their feelings by dancing with other girls." Luke purses his lips, inching back to take a sip of his blood-red drink, nodding to the dance floor. I almost forgot where we were.

When I look to where Jimmy should be, he's not sitting there, his yellow drink now abandoned. He's on the other side of the room, his now untidy hair pressed to his sweaty face as he dances with a blonde who doesn't appear to hold her liquor well — and I'm using the term 'dances' *very* loosely. I spin back around, irritated, swirling my silver drink around my glass. I twist back around, shifting forward slightly, and as I do, Luke catches my lips with his, gently keeping me there for only a second before he pulls away. *Holy shit.* Those are the only words that pop into my head at this fine moment in time. *Why did he have to say that now? Why did he have to kiss me?* I down my first drink, and the second quickly follows. It tastes like cookies. Luke revealed that he actually cared about me, might have even loved me — or might still.

I look at Uri, his eyes wide, a smug look on his face. *Yep! He definitely heard all of that.* Uri holds his soft pink drink up, toasting me and the love triangle I've found myself in, if I can even call it that, considering Jimmy hasn't even admitted his feelings.

Luke leans over again, "I'd ask you to dance, but it looks like they've found us." A cold hand falls on my shoulder. I tense, placing my drink back down.

"Follow me, Ms. Hudson." The man's breath, smelling of maraschino cherries and mint, is hot against my ear, his rough voice tickling my skin. I swivel, holding my breath, nudging Uri, but he's already on his feet, whistling for Jimmy to follow.

The man turns before I can see his face, but his build stops my heart. He's shaped like a bodyguard, gun outlined through his tight black shirt. His bald head is shiny, but the scorpion tattoo is absent from his skin. What if it's the man from the school? What if we've walked into a trap that Emma set up? I glance back at Jimmy. His reassuring smile is completely gone, his fighter's eyes taking over.

The man leads us past the rubies into a room identical to the one in my dream. Two flaming red couches face each other, a glass table in the middle — Emma sitting on one, her back to me and a woman on the other, so thin that every bone in her body almost pokes through her skin. Her nails are shaped in points, flames illustrated on the surface, and her hair is slicked back in a ponytail, the only difference being that it's knotted and ratty, not straight and perfect. She looks up, and I finally get to see her face. Her eyes are startling, with ember contacts, making them appear on fire. On one side of her face, migrating past her leather jacket, is a tattoo of a lively flame.

"Guess she likes flames!" Luke grumbles, using this comment to show the women and the men sitting on either side of her that they don't intimidate him. Uri nudges Luke's side, and he straightens because this is not the place to be tough.

"It's not nice to whisper about someone before you have introduced yourself," the woman purrs, speaking as if her voice is floating from her lips.

"You first," he replies, a little too bold. I wish he'd shut up.

"Ryker," she says, resting her arms on the back of the couch. Her left hand holds a cup, swirling the black liquor around, spilling some of the contents onto her hand.

At first, I think the way she sways her glass is her cockiness on display, but then I notice that the smooth rhythm is broken by a slight twitch, which makes the drink spill every so often. She can't control her movement.

My mom does the same thing when she's high. Ryker's a fiend, a person extremely addicted to harmful habits, in her case, drugs. They choose drugs over food, shelter, family, and over life. That's why she's so skinny and withered. That's why she can't control her muscles from twitching and swaying. Surprisingly, not many druggies get this way. Most of them have enough common sense to stop before it gets too bad and they end up destitute. The people who look like Ryker are usually drug dealers or connected to the Big Three somehow. This new-found information causes my chest to constrict further.

"Harley, weren't you taught it's not nice to stare?" she mocks. As I stare into her eyes, all the oxygen is drawn from the room. "Even if you've figured out my secrets." Her finger lifts and the men get up to push us to the couch where Emma silently sits. "Durçk told me you might show up, but I truly didn't expect you to. We knew you were in town." She scans over us. "They thought you'd stay in Dead Man's Hill for a while, but I didn't think you were stupid. I thought you'd be gone by now, but I guess I was wrong." She pulls a gun from between the couch cushions, placing it on her thigh. She taps the metal with her nails along to the rhythm of my heart, the barrel winking at me.

"Who's 'they'?" Jimmy asks, shifting closer to me, placing his leg in front of mine so if we were to fight them, he would be first to move forward. He does this all the time at Warehouse fights, but I find ways to slip around him.

"The Big Three, she works for them," I say, making an effort to appear calm, to keep my voice unimpressed. Ryker takes a sip from her glass, keeping her smile.

"Ah, I knew you weren't stupid," she praises with a hint of sarcasm, then holds up a finger, "But I'm not their little soldier. I'm not loyal to them — some would call me a double agent, but I prefer 'drifter,' drawn to the best offer."

"We don't have anything to offer you," Uri says tensely, straightening, making himself appear buffer, taller, like a bear does when it feels threatened.

"I am well aware of that Uri, so consider this a favour. I owed Durçk one. I guess he used it for you," she says smugly, pursing her lips into a line. She leans forward, placing her elbows on her thighs, waving the gun around and licking the drops of liquor from the side of her glass. She's prolonging our suffering by lingering on her words, pausing after every sentence.

"We need information on my brother, J Hudson," I blurt, not allowing her disturbed mind to be amused. In a way, she reminds me of flames: her inviting voice, her burning stare, manipulating the air to swirl around her.

"Bap, Bap, Bap, there's something you must do first." One of the men reaches under the couch, bringing forward a silver platter with a single line of white powder and a hundred-dollar bill on the side. "You have to prove your loyalty, and what better way to do that than put your own life at risk," she proclaims, keeping her eyes on me.

"It's just drugs," Luke huffs, getting up to pace back and forth behind me. The other man moves to the door so none of us can leave, but he doesn't make Luke sit back down.

"True, but it could also be flour, or sugar, or one of my new creations. You'll have to find out." She downs the rest of her drink, pointing the gun at me, the man beside her pointing his at Jimmy.

Suddenly I feel like I can't move. The silver gun and the way Ryker sits, reminds me of them dying. Her voice was in my vision — the platter was in the vision. Dying. All of them dying.

Jimmy reaches for my hand, only our fingertips touching. Ryker eyes them.

"Ooo! Lovers, I see. Best friends. Exes?" she questions with excitement, lowering the gun. Luke snorts, and her smile widens. "A love triangle! This may have gotten a lot more entertaining than I anticipated," Ryker says, sliding the platter toward us, one of her nails dipping into the powder. "You have one minute to choose who will be taking the risk or we will put a bullet in each and every one of your pretty heads. If you do it, you will get information on your brother. Promise," she says, making an X over her heart. "But if you don't, well, you understand."

Her laugh feels like knives digging into my throat. I need to do this, there's no question about it, but there has to be a catch. She might not follow through — I wish I had more damn time to come up with a different plan.

"I'll do it!" Uri offers, reaching for it, his hand slightly shaking as he sucks in a careful breath.

Jimmy stops his hand, "We need you to help get us back. I can do it."

This is a sick game to her. She likes to see her victims squirm before giving them what they need or before she kills them.

Luke shifts quietly behind me. Emma barely even breathes, but I can see shiny streaks under her eyes. The high-pitched voice sings in my head again, slowly, joyfully, taunting me. Enjoying every word he utters, *"You will fail. You will fail. Killing everyone you love. Too slow. Too reckless. You aren't strong enough to save them all."*

"No!" I pipe up, "She wants me to do it." Jimmy tries to reach for it, to pull it away from me, but I grab the platter before he can. "It's okay!" I say, looking away from him before he can convince me not to do it.

"You know you really remind me of a young version of myself. What a shame — also, the clock's ticking. You may want to skip the hero act. It's a little cliché."

I roll the bill up, placing it to my nose and leaning forward. But as the bill brushes over the white powder, someone pulls me back, yanking on my hair, the rose falling to my lap. Jimmy grabs the bill from my hand, bringing it to his nose, running it over the white line, and breathing in every last bit before my strangled objection can fight its way into the room.

For a second, nothing happens. He sits waiting with the rest of us, white residue rimmed around his nose. Maybe it was flour. But as soon as I move my hand to Jimmy's leg, he inhales sharply, falling to the ground, seizing. Instinctively I move forward, rolling him onto his side, pushing stuff out of the way, making a protective circle around him.

"Oh goody! It was my creation. That was intense for a second, I thought I accidently used flour," Ryker chirps, patting her men on the back.

"What the hell did you give him?" I yell, my voice frantic as I switch between glaring at her and making sure Jimmy's okay.

"Paraocybensinryker. It cuts the oxygen off to the brain, making the person feel like all their organs are on fire. It gives them the sensation of burning from the inside. Brilliant, isn't it?" She stands, walking to the dangling rubies.

"What about the information?" Luke asks, moving toward her, but her guards block him.

She glances back, almost frowning at me, "You have twenty minutes to get him to your front door, where the antidote waits. If you succeed, then we shall see."

"You promised!" Uri argues, leaning down and pulling Jimmy onto his shoulders.

"We never shook on it," she winks, her blonde hair disappearing behind the rubies.

Shit. I get to my feet, not trusting my legs to hold me up. *Think Harley. Think.* Don't focus on the foam starting to form on his lips, how his eyes are rolling back, and how if we don't move fast enough, he will die. "Uri, make sure his head stays on your shoulder," I order, readjusting Jimmy, his face too unnatural, scrunched up and shaking. I turn to Emma, "What's the fastest way out?" She hesitates, visibly crying now. I grab her shoulders, feeling my nails dig into her skin. "Emma, think!" I'm yelling now. I need to calm down. I need to stay calm.

"We can go the same way we came. It only took fifteen minutes. I remember the way," Uri says, running from the room.

I grab the flashlight Jimmy dropped and run after him. We push through the crowd, knocking drinks onto dresses, dodging angry dancers and sloppy drunks who beg us to stay a little longer. "Open the door!" Uri yells. The man turns, furious that someone dares to talk to him like that. Then he sees Jimmy shaking so intensely, I'm surprised Uri can keep hold of him. The man quickly obliges, shouting for people to get out of the way. I kick off my shoes and run into the tunnels. Broken glass, lit cigarettes and rocks dig into the soles of my feet, but I can't use the only flashlight to illuminate my path and protect my feet. It's occupied with lighting up Uri's path, so I'm only barely able to see when Jimmy goes still.

"Harley!" Uri calls back, debating whether he should stop to see if Jimmy's still breathing.

"Keep running," I pant, knowing that stopping won't help. It will only shorten his chance to survive. I listen for footsteps behind us in case angry drunks are following to start a fight. All I can make out are, hopefully, Luke and Emma.

"Left!" Uri takes a sharp turn, following the path he's memorized from walking to the speakeasy. I do the same before almost slamming into the rocks. Jimmy lurches, gasping, gulping for air, starting another round of violent seizing. *Stay calm, stay calm.*

"How much longer?" My voice breaks as I pray we haven't gone the wrong way. The tunnels have many different routes. For all I know, we could be headed to the Mayor's office.

"Not much longer," Uri says, his words almost lost in a loud thud and scream from behind us.

"What happened?" I yell back, not stopping.

"Emma twisted her ankle!" Luke calls back, his voice too far away for me to turn around and pull them forward. "We'll meet you back home," Luke assures.

Jimmy stops seizing again, following my voice, raising his head. "Harley," he moans. My throat has tied itself into knots, making it impossible to say anything back. I don't want to lose him. I can't lose him. He keeps me sane. He keeps me alive.

"Stairs!" Uri yells. The open door allows the street lights to shine onto the staircase. I shut off my flashlight, making a bit of an effort to keep curious eyes away from us. "This way," Uri pants, his shirt soaked in sweat and Jimmy's drool. His arms are shaking, almost losing their grip. I sprint faster so that I'm right behind him, prepared to let Jimmy use my body as a pillow if Uri lets go.

In minutes we reach the door, where a small orange bag sits, a black bow on top. Uri runs past it, hitting the door open, splintered wood flying everywhere. I grab the bag on the way in, careful not to break whatever's inside. Uri lays Jimmy on his side on the couch, then collapses into the chair, working to catch his breath and rest his tired muscles.

"What the hell!"

"No, no, Jimmy!" Tequila screams. She grabs at my shoulders as I reach Jimmy, her eyes pleading with me, distracting me with all her pain as she gives me the same look she had when she found Jimmy on the kitchen floor.

"Get off!" I shove her aside, not looking at her pleading eyes. Buckey holds her back, fighting with her to stay put, taking elbows in the stomach to let me help Jimmy.

"Someone hold his head!" I order. Finn rushes over to stabilize Jimmy, thinking of everything that could have gotten him to this state.

"What happened?" he asks, but I don't answer.

"Put him on his back."

Finn frowns at me, knowing that's not how you treat a seizing patient, and you sure as hell don't put anything in their mouth. I let my hand shake with Jimmy as I tilt the substance in the bottle to his lips, holding his chin up to make sure nothing spills, scared he'll spit it out.

Then everything stops, along with his breathing and my own. I can't give up. I slam my fist into his chest. "Jimmy, wake up!" I beg, starting compressions. "You can't leave me. You promised."

I blow air into his lungs, wanting them so badly to move on their own. He can't die. Finn leaves me, running up the stairs for supplies, but we have nothing that can help Jimmy. Nothing that can restart a heart. Tears start to cloud my vision.

"Please, help him, Please," Tequila whimpers beside me, cowering in Buckey's arms, letting them keep her from losing her mind. Rey, Johnny and Ace crowd around us, not able to do anything but stare and wait. I hear Luke and Emma come through the door, Emma crying out in agony, almost as if she's trying to divert our attention from Jimmy.

I keep pushing against Jimmy's chest, prepared to push harder and break his ribs if I have to. I blow air into his lungs over and over, feeling his chest rise and fall against my arm. After what feels like an eternity, Finn's hand falls to my shoulder, telling me I should stop. Telling me he's too far gone — telling me … he's dead.

"Did you find anything like adrenalin or nerson?" I ask, but I know he already looked, and the answer is no. I lie my head on Jimmy's chest, throwing my hands over him, protecting him, like someone's going to come in here and take his body.

"No — you can't stop!" Tequila cries. Her strained, hurt, terrified voice threatens to make me fall apart in front of everyone.

The room is almost too full of voices and mournful cries for me to hear the faint heartbeat against my ear. So slow, barely even there, for a second I think my mind made it up to trick me. Then Jimmy's chest lurches up, and he starts coughing. I lift my head so fast, tears are squeezed from my eyes.

"Harley?" He smiles, his voice coming out so hoarse, so broken, his eyes trying to stay open.

I expel a laugh that makes me sound as though I'm choking, "You idiot!" I sigh, and he winces, trying to pull himself up. "No, stay down, you shouldn't get up."

"Okay," he says weakly, without the strength to object. He lets his head flop back, and Finn slides a pillow under him before his head hits the rigid arm of the couch.

"You're crying." He wipes under my eyes, holding my face.

"Stop worrying about me." I lay my hand back to his chest, his heart racing.

"Harley, worrying about you is the best part of my day," Jimmy says, trying to laugh, but I can see how much pain his breathing is causing.

"I'll check him. Harley, you should sit down," Finn says, trying to pull me off, but I'm not leaving him. So I crawl onto his legs, resting my head on his side. He winces, but I don't move. I can't let him go. He understands this, wrapping one arm around me.

"I'm okay," he whispers. Every time he talks, a little piece of me breaks. I'm acting crazy and weak in front of the gang, but they know that I love him as much as he loves me. Tequila moves to his side.

"I'm sorry," I mouth.

"It's okay." She gives me a faint smile and lays her head on the couch, Jimmy stroking her hair.

Finn does his check-up around us, moving us only to let Ace and Rey remove Jimmy's jacket and shirt, his skin so hot and sweaty. "He's okay. It doesn't look like there's any nerve damage and his O_2 levels look normal." Finn shows me the screen, one I saw at his grandma's. "Whatever you gave him reset whatever he was experiencing. He'll probably only be weak for a couple of days, from his bruised ribs. None were broken."

"See, I'm fine," Jimmy croaks, lifting my chin and holding Tequila's hand.

"No you're not — now, stay down and shut up," Tequila says sternly, getting up and disappearing into the kitchen.

"I got it," Buckey says, touching Jimmy's shoulder before chasing after her.

"People deal with trauma in different ways," a voice whispers in my head.

"No!" I say back, *"not now."*

"What did I do?" Jimmy sighs in defence, trying to look for Tequila, but the effort to move his head is still too much.

"You kind of almost died, dude!" Uri pulls off his jacket, his shirt see-through from the sweat.

"Thank you, by the way." Jimmy nods.

"My pleasure," Uri says, hugging him and kissing the top of my head before heading up to the loft to try and sleep. Everyone else does the same, telling Jimmy they love him and promising me it will be okay.

"Call me if you need me," Finn says, bringing us water and leaving us alone, taking the empty antidote bottle to study.

I keep my head on Jimmy's chest, listening to his sounds of life, his normal breaths, making sure that it stays that way.

Sadness, anger and happiness rush over me at the same time. Why the hell did he do that, put his life at risk so I couldn't? We didn't even get information on where J is, so all of it was for nothing.

"Why did you do it?" I ask softly, moving my legs around him. He readjusts to suit my position, not telling me to get off as he flinches from the effort of holding me. I don't think I'll be leaving his side any time soon. I've lost my dad, my brother, my mom, and I almost lost him. He lifts my chin, his hands no longer clammy, now warm and comforting.

"To be a hero," he smirks. How could he be joking right now?

"Jimmy."

"I did it because I know how much that shit scares you — how you feel that if you took drugs even once, you'd be locked into that world like Eric, like your mom, never able to get out. You're scared you'd lose yourself. I don't want you to be scared, especially with all that's going on right now." He brings his other arm around me, locking me in his grasp and using all his strength to kiss my forehead.

"What about your addiction?" I'm always scared because no matter what I do, there is always something to lose. He considers this, then relaxes.

"This is different. I think I'll be fine."

The vision plays in my head again, making me watch him die. "I should have made you stay home." My words come out so weak.

"No. You couldn't have, because if I weren't there, she would have still selected someone and that someone would have been you. The problem with that is I don't know how to keep someone alive with mouth to mouth." He nudges me. "I'm sorry we didn't get the information."

I try to nuzzle my way further into his arms, but there's nowhere else to go. I have no more ideas to find out where J is. Everything was relying on tonight, so this could be it.

"Harley, I have to tell you something," Jimmy says. I look back up at him.

Whap, whap, whap. The pounding at the door nearly causes me to jump from the couch. Tequila storms out of the kitchen, gun in hand, "Show your faces, you cowards, bring it on!" she yells, flinging open the door. She waves her gun around like a madwoman, but then she stops. Bending down and shutting the door, she walks over to us, a letter in hand, passing it to me. "It's for you."

I rip it open, and a hard drive falls out, with a small note that reads, *'You have my respect, girl, here is the information you need on your brother.'*

"She came through." I turn to Jimmy. "We got it." He gives me a weak cheer, cut off by choking.

"At least she stuck to what she said." He smiles, pulling the letter and the hard drive from my hand, passing it to Tequila, then shutting his eyes.

"Maybe. But if I ever see her, I'm going to kill her," Tequila growls, tucking it in her pocket.

"I second that," Jimmy says through a yawn.

Tequila places a blanket over us and pushes the table against the door, throwing a pillow down. She curls up in a ball, reaching her hand up to hold Jimmy's as she sleeps. She's not letting him out of her sight either.

"Well, then we all agree," Buckey adds, laying a blanket across Tequila, then deciding that he'd better stay beside her.

I let my eyes close, counting Jimmy's breaths, listening to the music his heart plays for me as I drift off.

CHAPTER 13

(JIMMY)

I didn't fall asleep when everyone else did. When silence and even breaths filled the house. No one crowded me or fussed over me. They were too shocked and scared to comprehend it all. They told me they loved me, which was extremely hard for Rey to choke out, then they disappeared out of sight. Harley tried to stay up with my restless, wincing body, but her eyes couldn't resist the orders from her brain, which was soon closing them for her, while her tears were still sliding down my bare chest.

I couldn't tell her to move. I didn't want her to. I let her hold me because I knew it was the only thing that would ensure she got some rest. Besides, I've only been dreaming of this moment my whole life, but her presence, her body pressed to mine isn't enough to stop me from reliving what I saw when I was hallucinating and dying.

People always say that right before you die, you see your whole life flash before your eyes. I asked my mom about it when I was younger because every child knows their mom holds the answers to everything. She was sitting at her desk, sorting pictures. She turned to look at me with the most serious expression I have ever seen her muster and said, "No, you see what you miss most."

At the time, I never thought about the look in her eyes or how her voice saddened, as though she was thinking of a time it happened to her. I never thought she could be so right.

As the drugs burned into my nose and absorbed into my brain, I didn't remember going unconscious or seizing for what Harley told me was way too long for me to still have proper brain function. All I saw, all I recall, is living in a memory I had long forgotten.

I saw only light before becoming aware of the scratchy picnic blanket, chequered red and white, under my skinny young legs. A warm breeze lifted the edges up, blowing away napkins, and knocking over cups full of sparkling apple juice, a luxury my grandmother made only on my dad's birthday. My mom was beside me, echoing my laugh as we tried to pack the lightest things up and move rocks to the edges, making a game out of it, seeing who could be fastest. Then she paused to watch Tequila and my dad chase their yellow runaway kite.

"Jimmy," she said, pulling me onto her back. I was eight in this memory but still felt eighteen, so it surprised me when she effortlessly scooped me up. I was that kid again, skinny and light as a feather, with long hair and buggy eyes that were too big for my childish face. She galloped toward ten-year-old Tequila, who was wearing a muddy green dress, her fiery hair in long braids.

I squealed as my mom zigzagged and sprinted. I locked my fingers together and held my legs around her hips, trying so hard not to fall off.

"Jimmy," she said again, her voice almost bringing my dreaming subconscious to tears. I've longed to hear that voice for years — to hear her say my name one last time.

"Yes, Mama," I said, my voice small, squeaky. She stopped, facing us toward rolling fields of what my mom called yellow black-eyed Susan flowers, green grass filling the gaps, almost as beautiful as the flowers.

"I want you to take a mental picture."

"Like the ones Dad takes?" I ask.

"Exactly. You smart boy, but take it of the whole day. The beauty of it all." I tilted my head, not fully understanding how someone could do that. She moved her head so I could see a little bit of her face, her freckled cheeks and button nose. "Look at the field, then squeeze your eyes shut and try to recreate it with your imagination. I know you have a good one." She shut her eyes and turned back to the field. I copied her, taking in everything, then squeezing my eyes so tight I thought my brain would explode. "Now imagine the wind tickling your rosy cheeks, the smell of pollen mixed with dewy grass drifting through the air, circling around you. The sound of your father's silly laugh, and your sister's mischievous voice. How the colours play with the sun and the sky. The feeling of my hair tickling your nose." She tilted her head back and ruffled her hair against my face. I opened my eyes, brushing her hair away and looking around.

She spun me around, her arms outstretched like wings, ready to take flight, then she set me down. Both dizzy, we fell, disrupting the bugs with our laughter. My dad's rich voice called out. He and Tequila raced to see who could get to us first. "Now close your eyes again and tell me if you see it."

"Yes, Mama. I see it," I said, still not getting why I was doing this. Why did I have to imagine it if I was already here?

"Good, because now you have a place of refuge, where you can go when you are scared or lonely or can't find your way back to yourself. You merely have to shut your eyes and imagine. Take a couple of deep breaths and the field, the wind, and my voice will guide you to where you need to be and you'll be okay again." She winks at me, tapping my nose and smiling. The smile that made me feel safe, warm, at home. "Promise me you'll find this memory and let the wind lead you when you lose yourself, instead of the alternative." Her face broke then, making her look older, wearier than she ever let me see.

"I promise," I said, giving her a hug.

Only now, ten years later, do I understand what she meant by alternative. She knew I would lose my way — she's done it herself.

She scrambled to her feet in my memories, running over to my dad, his dark brown hair messy like mine. My mom jumped into his arms, yelling to the world — letting it know she loved him. I chased after her, the light shining and engulfing them, hiding them from me. I wanted so badly to follow them, but her voice told me not to — so I watched them leave.

The thing I missed most in the world was my parents: their voices, their smiles, their love. I wanted to pull Tequila with me after them because I knew she missed them too, but Harley's voice broke the light, telling me to come back. Telling me I made a promise to her that I'd never leave. I'd never leave her and Tequila behind, alone. She brought me back like she always does. I turned away from the light and walked into the field of flowers, not allowing myself to look back.

Tequila's light tread makes the floorboards creak, snapping me back to reality. She flops down to her makeshift bed where she and Buckey slept. Her hair is wet, eyes puffy, wearing new, clean, mismatched clothes. She takes a seat in front of me, staring at me for a while before Harley stirs, surely woken up by the heat of Tequila's eyes and the frustration she won't hesitate to share with me. Harley sits up first, looking at Tequila, then me. I try to be telepathic and tell her that I want her to stay so Tequila can't fully get mad at me.

"I'll go make some food," Harley says, giving me a reassuring look before she gets up,

disappearing into the kitchen.

I wait for Tequila to yell at me, to tell me how stupid and irresponsible I was for not only risking my life but also potentially reactivating my drug addiction. She keeps staring and staring, her freckled skin and red hair showing me glimpses of my mom, her different-coloured eyes displaying every emotion. Finally, quiet tears start to brim over her bottom eyelids, her shoulders shaking. I try to sit up to comfort her, but there's no chance of that happening without me passing out. So I slip my hand into hers, trying to take all the weight and pain off her shoulders.

"You almost died," she sobs, pulling the blanket tighter around her, still keeping her hand locked in mine. I never thought about the effect my decision would have on her. All I was thinking about was how to keep Harley alive, making sure she didn't end up like Eric — her mom — me.

"I'm sorry," I whisper, guilty of how much of a little brother pain in the ass I've been since our parents died. She's my big sister, yes, but I'm supposed to protect her, make sure all the bad stuff is directed to me, and all I've been able to do is deflect all of it and more to her.

"I'm not mad at you. I was last night, but then I thought about all the reasons you could have done it. It wasn't to get a quick high, or to end it all. It was to save her," she sighs, peering into the kitchen, lowering her voice. She's making me sound selfless, but I did it because I knew that if Harley died, I would too. "If you died last night, I wouldn't have been able to say goodbye or tell you I loved you. You would have been gone. Like Mom and Dad." Tears start to roll down the side of my face as her shaking voice makes her words very real. "You wouldn't have been able to tell her you loved her either — and we both wouldn't know what to do without your idiot comments around."

I feel a hint of a smile stretch across her face. She can so easily forgive me, so easily see the bright side when only darkness surrounds her. I've always envied her for that.

"I miss them. I'm sorry I did that," I repeat again, turning my head to her. I don't want to tell her about what I saw. She might not remember, but it would drag both of us deeper into grief if she did.

"Me too. You know, Harley loves you and you'd be a fool not to tell her now. Especially since she did every possible thing she could to save your life last night."

"Well, fool is my middle name!" I wipe the tears from her cheek, understanding that this may be the only time she's right, and I'm wrong.

"Can I tell you a secret?" she asks, obviously trying to change the subject so she doesn't start crying again. I nod. "I think Buckey might be the one."

I wrinkle my nose, then stop myself when I see she's serious, "Really?"

"Yeah — I mean, I think so." She looks at the stairs, remembering something. Something that makes a bashful smile stretch across her face. "You know I talk to a lot of lovers."

"A lot is an understatement," I say, rolling my eyes. She punches me lightly. She's had a lot of romantic interests walk in and out of her life. Some I've liked, some I haven't. But it's never bugged her, so it's never bugged me, even though sometimes I wished, without really knowing why, that I could beat the guys up.

"Whatever! But like, he's the only one I've ever really seen a future with. The only one I've been able to tolerate without moving onto the next. And he doesn't think I'm weird or scary. He sees me the way I see myself. Kind of like you and Harley."

"I'm happy for you, T." She flings her arms around me. "I like him, but I'm prepared to beat him up if he does anything stupid," I add as she turns to face the TV, clicking it on and resting the back of her head against my side.

"Don't worry. Johnny does enough stupid things for the both of them," she reassures me.

"I heard that," Johnny yells, jumping over the couch, slamming his knee hard against the table. He winces, falling dramatically into the chair, covering his face with a pillow to hide his embarrassment.

The rest of the gang piles into the room, squeezing onto the chairs, sitting on the floor, purposefully leaving me the whole couch. I try to get Finn and Uri to sit with me, but they refuse. Uri helps Harley pass out the food, and Finn pokes me, shining a light in my eye, to see if anything has changed overnight, but as I expected, it hasn't. My ribs are still bruised, and my nerves are still fine. That antidote Harley gave me reversed any reaction or side effect the drug should have had on me, but I still feel weak, like all life has been drained out of me. I'm waiting, like everyone else, for the addictive side to come out of hibernation and drive me back to the speakeasy to get more of Ryker's creation. A small part of me says this time will be different. I won't relapse. At least, I hope I won't. I can't afford to become irrational and paranoid. It's hard to tell when I'm high, but when I'm craving the stuff, hell, I'd break my own arm to get it.

Emma flings her bedroom door open, frowning before realizing everyone is staring at her. She quickly puts a smile on her face, but her eyes are still grumpy and tired. She moves to sit where my legs are. Harley bumps into her, making her stumble forward. Emma gives a frustrated grunt as Harley props my head up with a pillow, hands me water, moves my legs and sits down, placing them on her lap and adding a pleased smile. Emma grimaces as she takes a plate of food and settles for a spot on the floor, elevating her ankle on the table.

"What happened to you?" I ask, the events of the night not coming back to me anytime soon. The mood in the room drops to what I can only describe as resentment.

"I twisted my ankle," she starts, but Tequila doesn't hesitate to interrupt.

"She failed to remember the quickest way out of the tunnels, even though she's been there hundreds of times, and then *'fell,'*" Tequila puts that last word in air quotes, "Both times lessening the already short window they had to get you back and keep you alive."

"Woow tiger! It was stressful and really dark in the tunnels. It could have happened to any of us," Uri defends unconcernedly. I look at him for the first time, noticing the bags under his eyes and bruises on his shoulder from where I thrashed around — more guilt piles on top of me.

"I still think she tripped on purpose," Ace says, his eyes shut, sitting in an awkward position so his head can rest on Harley's shoulder while he sits on the arm of the couch. I genuinely don't understand how he sleeps anytime, anywhere.

"Watch your mouth. You weren't even there," Luke argues, but Ace keeps his eyes closed, not even slightly intimidated.

"She didn't even let Finn look at it," Johnny adds. Finn stares at his food, trying to stay out of the confrontation.

"Unlike you, I have enough money to get coverage to go to the hospital," Emma argues, "I don't need to rely on someone who's dropped out of school."

She's done it now. The whole room erupts in rude comments. All of them team up on Emma, accusing her of being responsible for falling, as if she had control over it. Finn and Harley are the only ones trying to stay calm.

I would say something, but my head starts to get mad at me. It's complaining about all the noise, so I focus on Harley as she pretends like nothing's happening, merely enjoying her food and sipping her water. When she finishes eating and slowly drinking her water, she says in her usual calm voice, "Shut up!" And all at once, everyone does, as if they've gotten tired of what they were arguing about. They turn to us, Luke the only one resisting her voice. A snarling look appears on his face as though he doesn't want to stop fighting, but since everyone else did, he has no choice. "What happened, happened. The important thing is that Jimmy is alive and we now have the information on J," she says, grabbing the hard drive from Tequila. "Emma, may we please use your computer?"

The hard drive looks like the one in the phone, the one I keep forgetting to tell Harley about. If I'm going to tell her how I feel, I have to tell her about it. I nudge her with my foot, but she's too caught up in finally getting information on her brother to pay attention to me. *This isn't the time*, I tell myself, realizing that's been my excuse for days.

"Of course. I'll be right back," Emma says, in her cheery voice, running into her room and coming back with the newest kind of computer.

How does she afford all this stuff? I think about what Harley told me last night, taking another look at Emma's small, run-down house, the paint chipping from the walls. I know that some people live in poorer homes to save money and spend it on other things, but I'm starting to see why Harley is suspicious. The clothes, the food, the computer. Not even the Opulents have all this stuff. They usually have one or two expensive things, but not like this. I truly can't get a read on her. She looks so nice and acts like she'd give her soul to save even a single person.

Harley slips in the hard drive, a white light shining on her and Ace's face. She squints at the screen, studying it. Ace finally opens his amber eyes, looking confused, then intrigued, then confused again. She turns the screen to us, a small smile playing across her face.

"X marks the spot," Uri says, getting up to take a closer look.

The screen displays a blueprint. On one half, there's a floor plan, and on the other, there's a building labelled 'Aron Clarke's building, closest to Dead Man's Hill.' The building has an X on floor two, on a piece of the foundation that protrudes from the rest. On the left side of the blueprint, there's an X over the cell J could be in, and along the side, there's a room number for where J would be if he were being tortured. I choose to ignore the last part because Harley either hasn't noticed it or skips over it, she only looks motivated by the information.

"Guess I can't kill Ryker after all. She went all out," Tequila says in awe, staring wide-eyed at the computer. She's right; Ryker put our plan into motion and gave it all its bells and whistles. Even if I did die, I have a feeling Ryker would have given Harley the information anyway. She worked too hard not to.

"Guess you're right," Harley says, holding the computer out for Emma. "Do you have a printer?" she inquires in the voice she uses for old people and puppies. Emma glares at her, probably wanting Harley to get up herself so she can steal her spot, but Harley is in protective mode, and that means she is not letting anyone she doesn't trust near me. She does this for everyone who's hurt or in trouble, not just me.

"For sure," Emma says, snatching the computer from her hands. Johnny and Rey mimic her, and even Luke is trying not to laugh.

"Uri, what's the best way to get there?"

He sifts through the documents and the maps that fill his head. "Probably straight through the thicket of No Man's Land. It would take way too long to travel to the clearing and we'd risk being seen."

"No Man's Land gives me the creeps," Buckey says, physically shivering.

"You can get lost pretty easily in there," Finn adds, practicing stitching up a banana with a piece of someone's hair.

"We'll have to risk it," Harley decides, moving on to the next obstacle she finds.

I've always hated No Man's Land. The poisonous bugs, the skeletons and sinkholes that absorb your screams so no one can find you. No Man's Land is a thick layer of trees that separates us from the Big Three, a day-long trip on foot if you don't get lost or eaten along the way. Basically, it's a graveyard where people get banished, given no food, no water, no shelter. No one ever survives alone in the forest. Criminals are supposed to be the ones who are sentenced to banishment, but since the Big Three favor them, the nicer and more genuine ones, who may have only stolen food to feed their starving families, end up in No Man's Land, and since they aren't hardened criminals, they have no fighting chance.

"So what time are we leaving tomorrow?" Emma chirps, handing Harley the blueprint. Harley takes the hard drive back and clears the screen, pursing her lips.

"Before sunrise, before anyone wakes up. But you will be staying here. Ten is already too many to travel with and Luke will need you to take care of his car and trailer," Harley says, trying to make Emma's job sound important.

Tequila stands quickly, clearing the plates, working on hiding her approving look. "You are no longer needed," she remarks, winking at me and walking into the other room.

Emma crosses her arms, bunching her lips together, making a pouty face that only makes her look like she's constipated. "But I've helped so much, you need me," she whines, making Johnny cover his ears.

"Yes, you've helped us in many ways and we thank you for your hospitality and hope that you keep your word and don't tell people of our whereabouts. But, you are needed here, with your job and with your mother." Harley's voice is breathy and calm, relaxing my muscles and my eyes. "We do appreciate everything you've done."

"Whatever, I'm going to work," Emma grumbles, grabbing her coat and leaving in a storming fit.

Tequila appears by my side again, holding a steaming cup of tea. "To help you sleep," she says, sliding it into my hands. I'm so weak it's hard to hold it up, the heat tickling my fingers. I don't question it, sipping until all of it's gone, giving it to Harley to place on the table. The tea is hot, but it isn't too unbearable, and instantly, I feel heavy and sleepy.

The gang gathers around Harley, feeding off her plan, giving her good and bad ideas. Their words go in one ear and out the other, so I only catch bits and pieces.

"No Man's land."

"Flashlight."

"Finn and Rey go find supplies."

"The rest of you pack what you need, leave what you don't."

"I'll pack for Jimmy."

"Cherry Pie"

"You're pretty," I sigh, watching Harley's lips, her concentration. Only she looks at me, giving me a timid smile as the others pretend they didn't hear. Her eyes are less puffy now, and when the light hits them, gold reflects back at me. She looks comfortable when she's helping people, forming plans and giving ideas.

She tells everyone to talk softer when she watches my eyes flicker shut, warmth flowing throughout my chest, reminding me of the burning building. The warm flames, my aching muscles as I carried Harley through the hall as she muttered, *"I want to sleep."*

Me too, Harley. Me too, I think before everything goes dark.

CHAPTER 14
(HARLEY)

I spent hours with the gang going over the blueprints, taking us step by step through the next day, until only Uri sat by my side. He reassured me that I left no holes in my plan, no ways to be seen or taken. Eventually, the sun disappeared behind the trees, and only I remained, checking and rechecking everything, with just a sleeping Jimmy sprawled across the couch to keep me company.

I'm wary about tomorrow. We have to travel by foot across town. Twenty minutes in the open to No Man's Land, where little light shines through the trees and mysterious creatures lurk. Vines and bushes look identical, making it easy to walk hopelessly in circles until you have to break for camp, drifting off into a defenceless sleep with the help of sickly-sweet fragrant flowers. I've never been past the tree line and have never met the banished; no one has, so they are somewhat of a myth. When someone does travel to the Big Three, they go through the clearings located in the worst towns, with Hunters at both ends, making it practically impossible to move through without being noticed.

I accidentally knock Jimmy's leg with my elbow as I move to readjust.

His eyes open. "What time is it?" He stretches, yawning so wide I can see his molars. I check the clock on the TV. I always find myself losing track of time, hours seeming like minutes.

"Just after ten, go back to sleep," I whisper, using a lulling voice.

I've only moved once to go to the bathroom and change, but other than that, I haven't let him out of my sight. I almost lost him, felt his heart stop, watched his life slip through my fingers.

I almost considered waking him after Uri left when I ran into a little problem in the plan, but he looked so at peace. His hand rests on his chest, rising and falling with his breath, along with the hair on his forehead, moving as the air leaves his lips.

He doesn't look any better, his skin still pale, dark circles under his eyes and too weak to even hold up a cup of tea, but Finn keeps telling me that not everyone heals as fast as I do. It takes time, but I can tell he's as worried as I am about Jimmy beginning to crave drugs. We have no more detox pills, so all we can do if we run into the problem is give him small doses of morphine to dull his symptoms, and hope that as we walk through the forest, we happen to come across Noves root, the plant which the detox pills are made from, but we have no idea where to look.

"What are you doing?" he asks, pushing himself up, having no trouble this time. Maybe he is getting better. Maybe Finn and I have seen too many mishaps to acknowledge the positive.

"Going over the plan," I say, dropping my pen and leaning back to let myself relax. He looks so young in this light, with extremely messy hair, always and forever smiling, the kind of smile you only come across once in your life. I catch myself staring for too long and end up blushing, averting my eyes.

He sighs, getting to his feet, wobbling at first, then finding his balance, standing tall and strong, showing me he's okay. "If I know you — and I do — you've gone over that hundreds of times already." He sticks out his hand to me, "Come here."

I narrow my eyes, hesitating before placing my hand in his. It's warm and clammy, but that never bugs me because every time his hand finds mine, butterflies fill my stomach, even after fourteen years. He squeezes it gently, guiding me to my feet, his muscles powerful, even when he's at his weakest. He spins me into his arms, our bodies beginning to move as one, turning in circles, swaying back and forth.

"You shouldn't be up, let alone dancing," I say, not really wanting him to stop. I like it when he does this. We used to have random dance parties all the time. We ached with laughter as his mom taught us new moves, pretending we were the best in the world, entering competitions with ourselves that we always won. Lately, however, we've been too caught up with life.

He replies by starting to hum, 'Can't help falling in love,' the first song his mom taught him and my favourite. A smirk pulls at his lips, his clear blue eyes playing with the light, glistening as he spins me again, and I spin him.

"You're an idiot if you think dancing will prepare us for tomorrow," I joke, resting my head against his chest, breathing in his shirt — his scent.

"First, goof is a better word to describe my dashing personality, and this isn't to prepare you, it's to give you a break from being *so* uptight." His hand brushes down my back, drifting slowly to my waist. Surges of everything I've ever felt about him move with it — the hate, distrust, secrets. The loyalty, the happiness and the pain of never getting to love him the way I should have.

"You're the one that told me to do it," I offer. "Be the leader," I mimic, making my voice deeper, furrowing my eyebrows. He dips me, and a squeal escapes my mouth, a sound I've never made before, not even when I was younger.

"Well, I don't follow my own advice, so I'd never expect you to."

"Exactly what I've been telling myself the past couple of days," I giggle as he pulls me up, blood rushing to my cheeks. He pouts, pretending to walk away, but he doesn't get far before he comes right back. He pulls me in closer, keeping one hand in mine and the other on my hip, his heart rate fluttering to the sweetness of his voice.

"You're the most beautiful person I've ever laid eyes on," he admits, leaning his head down to press his lips to my fingers. I laugh because Jimmy only ever says this jokingly. "No, I'm serious." He spins me out, and when I catch a glimpse of his face, I can tell there's no trace of sarcasm anywhere. "I'd never joke about that — I never have," he adds, making sure I see his seriousness. I nod, speechless, and even though we aren't dancing to any music, our bodies move rhythmically together, gliding across the creaky floor, easily avoiding the tables and chairs.

His lips fall to my ear. "Do you remember the first time we met?" he whispers, moving back to look at me, his mouth leaving a shadow of lust on my earlobe. I tilt my head so his pink lips hover over mine.

I don't remember much from my childhood. My brain is simply too full of new traumas and memories to have room for all eighteen years. I remember mainly glimpses of my dad and my brother, some of Jimmy after eight, but a clue of what he means tugs at my tongue.

"We were four," I breathe. His low delicate chuckle tells me I'm right. "But all I remember is you introducing yourself with a mouth full of dirt," I laugh as he squeezes my side. It seems like we're in a dream, floating, on a fluffy cloud, so high up no one could touch us, too good to be true.

"That's true, but I remember everything. It's literally my favourite memory." He moves my arms to rest around his neck, his other hand falling to my hip. I close my eyes, searching for that day, but all I see are the little details — the red roses, the wind rustling my hair, clouding my vision, and the sound of my dad's laugh when I stood on his feet as he taught me to dance.

"It was right after someone's wedding. Everyone was celebrating in the garden behind the old church that no one uses anymore. There were so many people. Happy people, laughing and dancing, thriving in the first summer's sun, and the fact that Hunters can't disrupt weddings." He speaks as if the memory is playing out In front of us. I keep my eyes shut, imagining every word. "My mom dragged me everywhere, introducing me to people that pinched my cheeks and told me how much I looked like my dad. But all I wanted to do was get my clothes dirty and play with the other kids. Then I saw you. Dancing with your dad. Your mom holding baby J, actually content with life." He brushes his fingers across my cheek, gliding them down to my neck. I hold my breath, not wanting to make a sound, not wanting him to stop. "Your hair was so messy, falling all over your face. You weren't like the other girls, perfect and trying too hard to appear Opulent, with their puffy homemade sparkly dresses, but yours — yours was simple. You were free. You were giggling and so happy, more beautiful than the roses along the fence. Every damn boy couldn't keep their eyes off you. That's when we all started fighting for you, even though we thought girls had cooties. They were all scared to go up to you 'cause you were with your dad, but I sure as hell wasn't. I saw my chance to ask you to play with me, to dig for worms or whatever a four year old does — I went sauntering over, with confidence I have never possessed since that day."

"And you tripped," I smile, giggling, the memory slowly coming back to me.

"More like a rock knocked me over. But yes, the rock pushed me right into the dirt and I wasn't smart enough to put my hands out and protect my face. I was a little embarrassed because everyone was laughing at me."

"I remember your face turning bright red," I tease.

"Who's telling the story?" He pulls me closer, kissing the top of my head, his lips lingering there.

"Sorry!" I breathe, nearly losing my voice, my mind.

"Okay, so I was very embarrassed because I blew my first shot at talking to a pretty girl, and making a good first impression. But you know what you said to me?" He stops swaying, taking my face in both his warm, calloused hands. I press into them, letting them support me.

"No," I sigh.

"You pretended to fall and landed right beside me, and all the kids stopped laughing — they followed you, flopping into the dirt, thinking it was a game. The parents were fuming because their kids were dirty, but yours smiled. You giggled, the most beautiful sound I've ever heard and you said, 'I like you, we're going to be best friends.' And fourteen years later

I'm still in the friend zone." He exhales, frowning slightly, lifting my chin. "Though, I promised myself something that day — I promised that no matter how long I had to wait for you to come to your senses, to notice me in a different way — I would never stop fighting for you. Not even if we hated each other. Not even when we're on death's door." He leans his forehead to mine, taking a deep breath and closing his eyes. My breath hitches, my chest filling with tension, longing, and desire. "Harley, I — I have been so insanely, painfully, in love with you since that day and not once have I ever changed my mind." He laughs nervously, letting out a deep exhale as if a ten-thousand-pound weight has been lifted from his chest. "I love you," he whispers again, as if those words are keeping him alive.

His eyes open, scanning my face for any signs of withdrawal or disgust, but I feel none of that. For years I've been coming up with reasons not to be with him, not to cross that line. I was scared of him rejecting me, of Eric having another person to hurt me with or even the gang getting mad. But now, all I feel is happiness.

"You don't have to say anything back, I know this is out of nowhere. Kind of but—" he babbles, dropping his eyes to my lips.

"Shut up," I laugh, silencing him as I press my lips to his, so soft, so unfamiliar, a part of him I've never had the privilege to touch. Heat blankets my skin. All my fears, all my pain, everything unravels with the influence of him.

For a second, he's caught off guard, but he quickly recovers and pulls me closer. He runs one hand through my hair, moving the other to the small of my back, where he grips my shirt as he parts his lips to make room for mine. He leans down, and I stand on my tiptoes, but he eventually lifts me off the ground. I swing my legs around him as he moves to sit on the couch. My hair falls around us like a curtain, and he pushes it behind my shoulders, running his fingers across my neck as they retreat to my hips. I pull back slightly, watching him move with me, his eyes fluttering open, mystified. Our heavy breaths mix, no trace of whiskey on his this time.

I trace my fingertips over his pink lips, trying to memorize them in a new way and forget the fact that I'm sitting on his lap. "I love you," I whisper. A smile stretches across his face as my words sink in. He pulls me into a hug, nuzzling his face into my neck, his silky hair soft against my cheek.

"I love you," he repeats, kissing my forehead, my chin, my cheeks, my neck, before bringing his lips back to mine.

Tingles rush up my arms and down my legs, exciting my heart, sending butterflies from my head to the tips of my toes. I want to stay here forever, let my mind go blank, my lips stay locked with his and let our hands make all the decisions. I want so badly to forget where we are, to lose myself in him and never have to worry about finding who I am, who everyone needs me to be. But I can't. I move back, touching my palm lightly to his chest.

"Jimmy."

"Yes, what is it?" He asks, concerned like he's done something wrong.

"Nothing," I smile, kissing him again softly, slowly, letting my lips hover and our noses touch, "but we can't do this here and — I'm nervous." I look away, embarrassed because I know for a fact that all the girls he's been with were never nervous or never admitted it if they were.

He moves his head so I'm forced to look at him, "Harley, I am too," he agrees, surprising me. "And I've waited years to tell you how I feel. So I can wait a bit longer to do other things — not that that part of the relationship is all I want."

I shut him up with another kiss, "Hey, I kind of like this — now I have a sure way of stopping you from talking." I crawl from his lap, but he only follows me, lying down beside me, holding me so that even if I wanted to leave, I couldn't. I never would.

"Harley."

"Yes." I rest my hand on his cheek, looking at all the places my lips wish to discover.

"I've only ever loved you. I know it's different for you because you have Ace and so on, but you have no idea how happy I am right now," he says, lightly touching his lips to mine, his eyes flutter closed as tiredness takes over, his breaths slowly becoming even, his arms still staying locked around me.

"I love you," I breathe, kissing the spot where a crease appears between his eyebrows when he's concentrating. I kiss his cheek, his nose, under his chin, the nape of his neck, his collarbone, almost giddy with this new feeling coursing through my veins. I smile as he lets out a longing sigh, guiding my lips back to his.

"Now I'll never let you go, especially when you want me to."

I run my fingers through his hair. I can see why he does it all the time. It feels like fluffy clouds moving between my fingers. "I don't think I'd ever want you to, even if it seemed like I did," I say, letting my eyes close too. "I'm happy."

"I — I have something I need to tell you," he says, touching his fingertips to my lips, his voice taking on the tone he uses when he's attempting to tell me he's lied.

"I know," I whisper, the butterflies in my stomach starting to die down as stress, sadness, and guilt try to take over this moment. "Ace told me about the hard drive already."

Ace told me about the phone, the hard drive and the hiding spot in Luke's trailer the same day they found it. I had been waiting for Jimmy to tell me himself, but I figured he had a reason not to, or he knew Ace told me, but I guess not.

"Oh!" he says, putting his arm back around me. I press my lips to his — the tingling sensation still running through my body — not caring that he never told me the truth. I don't want to ruin the moment by starting a fight.

"We went looking for it when everyone was asleep, but it was gone. We figured he traded it or sold it when we got to town."

"I saw him do it. He traded it to a man, but I never saw his face. Luke told me it had something to do with you," Jimmy utters, "I just forgot to tell you." I can feel his eyes on me, waiting for me to get mad or suggest ideas about what Luke could have been doing with the hard drive. I'm too tired and stressed about tomorrow to care, and he's still weak. Luke is not the priority right now. I have to focus on getting everyone into No Man's Land without getting killed.

"Jimmy," I snuggle my way further into his arms, "We can talk about this when we get out of town. If Luke says it's about me then he's probably trying to get in your head. It's okay, I can handle myself," I say, but a part of me knows his worrying is for a better reason than a petty fight over me. It was condescending of me to say that. "I love you and I never want this moment to end, okay?" I whisper, understanding now why I've only ever said, 'I love you,' to three people. Those words hold more power than anything I've ever said.

"I'll freeze it for us right now," he whispers, covering his hurt with a joke as he squeezes his eyes shut.

I kiss him again, feeling his warmth blanket me, feeling free for the first time in my life. I love him. He's always watching over me, protecting me. I want to stay up, kiss him forever, but, safe in his arms, I let my mind go blank as his breath becomes even as we drift off.

CHAPTER 15

(JIMMY)

"Well, isn't this interesting? Never expected to one day wake up and see these two sleeping together," Rey huffs, poking my face.

"Shut up, they're *so* cute." I know that's Tequila; she's the only one who would willingly call me cuddling Harley cute.

Cuddling *Harley*. I open my eyes to see she's still beside me, hair covering her eyes and moving with her slowly waking breath.

"Well, we have to go," Luke grunts, shoving my head hard, knocking it into Harley's, the motion making her hit the back of her head on Rey's knee. She brings her hand to her forehead, confused, then kisses me in front of everyone. A small peck, but my cheeks still go red as whistling, gagging, and sighs follow from the group.

Last night wasn't a dream. I feel stronger, no longer held down by the after-effects of almost dying, no longer scared that she'll never love me back. In a way, I feel liberated.

"Buckey, pay up! Told you he'd tell her before he turned twenty-five," Johnny cheers, tossing two backpacks on top of us.

"I ain't got any."

"Don't worry, I'll add it to your tab."

Harley grabs a jacket, slides it on, slings her bag over her shoulders, and ties her hair back. She helps me do the same because the effort is still too much for me to handle without breathing heavily. I guess my strength was just a mirage.

"Hopefully only one more day of feeling like shit," Finn says, handing me a blue pill. "It's a low dose of muscle pain relief, don't worry." I look at Harley, and she nods. Even giving me muscle relaxers is a dangerous game to play, but I trust both of them with my life, so I take it.

"We have to go," Luke groans again, giving Emma a goodbye hug before flinging the door open and walking out.

"Oh, chill out man," Rey protests.

"You're only jealous," Johnny piles on.

They chase after him, ecstatic they have a new person to torment on the long walk. Harley snaps out of her happy daze as she goes into street mode, where she sees and hears every little thing, even the buzzing of insects that are nowhere near her.

"Uri, go get in front of them. We're moving in twos. Make sure those idiots stay quiet," Harley orders. Uri sprints after them, his black backpack flopping up and down, hitting the gun in his waistband. "Finn, you have the supplies?"

"Yes, all in here. Stem 47, extra cloths and stitching supplies. There wasn't much else we could find," Finn states as he and Tequila walk out next. Tequila winks at me as she pulls her fiery red hair into a toque and flashes me her gun.

"See you on the other side," I say, wishing she could stay within six feet of me as we leave town so I can keep an eye on her. But she's smart enough and in better shape than I am.

"See you there," she calls back.

"Are we taking all the guns?" I ask Harley, thinking that walking around with loads of firearms and ammo likely wouldn't end well if someone caught us. She pulls an oversized jacket over me and my bag, ties a bandana over my mouth and yanks my hood up.

Everyone's wearing jackets, dark clothes and something over their face to hide their features. I have no idea where they managed to find all of this extra clothing and these bags. I hate being out of the loop. It makes me feel helpless because I'm usually the one helping Harley put the plans into motion.

"Yes, Uri has the bullets, every group has a gun and a walkie talkie and I have the extras and the knives," she says, zipping her jacket all the way up to her nose, pulling her hair in a black toque as well.

"But your clothes?"

"With Ace," she replies, gesturing to him and Buckey. "Buckey's going to take you. Ace and I are going to bring up the rear. If you get too tired, Buckey's going to tell Ace to come help you, so one can support you and the other can still fire a gun if necessary. We're all meeting in the tree line so I'll see you in a bit, okay?" She kisses my forehead, then lets Buckey help me out the door. I want to object and tell her I want to stay with her, but I know I'll only slow her down and make her a bigger target, so I say nothing.

The crisp air nips at my skin, stinging my eyes and making my nose run. Winter is coming, which is going to make travelling on foot even more unbearable. Weak light from the rising sun and dimming street lamps project shadows on drawn shutters and pitch-black houses, making the town feel more ominous than I thought possible. I miss The Sticks, not because I had my own bed and only Hunters as a threat, but because it was predictable. We knew the other gangs would have our back if we had theirs, but here, the people seem divided, like if they saw someone dying on the streets, they'd unquestionably walk the other way. That's the one plus of The Sticks; It's everyone against the Hunters.

We're barely halfway to the trees when my legs start to feel like molasses. I lean my weight on Buckey's shoulder, which has no effect on his fast pace. I wish he'd slow down a little. In the distance through the morning fog, I can just make out a piece of Tequila's red hair that escaped from her toque before Finn tucks it back in, and she disappears into the shadows once more. I look back to see Harley, but she must be too far behind for me to make out. *Good, If I can't see her, maybe no one else can.*

"So you finally made your move," Buckey grunts, his breaths making small puffs of steam.

"Yepp!" I answer, my breath noticeably heavier than his. I consciously work on breathing evenly, but that only makes it worse. I don't understand why I feel this way if the antidote was meant to reverse everything. Maybe it still has an aftereffect.

All of a sudden, I feel eyes on the back of my neck, and my heart quickens. "Move to the wall," I say urgently, hobbling closer and using it to help me walk so Buckey can stand guard in front of me. As our feet shuffle over the gravel, I scan the roofs, alleys and windows to try to be more helpful. Sweat drips down my face, soaking my shirt, but I see nothing — not one person, not one light to reveal company. Maybe I'm just paranoid or seeing things.

"Do you see anything?" Buckey whispers, pulling his gun and raising it to the buildings. A street light catches the silver, allowing the metal to glimmer in the darkness. I push Buckey forward faster, and for a second, nothing happens — the town stays as it is, quiet and empty. Then the first shot goes off. We scramble, and Buckey locks his hand around my arm, dragging me forward, zig-zagging from shadow to shadow. A second shot goes off, the sound bouncing off the walls, the bullet not hitting anywhere near us. They're not firing at us, and even if they were, Buckey wouldn't be able to shoot back; he's too busy making sure I stay upright. Besides, he's not used to shooting with one hand, and there's always the risk of hitting other civilians.

My mind goes to Harley. They're shooting at her. My first thought is to go back, but I convince my body to move as fast as it can. *I'd be no help to her,* I tell myself. I look around, but still, I can see no one. They have to be in the houses, using windows as sniper nests.

We pass the tree line when a third shot goes off. Buckey jerks to the side, letting me go, groaning through rigid teeth. I stumble forward a couple of feet, unable to stop myself before slamming into a tree. Tequila rushes to my side, pulling the bag from my shoulders and helping me sit up.

"Are you okay?" Her eyes are wild, distracted by Buckey, who lies against a tree, holding his shoulder.

"Yeah, you?" I ask, trying not to throw up. She nods. "We have to move further in," I yell, knowing that the Hunters can shoot into the opening of the trees and hit each and every one of us with no problem. Uri and Johnny grab Buckey by his bag, dragging him further as Finn yells at them to watch his shoulder. They set him on a rock, cutting away the straps and pulling off his bag and the jacket that covers his wound. A trail of blood leads straight toward him. Tequila holds me, leaning me against a tree.

"Where's Harley?" Luke asks, grabbing me. I slap his hands away, not able to do much else.

"She was behind us — she's coming," I affirm, more to reassure myself than him. He starts forward, but I grip his sleeve, yanking him back. "If you go out there you'll get yourself, and her killed when she has to save you," I say, a little reluctantly, but to my surprise, he listens, raising his gun, watching the trees.

"Did the bullet go through?" Buckey moans, his voice strained, holding his left shoulder, blood seeping between his fingers. Johnny presses both his hands to the back of Buckey's shoulder, making an effort to hold back his tears for his brother's sake. Finn moves their hands, checking the bullet-sized wound.

"Yes! You're lucky, and by the looks of your arm and how you have little trouble moving it, it also doesn't look like it hit anything important, and won't cause much muscle damage." Finn starts pouring supplies from his bag, his hands moving fast.

"Little trouble moving it, hey," Buckey echoes, grimacing.

"I have to get it to clot. Here, hold this, both of you," Finn orders, passing them cloth. "Then I can either use the Stem 47 to make it heal fully and faster, or I can stitch it."

Buckey looks at his brother, then at Tequila, who places her hand on my arm, facing away from him and closing her eyes. She may be tough, but she sucks at dealing with this stuff.

"Save the cream for something else," Buckey says, his face turning pale. Finn nods, placing the cans back in his bags before wrapping a long piece of cloth around Buckey's shoulder to hold the gauze in place, all of their hands and clothes stained.

"I'll give you some morphine."

"We have to move further in," Uri decides, peeling off his jacket, removing his shirt so Finn can use it for a sling. Uri looks defeated as he zips the jacket back up, putting on his bag and throwing Buckey's over it.

"What about Ace and Harley?" Rey asks, eyes trained on the blood. I tell Tequila to go stand with him because he looks like he might pass out. I get to my feet, adrenaline yelling at me to go after Harley.

"She knows where to go," Uri assures us, directing his stern, sympathetic look at me. He's right; she's smart, she's a survivor.

"Harley, come in — Harley, do you hear me?" Luke says over the walkie talkie, but there's no answer. "If you hear me, we're going deeper in." I move forward, working on balancing, training my eyes on the forest floor.

"Luke, help me with Buckey. Finn, Rey, Tequila, go. Johnny, take up the rear," Uri commands.

Buckey bites his hand, stifling his screams as they pull him to his feet. I know he's trying, but the noise is going to call more Hunters to our location. Two more gunshots go off. One bullet hits the tree where I rested a couple of seconds ago, and the other either misses its target or wasn't directed at us.

She's fine. She's fine, I repeat to myself.

"She'll be fine," Tequila says, repeating my thoughts, stopping me where the vines and roots begin to blanket the ground. The bushes and trees are thicker here, cutting off most of the light, a good place to stop. Besides, Buckey is screaming so loud now, we are not only drawing in Hunters but other creatures. The forest is starting to feel more alive.

Something's off about this whole thing. It sounds like there are more than a couple of Hunters firing, which makes no sense because usually, no more than two or three Hunters are in one area at a time. Even if the

Hunters called for backup, it would have taken longer than two seconds for them to get in position. They must have known we were leaving at this time. But how?

Luke crouches on a rock, gun held up, finger on the trigger. "Look before you shoot," I say, scared that Harley and Ace will come running at Luke, and he'll become trigger happy and shoot them.

"I'm not an idiot."

"Tequila, you okay?" Buckey calls. Finn holds a flashlight in between his teeth, cleaning the wound, his eyes fixed in concentration. I bet he can't hear anything or anyone around him.

"Yes," Tequila says timidly, taking a deep breath before walking over to Buckey and taking his hand, still keeping her eyes trained on the trees. Uri stands, checking his watch, tapping his foot on the ground, distracting himself with a map he must have drawn up last night.

"They should be here by now," Johnny says, standing over Buckey, gun ready. This is the first time I've seen him genuinely scared. He's almost in tears.

I lean against a tree, dropping my bag, trying to catch my breath. I focus on the moss, the different coloured leaves and how dreary and cold this hellhole is.

"We'll go look for them in ten," Luke offers, appearing distressed and scared. I might have to apologize to him for saying he doesn't care about Harley, because all I've seen him do lately is help me protect her. At the speakeasy, we made an unspoken agreement for me to take the drug and stop Harley from doing it.

A sound to my left pulls me from my thoughts.

"Shut up," I hiss, tilting my head toward it.

"What?" Luke starts to argue, but I interrupt again.

"No, shut up!" The leaves start to rustle. Everyone goes still, pointing their guns toward the noise. Harley isn't big enough to disrupt that many leaves; she's quiet and stealthy, but I still want it to be her.

The bushes fall quiet, a branch snaps, and Harley stumbles through with an unconscious Ace draped across her shoulders. One of us shoots, the bullet just missing her leg, lodging itself in a tree behind her.

"Good thing you're a bad shot, Johnny," she huffs, barely audible through her heaving breaths. She falls to her knees, rolling Ace onto the ground, positioning his bag so his head rests on it. Johnny smiles, dropping his gun.

I lock eyes with her, feeling all my stress and her own fall from our shoulders. I feel like I can focus again. I run to her, folding her into my arms, feeling her body curl into mine. I look for words, but nothing comes out. I hold tighter, breathing her in. Uri leans across us, checking Ace's pulse.

"Thank god you're alive!" she mutters in my ear, opening a new part of me — the part that knows someone cares if I'm alive. "But I need both my arms to check Ace. I promise I'll let you hug me for as long as you want, later." I let her go, seeing for the first time the big gash on her shoulder. Both her jacket and shirt sleeve, torn away.

"What the hell happened?" Luke asks, keeping his eyes on the forest. I take gauze, pressing it to her cut while she works on Ace, checking for bullet holes and looking at his pupils.

"Ace saw something on the roof. So we moved into the shadows, sticking to the wall, but they had already spotted us. The first shot skimmed my arm — flesh wound," she says to me, the bags under her eyes heavy. "I ripped off my sleeve to wrap it around my arm so we didn't leave a trail."

"You're looking pretty tough now, hey Buckey," Johnny snorts. Buckey punches his leg, already looking better, the morphine finally setting in. Finn finishes the rushed stitches on both sides of Buckey's shoulder when he finally notices Ace and drags his bag over with him.

"But before I could, two Hunters were on top of us fast. One had a gun. He took a shot and luckily missed, giving me enough time to pull a knife and throw. I hit him in the throat. I killed him..." Harley trails off, her voice flat. She places her hand on Ace's chest, using his heartbeat to calm her. "The second Hunter was faster. He hit my arm and got me into a headlock. Ace managed to pull him off of me but got knocked out when the Hunter slammed him into the wall. I grabbed Ace's gun and shot the Hunter in the chest." She looks at me again, placing her other hand on the one I have pressed to her arm. "I tried the walkie talkie, but it wasn't there — I carried Ace the rest of the way, hoping the Hunters didn't have good aim. They didn't. They only shot at us once more before we made it into the tree line further down. It was hard to find you, but I heard Buckey." She sits back, going through her bag, "Finn, do you have any smelling salts?"

"Yeah," he grabs one, breaking it and waving it under Ace's nose. He gasps, coughing, taking in deep breaths.

"Sorry, Harley," Ace coughs, holding his hand back to her. She smiles and takes it, grasping it tightly, finally able to stop moving so fast.

"No, you saved me!" she breathes.

The gang moves around us. Luke shifts to Harley's back, watching the trees. Uri does the same on the other side. Finn moves my hand off Harley's arm slowly, cautiously, as if I'm the one who's hurt. I sit back, letting him take over. Her cut isn't deep, but blood still streams down her arm.

"Where did Buckey get hit?" Harley asks, barely twitching when Finn pours something over her shoulder.

"Same place. Went all the way through."

"Lucky bastard," She yells to him. Buckey gives her a timid smile, his arm now in a sling as Johnny helps him to his feet. I watch her face, convinced her arm must be numb or something. It seems as if she has no nerve endings. The wound that makes me fall only makes her flinch.

"Do you think this was planned?" I ask, sitting back, even though all I want to do is kiss her, hold her and tell her I love her, because I'm soft, and she makes me want to be sentimental and shit. I also thought she might not make it. I thought I was going to lose her, but I have to let her lead. She pulls off her toque, hair soaked in sweat.

"Could be. The walkie talkie was in the bag last night. Ace packed it. And there were too many Hunters in one place."

"I counted seven experienced, meaty boys. Saw a couple of sharp-shooters in the windows before I got knocked out," Ace adds, rubbing his hand over a goose egg on the back of his head.

Harley's eyes narrow as Finn finishes patching her up and steps away, massaging his hand. She looks at me, considering something, and I think I know what she's found out.

"Emma," I mouth. She nods, looking at Luke's back, frowning.

"Buckey, can you walk? You're not too dizzy?" she asks, getting to her feet and dragging me up with her.

"I'm good," he confirms, pulling Tequila up, Johnny close on his heels.

"Jimmy?" She squeezes my hand.

"Yeah, I'm fine," I say, but I feel exhausted, thinking that if we have to walk another hour, I might pass out. Harley nods, even though she knows I'm lying.

"I'm good too," Ace says, wobbling when he stands, but he flings his arm around Finn. The weight from Finn's bag, along with Ace, starts to pull down his already tired body, but Finn simply smiles.

"Okay, Uri, you go first. Finn and Ace next. Then Tequila and Buckey. Johnny, you take Jimmy, me and Luke will go last."

"No," I object. I don't want to leave her again.

"Jimmy, I'm the best shot. Luke's next. I'll be fine. Rey will be guiding me as I walk backwards, so he'll have his hand on my shoulder at all times. I'll even hum so you can hear me. Okay?" she kisses me softly, the heat from her lips sending a wave through my body. I nod, turning away, listening to her hum as we walk. "I love you," I whisper.

"I love you too."

I wish she wouldn't do that — act like nothing wrong has happened just so she can keep moving forward. We're not in danger at the moment. The least she could do is take a minute. She just killed two people, and how the hell did she carry Ace all that way and still have the energy to keep moving? I ran for two minutes, and now all I want to do is sit down and make camp for the night. But her drive is what's going to keep us alive.

When my weakness subsides, and I can keep up with her, I'm never letting her out of my sight. In an attack, I'm going to do every damn thing I can to protect her.

My mom used to tell me how much she loved walking and playing games in the forest as a child before the cities were made. She talked about how the trees whispered secrets, the animals brought her safety, and the smell of sweet dewy pine brought her comfort, but now, our feet shuffle through debris, branches creaking, the wind whistling around leaves. I feel no comfort or safety here, and no sounds of birds chirping or squirrels chattering fills the air. The stale earthy smell mixes with rotting wood and an unpleasant odour that stings my nose. The forest is so damp and musty that my body keeps fighting between hot and cold. Hardly any light comes through the changing leaves, enough to see in front of us but not enough to walk without flashlights or to keep me from losing my footing and stubbing the same toe on the exposed roots underfoot. Dust and debris fall on our heads and down our shirts. Every other step, Tequila squeals, batting at her clothes. Buckey clasps his hand over her mouth so her voice doesn't travel and promises there are no spiders. The trees echo and carry our sounds. Uri can hear Harley humming from all the way up front and makes her stop. My only knowledge of her presence behind me is the hope that Rey won't let her go.

Shadows continue to dance around us, playing with our eyes, making Johnny so antsy that I decide it's best if I hold on to his gun for now. The eerie silence is killing me. I glance over my shoulder to watch Harley move in easy steps, dodging everything without looking.

A gust of warm wind passes over us, playing with the loose strands of hair her toque can't keep contained. Luke nudges her, and for a moment, they share a concentrated, terrified look. I don't understand.

As the warm wind glides across my skin I start to feel heavy — feathery. "No that's not right," I mutter, smirking to myself, "I can't be both." Suddenly I understand why my mom likes the forest. I want to lie down, cover myself in a blanket of moss and leaves because it smells so sweet, like my mom's homemade apple pie.

"Tequila, do you smell that?" I ask. She looks back at me. Well, actually, three of her look back at me — all her faces, hazy and confused. I find myself playing eenie, meenie, miney, moe to decide which face to focus on.

Tequila's eyes widen. "Apple pie," her voice sounds deep and slow, traveling a million miles to reach me.

"What do you mean? It smells like chocolate chip cookies," Rey decides dreamily. When I turn to look at him, he's walking with his eyes squeezed shut, almost floating with the scent. I swing my fist out to hit him, to wake him up, but I miss, hitting the fluffy bark off a tree. I burst into laughter, Rey joining me.

"Something's wrong," Uri says, giggling too, sitting on a giant mushroom, his voice flying by my ears in a train, waving at me. I wave back, deliriously oblivious to the fact that what I'm seeing isn't possible.

"What's going on?" Harley asks, obviously not seeing the hilarious scene floating around my head. One by one, everyone in front of me starts to drop, descending into an impromptu sleep.

"D-R-E-A-M--R-O-O-T," Finn says, his words falling from his lips in slow motion before he trips over a vine that's shaped like a candy cane and knocks himself out on a giant gingerbread tree. I feel Johnny's hand slip from my arm and hear a thud behind me as he crumples to the ground.

"Stay awake," Harley says, shaking Luke's shoulders, but he looks so out of it, it's funny. He also looks like he's about to kiss her. I move toward them, no control over my muscles; they're literally noodles, yellow and wiggling. Luke starts to point and laugh at Rey, whose face is in the dirt, his butt pointed to the sky. I tackle Harley to the ground, kissing her cheek, her forehead, her lips. They're petal-soft.

"Jimmy." She looks at me, scared, apprehensive about doing anything that would make my mood change.

Why is she scared of me? Why would she be scared of me? Luke loses balance, piling onto Harley and me. He's surprisingly light. "He must have left his ego at home."

"Hey," he slurs, trying to hit me, but he only manages to tap my head.

"Didn't mean to say that out loud, man," I laugh. My cheeks start to hurt, and I try to use my fingers to turn my smile upside down.

"Jimmy." I can see her lips move, but her words seem like they're coming from behind me. Her brown eyes and her voice tell me to focus, to pull myself back to her. "Jimmy, look at me."

I am looking at you, but as soon as I think that, my vision becomes unfocused, almost like I'm doing it on purpose. Tequila and I used to play a game at night to pass time, seeing who could unfocus the street lights longer. It made my head hurt and almost made her go cross-eyed. I attempt to refocus, but all control over my body shuts down.

"Jimmy, tell me what's wrong!" Her voice is restricted, as if someone were holding back her air. I furrow my eyebrows, crinkling my nose. Thinking. Thinking. *Oh! Luke and I are pressing on her chest.* I move my lips to hers, but she slaps me, and it only tickles.

"You don't see the things around you?" I ask, pointing to the glowing butterflies and dancing fairies.

"No, I'm only hearing things," she says, trying to wiggle her way free.

"You're very intimidating," I slur.

"Jimmy."

"But, you—" I start to say. I feel Luke get lifted from my body, and then I feel weightless as hands clamp over my shoulders. Black combat boots move beside Harley's head. The last thing I see is her face hardening, her mouth pinching shut and the boots pinning her hair down. Then everything goes black.

CHAPTER 16
(JIMMY)

The sound of metal grinding on metal and wood jingles in my ears, along with suppressed voices and wood crackling with the flames. For a moment I'm terrified that I'm in the burning building again, the fire licking my legs, its teeth digging into my flesh, its hands pulling Harley into its gleaming mouth, and the voices of the dying children begging us to save them.

"Who are you?" I freeze when I don't recognize the voice. It sounds like a woman, irritated and tense.

"I could understandably ask you the same question," Harley retorts, her voice steadier, demonstrating that she has all the power. I open my eyes to see her against a tree with Luke in between us. On the other side of me is Finn, the rest of the gang further down in a line, all chained to trees. Not trees — wooden stakes, adjusted to our heights to prevent us from standing and lifting our hands over the top to escape. Harley and I seem to be the only ones awake, the rest of the gang slowly coming to.

"What do you want with us anyway?" Harley presses, fidgeting with her chains.

Two girls who look similar stand over Harley. One has dirty, cracked bare feet, and the other wears black shiny combat boots. They both wear worn, patched jeans and shirts, but the one with the boots wears an animal pelt over her shoulders, possibly wolf's skin, and has a tattoo of a moon curved around her eye. Her long black hair is braided down her back, small white flowers woven into it. When I look at the rest of the village, I notice she's the only one dressed that way.

The people are dressed like the Barefoot girl, their clothes ripped and worn, their appearance somehow cleaner and healthier looking than the people back home. They move as if we aren't here, cooking, cleaning and repairing small huts. Children squeal as they run around, playing some kind of tag game where they freeze when someone touches them and unfreeze when another runs under their outstretched arms. Their village is built in what seems to be the only possible place where the trees create an opening for the sun to shine through.

"We want to know why you brought Hunters into our land," says the first girl with the wolf skin, her voice almost playful. She and Harley volley questions back and forth, neither answering.

"Your land?" Harley questions. The Wolf girl grunts in frustration, and when she turns to me, I consider knocking myself out again. Her eyes are a screaming, piercing dark blue, her mouth drawn in a stern line, showing not even a stitch of curiosity or interest in me. Though the thing that makes me freeze like the children in the game is the thick red scar around her throat with two thinner white scars on either side.

"He looks like he'll answer my questions," she smiles, only one corner of her mouth turning up.

"You're a horrible interrogator," Luke jumps in, his voice raspy. He looks almost as delirious as I feel, waking up to find he's in a new place with a new threat in front of him. "You have to know that she's in charge, so if she's not talking there's no chance we are."

The Wolf girl purses her lips, turning back to Harley. "Why were you the only one who didn't get knocked out by the dream root?" she asks, beginning to sound out of control as Harley burrows her way under the Wolf girl's skin. She glances to her side as more chains jingle, signaling the consciousness of everyone else. Harley only smiles and shrugs, not looking at us, as she continues to stare at the Wolf girl while the Barefoot one goes around checking the gang, whispering apologies.

The Wolf girl looks around, then punches Harley full force, splitting her lip, but Harley doesn't look away. She smiles, spitting the blood from her mouth onto the girl's shiny boots.

"Fine. Even if you were going to talk, it's our law that you have to win a fight in order to pass — and no one ever wins," the Wolf girl says, sliding her tongue over her teeth.

"Fight?" I echo, feeling my heart climb into my throat. We are in no condition to fight. I'm still weak. Buckey is injured, Ace has a concussion, and everyone else is too exhausted. When she turns to me again, I wish I'd kept my mouth shut because her expression has drastically changed. Eyes flaming, enraged, irritated, a polished dagger gripped in her hand. I bet she's used to getting people to break with one word.

"Yes," she grits her teeth, "We don't like trespassers, especially ones who bring Hunters with them, but we think it only fair to give people an opportunity to fight for passage. Exactly how the Big Three so kindly gave us the opportunity to be banished. If you lose, you must go back, and by the looks of your lot, you can't afford to." She walks away, deciding we're no longer worth her time. She takes a seat in a wooden chair with spikes coming from the top and various weapons moulded to it.

"Harley, you good?" I whisper. She only nods, now focusing on the Barefoot girl who is checking Luke.

"Excuse me?" Harley whispers. The Barefoot girl tries to ignore her but ends up giving into Harley's sweet, breathy voice. She moves to Harley, keeping her eyes trained on the ground. "Where are we?" Harley asks, moving her head so the girl has to look at her; the girl shrinks away. "I'm sorry, what's your name?"

"Anna," she says, her voice almost a whisper, not fighting against Harley's words like the Wolf girl did.

"My name is Harley, that's Luke, Jimmy, Finn, Tequila, Rey, Johnny, Buckey, Ace and Uri. Can you please tell us what's going on?" Harley asks in a neutral tone, nodding her head toward us. I don't think it's a good idea to tell Anna our names, but there's no going back now, and she seems trustworthy enough.

"That was Até, she's nicer than she seems. She's my sister and our leader — the leader of the Nomads, the banished."

"Nomads?" Harley echoes, her eyes brightening, "My dad used to tell me bedtime stories about the Nomads, but I thought that was all they were, stories. He told me he lived in your village and taught you how to heal. You gave him refuge and showed him kindness."

Something in Anna's expression changes with Harley's words — recognition. She looks over her shoulder, telling the guards to give her space. They move with no question as Anna pretends to check Harley's pulse.

"Harley?" she asks. An aching smile pulls at Anna's mouth, forming smile lines in her cheeks. "Your dad's Robin and your mom's Lucy," she whispers, bringing her hand to her mouth.

"You knew them?" Harley lurches forward, scaring Anna, causing her to draw back. She looks around, debating something before she leans forward again.

"I assisted your father with your birth. You were born on my seventeenth birthday — Here," Anna says.

She's younger than I expected, but the roots of her hair are entirely grey with long streaks slicing through the black. Persistent wrinkles are creased into her forehead and under her light blue, almost grey eyes. Anna gives off a motherly aura, caring and kind, unlike her sister. As she talks, she keeps unconsciously massaging her hands like Finn does, which probably means she's the most experienced and overworked healer.

"They came to us when Robin was nineteen and Lucy was eighteen, eight months pregnant. They didn't want to raise you in a place where you kill or are killed." Anna gets to her feet, wiping her hands on her pants, pretending that she's talking to the people around her, but Até is too distracted by the dagger she sharpens to notice. "My mother was the leader at that time, but the same rules were in place, to fight and win for safe passage.

Your father was a peaceful man and your mother was in no condition to fight. Robin saw that our people were battling an infection that was raging through our community. He offered to teach us healing in exchange for safe passage. He was extremely wise for his age. He saved a lot of people ..." She trails off, smiling at her hands. "He stayed with us for two months while they waited for arrangements to be made in The Sticks. He never told us who was helping him. After he left, he travelled back monthly to teach and bring supplies to us, until eight years ago, that is."

"He disappeared — when I was ten," Harley interrupts, her voice distant. A single tear runs down her face as she repositions herself on the tree, her wrists rubbed raw by the chains.

"Anna," Até calls, jamming her dagger into the arm of her chair.

"You will fight in an hour. I'll make sure I'm the one who gets you ready and I'll try to talk to Até. Your dad was very well respected among our people, so perhaps she'll change her mind." Anna pauses, "May I ask why you are going to the Big Three?"

"They took my brother. He's thirteen," Harley says, dropping her head, taking a moment to miss him.

"I'll try to help," Anna says, hurrying over to Até, who is staring at me so intensely I feel as if she's ripped out my soul and dissected it before shoving it back into my chest.

"Harley," I whisper, fighting to keep my voice as calm as hers. She doesn't look up. All she lets me see are the teardrops dripping from her cheeks, her foot drawing lines in the dirt. "Harley, please talk to me," I plead urgently. I don't know why I'm becoming so persistent. I feel responsible for getting us in this situation, for making her so vulnerable, for being such a burden to everyone.

"Jimmy, chill out," Luke spits, working on sliding from his chains. He's the only one still trying to get free. "If you found out what she just discovered, would you want to share your feelings with everyone?"

"Yes," I blurt, but he's making a valid point. If I found out my parents had a secret life, and I was born here, I wouldn't talk to anyone, only Harley.

"It's okay," Harley mutters, dazed, swivelling to face us. Her lip has already stopped bleeding, but a thin red line runs down her chin, making its way to her neck. The group is fully awake now, listening, Rey and Johnny making the occasional snarky comment. "I'm fine," she says. "If we do fight, I'm not letting you, Ace or Buckey join, even if that means surrendering and turning back," she continues. We give objections, only to be silenced by her gentle stare. "If I can help it, none of you will have to fight, but I believe she has a show in mind and we're the main event." She nods toward Até, who is standing on her chair, stomping her foot, Anna by her side, calling for the attention of her people. Instantaneously, they stop, drop what they are doing, and turn to give their leader their undivided attention.

"Thank you for stopping to listen." She acknowledges them by moving both her hands from her chest toward them, and the people do the same. "Today you all know we have ten visitors."

"Oh, now we're her visitors," Rey mutters. We all shush him.

"We will be witnessing a great and honourable fight tonight." The people cheer, stomping their feet, applauding her instead of us — the people who will be giving them that great and honourable fight. Até holds her hands out, and they fall silent once again. "Harley, daughter to Robin and Lucy, has wandered into our land in search of her brother who has been taken by the Big Three leaders, our greatest threat." Everyone turns to Harley, some giving their condolences, others staring cynically. "Since we have great respect for Robin, we, the court …" She gestures to four people sitting in lesser chairs on either side of her: Anna, two elderly men who both use canes to walk and a woman who looks to be in her seventies with muscles bulging through her shirt and a faded moon tattoo curved around her eye. "… have decided that Harley and her best fighter will be fighting against our two best. If she wins, we will grant her safe passage, a place to stay and help to rescue her brother. If they lose they must turn back." Até nods, hopping off her chair, strutting over to Harley. The crowd cheers, then disperses, continuing on with the daily chores. Their community looks like a well-oiled machine, specific duties flawlessly performed as they move with and around others. "You have twenty minutes to decide who will be fighting beside you. Then Anna will prepare you." Até moves past us, Anna giving us a sympathetic smile before they both disappear into a hut with an animal pelt as a door.

I don't even care about the new information — that the banished managed to survive and create their own world. I'm too caught up in the excitement rushing over me. This is the best deal Até could give us and the best-case scenario. If we win, we can gain refuge and maybe even have a place to lay low after we retrieve J, though Harley doesn't seem to feel the same way. She slumps further down, intentionally rubbing her chain against her now bleeding wrists.

"Two of us have to fight, probably to the death, and win so the rest of us don't get sent back to Dead Man's Hill where Hunters are waiting to ambush us." Ace's words hit me all at once, knocking the air from my lungs and squeezing my heart to the point of rupturing. I never even thought about that. I was too busy thinking of the good.

"No!" Dizziness spreads throughout my vision, and I feel the urge to disappear. "No!" I repeat, understanding that I have failed her again. I stare so intensely at her as my emotions overflow from my mind. I'm usually better at controlling myself.

"Jimmy," she sighs, her eyes glossy, vulnerable, glinting their golden colour.

"No!" My voice breaks, cracking and crumbling onto the dirty, muddy ground. I failed to keep her out of harm's way again. I failed to put myself in front of her. "I'll fight in your place!" I beg, more than offer. I wait for Luke to tell me to shut up, make fun of me for acting weak and out of control, but he's busy averting his eyes, giving us privacy in a place so public.

"Jimmy, Até purposely picked me because of my dad and my stubbornness. Her fighters, hopefully, are less experienced than us. It'll be okay. Don't blame yourself for something you had no control over," she says.

Always in my head, understanding my thoughts and feelings before I have a chance to comprehend them. My hands start to shake, the movement climbing up my arms until my whole body threatens to do the same. I'm usually more rational. I trust Harley, root for her, believe that she can fight for herself, but I have no control over any part of me. My thoughts, my actions, my strength. All I want to do is find the dream root and inhale every last bit of it.

I look at Finn, his head lowered and wearing the same expression as Harley. His cheeks are shiny, his shoulders slumped. That's when I recognize my fatigue, Harley's cautiousness around me when I was high on the dream root and my lack of ability to control these familiar emotions. She didn't mean that us getting captured was out of my control; she meant the addiction, the withdrawal, and making everyone's pain my fault is out of my hands. I'm also craving drugs that will bring me peace, take me from this dark reality. It explains my urge to disappear.

"You know about that too," I say, coming to understand what Finn and Harley have known ever since I got up this morning. That's the reason they gave me the blue pill, the same one Finn gave to Buckey to numb his shoulder after he got shot, to numb his feelings. I knew it tasted like morphine. It was so familiar. Harley looks up, holding my stare, tear tracks mixing with the blood on her chin.

"Yes — but my last detox pill went to Eric."

"What is she talking about?" Tequila strains, pulling her chains, Buckey begging her to calm down. I forgot they were here. They've become uncharacteristically quiet.

"So you're fighting for me because they can help. We could have easily declined the fight, turned around and moved back into the trees in a different direction to avoid them, and been more careful." I feel a sense of betrayal rise in my chest, starting to realize a secret has been kept from me. The whole world is whispering behind my back. *Fatigue, lack of control, sweating, shaking and now paranoia. Great! More reasons to keep me from the action and not trust me.* "But you and Finn don't know where to find the plant that created the detox pill. You only know the name," I guess, my voice bitter.

Finn confirms my suspicion, but Harley studies me, checking for more symptoms, the ones that I connected to running and getting shot at, not addiction. I inch my way around the wooden stake, isolating myself from the gang, ashamed and mad at her for not trusting me with the information, not trusting me with my own problem. It shouldn't matter. I get why she's done this. When in withdrawal, an addict is in denial and becomes irrational, unpredictable, willing to do anything for the first euphoric feeling they experienced, the feeling that can never be replicated. I know that feeling all too well. That's why whenever Eric sees me, he smiles because he has a soft spot in his heart for the customers who will do anything for drugs. Anything. Especially betray the ones they love.

I watch my torn, taped, muddy shoes brush over the ground as I try to calm myself down without being able to run my finger through my hair. I can't bear to look at Harley, or even see Tequila, not that I'd want to see the pity masked on her face. I can't even protect her — my own blood.

Harley doesn't try to talk to me. She carries on, telling the gang that she won't pick anyone, but Luke and Uri volunteer. Uri is selected because he can fight as if he were three people. They might have a chance. I listen to everyone. Tequila, Finn and Luke help Harley form ideas and create a plan for J's rescue for us to carry out in case Harley and Uri are killed during the fight. The Nomads are unpredictable. We have no idea if they are trained to fight, if they fight fair or if they fight with weapons. I tune the rest of their words out, scanning my day, recounting everything I've done and realizing it was all one big symptom controlling me.

When I finally come to my senses, I spin back around to apologize to them, but Anna and two guards dressed in leather armour are unlocking Harley and Uri, escorting them into a small hut. I don't get a chance to tell her good luck or that I love her. Too busy making everything about myself. I didn't put into perspective that she and Uri are fighting to the death so the gang can live. I'm stuck sitting beside the people I have let down, soaking in all my self-pity.

CHAPTER 17
(HARLEY)

Dust particles and sunlight sting the raw skin on my wrists, but it's nothing compared to the ache in my chest. I knew Jimmy would hate me for not telling him he was slipping from this world, but I had no reason to get him riled up. He thought the symptoms were related to fatigue and stress on the body, caused by the chaos of escaping Dead Man's hill. Only Finn and I knew he was in withdrawal because he was mumbling the names of drugs in his sleep. We were keeping an eye on him, making sure it wouldn't get to the point where he'd put the rest of us in danger, but when the dream root knocked everyone out, he looked so happy when he was kissing me. His distracted and euphoric expression was exactly how he looked before he got clean.

I was relieved when Até found us. She stood over me in a wooden mask while I had Jimmy and Luke sprawled across me. When they led us to their camp and took off my blindfold, I was reminded of a story my dad once told me. It was about an area where light rules the leaves and Nomads rule the land, a place where the roots grow as a border around the huts. I figured this was the place he meant when Anna told me she knew him. Having seen Anna's love for healing, I was also relieved, knowing that she wouldn't be able to let Jimmy go untreated.

Jimmy never gave me time to comprehend all that Anna said about my parents before figuring out what was going on with him. A couple more minutes, and Finn would have had to explain everything. Then Jimmy would have taken his bitterness out on him.

My thoughts drift to my parents. They had stayed here for months. They gave birth to me here, built friendships and a family. My dad visited regularly and never told me once, besides trying to make this place seem like a bedtime story. I was a child, yes, but I still could have understood. I could have gone with him, met the people, and kept his secret. My dad kept me in the dark about so many things, most of which I haven't figured out yet. I'm starting to think that what I thought was my dad's kindness was a mirage made up by my grief.

On top of all of this, I didn't get to say goodbye to Jimmy. I couldn't help him with a backup plan in case Uri and I don't return but Ace promised me he would catch him up.

"Harley," Uri says, placing his hand in between my shoulder blades, so gently I barely feel it.

"Yeah?" My mind's not in this reality; I'm too busy worrying about everyone else when I should be focusing on protecting Uri and trying to keep us alive. Sometimes my brain becomes too full of disjointed thoughts leading to long-forgotten ones, removing the spider webs and dust that had obscured them. I zone out, begging to be taken to a new world where my brain has no restrictions — where I can spend forever sifting through my thoughts until they fall back in line, placed back into storage. But I can't afford to lose myself down that path.

I notice my surroundings and find we're in a damp hut full of weapons — no guards protecting the entrance. Trust must be one of their biggest policies here, or everyone is too scared of Até to disobey her. In the hut, knives, spears, bows and arrows line one wall made from light wood, flint and other tough rocks. On another are factory-made weapons: guns, bullets, crossbows, polished daggers and swords. The last wall holds leather armour and wooden helmets, along with six iron breastplates and two vests

I've seen on the Hunters. They all must be heavy as hell and restrictive in a fight. The pure number of them surprises me, no doubt built up over the years. Maybe my dad even brought some of them.

"Anna has something for you," Uri says, pushing me to the table and helping me into a seat. I need to snap out of this daze before the fight, or I'll be walking into a battle I can't win. Anna slides a wooden box toward me, undoing the latch and flipping open the lid.

Inside is a pile of letters, creased and brown, along with four pictures. Three of the photos are of my dad, teaching eager people sutures and how to set bones. The fourth is a small group of people, my mom, strikingly similar to me in a newly washed white dress, skin clear, eyes lively, not yet introduced to her fate. She's standing beside a young black-haired Anna. An even younger Até, four or five, is holding tightly to her sister's arm, a dulled version of her dagger in her hand. No scar is covering her neck, and no tattoo is curved around her eye, but her expression is as cold as ever. In the middle is my dad, young, smiling, creases around his eyes, light playing with his long and shaggy hair. He's holding a swaddled baby asleep on his chest. This was probably taken days after I was born. Rather than sadness blanketing me like it always does when I see my dad's face, it feels as if someone took hundreds of needles and injected the feeling into every inch of my body, leaving me nowhere to retreat. They look happy together, like the family I've always dreamt of having.

"He wrote to me every day, mostly about you, and brought the letters when he visited." Anna runs her fingers over the worn, crinkled edges of an envelope, my dad's messy cursive on the front. "I kept every last one." She takes a shaky breath, moving away from us, gathering and preparing things.

"I'm glad you did," I smile weakly, setting the picture back inside and running my finger gently over their faces before closing the box. When I read these letters and get a piece of my dad back, I don't want it to be just before a fight and in front of a bunch of people in this musty, dark room. "Thank you," I whisper, breathing in musty wood, old leather and the stray pine needles under our feet. Anna hands us a piece of wood with the names of weapons carved into it.

"We have to use weapons?" Uri asks, and I can hear the anxiety in his voice. When he lived in the Big Three, he undoubtedly was a part of these types of fights to the death. The Big Three leaders organize certain fights they know will attract spectators. All of it is for the leaders' pure entertainment, and it seems Até does the same. Uri thought he'd gotten away from this life, but now he's volunteered to do it all over again, sacrificing himself to save the only family he has left.

"Not necessarily," Anna says. "If you talk to Jasper and Malick, the people you will be fighting, you can ask to have a weaponless fight. However, if they reject your request, then you have no choice."

"Can we meet with them?" Uri asks, deciding for us.

"Please," I add. Anna will be kinder if we don't order her around like her sister so clearly does.

"Certainly." She gestures to the guards behind us, one of them leaving. The other moves closer to my side as a precaution, thinking I'm the most unpredictable at this moment, but I've never seen Uri so antsy. He wipes his hands on his pants every couple of seconds while bouncing his knee up and down. I rest my hand on his, willing all his stress to travel through my fingers and become my own.

"Anna?" She looks up at me, pausing her search through the armour for a moment. "My dad made a pill to detox addicts, getting rid of all their symptoms and cravings, with only one dose. He made it from a root called Noves. I believe he got it from here," I say, hoping I'm right and don't sound like an idiot.

"Yes, I helped him with that, but we make tea out of it. We haven't had a need for it in a long time, but I keep it growing in my hut for your dad." Her gaze falls back down to her hands. She must have loved my dad. Probably in more ways than one. I let my anxiety fall to the floor because even if we don't win, Jimmy will be fine. I know I shouldn't be thinking this way, but I've had too many close calls these past days. My luck should be starting to run out. "You want me to give it to Jimmy?" she offers, handing us two leather parka-like coats. I'm impressed by how good she is at healing, noticing the little things that others miss. I'm sure Finn and I could learn so much just by watching her work.

"Please."

"Of course. And you don't have to wear these in the fight, only when you walk into the arena," Anna says, giving us a kind and sympathetic smile. I now see she doesn't belong here, in a place where violence is a game, exactly like in the Big Three. She belongs somewhere free and supportive, but that's never existed. The discomfort of the weight she carries from watching her sister and mother create havoc has made her age quickly and made her heart beat slower. They are very close in age, both beaten by time, yet one has been burdened by drugs and alcohol, trying to kill herself faster. The other is kind, unable to hurt anyone, slowly being killed by the pain of others.

"You asked for us," a gruff voice calls. Two burly men walk into the hut, tall and thick. One is maybe a couple inches shorter than Uri, with a bow strapped around his upper body and a quiver of arrows peeking out from behind his shoulder. The other, shorter than the first, has a long silver sword held in his belt. They both wear the same clothes as the guards, layered armour, with what I suspect is deer hide on the bottom and strips of leather over top. They wear Hunters' pants, stolen either from the dead or from the factories. Uri starts to talk, but I quickly get to my feet to interrupt. Uri can come across as arrogant with strangers, especially men, in an attempt to assert his dominance; all men do this. Sometimes it's useful, but most of the time, it leads to a more aggressive fight.

"Hello, my name is Harley, and this is Uri." I stick my hand out to them. They both size me up, considering me before shaking my hand, briefly acknowledging Uri. Anna pulls two chairs up. I offer them mine to show respect, but they reject it, moving to the others.

"I'm Jasper," the blonde one says, his ocean eyes bold, his smile clumsy, a wide gap between his teeth. His arms are covered in peculiar tattoos, ones I've never seen. Come to think of it, all of the guards I've seen so far have something similar. Jasper notices my eyes drifting up and down his arms, so he moves his hands to his lap, preventing me from observing his forearms any further. "And this is Malick." He nods to a man whose black hair is cropped short, his skin caramel, tattoos on his neck. His gentle eyes take in every detail of us, his bow now resting on his legs.

"Very pleased to meet you," Uri smiles, his voice screaming sarcasm as he places his elbows on the table, showing off the number of tattoos he has. I roll my eyes.

"You're Robin's kid?" Jasper asks, blatantly ignoring Uri.

"Yeah."

His eyes brighten, looking almost amiably at me as he loosens up. "He saved my mom from a virus."

"He helped my trainee ten years ago, when he wandered in front of my arrow while I was practicing," Malick adds, taking off his quiver and setting it by his feet.

"I'm sorry for your loss," they both offer, letting their walls down and allowing us to become a part of their group. They seem like good people, their smiles gentle, their friendship toward each other genuine. They act like brothers.

"Would you be willing to fight with no weapons?" Uri blurts, impatient but less dominant. I know he trusts me and is starting to trust them. Jasper and Malick don't tense or seem irritated. They surprise me by smiling and reaching for my hands.

"No weapons it is! I prefer to not look any more beaten than I already am. I have a newborn at home," Malick laughs, sliding his jacket off, making himself more comfortable. When he does, I see that his tattoos extend from his neck down to his wrists, and there look to be more under his shirt. They must mean something.

"Anna, I think we'll stay and get ready with them. You know, scout the competition and what not." Jasper places his sword on the table allowing the gentle light to glint across the silver blade engraved with the words '*Sacrifice For Our People.*'

My dad's voice pops into my head, another story, this one about the protectors of the trees: 'They are kind. They are smart. If they trust you they will protect your heart. But they are cruel. They are reckless. They see power as the only thing to protect them.' Pretty interesting story to tell a kid, but I think there might be some truth to it. The guards are carefully selected and trained in extreme ways, prepared to beat the Hunters in case they come across them. They are trained to be intense, but I don't think they're heartless.

"What do we have to get ready anyway?" Uri asks.

Jasper's smile grows, showing most of his teeth are missing, probably from past fights. "Well, Até likes to think that leather armour and appealing faces make the people find the fights more entertaining, right Anna?" He leans over, pinching her waist, but she pushes him away, clearly not impressed. "Sorry, love, didn't mean to say it that way." He shrinks into his chair, not so severe around her, but I can tell by the way she looks at him, worried and scared, that she loves him.

"My sister wants me to make you look presentable, do your hair, clean your faces and change your clothes." She pulls a brush from a bag, approaching me. "May I?" She loosens the elastic from my hair.

"Yes," I say, relieved to get the knots and leaves removed. Anna starts at the bottom, coaxing out the bigger tangles, her movements so gentle that it doesn't hurt. Anna does my hair with a braid on the top of my head, pulling the rest into a ponytail.

Malick tells me of his position in their guard — top commander. He was nineteen when he was banished from AC's city. His parents weren't given a choice, executed in their living room for not paying their outstanding debt of twenty-one dollars, but a guard spared Malick and told him to choose banishment. He made it five months by himself, foraging rainwater, eating roots and already dead animals until he collapsed, ready to die. That's when Até and her mother, Nya, found him, skinnier than a twig and hallucinating like he was on dream root. When he got better, he became Nya's right-hand man, and now Até's, working with the family for thirteen years.

Jasper is second to Malick, younger too, born in No Man's Land. His thirtieth birthday is in two days, and he is waiting desperately for Anna to let him marry her. Even though Malick is ranked higher than he, Jasper seems to do most of the talking and gives the commands. It's not because Malick is lazy or has no desire to be in charge; he's doing it to let Jasper learn from his mistakes and because he trusts him. *That's what a true leader is*, I think, running my hands over my bumpy hair.

Uri and I tell them as much as we can without giving our whole lives away. About the fire, the wanted poster, the speakeasy and the ambush on our way here. As we talk, Anna cleans Uri's face, picking the small twigs from his short hair. They tell us we're lucky to be alive and that I've faced more trouble from the Big Three than any of their guards. Anna moves past Jasper, planting a kiss on his cheek.

She hands us a pile of clothes, shielding me with a towel while we all change. I trace my fingers over the scars and bruises that have turned to white lines and yellowy-green blotches, even the ones from a day ago. I knew I healed fast, but this is crazy.

I can't focus on this right now, I tell myself, pushing the thought from my mind.

The outfit I wear now consists of flexible black pants with multiple pockets for knives and a loose shirt that's soft and airy. Anna drapes the leather over my shoulders, the heaviness choking me, pinching at my neck.

"I'm sorry," she says sympathetically, hiding her tears when she embraces Jasper. They hold each other for a long time, Jasper kissing her cheek, stroking her hair and not wanting to let her go, but eventually, he does. Uri moves beside me, dressed in similar pants and a black muscle T, showing his flexing biceps.

"I don't want to fight them," I whisper, feeling empty as we walk outside. Malick runs over to his wife, kissing her and the top of his child's head. His wife doesn't seem distressed or worried. She has the expression of someone who is used to seeing her husband fight.

"Neither do I, maybe they'll take it easy on us," Uri sighs, adjusting his leather. It makes him look like one of the guards, with his tattoos and hefty build.

The air has cooled drastically, the setting sun painting the sky a soft pink and bold orange, the leaves sparkling. It had to have just been dinner time because the smell of cooked meat and roots lingers in the air, waking my stomach.

I stop in my tracks. The guards shove me forward. The gang is gone, no longer bound to the wooden stakes. I start to panic. Maybe Até changed her mind. She might have sent them back, or she might have killed them. Anna holds my shoulder, making me jump.

"It's okay. She's moved them to the arena to watch. Also, I'll get Jimmy the tea before the fight starts." She touches my cheek before running off, not letting me say thank you. The moment she leaves, the guards take our arms. They must trust that if we were to do something, Anna would be able to stop us, but without her, they feel they have no control.

"Back off! They aren't stupid. They won't run," Jasper scolds, pulling their hands off me. One of the guards leaves nail marks on my forearm, but he apologizes when Malick and Jasper glare at him. In that instant, I feel as though they would protect me, no matter what, as if they genuinely trust me because of my dad.

Jasper fills me in on what will happen. We are to walk into the arena and stand in front of Até, Anna and the former leaders. Até will tell us the rules, and the people will give us thanks for our honour and pride. Then we'll remove our leather, handing it to Até piece by piece, and when the whistle sounds, we will begin to fight. I zone out for the rest of his explanation.

For some unknown reason, this feels like any other Warehouse fight as I run through my routine, emptying my mind one problem at a time. I notice my muscles flex and relax, warm and cool. I study my opponents, getting to know their weaknesses, their strengths. I didn't mean to observe them. I didn't want to. But I noticed, since Jasper wields a sword, he has strong arms and heavy hands. His punches have to pack some power, but he's overconfident. He wears his wounds as medals, so in a fight, he underestimates his opponent and doesn't protect his face. That's why he has so many missing teeth. Malick, on the other hand, is more disciplined, patient and accurate. That's why his weapon of choice is a bow, making him agile, most likely fast. However, he's distracted by his child. He won't put his life at risk for a meaningless fight. If it comes down to it, he'll tap out to prevent further damage to himself. He won't be reckless.

"When we fight, I'll take Malick," I say to Uri, wanting to protect him from Uri's wrath. When Uri fights, he loses control and doesn't see the person, only the victory, leading him to take the fight too far. Jasper can handle himself. He has Anna as his personal healer.

It's starting to get darker. I haven't been able to tell time since they took Uri's watch. I begin to wonder if they'll make us fight in the dark, when torches, one by one, illuminate the crowds that scream Jasper and Malick's names. We walk into a small ring surrounded by wooden fences and benches that are staggered so everyone has a chance to see. I wonder how often people pass through No Man's Land and have to fight, since they've invested so much time and effort into building a dedicated arena.

On the opposite end of the ring is a raised platform holding five chairs. The biggest one, covered in fur pelts, holds Até, who wears a long black animal cloak, pants similar to mine, and a purple shirt that matches the paint enclosing her eyes and dripping down her face. Her hair has been taken from its braid and falls loose on her shoulders, the black strands kept from her face by a wooden crown that sits atop her head.

On her left side sits Anna, dressed relatively the same, only less dramatically. On Até's right sits Nya, dressed in the clothes she wore this morning. The only difference is the wooden half-crown sitting on her bobbed gray-streaked hair and her lack of shoes, her feet the same crusty colour as the dirt. Two older men sit in chairs too small to be thrones, being lulled by the crowd. Obviously, these frivolous events have lost all their interest.

It's funny how drastically different Anna is from her sister and mother. Physically, only her bone structure is the same, but mentally, she is on the moon while her family is on earth.

In a heavily guarded area, pressed as close as possible to the platform, is the gang. Rey, Buckey and Johnny chirp at the crowd, calling them names I'm sure will get the boys some spit in their food. Tequila is moving in a circle, stealing from the guards, putting their things in different places and pockets and keeping little weapons like darts and knives. Finn and Ace sit cross-legged on the ground — Ace counting all the medical supplies, turning them over and over in his hands. Finn grabs them from him, sorting his bag neatly, precisely as he wants it. Luke and Jimmy stand as close as they can to the edge of the ring, where the guards' arms prevent them from moving any closer. A little relief washes over me when Jimmy's face comes into focus. Anna must have gotten him the tea already because he's back to his tanned self, his crystal eyes piercing my heart, no longer shaking. He looks saner.

His eyes shift away from me as Jasper and Malick move to our sides, towering over me. They snarl, exciting the people, their leather armour flexible and light on their shoulders. Red paint drips under their eyes, like Até's. *When the hell did they do that?*

Malick finds his wife in the sea of people, pointing to her and smiling as she moves her child's hand so the baby is waving. Jasper blows Anna a kiss, only to have her ignore it, but at her side, I see her hand move to catch it and press it to her heart. Até rolls her eyes in response, getting to her feet. Jasper leans in to whisper something in my ear, but the nauseating cheers and my heartbeat makes it impossible for me to understand him.

Suddenly my vision goes dark, all sounds disappearing as J appears in front of me. I feel a cold rock floor under my bare feet, the thirst and the itchiness from untreated wounds creeping into my pores. J sits in a corner, squeezing his arms around his legs, burying his face between his knees, and when he looks up, I see his glasses are missing and cuts line his face.

"J, J," I scream in my head, and for a second, I feel like he can see me, but then a shadowy figure stands where I do, taunting me in a high-pitched voice.

"J, J." His scratchy metal laugh only fuels my anger. "Have fun losing," the voice snickers before kicking me out of the vision, back into the fire-lit ring.

I shake my head. Até comes into focus, too comfortable in this environment. I know that was really J, and I could feel the life draining from him, but I can't think of that right now.

Something inside me switches to anger, and a different voice speaks to me. It's hard and cold, one of a warrior. *"Born from rage, we rise to fight the battles of a thousand lost souls. You hold our strength. You hold my skills. You will not falter."*

"Yes," I say back, pushing the high-pitched voice further down, imagining locking it away. Até struggles to silence her people, first using hand motions, then working to make her voice heard but failing.

"Hey," I mutter, only grabbing the attention of the people closest to me. "Hey!" I say again, below a yell. The crowd falls silent, staring at me, and Até tilts her head questioningly.

"Well, shall we begin?" she regroups, screwing up her face and continuing to glare at me. "In this very ring many people have fought for their honour and our respect. We thank them for their courage."

"Thank you," the crowd echoes. Jasper and Malick do the same, bowing their heads. I don't look around me, at Ace, Luke, Jimmy. I can't look at their scared, stone-cold faces. I don't want to mouth, 'I love you,' as a tragic goodbye.

"Today, Jasper, Malick, Uri and Harley are taking on this great battle of pride. Two fighting for passage, refuge and help. Two fighting for respect and to remain undefeated. Also, all four have decided not to use weapons and to fight fair." The excitement deflates from the crowd as stray boos filter onto the forest floor along with a rock, landing at Jasper's feet. He kicks it aside, glaring in the direction it came from. "I know, I know, but I feel this fight will be the most entertaining yet," Até assures. Anna stands, placing her hand on her sister's forearm, waiting for Até to stop, to get to the point. Até sits back down, slumping into her chair, letting Anna take the stage.

"The fight will start when the whistle sounds, and will last until one team can no longer continue, or until we say. You may remove your armour and place it at the feet of our leader." She hesitates slightly on the last words, feeling the resistance in me.

Jasper and Malick move forward, lifting their armour over their heads, bowing and placing it near Até's black combat boots. Uri moves back, but I pull him along with me. We copy Jasper and Malick by placing the leather at her feet. Até smiles at me as if she has already won, as if I have submitted. I refuse to give her the satisfaction, so I focus on Anna, who is now sorting and preparing her medical bag, similar to Finn.

Uri and I turn to face our opponents. I shake my arms and legs, warming my muscles. Uri swings his arms, doing the same. Jasper and Malick shake our hands, wish us luck, then step back.

I squeeze Uri's arm. "Together."

"Together," he agrees, winking at me. Then the whistle sounds.

Jasper throws the first punch, catching me by surprise, forcing me to stagger back. Before he can step toward me, Uri comes to my aid, grabbing Jasper's arm, easily flipping him onto his back. The impact draws all the air from his lungs. I don't have time to see what happens next.

"*On your left,*" the cold voice says.

I whip around in time to block Malick's punch with my tricep. I grab his arm and twist, but he's far stronger than me. He jerks me forward, using the momentum to plant a punch in my ribs, his second punch hitting my shoulder. I was right; his punches aren't powerful. He's subconsciously slowing them down to protect his hands. I quickly move around him, squirming, weakening his grip so he'll let go. I jump, hitting the pressure point in his traps with my elbow and kicking the back of his knee in. He doesn't fall. He sweeps his leg back, knocking my feet out from under me. I land on my side, hearing a pop in my shoulder. *Dislocated,* I think. I cover my face, letting him punch me as I try to remember how to pop a shoulder back in.

"*Slam it on the ground,*" a different voice says, but I don't have time to wonder who it is.

I oblige, grasping Malick's shoulder. He moves up as I expected, and I let go, angling my body to the side, the hard, bumpy ground providing enough force to push the joint back into my shoulder socket. I crawl away, dirt fusing into my nails, the grimy, musty taste coating my tongue. I focus hard, imagining my pain to be the size of a pin, only able to live in my pinky toe, and that's what it becomes. I push myself up, waving Malick forward. He runs at me, light on his toes, telegraphing where his movements will take him. I jam my knuckles into his throat, sweep his feet from under him and slam him onto his back as he gasps for air. Using all my weight, I try to keep him down, working his arm into my hands, as I did to Luke, but sometimes size trumps skill. He moves so quickly that he has me in a headlock in no time. I swing my elbow back, snagging his nose. The feeling of blood dripping down my neck tells me I broke it, but he doesn't loosen his grip. I can't get out of this.

I could give up. Let him hold me in this headlock and stop my breath. I'm so tired, no more than four hours of sleep in two days. I should give up. Lightheadedness and fatigue aren't a good mix. After they sent us back to Dead Man's Hill, we could easily move back into the forest and navigate our way around them. *No*, I think. They said they'd help with J.

Malick keeps his grip on my neck as he digs his nails into my chest, dragging up.

"*Relax all your muscles. Breathe.*" I do as the cold voice says, going limp. Malick lets go, thinking he's won. I swing my elbow back, hitting his groin. It's unfair, I know, but it had to be done. I hit his forehead with the back of my head, pushing away from him. I turn to face him, half expecting his fist to connect with my jaw, but he only watches me, mouthing something. To knock him out. *Where can I hit him and not cause damage?*

"*Hard uppercut to the corner of his jaw,*" the cold voice yells in my head. I'm beginning to like this new voice. I see Jimmy out of the corner of my eye, motioning the same thing.

"I'm sorry," I whisper as my knuckles crack against his jaw. I have to do it two more times before his eyes flutter shut. One more would have broken my hand or his jaw, most likely both. I catch him, lowering him softly to the ground.

Someone grabs my hair, yanking me back. I scrape my hands on the dirt in an effort to stop my head from slamming into the ground. My arms don't shield my face fast enough when I see Jasper towering over me. He grimaces as his hand collides with my cheek, my mouth, my ear. He looks startled when I don't cry out or back down. His foot presses down on my knee, and I can barely move enough to prevent him from breaking it. I flip to my side, thrusting my other foot into his stomach. Exhausted, he falls on top of me, dazed, holding my legs down with his knees. I move my hands to his throat, squeezing my thumbs into his windpipe. Uri comes from my left, elbowing Jasper hard in the temple, all the light leaving his eyes as he collapses onto me. Uri rolls him off, giving Jasper one more good punch in the face before it's over. We've won.

Uri collapses to a seated position, holding a cracked and bloody hand to his face. I crawl over to him, seeing now that he has an already forming black eye and his lip is split wide open. Even with his mouth closed, I can see his teeth stained pink. I can feel my eye starting to puff up, so I will it to stay open a little longer. I can still move my shoulder, meaning there is no damage to the tendons or muscles. Uri starts to groan, coughing as he keels over, spewing blood. I know he's broken his ribs.

"Anna? Finn?" I yell, waiting for them to rush over to the injured, but no one comes. I look up to see Finn struggling to get past the guards, Anna at his side. "Let them through," I say, scared. I don't know what's happening. Anna looks panicked as Jimmy and Luke work to pry the wall of arms apart. "Let them through," I yell again as loud as my raspy voice will allow. The guards hesitate for a moment, looking at me, but still they don't move.

"Help them," Uri groans, waving me away, pointing to our opponents as he rolls onto his side, letting the blood drip freely from his mouth. I move to Jasper and Malick, both still unconscious.

Malick doesn't look too bad. A wide bruise is starting to blossom around his jaw, a nice-sized cut above his eye, and the only thing I broke was his nose. I pinch it between my fingertips, resetting it, the pain enough to wake him. He sits up, startled, holding his side. He lets me lift his shirt to check it, and I suspect his abdomen is only bruised.

When I move over to Jasper, the sight of him sends me into a state of emergency. Uri didn't hold back one bit. Jasper's face is so swollen I'm afraid he can't breathe. I lean his head back, checking his airway, the sound of moving air faint. Jasper's hand is broken, and I'm sure his shoulder and ribs are too. Why isn't Até helping her own men? Her two best fighters.

"Finish them." I almost don't catch her words from pure shock. She. Até. Their leader. Ordering me to kill them. No!

She hops from her platform, strutting over to me, her face blank as she tosses a dagger at my knees. The handle takes the shape of a snake with rubies for eyes, the blade so shiny I can see my reflection. The bruises and cuts, along with the braids, make me look like a warrior. I'm so busy staring at myself that I almost don't notice that the whole world has gone quiet — still. The crowd no longer eggs us on, and the guards no longer fight with Finn and the others, their faces as shocked as mine. But Anna. Anna is crying tears of anger and rage directed toward her sister, who is ordering me to kill the man she loves.

"You want me to kill your best fighters?" I sit back on my heels, catching my breath, the dagger inches from my fingertips. "The man who has served your family for years. And the other, who loves your sister and is second in command — Até, this fight is over."

"I didn't say it was," Até yells, losing control, pulling her dagger from one of her pockets. She is threatened by me. I have won an unwinnable battle and have swayed her people to listen to me. I didn't want any of this. I grab the dagger, the jagged scales making the handle slick. I throw it past

Até's head, aiming for the back of her chair, but I'm so tired that the blade shifts too far to the right, knocking Nya's crown off and burying its tip in the wood.

"That could have been bad," Uri coughs at my side, a small red puddle starting to pool around his head.

"You are extremely over-confident for the situation you're in," Até says, inching closer. Scared that I will have a surge of energy and go after her, she drops her cloak to the ground, readying herself, revealing more tattoos. I notice one is of a wolf howling and another one of my dad's stories clicks in my head.

"Maybe," I agree, forcing my eyes to stay open, to stay on hers. She smiles an evil, manipulative smile, the same one Eric gives me the moment I walk through the door. "But I will not kill people who lie defenseless by my hands. I do not kill for entertainment." Até's eyes shift from me to her people. Some turn away; others frown at her, and very few are backing her words. She's losing support, and she knows it.

"You are not honourable. You are weak and a coward, like your father. He did not reject a fight out of strength or peace. He did it out of cowardice. That's why he's dead." Até spits the words at me, burying them in my chest where a fiery storm of hate burns. The crowd erupts into fitful objections. My dad was their saviour. They are trying to fight for me, only to be silenced by Nya hitting her staff on the arm of her chair. The fire starts to boil into my throat, provoking an attack, but that's what Até wants — for me to show her people that I am more reckless and vile than she. So, instead, I bow my head.

"Fight me," she urges, gripping my hair in her fist and pulling my head back as she places her blade against my neck in the same spot the earringed man did. My mind tries to pull me into the past, showing me the school hallway, the white masks, J's face.

I focus harder on Até's eyes, noticing for the first time how young she really is. Probably no older than twenty-three. Thirteen years younger than her sister.

"It's okay," I whisper, no longer scared. "If offing me in front of your people will make you feel stronger, braver, more powerful, then by all means." She moves the blade down, drawing a line in my skin, connecting it to the nail marks.

"Fight back!" she screams, yanking my head back further so I can now feel the cold blade on my windpipe. I make my breaths smaller and more controlled, not wanting to accidentally quicken my execution.

"No," I say. All she wants is to appear invulnerable by fighting me, but a good fighter must know their opponent, and she doesn't know me. I know that Até feeds off others' fears, and if I am not scared, she is lost.

"You are a coward," she repeats, fighting with herself now, weighing the consequences of killing me in her head and debating if the burden would be worth the small victory. She's scared. She's been raised from a very young age to see power as the only way of life, and I threaten it. She understands she can't fail and allow the leadership to be taken from her. Leadership would automatically fall to Anna, and Anna could never handle the burden of punishing and killing people. That is why Até took Anna's spot in the first place.

"You are far from a coward," I say, treading on thin ice.

"I never said I was." She digs the blade further into my skin, and all I can do is pray it's far from my carotid.

"Didn't you?" I question, willing my voice to be louder so no one can miss a word. "You are scared, and young. You think that killing me will help you gain respect and willing followers, but that's not true. You will lose your people. They don't believe in you because of your ruthlessness. They believe in you because of the sacrifice you made for your sister."

Her grip falters on my hair, her blade slipping down my neck. I force more words out, hoping that even if she does kill me, she will at least see a different way to live. "You knew Anna wasn't made for the responsibility and pressure that came from this job. It would destroy her; it almost did. So you fought the wolf, the highest honour of the ruler. That's the pelt you wear across your shoulders, the tattoo on your arm and the scars on your neck. You risked your life to save Anna's."

She grunts in frustration, moving the blade from my neck and digging the point deep into my arm. She pulls it out and wipes my blood across my lips. I keep my eyes on her, surprising her when I don't flinch or scream. The arm she chose was already over-stimulated from being dislocated, so all I feel is a pinch in my toe.

"How—"

"My dad told me stories about you," I interrupt. "The princess of the Nomads. Nobler and fiercer than anyone he's ever met." Até's so confused as to why I'm not passing out and why my dad told me about her, that she doesn't move. "You can hurt me all you want. You can kill me and parade me around as your greatest victory, but the moment you do, your people will no longer see you as the person they learned to love — you will also have to deal with the eight people over there calling for your blood."

"Yeah!" Rey pipes up.

Até shuts her eyes, bringing the blade coated in my blood back to my throat. "Do it." I'm exhausted, done with getting hurt, healing and getting hurt all over again. Shifting my eyes from Até, I look at Jimmy, so he is the last beautiful thing I see. "Do it," I press, testing her now.

Her jaw tightens as she grits her teeth, her hand gripping the blade so hard it shakes. Then she sighs, releasing my hair, pushing me back; she wipes the blade with her sleeve before pocketing her dagger. She moves to her throne, waving her hand for the guards to let Finn and Anna through. I lie beside Uri, whose eyes are shut. Placing my two fingers to his neck, I check for a pulse. He's okay. Two hands rest on my arms, and I notice now that Malick and Jasper are both conscious and staring at me with wide eyes.

"Harley and Uri have won and are now granted free passage, refuge and help with her brother. But since they have proven they do not work for the Big Three, this would have been the case whether they lost or won." Até reveals smirking at me, taking hold of her mother's arm and helping her to her feet. I feel Jimmy at my side pulling me up and Luke carefully holding my other arm, blood rolling off my hand. Johnny and Ace rush to help Uri. Rey, Buckey and Tequila run past me with some guards to help Jasper and Malick. Finn and Anna frantically working to stop our bleeding as they guide us to a hut. People urgently speak close to my ears, but I'm too busy watching Até to care what they say. She smirks at me, saying one last thing. "In honour of this, Harley has won my dagger, one that only the most powerful warriors may hold." Then she turns away, disappearing from my sight.

I can feel my eyes start to become puffy and close up, blood flowing more heavily, quickening the throbbing in my neck. Lightheadedness blankets me as I no longer need to be invincible. My right leg gives out, so Luke sweeps me into his arms, Jimmy holding my head up.

"You will not die, brave warrior," the cold voice says. The voice that prepared me for battle, quieting my thoughts. *"Even if you were close, you cannot die by the hands of an equal who craves more power than they deserve."* Somehow, I understand her, letting her words numb me. I will heal, and I will live.

CHAPTER 18
(HARLEY)

"Harles, you're disrupting my concentration." Ace sits at the edge of my bed, sorting our bullets, knives and guns into ten different piles. Até must have given our packs back after Uri and I won. Ace looks fresh and clean, his wet, dark hair soaking his shirt as water droplets drip down his neck without bothering him.

"Sorry my breathing is an inconvenience to you," I mutter, rolling onto my back. When I look up, I find that the dagger Até threw at my knees after the fight is jammed into the wall above my head, the snake's ruby eyes sending chills up my spine. I pull it from the wall. The lightness and the ease with which it balances on one finger surprises me. On its freshly polished silver is the same writing as engraved on the blade of Jasper's sword, 'Sacrifice For Our People.' Ace ignores me, sliding the bullets into leather pouches.

The hut we're in is much bigger than the armoury, more airy and homey. There's a window by my bed, light seeping through the big leaf covering it. Somehow the inside seems cleaner, with rough wood covering the ground. A large sheet separates my bed from the rest of the room. Through the gaps, I can see that the floor is scattered with makeshift beds, clothes and blankets.

"What happened while I was out?" I ask, but Ace doesn't acknowledge me until everything is in its proper bag. Once he has all of our packs under the bed, he starts to talk.

"The whole place broke out into a kind of organized chaos. Most of the civilians formed a protective circle around the medical hut, calling for Até to show her face and give you a formal apology. It was actually rather funny because they didn't know how to rebel against their leader. They made it look like they were calling for blood, but they only wanted her to apologize." He smiles, replaying the events in his head.

"Did she?"

"They think she did, but in reality, she waited for you to get to our hut, then jammed the dagger over your head and whispered something in your ear. She almost provoked us to attack her, but one of the guards got hold of Johnny and knocked him out so easily we decided to back off. We didn't want to lose more healthy people, ya know." He grabs the dagger from me, tracing his fingertips over the blade and looking deeply into the snake's eyes, as if he can hear it hissing.

"Ace, focus," I say, starting to notice the perspiration clinging to my body. I push the blanket off me, sitting up and realizing I'm only in my rainbow sports bra, which is covered in so much dirt and sweat it makes me feel grimy. I fling my hands across my chest, blushing. Ace tosses me his shirt, pretending to cover his eyes, but he peeks through his fingers.

"Not like I haven't seen it before," he laughs, shaking his wet hair over me like a dog. I forgot how easy it is to be with him. How comfortable he makes me feel.

"You haven't seen me like that — whatever, carry on," I say, checking to see if they managed to put me in pants, and to my luck, I'm wearing someone's old baggy shorts.

"Well, Finn got to help Anna stop Jasper's internal bleeding. He said it was the most riveting thing he's done in his life. He'll probably tell you about it in endless detail tonight," he says, stopping to reach down, bringing up the wooden box that holds all my dad's memories. I panic for a second. I don't want to open them and find something that will further ruin my memories of him.

"I didn't open any of them," Ace defends quickly, pulling up the lid and taking a picture out. "There's over three thousand of them, and I couldn't help but look at the pictures, since they were right there staring at me — I never got to meet your dad, but he and J look a lot alike, and you are a spitting image of your mom. Even if you wish you weren't." I choke a little on his words, and he quickly moves on. "Also, we know you're superhuman and all, but man, was that fight insane. Someone said it was the longest one yet. But you scared the living shit out of me when you let Até hold her dagger to your throat and you told her — you know — did you know she was going to drop it?" He leans forward, waiting to soak up all the information he can from me.

I don't want to talk about what happened, but eventually his amber eyes will persuade the words to escape my lips. So for a second I focus on him, how every part of him makes me happy, his crazy mind, his smooth face and his untidy eyebrows. But the best part of his physical beauty is his birthmark. It takes up half his neck, stretching from his collar bone up to his ear and reaching its fingers over his chin, stopping inches from his bottom lip. He used to tell me it was the button that activated his superpower, and when he tapped it three times, he could see all the information in the universe. To us, it was an inside joke when we were in school. He tapped it every time we took a test together or when we were straining our minds to remember the answer to a question. When he dropped out of school, the joke faded over time. In some ways, I suspected it was true because he lives for information, needing to know everything possible.

"No," I say, feeling for the scabs along my neck and chest, but I feel nothing.

"Oh, also, you healed way faster than ever before. Finn said that when they moved over to you, you muttered an ancient word in a different language. I couldn't even figure out the origin. I think it was Sana or something."

"Heal," I interrupt, not sure why I knew that or when I decided to say it out loud. Ace tilts his head, scratching his cheek.

"I mean, it makes sense, because when they were working on Jasper you said that and all your neck wounds turned to old scars and the swelling in your eye deflated, the bruising barely there, and Finn said when he checked your shoulder it didn't even feel like it had been dislocated. I didn't see it happen, but it sounded amazing," he says in awe, only focusing on me now.

But I don't share the same interest as him. I'm scared — terrified of the mysteries of my newfound gifts and the new voices popping up. They seem to control me; they give me orders I don't think to question. "Ace, something is wrong with me," I mutter.

I tell him about my dreams, the voices and how I can control the pain and the injuries. I tell him how I convince people to listen to me and how I saw J seconds before the fight and felt everything he did. All the emotions I've suppressed for days crawl back up, and I start to cry, unable to stop the overwhelming tears from flowing freely because, with Ace, it's so easy to be vulnerable. He doesn't expect me to be anything but myself.

He moves the box from the bed and crawls beside me, letting me press my ear to his chest, allowing me to match his heartbeat to my own racing one.

We developed this tactic when we were fourteen and I started having panic attacks whenever I heard Eric's name or when certain memories resurfaced. Ace would let me hold him and stayed with me till my breathing was even, never letting go, not even if he had somewhere important to be. He's seen my weakness more than Jimmy has.

"Nothing's wrong with you. Something different and extremely insane is happening and, yes, we have no idea what it is, and that's scary, but man, is it cool." He takes my hands, looking at the places where raw, cracked skin should be but instead are patches of pink. "I'll work my hardest to figure it out, but do you want to know what else I found out?" he asks. My body is done shaking. My eyes are now dry, steadied by the familiarity of his presence. "You, my friend, look a lot saner when you sleep." My face breaks into a smile as he jostles my side.

"Ace, you've been known to look less sane than I do."

"Insanity is a gift given to brilliant minds," he states in a bit of a daze, looking at one of the pictures where one man has his arm slung across a younger man.

"Your brother said that to you when everyone used to call you a freak." I sit up to look at him, watching how his face saddens with the memory of his brother. He didn't even get to say goodbye to him. Ace leans back, using his hands as a pillow, shutting his eyes and wiggling his toes under my calves.

"Yep, and he was right because I'm smarter than ninety percent of the town, more insane, and I'm a dropout." He reaches for the box, resting it on his belly, taking out a letter, and rubbing it between his thumb and forefinger. I'd rather read them alone in the privacy of my own head, but I know he's too curious to leave the subject alone. He'll bug me until I tell him every little detail.

"Yes, you can read it with me, but I want to get Jimmy too. Do you know where he is?"

Ace twiddles his thumbs, continuing to wiggle his toes and smiling at the letters. His love for these types of old notes and historical artifacts is unreal. He can sit and sift through things for hours, days, until he feels he knows the person behind it all. He loves them so much that when he had to drop out of school to help run his gang, he was devastated.

One time he was so caught up in something new that his brother Gunner didn't know where he was for four days. Gunner showed up at The Shed, worried out of his mind, begging me to help him. I smiled, making him take a walk with me and climb onto the roof of our school. There Ace was, covered in a pile of books, passed out with his face on his notepad, a pen in his hand. Gunner nearly threw Ace off the roof for scaring him so badly.

"He's got chores. Até gave everyone something to do. But I think it's his turn to wash up."

"What's yours?"

"I didn't get one. I told her I couldn't function without a piece of cake first, to spike my sugar levels. She refused and tried to act all scary. So I lay down in everyone's way and pretended to fall asleep, because I am a genius," he says, tapping his head. "She finally gave in and told me to watch you and stay out of everyone's way, and I was happily minding my own business till you started making noises." I pretend to punch him, and he flinches, covering his face but laughing as well.

"You don't even like cake," I say.

"This is true, but she one hundred percent doesn't have anything to make cake with, and she probably doesn't even know what it is. I figured I'd roll with it — anyways, Jimmy would be down at the river — did you know it runs all the way around the Big Three and is their primary source of water? Kind of gross how people wash up in it, but I guess we rinse off on the side of the river, and they boil their water," he says, his mind going a hundred miles an hour. He starts to count his fingers to slow himself down.

I jump out of bed, feeling steadier than ever, more like I could run a marathon and not like I got beat up yesterday. "Ace, you can read one letter while I'm gone," I say reluctantly, emphasizing the one with my finger. I know it will calm him down. He nods, already carefully opening the first one as I push past the curtain, jumping over the clothes and underwear on the floor. You'd think the boys would be less messy when sharing a room with two girls.

When I walk out the door, people passing me stop to stare. They ask how I am, if I need anything, and if I do, can they run to get it for me. I start to say no but realize Ace didn't tell me where the river is. A young girl takes my hand, offering to lead me there.

She takes me past a garden, where six rows of arranged plants grow, a tightly woven wire fence around it so the animals don't get in. She tells me that she takes care of it all by herself with the help of her mother. The banished have not only survived but are living better than anyone in the towns or the Big Three.

"You're the magic doctor's daughter, right?" she asks, swinging my arm back and forth as she skips, dodging the branches and roots, her ponytail swaying with her steps.

"I guess you could say that," I nod, distracted by how beautiful the forest is. White flowers connected to vines wrap around mossy wood. Weird plants sticking out of the ground look like horses' tails, and in this part of the forest, more birds and small animals roam around in the sunlight. The air is sweet and inviting.

I can hear the sound of rushing water in the distance, far more powerful than the sink at home. As we get closer, I can see the clear liquid running over the ground, crashing into the rocks and the edges of the river bank. I stop, not wanting to take the girl any further. "Thank you for taking me here — umm," I stutter, realizing I never asked for her name.

"Mya," she beams, hugging my waist, her head barely reaching my belly.

"Thank you, Mya," I say, watching her run off, disappearing into the trees.

In the distance, I hear her sing, "I hugged the magic daughter. I hugged the magic daughter," she giggles. I wonder what the people tell their kids about my dad. It must be good, or I would be called much worse than the magic daughter.

I take a deep breath, smiling brighter. For the first time in a while, Jimmy and I will be alone, with nothing in the near future to worry about — no running across town or walking to an underground bar. It's just me, him and the water.

Jimmy stands at the edge of the river in only his boxers, scrubbing himself with weird-looking soap and dumping a bucket of water over his head, the droplets sparkling on his bare skin. He flexes his back, the muscles defined and rippling with his movement. He's not big and bulky like the guards or Uri and Buckey. He's leaner than Luke but not as lanky as

Finn, who only has muscle from fights and factory work. Jimmy's build shows little fat from years of giving his food to Tequila or J, keeping only enough to sustain him.

I never noticed how defined his whole body is. But then again, I've never seen him almost naked. In this light, he looks like a regular boy. He's clean with minor scars on his face and across his skin and only a couple of bruises, small and irrelevant.

Walking through the bushes, I feel a little weird invading his privacy without him knowing. I go to call out his name but stop myself when his mouth moves, startled as someone walks toward him. Até's flower-braided hair comes into focus, her wolf pelt falling to the ground as she struts toward him in a flimsy white tank top.

Everything inside me tells me to move forward, make a noise to stop whatever she has planned, or even to leave. But I keep myself hidden behind a tree, peeking around it as if I'm spying on a forbidden romance. Jimmy reaches for his towel, positioning it around his waist, still leaving himself half-naked. His shoulders tense as she gets closer, saying something I can't make out. It seems to be interesting to Jimmy as it keeps him from reaching for his clothes.

Turn away. I tell myself. *If anything happens, he'll tell you, and at least you won't have to watch it.* But I'm not convinced, because what if Jimmy hides this from me as well? She traces her nail along his bicep, leaning over to whisper something to him. I can't see her face, but I can tell she is smiling with all the joy and trickery in the world.

I had a teacher once who spouted on about gods and goddesses roaming the earth before us. One of them was named Até, the goddess of mischief, delusion, ruin and folly, who played tricks on her brothers and sisters for fun. I guess Nya picked the best name for her daughter without even knowing the meaning. Até will do anything to throw me off my game and distract me, to make me weaker than her, even if that means pulling all of us apart, one by one.

Até moves back, then quickly touches her lips to Jimmy's, holding them there for as long as she can. Jimmy wasn't expecting it, he was caught off guard, and even though they kiss for only a second, it's a second too long for both parties not to get involved. Too long for his lips not to move with hers before they move away. I can't describe the feeling that falls over me when this nightmare plays out in front of my eyes. I've never felt it before. Not when Ace and I broke up. Not when Luke dumped me.

This feeling is one that builds up over time when you give in to the fantasy in your head that your life can change for the better because one person makes you feel so right and safe. You know, no matter what, that person will choose you and love you over anyone else. It's the feeling you get when you let someone all the way in, oblivious to the fact that the way you feel toward them could simply be one-sided. It's the feeling you get when all of that gets blown up in front of you, rendering you speechless because you don't know what to do as you watch the person you love turn back to your best friend who kisses everyone but you.

He pushes her back, shocked, then angry, running his fingers through his hair as he hurriedly puts on his clothes. Até simply smiles. Proud of herself for what she has done. Até looks in my direction as if she knew I'd be in this exact spot.

Maybe if I turn away, I can act like it never happened, I think as I take a step back, but I hoped for too much. My careless step cracks a branch in half, the sound carried by the soft breeze all the way to Jimmy. He looks up, suspecting it's me because the look on his face is the same as when a child gets caught sneaking candy before dinner, ashamed and momentarily petrified.

I move through the trees, scanning the roots and stumps to figure out the direction I'm going, but my mind is so distracted, I'm having trouble seeing straight from the buildup of frustrated tears. I slow my pace down to a walk, knowing if I run, I'll fall or go face-first into a tree, and some part of me wants Jimmy to come after me. I know he is. I can hear his light tread behind me, calling for me to stop. In seconds he grabs my arm, gently stopping us. He moves in front of me, face red, lip quivering as he searches for words.

He stares at me for a long time trying to read my expression, but I've perfected my poker face over time. He clenches his jaw, anticipating me slapping him, but why would I do that? I've told him before that inflicting pain on the people who hurt you only makes you hate yourself more.

"It wasn't what it looked like. I swear on my life," he says, pulling at his hair, then pointing a finger to his chest, drawing an X over his heart. I keep my emotions locked away. The only thought popping into my head is that he could have chosen a less generic opening. I cross my arms, biting my tongue, waiting for him to continue, but he opens his mouth. No words come out, and his lips stay in an O shape as his eyes gloss over. "She kissed me," he finally says, reaching for my hand, but I back away.

"Did you kiss her back?" I ask. A part of me knows he's telling the truth. She did lean in first, and he was taken off guard. When Jimmy lies, he drops his gaze, and right now, his eyes are locked on mine.

When boys hurt me, I never stick around or ask for an explanation or anything. If they mistreat me, I don't pursue them further. If they play games, I never engage in them. I have enough bad men in my life. I would never willingly let in more. However, Jimmy has a VIP pass with unlimited access, no matter what happens. Maybe it's because he's always been around, and I couldn't imagine a world without him, or I love him too much. His crystal eyes drown me, boring into my chest, sinking me in a way that still allows me to breathe. I have spent my whole life fighting to let myself love him, only to have a petty girl ruin it.

"No," he explains, tugging at the collar of his soaked shirt. "If it looked like that, it's because I was shocked. I didn't know she was going to do that."

"What did she whisper to you?" I ask, despising myself for becoming like those jealous girls in school who fight with their boyfriends in the hall every other day. Boyfriend. We never labelled it. We never made it official.

"She said I could get more protection for you if I did a job for her. She leaned in and didn't say what the job was. I know now she needed a reason to get close."

The more he talks and keeps his eyes on mine, the heavier my heart gets, draining all my energy as confusion scrambles my brain.

"You're being weak," a voice more dominant and powerful than the ones I've heard before says.

"Love is not weakness, it's power; even you should know this," a second voice says, dreamy and beautiful. Like a rose would sound if it could talk. The second was more talking to the first than to me.

"How can I sway crowds to listen? Heal instantly? Make my pain a pin prick? But one boy makes me forget everything, makes me helpless," I ask the voices, but of course, no one answers me. They can intrude whenever they want but can't answer my questions.

"I have to go help Ace," I say, moving past him. He lets me go easily, his eyes on my back as I walk away, folding my arms over my chest.

"That's all you're going to say?" he calls, his footsteps annoyingly following me again. I wish he were less persistent and stubborn.

"I don't know what you want," I say, tired, waving him off. I am losing the time I need to make a plan to save my brother and find more information out about my dad.

"I want you to yell at me, fight for me," he mutters under his breath, not really wanting me to hear his words, but I can't miss them. The cold voice curses in my head, forcing me to turn around and face him. Irritated and enraged, I fix my stoniest glare at him.

"Fight for you," I echo, marching forward, catching him by surprise. My voice grows harsher as I get closer to him. He nods, fluttering his eyes, making himself look so sweet and innocent. "All I have ever done is fight for you. When we fought at the Warehouse I always put myself in front of you and everyone else to take all the hits. When you were on drugs I knew the whole time. I didn't want to send you over the edge, so I tried to make it harder and harder for you to buy the shit. I tried to make you want to get clean by showing you what the druggies looked like, what my mom looked like. I fought for you to get sober, to stay sober. I fought for you to breathe again. Yesterday I literally fought so you could get treated and so we didn't have to go back." I finally stop, taking a deep breath, reaching up to his face and placing my hand on his slightly prickly cheek. I lower my voice, "Jimmy, if you were anyone else I would have walked away, because I'm not a person who needs a man, but I've been fighting for you my whole life and no matter how much I hate you I will never stop. How can you not see that?" I feel small as I lower my hand, allowing him to grab it and intertwine his fingers with mine. I can't stop the uninvited butterflies from flapping around in my stomach as the warmth from his hand travels up my arm.

"I'm so sorry," he whispers, leaning his forehead to mine. "I never wanted to hurt you. I'm so sorry." His breath is hot against my nose as he sniffles, not holding his tears back as well as I am.

Is love weakness or power? I ask myself. *Both*, I decide.

"I love you," he whispers, leaning forward.

I can't stay. I can't kiss him. Not when Até's lips were pressed to his just two minutes ago. I close my eyes and move away because maybe if I don't look at him, it won't hurt me as much to walk away.

"Harley," he chokes. I have to open my eyes.

"Nothing could make me not love you. But right now I — I need to go."

His hand loosens and drops from mine, and we walk back to camp in silence because he will follow me, like he always does, until I forgive him, like I always do. I feel heartless for not saying, 'I love you,' back, but I can't feel anything right now. All I feel is the chronic pain, guilt and worry that my brother is being tortured right now while I'm having this stupid argument. I know Jimmy didn't kiss her back, but watching it happen sticks with me. I don't want to think about it.

"Harley — Jimmy." Tequila runs toward us, stopping as she sees our faces. Jimmy wipes tears from his cheeks, and my anger is showing. She keeps her awkward smile, understanding instantly that we've gotten in a fight. "Umm, Anna said we're having a meeting right now. Come on," she says, not asking us any further questions.

The thing about being mad at any of the gang members is that we're always with each other. If we fight, we can manage a couple of hours apart, but circumstances always force us back together — a fight, a problem with the Hunters or the fact that no one likes to be at their own homes, so we can never stay mad for long. All I wish is that the universe would give me more time to regroup before throwing me into another problem.

At this point, all the huts look the same. Only this one has a long table in it with over twenty chairs, meant to hold large numbers of people for long meetings. With the ten of us, Até, Anna and her five guards, this room is stuffy and crowded. The dust tickles my nose and the humidity makes my head sweat. Anna offers me a seat next to her at the table's head so everyone can see me when we hash out a plan, but since it's one chair over from Até and having all the attention on me isn't appealing, I respectfully decline. I slide into a chair next to Finn, who is poring over a notebook that must be Anna's.

He ignores me mostly, but every so often, he'll ask me what something means or teach me a cool way to do stitches faster and neater or show me plants that can be used to slow bleeding. When I look over at Jimmy out of habit, I can only assume he has just finished explaining the whole situation at the river to Tequila. She switches between glaring at Jimmy and Até, her eyes burning with flames, and managing to give me a timid smile. It lifts my spirits a little. Jimmy walks over to me slowly, approaching me like I'm a wounded bear. He reaches for the empty chair on my other side, but thankfully, Ace jumps over the back of it and slides gracefully beside me, leaving Jimmy with the empty chair right beside Até, who won't stop smirking at me. The more she does it, the more disfigured the moon tattoo looks.

"I overheard Jimmy talking to Tequila, 'cause I'm a master at overhearing things I shouldn't." Ace grabs my hand, making me look at him, "Are you okay?"

I shrug, scared that if I talk, my voice will break. Ace throws a protective arm around me. He directs his fakest smile toward Jimmy, Ace's best attempt at being mean.

I'm distracted by a guard who brings in a large roll of paper, unravelling it to reveal the most beautiful, detailed map I've ever seen, one that makes Uri's drawing and my blueprint seem like something a child created. It has realistic sketches of each leader's tower, with the essential rooms in green and the number of Hunters in blue, along with the population and how many people work in each government position. It has all the streets labelled, showing which ones hold gang fights, on which days and how many Hunters work in each area. This map must have been developed over the years because you can tell where things have been erased, and a new pen has scribbled over top.

"This is amazing," I gasp, hovering my fingers over a floor in JC's building labelled 'weaponry for all your needs.'

"Why, thank you, Ms. Harley," A nasally voice says from behind me. A boy no taller than me when I'm seated walks over, shaking my hand. His hair is slicked back with what appears to be sap, giving it a sticky, crunchy look. His glasses show a layer of dust, and he wears a worn, sky blue tie around his neck, not matching his grey shirt and tattered pants. "Asteroid at your service, newly banished, pleased to make your acquaintance," he says, whipping out a pen and paper and jotting down notes. He's not as big or powerful-looking as the other people in this room, but by the jagged scars on Asteroid's face, he looks like he can hold his own. He leans closer, eyeing Até. "Well, by new, I mean 'been here for four years,' but Até still has me on probation."

"Asteroid," Até yells, slamming her fist on the table.

Asteroid bows, stepping back to his place, pressed against the wall. I can tell he's silently pleased with me for loving his creation and understanding it without explanation.

"So what's the plan?" Luke asks, opening and closing his switchblade. He looks clean like everyone else at the table, washed and newly dressed. Even Uri is. He has stitches on his lip and shiny cream on his face. He didn't bother to put on a shirt, so you can see the cloth wrapped around his ribs. He won't be able to move properly for a week, but he won't sit out of this rescue mission, and I'm selfish because I don't want him to.

"Can't you see I'm about to speak to that?" Até snarls, standing and pressing her palms into the table.

"Get there faster. I have a class to teach," Rey says, sticking his tongue out as he scribbles madly on paper. Johnny peeks over at it, chuckling. They've both chosen long-sleeve shirts that have a mouse cartoon character on them, its face disfigured from years of being passed from person to person.

"What are you talking about?" Até asks, as confused as the rest of us, but I've learned over the years not to ask Rey what he's doing. It's never good.

"Let's call it chemistry."

"Rey, put it away," I pipe up, not wanting to waste any more time, and frankly, I'm annoyed with the lack of control Até has over a room. If she had treated us fairly and like people when we showed up, she could have gotten our respect faster, but now the boys will only make it harder for her. "I know you don't trust or like Até. I understand. I have more than enough dislike for her to go around, but she is helping us find J, which is the reason we are here and like it or not they know how to get him out," I say. Their faces all go blank because, like me, through all the chaos of the fight, they have forgotten the bigger picture. Even Até backs down a little.

Rey slides the paper onto his lap, mouthing the word 'moonshine' to Ace, who smiles at the notion, taking his arm from my shoulder and squeezing my leg. I look to Jimmy, who is focusing his attention on his hands.

"We will move out tonight, to scout out the prison and the surroundings. We'll watch the Hunters' rotations and activity, since we don't usually bother to keep watch of that section," Até states, pointing to the east part of AC's building. It's a challenging area because it's in the middle of the Big Three, beside MC's and JC's buildings. There will be no shortage of eyes looking for us.

"How many people can we take?" I ask, scanning the gang. Buckey is out because of his arm. Uri won't be able to keep up. Tequila doesn't usually participate in stakeouts because she gets too distracted and ends up disappearing and coming back with stolen goods. Rey is the same way, only he talks too loud and starts playing tricks on us, and I can only assume Johnny is similar, unable to stop talking or stay still, so they're out too. And Finn, well, it's not in his nature, plus he can't hold a gun, so if we run into trouble, he'll be an extra body to protect, and I don't think I could bring myself to put him in that situation. That leaves me with Jimmy, Luke and Ace. Ace is second to Uri in memorization since he counts everything; steps, turns, trees, buildings. I can trust him to relay the directions back to Uri. Luke is good to have around because he's good at sensing things, and despite the fact that there are many reasons I don't want to take Jimmy, he is the only one who understands what I'm doing without me telling him.

"Three of mine and three of yours. We'll have two groups scouting from two different angles on the roofs. The rest can stay in the tree line for extra eyes. I'll be taking Em, Malick and Jasper," she says, sitting back down.

I don't trust her not to leave us behind if we separate. Anna shifts nervously in her chair because everyone knows Jasper won't be ready by tonight. "One of us can go with you and one of yours can come with us to help us navigate," I say, looking to the gang. All of them raise their hands, and by the look of everyone around us, I can tell they aren't used to seeing people have a choice in whether they risk their life or not. It's how we aperate. If a person doesn't feel comfortable enough to do the task, no one can judge them for not volunteering. "Jimmy, Ace and Luke," I decide, looking at Jimmy, whose eyes are still trained on the table. So instead, I look to Luke, who nods. "Luke will go with you," I say to Até, who looks a bit shocked.

"You can have Em, then," Até offers, leaning back, grinning because she gave me her third choice, and I gave her one of my best.

"No," I say, turning back to look at Asteroid. "How well do you know the city? A spark lights his eyes.

"I used to be head of surveillance and worked in the labs to graph the activity in the streets and make maps." He smiles because I bet no one ever asks for his help. "Very well, ma'am," he adds.

Até glares at me when I turn back, and I'm starting to like Asteroid a lot more. Not because Até hates him but because he is like us, underestimated.

"Since I gave you one of my best, Asteroid will come with me," I declare.

"He's not a guard," Até interrupts.

"Asteroid, do you know how to run?"

"Yes, ma'am."

"Do you know how to fire a gun?"

"Yes, ma'am."

"Then I see no problem with taking him with us. This way Jasper can stay back and rest, because if he opens his stitches or damages anything further you won't have him by your side when you need him," I say with authority, not backing down. Anna gives me a grateful smile and leaves to check on Jasper. Finn runs after her, clutching the notebook.

"Very well," Até concedes, writing something down and passing it to a guard who hurries off. "Anything else?"

"Yes," I say, even though her question was rhetorical. "We can stay in touch with walkie talkies. Luke will have one, Ace will have one and the people in the trees will have the rest — we'll also change their channel because the Hunters might have one too."

"We have night vision goggles. Robin brought—" one of the guards blurts, backing down when Até glares at him sharply. Até is keeping that information from me, making me wonder what else she's holding back.

"Sick," Johnny says.

"Perfect. The prison is pretty visible from the trees, and it's a straight shot down the road," Até says, drawing a line through the map, crossing through some numbers. Asteroid curses as she ruins the detail.

"We leave after dinner then?" Tequila asks, rubbing her stomach. Come to think of it, I haven't eaten since yesterday morning. I feel hollow.

"Yes. Until then you can go to the armoury and pick out what you need if you don't wish to use your own weapons," Até offers, becoming suspiciously generous.

"Oh, sweet." Rey cheers.

"Race you," Rey and Johnny yell, springing from their seats and stampeding out the door. Tequila and Buckey roll their eyes and chase after them to make sure they don't blow the place up or get us kicked out.

"She is leaving something out," a voice says. It sounds like Finn's grandma, wise beyond her years.

Até is taking all of us away from the camp. Even if Luke is with her, she can still lose him and abandon all of us, giving us no way back. She could make Asteroid leave us, and we would have to rely only on Uri's memory to guide us back through the maze of trees.

"I want one person to stay here with a walkie talkie," I demand, quickly realizing that if she is planning to abandon us, she'll leave us without any supplies, lost and easy for every Hunter to find.

A smile hides at the edge of Até's lips. "Why?"

"Trust," I reply.

"Fine. After dinner we will meet at the fire," she says, dismissing us and turning to Jimmy to carry on their conversation. She leans her elbow on the table, pulls her chair closer to him and bats her eyes as Jimmy moves as far back as possible, his face full of annoyance because he does love me, but a hint of amusement shows because he can't help his natural love for attention.

"Very good," the voice says, praising me as if I were her student and have solved a high-level math problem. I think that's now six different

voices in my head, but I'm starting to lose track. Next time they talk, I have to give them qualities to tell them apart.

"Is that all?" Até asks, directing her question more to Jimmy than to me.

"Yes," Luke says, moving to my side. Ace is standing on the other, both of them protecting me. I understand why Ace is; he knows what Jimmy did, but Luke doesn't. He glares at Jimmy, unsettling me.

"Let's go read, I found something interesting," Ace offers, hovering his hand over the small of my back, guiding me out the door. I look over my shoulder, seeing that Jimmy's face is suffused with anger as he hisses words at Até. This gives life to an idea.

"I am assuming that if we are scouting at night we are planning to get J at night the next day?" I stop at the door.

I'm testing whether Até is too caught up with trying to get in my head to lead her people and develop an effective plan or if she's hiding something from me. This same issue is probably the reason she's having trouble getting people to listen to her because her thoughts are somewhere else.

"Obviously," she huffs, not drawing her attention from Jimmy.

"And are there more guards during the day than at night?" I ask.

"Two or three more. We scout that building during the day mostly and have one person stationed there at night," Até says, not realizing that she's admitted to her lie. Jimmy's mouth twitches. He knows what I did.

"I thought you didn't bother scouting out the prison," I say, winking at Asteroid, who is redoing the place where Até drew the line. I turn to Até with an air of innocence, and she drops her gaze, knowing she's screwed up.

"I'm assuming somewhere around that area," I point to the floor above the prison, "Is where most of the Hunters sleep," I say, picturing the blueprint that had the initials HSQ on the third floor of the building. If I'm correct, it means Hunters' sleeping quarters. "That's also why you drew the line — to make it hard to see the number of guards. Black numbers for night, blue for day." Asteroid gives me an approving look. It confirms I'm not too far off. Jimmy looks at me for the first time since we sat down. The whites of his eyes are a scratchy red, the saddest I've seen them in years. I know he wasn't lying to me. "Asteroid, can you please get me all the information you can on the prison?" I ask, looking at him when I talk, making sure he knows I value him.

"Yes, ma'am," he says, rolling the map up carelessly and hurrying out the door, bumping into things as the paper covers his view.

"You can't do that," Até grunts, frustrated that I have not only caught her in a lie but that I am now ordering her people around like they are my own.

"I must remind you that we are doing this for my thirteen-year-old brother, my only family, who is in this situation because of me, because the Big Three, our mutual enemy, used him as collateral. What if it were Anna? You can play all the games you want with me, but I don't have time for this. So stop lying to me, because I will find out one way or another." Até almost looks ashamed. I look at Jimmy again, locking eyes with him. "Be better," I sigh, walking out the door.

CHAPTER 19
(JIMMY)

One thing I hate more than anything in the world is pushing Harley to the point where she wants nothing to do with me, well, and snakes, but that's not the point.

When she's annoying me, I'll start arguments on purpose, but I would never do something like this — something that could cause her to lose trust in me.

When she left the meeting, I was so mad at Até I lost the ability to pronounce words correctly. Até kept trying to get closer, even though Harley was no longer there. She said, "You will find better." Like she suspected Harley would never forgive me. Maybe she won't.

I have done many horrible things to girls' hearts in my life — led them on, kept them around for entertainment, and paraded them in front of Harley to make her jealous — but by far, this is the worst, and I didn't even mean to do it. Até caught me off guard. Got close to me by using the one person I could never abandon. Até kissed me to get into Harley's head because to Até, she is a threat to her power. Até was stupid to think that would work. Even though Harley loves me, at least I hope she still does, she will always prioritize the most dire situations first, and nothing will stop her from giving her full attention to that.

Harley is more morally sound than any of us and is the most unbelievably badass woman I have ever met. I mean, she called Até out on lies none of us caught. She persuades people to listen to her by playing to what they see as kindness, and I notice all of that. I love all of that. I wish I could tell her without making her think I'm lying. Fuck my stupid ignorance. I should give her space to hate me, but the more space I give her, the more her ability to ignore me will increase.

My feet carried me to the hut while my mind abandoned me. Ace worked on blocking the door when I showed up, but his inability to leave people out gave way. Now I lie on Uri's bed where I listen to their whispering and the turning of papers muffled behind the sheet. I'm working on ignoring my jealousy toward Ace because maybe he is the best person for Harley, and the more I mess up, the harder it is for me to change that. Ace and I are the only people she relies on and tells everything to, because he's annoyingly easy to talk to, and I've been with her the longest.

Feelings and being in love suck. It's as simple as that. Maybe that's why I've never loved before. I'm protecting myself from a mind-melting, heart-dissolving experience that makes me crave life. No. It's because I've only ever loved her.

The worst part about being so close to her, yet utterly alone, is my overactive conscience that switches back and forth between wanting her to give me all her attention and being ashamed for forgetting why we are here in the first place. J is what we all have to focus on, and Harley made that pretty clear. We are starting to lose sight of that.

I wish it were only the two of us in a different world where we didn't know what running and fighting felt like. *I'm delusional and selfish*, I think. Harley would never let me or anyone else get in the way of her and her brother, and I understand — I would expect nothing less. She would pick J over me, and I would pick Tequila over her. Fighting for our blood is what makes us human. I'm so frustrated with it all, "Ugggh," I accidentally let a groan escape.

"Jimmy, I need you for a second," Harley calls. The words, 'I need you,' make me have to slow myself down when I jump up and rush over to the sheet.

I can't tell if she's still mad or not by the tone in her voice, but I hesitantly move the sheet aside and step toward her. Papers are scattered all over the bed, some neatly in envelopes, others carelessly shoved into a carved wooden box laying open on the floor. Pictures poke out of it. One I swear is of Harley, but when I lean closer, I realize it's her dad and mom.

"What is all of this?" I ask, looking up only to notice how close Harley and Ace are sitting together. Harley's perched on her toes, rocking back and forth, eyebrows furrowed in concentration. Ace leans against the wall in his knowledgeable daze, their arms brushing against one another. A single piece of paper is held between them with only a paragraph pencilled on it, whereas the rest of the letters are filled with writing.

Ace smiles at me for a moment, then remembers that he's supposed to be mad, so he works his hardest to frown. It doesn't have the same effect given his permanent smile lines. When Harley looks at me, she seems to hate me a little less, giving me the 'I could kill you but maybe not today' look. It's a lot better than her poker face where you have absolutely no idea whether you should be scared or terrified. I've only ever gotten her poker face twice, and once was because I stupidly wrote in permanent marker, 'Jimmy's number one,' on her face while she slept in the alley. I'll just say it wasn't my best idea.

"Over ten years of letters Robin wrote to Anna," Ace says, gently placing some letters back into their envelopes to make a corner for me to sit. I keep my distance, sitting half on, half off the bed as Harley swallows hard, passing the letter to me.

"He wrote mostly about me, my first steps, going to school and meeting you." She rolls her eyes as an unconscious smile fills my face. "And other things like J being born, new medical discoveries and so on, but — this one is different. We need some help figuring it out," Harley says, nodding for me to start reading. I clear my voice speaking aloud, the letter feeling crackly and brittle between my fingertips.

Anna, my dearest friend,

The world has finally caught on to my secrets, and I am afraid it will not be lenient with me. Ever since I heard my baby's heartbeat in Lucy's belly for the first time, I vowed to give my life to protect her. I have given my own heart to make sure that my sweet daughter's blessing and curse would stay hidden from the leaders of the Big Three until she is ready and can understand.

I gave my soul and left everyone I loved to start a new life with a new identity, but they have finally found me. Finally figured out the truth. Tomorrow is her tenth birthday, and they will know for sure if her soul is not just her own. Her abilities will become stronger and more noticeable. The leaders will be watching her until she is eighteen, an adult. I cannot tell you why the leaders cannot kill her or harm her, in the fear that Lucy will find this letter and be an accomplice to my lies. That is also why I cannot tell you the whole truth.

I am writing this to drain my mind of the pain I will be facing soon and give you a memory of her so if she were to appear in your land, you would see her as an ally and do what I could never do. I need you to protect her, Anna, and to know that she is not only important to me but to the world. I'll tell her the truth one day, if I make it that far that is. However, if I don't, someone else must bring you this letter. All I can say in case of interception is that the words I muttered when she was first born were the most literal things I have ever said in my entire life. My bloodline holds the answers. Protect her at all costs, Anna. She has the strength of the seven and may be the only one to free us from this dictatorship and give the people justice. I love you.

-Sincerely, Robin

P.S. Happy Birthday.

We sit in silence, all the words settling over us like the dust drifting through the air. Robin knew the Big Three were coming for him, for Harley, the person who will free us all and lead us. He knew about her abilities, about everything.

"He left the Big Three to save you?" I ask, breaking the silence, thousands of questions bubbling into my head. *Is Robin his real name? Why didn't he tell his own wife what was happening, but he was willing to tell Anna? Did he get run out of town by the Hunters, or did he willingly leave?* But those are pretty touchy questions to start with. This one seems to be safe.

"Yes," she says, reaching for the paper and running her fingertips over the words, maybe trying to feel what her dad felt when he was writing this. The writing almost seems rushed, some of the words swooping as if he jumped at every noise, and at the bottom are small dots, yellowing faster than the rest of the paper, either from his tears or Anna's.

"Maybe he left because he knew they were going to kill him," I offer, moving closer to Harley, wanting to make sure she knows he didn't abandon her — not on purpose, anyway, but I'm not even sure of that.

"That's what we thought, but that would mean—" Harley trails off, not finishing her sentence.

He abandoned his family without knowing if they would live or die, I think, finishing her thought in my head. For years she has hung onto the hope that the Hunters made him leave, that he wasn't dead and was being kept away from his family unwillingly. That's why he couldn't come back for Harley and J. But now — to think he left her to save himself — well, it's killing her.

"But he also brought the letter to Anna. He could have made it here and couldn't get back," Ace says, carefully inching the letter out of her grasp and sliding it back into the box.

Right now, they are repeating the same thoughts they've already had. Their two minds together are infinitely better than my one. They want me to confirm or deny what they have found out, and right now, I wish I could.

"The seven? And his bloodline holding the answers?" I ask, wanting to move on to a different problem, but it's also the one thing I can't think of an answer for.

"Your guess is as good as ours," Ace grunts, but I know there's an idea floating around in Harley's head. I place my hand on her leg, getting her to sit back and not look so tense. She spaces out, looking at one of the pictures on the wall, moulding her idea into words.

"What are you thinking?" I press slowly, moving further onto the bed, waiting for her to tell me to move, but she is too busy to notice or doesn't care. She looks at Ace, who nods like he's agreeing with her thought process.

"Do you know anything about seven rulers or warriors? Girls, or sisters, maybe?" she asks Ace. He moves his fingers over his birthmark, eyes shifting side to side as he focuses.

"In the time before the Big Three there were eighty five female leaders. But by the way your dad was talking about it, it seems like not very many people knew what he was referring to — only the leaders, people closest to him and, well, his relatives would know. It also might be a way older reference than we think."

"I think it has to do with the voices in my head, but I've only heard six," Harley adds.

"Six," I echo. At the beginning of this, she had only heard two — that she told me of, at least. Also, she only saw her futuristic dreams at night once in a while, but now they are happening more often. I noticed that before the fight, her eyes went blank, and she had to shake her head to get rid of whatever she saw, which makes me think she had one then too.

"Can you tell them apart? Can you talk to them?" Ace asks, carving one through seven on the wall with question marks beside them. Harley shakes her head, pulling at the skin on her arm.

"We should ask Anna about it," I suggest, picking the box up, plucking the letter from its pile and looking at the picture. I think that Anna could have been more than a student to Robin, maybe best friends like Harley and me or more than that — also something I can't say aloud.

Robin trusted Anna with his daughter's secret and her life. He expected Harley would go to No Man's Land one day, and he needed Anna to take care of her. Robin knew the Big Three would come after Harley, most likely knew they could capture her, torture her or kill her. He left without even sharing this information with his wife. I can't believe it. If he somehow comes back, I'm going to give him a nice knuckle sandwich.

We walk to the medical hut, the one letter flapping in Harley's hand. All of us are lost in our thoughts, barely noticing the people around us. Something inside me tells me that even if Anna does know, she might not tell us. I trust her, but still, she is Até's sister, and blood is thicker than water. If Anna told her sister and Até told her not to share the secret with Harley, then it won't surprise me if she doesn't. Even if it means Harley would be driven mad by whatever is happening to her.

I can't — I won't, ever completely understand what's going on in her mind anymore. She thinks differently now, moves as if she were a trained warrior. What if the voices change who she is entirely? She might never love me in the same way. *Man, am I selfish*, I think. Besides, none of us will ever be the same as we were before we left The Sticks.

"Anna," Harley calls, peeking in through the open door, where a shadowy figure moves back and forth, scrubbing dried blood off surfaces.

This hut is the most high-tech one I have seen yet — solar panels on the roof and smaller versions of wind turbines around the outside. All the walls and the tables are made out of some sort of metal, and where a fur pelt would be, instead a piece of plastic seals off the sterile inside from the dust and dirt-ridden outside, only letting the faint smell of bleach and iron seep out. They have to have more connections than Robin. There is no way all of this came from The Sticks. There are even heart monitors, a cabinet of medicine and new-looking supplies. It's expensive and hard to come by equipment even if you did work in the hospital. Harley isn't interested in any of that. "Anna," she calls again, but Finn walks out instead, pulling off blue gloves.

"What is it?" He looks tired, packed to the brim with new information. I'm glad we're leaving him here. I couldn't live with myself if he got hurt or killed. He and Harley are our healers.

"I need Anna," Harley insists.

Finn frowns, knowing it would be best for him to walk away and get some rest while Harley is on a mission. She never stops until she gets the answers. We all find it best to move aside. Anna pushes the plastic back, stepping into the sunlight, letting the fresh air absorb into her skin, and the fragrance fill her lungs. Somehow she looks less tired than Finn.

"Yes?"

"Tell me what you know about this letter," Harley says, shoving it into Anna's hands.

Harley needs to take a breath and calm down like she can usually do so effortlessly. Lately, it's like her body has been fighting between anger and peace. Anna squints at the paper, eyes moving down the lines. Then, as if her world breaks, she pales. Her bottom lip trembles slightly. Her breath becomes shallow, and everything about her closes off.

"He—" Anna tries to look at Harley, but it appears to be hurting her more than looking at the paper. "Robin never made it here, someone named Eric brought this to me. Your dad trusted him not to tell anyone the Nomads existed," Anna mutters, holding the letter out to her, but Harley's hands stay bound to her side. Harley's wild eyes are scaring all of us, so I take the letter instead, folding it into my pocket.

"Eric," Harley whispers to herself. Everything he said to her is now dreadfully real. At this point, Eric has been more honest than her own father.

"Yes. He told me Robin was gone — he didn't tell me why, but he told me that you were the reason. He—"

"What else did he say?" I interrupt before Anna says the words that will make this already terrible situation worse. Robin left everything, everyone he loved behind, as he did when he left the Big Three. Harley being the reason he did both.

"Eric said he would watch you and take care of you, make sure nothing happened till he could no longer help. If Eric knew anything more of what you are, he didn't give me any indication of it. I can't help you. For years I spent day and night researching what the strength of seven means and the only documents of bloodlines are locked away in MC's building. I found nothing."

"The only ones that can tell me are the leaders," Harley whispers, seemingly disconnected from the world.

"We can keep looking," Ace says, attempting a positive outlook on all this.

The sun no longer feels warm, this place no longer feels safe. It feels empty and threatening because, no matter where we go, Harley will never be beyond the reach of danger. If she is this important, they will chase her until she is in the custody of the Big Three. Harley will never know what is happening to her unless she hands herself over. I know her mind, and I know eventually, whether to save us or someone else, she will give herself up and find out what all of this means.

"What about the words my dad said when I was born?" Harley asks, ignoring us and biting down so hard on her lip that it starts to bleed.

In an attempt to calm her down, I take her hand in mine, moving my thumb in circles. I expect her to pull away, but she doesn't. She pushes out a held-back breath, releasing every muscle in her body. Her eyes close for a second as she pulls herself back to me. "I'm sorry," she mutters under her breath. I'm not sure if it was directed to Anna, Ace, or me. Anna relaxes as well, and Ace sways as if he might drop right now and start snoring.

"He whispered to you — no one was meant to hear it, but I did. He said you came from a great bloodline of powerful women. You were the last soul ruler. Our last hope," Anna's voice breaks, and she looks like she's about to cry. Ace crosses over to Anna, taking her hand, thanking her for the time she has given us and telling her she can go.

Harley squeezes my hand, thinking. She's wondering, as I am, what soul ruler means, why she was burdened with being our last hope and if her dad may simply have been crazy, but the Big Three wouldn't put so much effort into getting her if her being the soul ruler was based on a crazy man's conspiracy.

"What does that mean?" Ace asks, moving closer to us, but I can tell by how Harley's eyes cling to my face, she doesn't want to talk anymore.

"I don't know," she sighs. "All of that is out of our control right now. We have to focus on the upcoming task." She slips her hand from mine, her demeanour deflated, saddened. I want her to talk to me because it helps empty a racing mind, but I know it will make things worse right now. "Ace, go to the armoury and get ready." She smiles lightly, grabbing his shoulders. He looks sorry for her, scared and helpless all at the same time, before agreeing to do so and taking his sweet time walking toward the noise that is undoubtedly Rey and Johnny breaking things.

"I'm going down to the river. I think dinner is almost ready and I want to feel clean," she says, turning to me, making me notice the faint smells of cooking meat and vegetables.

"You do smell," I tease, grimacing, wondering if it's too soon. A stray piece of hair falls over her face. Out of habit, I tuck it behind her ear, letting my hand linger too long on her cheek. Her brown eyes catch the light, glinting gold. Her expression turns vulnerable as she looks up at me.

"Promise you won't leave me," she says, her voice small, her expression so gentle it almost scares me. She breaks me down in every way possible, makes me want to be better and selfless, not only for her but also for myself.

"I promise on the sun," I say back.

We have used that type of promise ever since we were young. The sun is always there. Always reliable. Even when the moon takes its place, it shines on the other side of the world. Even when the clouds fill the sky, it still shines behind them. That is its promise to the world. To shine until its light burns out. I have promised to fight for her, protect her, love her until my light fades away. Harley stands on her tippy toes, placing a kiss on my lips. However small and short, it still leaves tingles in my body and a warm shadow as she walks away.

CHAPTER 20

(HARLEY)

I only remove my shirt when I rinse at the river, not wanting anyone to walk down and see me in my underwear. I wish I could remove my rainbow sports bra to wash away the grimy bloody memories from the fight, but for some reason, it feels like a part of me, like a good luck charm.

I'm not a superstitious person. I don't wear the same unwashed, rotten-smelling socks every fight like Rey does or put my hair on my left shoulder when I go on dates like Tequila. I know this stupid bra doesn't keep me from getting shot or dying, but it doesn't hurt to wear it.

Death, I think. I haven't had time to think about death in a while. I killed two Hunters in Dead Man's Hill and haven't given them a second thought until now. It seems so long ago, but I'm sure they will appear in my nightmares at some point. Ghosts and dead people don't scare me, and neither does dying. My mom used to tell me that when a soul is taken from the world, it finds an unborn creature to give life to. Death seems peaceful, fulfilling, and being tossed into an empty void of darkness doesn't seem so bad right about now.

"*Down by the river, we send off dead bodies to drift to the places they wish they could be,*" the high-pitched voice giggles, the feeling of his smile sending goosebumps up my skin. I can feel bags forming under my eyes and my mind saying, *Here we go again.*

"What do you want with me?" I ask, my voice in my head taking on a gravelly, distorted sound.

"*I wish I could tell you because I have grown quite fond of you, but it would make things less entertaining.*"

This time he sounds like he's standing directly behind me, his words floating in the air. I know if I turn to face him, something will change, and I will no longer have the mud squishing between my toes or the icy river spraying mist onto my face.

"*Yeah, entertaining,*" I mutter. Without shutting my eyes, I slowly inch around, although I know no matter what I do, I'll only see what he wants me to. As soon as I think that, my surroundings change to an endless barren field, dried grass reaching my hips. This place must have recently been overcome with fire or hasn't seen rain in a long time. Ashes and humidity warm me instantly as rays of sun beat against my back. Rain would be nice, but not a cloud crosses the sky. Only hungry, angry vultures hover in circles overhead. "*Are you one of the seven?*" I manage to ask, but a wave of disgust rolls over me instantly once the words leave my lips. "*I'll take that as a no,*" I say as a nauseated sensation fills my stomach. The ground shifts, creating a path in the grass only able to fit one person, with no end in sight. Within seconds, my tongue dries, and my throat burns as the heat steals all the moisture in the air I breathe.

"*Walk with me, my dear,*" he squeals. A large wide hand presses into my back, shoving me forward and throwing me off balance, causing me to scrape my knees and hands on the protruding rocks. A shiver rolls up my spine as my fingers run over the bumpy earth. Those aren't rocks. Rocks aren't that pearly, distinct colour. Rocks don't have that consistent long, narrow shape.

"*Bones,*" I gasp. A small scream escapes my mouth as I scramble to my feet, looking for answers, but no one's there.

"*Walk.*" His high-pitched voice surrounds me, coming from every direction, though the same hand still guides me forward.

The longer we walk, the more my muscles tighten and weaken from dehydration and my mouth withers like a desert. My eyes start to play tricks on me — at least that's what I tell myself as skeletons crawl from the earth, grabbing at my ankles, poking at the bottoms of my shoes. *"Now, girl. This time, this is not so much a vision as it is a warning."*

"What?" I squeak, my voice leaving me, forced breathing becoming my main focus as my lungs shrink to raisins.

"What you normally see is the future, which shifts a little, but is mostly the way it appears. You, however, have a way of manipulating it. Your beloved Jimmy should have died in that speakeasy, but you saved him — I have never seen that ability before. You're stronger than the rest," he says, his words sounding more sinister than complimentary. His voice stings my ears, giving me a migraine, as if he's knocking a tuning fork against my teeth. I ask myself, *Is he the one giving me the visions, letting me see the future all the time?*

"No. That is one of the seven. I can sometimes give the visions more of a dramatic flare, like the head on the platter — that one was my favourite," he smirks.

I forgot he could hear my thoughts. His hand pressed to my back feels so real. This place, my fatigue, the sound of clicking insects and flies tickling my skin feels so real. I know it isn't, yet I still can't get my feet to still. I can't wake myself up, and I almost miss the paralyzing feeling that accompanies every vision.

"You know them?"

"Of course I do. I live with them in your head, and don't ask me who they are because it's not my secret to share — well, I guess in a way it is, but I'm still not going to tell you," he taunts. Blisters form on my toes and the backs of my heels, my knees in danger of buckling as every step drags me down.

"Stop playing with me. Why am I here?" I snarl, trying to shake the feeling of his jagged, dirty fingernails pinching into the flesh between my shoulder blades.

"I told you, it is a warning."

"Of what?" I blurt. Sheer exhaustion from this neverending walk makes it harder and harder to speak, to think. I stumble, not able to hold myself up. His hands move to my armpits, supporting me and lifting me like a puppet.

"What will happen to you if you let the seven become a part of you? At this moment there's a wall in between you and them. Only one or two are able to be present with you at a time." He lets go, dropping me onto sharpened bones that stab into my knees, digging into my tendons and muscles, ripping through them with ease. I scream as the feeling of knives, warm lava and speeding shrapnel fusing with my skin sends white dots into my vision.

I can't stop the pain — I can't make it smaller. I've never experienced anything like this before. Pain is usually an easy thing for me to get rid of. Dehydration and relentless sun shouldn't bother me either.

"Harley, don't listen to him," the soft voice breaks in. It's more panicked than usual as she tries to gain control, her presence cooling my body with beads of sweat.

"She can't help you here. I have all the control but not for much longer. Lucky for you," the high-pitch voice huffs, lifting my head. A cliff edge appears in front of me. The sweet voice's disappearance causes my skin to wither along with my eyes and blood.

Hot water spills across my face. Fingers wipe roughly at my eyes, stinging them but making my vision clear. In front of me is a quarry filled with — people — millions of bodies decaying, the smell gagging and strangling me. All of their facial features are ripped away. Anything that can tell me if I know them, gone. "The seven did this. Claiming they wanted peace, they took the women in your bloodline and made them into murderers. They convinced innocent people to follow them and work to make the world safer, but look at this. Think about the world you live in now." He pushes me forward, so I'm forced to look down, my chest hanging over the edge, all my blood rushing to my brain. "If you allow them to break that wall, you will be the next to add bodies to the pile."

My mind starts racing, trying to follow his words, what he's trying to tell me, but it's filled with so much fog that I can't find my way around.

"Why me?"

"I thought you were supposed to be intuitive," he sighs. "Fine, I'll explain — it is you because you are the last female in your bloodline. After that nasty toxic gas disaster, most of your remaining family died from starvation and Hunters. Your father was the only survivor of the bloodline. You have no grandparents, aunts, uncles or cousins, and the men are only carriers of the gene. So since you aren't going to continue the bloodline anytime soon and your brother is even further from that, you, my friend, are the last of your kind. If you and your brother die, the line will be no longer — no more power struggles or deaths. "You are the biggest threat to the Big Three because they can't kill you without hurting themselves thanks to your ancestors, and they can't hurt you without you healing. They can kill your brother whenever they want. Until you are dead, J lives."

"How — do — you — know — this? I don't understand." I force the words into my mind as I start gasping, grabbing at the invisible hands around my neck, feeling all the blood rushing to my head

"The seven don't think it's time for you to know everything, it might make you lose your mind and, as much as I want that to happen to you, they're blocking me from telling you the whole truth." Pure anger and disgust overtake me, as though I'm feeling all of his emotions. "And, to answer the question as to why I know all of this — I raised the seven. I summoned the powerful abilities that kept them alive, that keep you alive. I did all I could to keep them safe, and my daughters — my own blood, betrayed me and broke promises for something as meaningless as love." A bitter taste forms in my mouth.

"How am I supposed to trust you?"

"You can't. He's not supposed to be here," the cold voice snarls, pushing against the high-pitched one. It stretches the sides of my skull, straining my brain. I can't feel my face anymore, my lips swelling like balloons, almost as if I'm having an allergic reaction to their presence. Everything hurts too much.

"Harley, breathe. Relax and keep breathing — he's almost gone." The sweet voice makes me do as she asks, without me having to process her words.

Clouds begin to cover the blue sky, the sun disappearing, the humidity making it more difficult to breathe. A fire ignites among the bodies, ashes scattering around me, getting in my eyes, up my nose, in my mouth — the potent, gut-wrenching smell threatening to knock me out.

"Please help me," I beg. This is the most out of control and hopeless I have felt in years. I don't know what to do but lie here and watch them burn.

"'Your 'bloodline' is the reason they didn't get to live," the high-pitched voice laughs, sounding further away.

I can't pull myself back over the edge as I slip further with every strangled breath. Screams and cries from the pit plug my ears, but they're dead. They have to be dead. A small hand reaches up to me, shaking, fighting to escape its fate — the fate I had a part in making. Someone grips my ankles, pushing me over the edge until I am weightless, tumbling down into hell, my stomach flipping into my throat.

When I come to, I'm still standing in the mud puddle I've created on the bank of the river. An area of skin on my stomach is rubbed raw from the now-dissolved soap. My tongue is dryer than ever, the feeling of tight muscles lingering, though I can move with no problem or pain. The smell of burning flesh is a hundred times worse than the school fire.

How does this keep happening? Another person having control over my cognitive and neurological functions makes no sense. I hope this doesn't happen during a fight or when someone else's life is in my hands. If I were normal, the voices, the visions and being so close to finally getting J would terrify me, paralyze me even, but I am far from normal.

"Harley, you can't trust him."

"Get out of my *fucking* head," I yell out loud, crouching down so the fall won't be too far if I decide to black out as I sometimes do. My heart is running a one-hundred-metre sprint against my rib cage as I press my palms against the sides of my head and squeeze my eyes shut.

"Harley." A chilled hand prickles my skin, sending me into the mud as I spring back, getting dirtier than I was prior to my river bath. Johnny stands over me wearing clothes similar to the ones Uri and I wore for the fight, a silver spear in his hand, a sword hanging from his belt.

"What are you going to do with a spear and a sword?" I ask casually, though the words feel like dry clumps of crackers as they slide over my tongue. He stretches his calloused hand to me, not caring that it's covered in mud as he's yanking me to my feet and wiping his hand on my shorts.

"I'll show you," he says, trying to sound mischievous as usual, but I can tell by the way his eyes don't meet mine that he's worried but is too scared to ask what's wrong. He looks from side to side, lifts the spear over his shoulder and in one quick motion, he buries the tip in the bark of a tree fifty feet away.

"You and Rey learned how to do that in that short amount of time?" I gape as he turns proudly toward me.

He frowns, moving to retrieve his weapon. "It's been almost three hours. I was sent down to find you because dinner is in twenty and everyone's still getting ready," he says. I look away, scrubbing my hands in the river and pouring a bucket of water over my head, embarrassed that my vision not only scared me but disoriented me as well. "And I'm only good at this because my gang plays this game where you throw pointy sticks at each other to see who has the fastest reflexes. I got good enough to aim for places that wouldn't cause damage." He moves around me, passing me a towel. He stares at the angry flesh on my side but doesn't linger on the fact that he interrupted my mental breakdown. I catch his hand.

"Johnny, you can't tell Jimmy about what you saw or anyone else, okay? It was nothing."

"It wasn't nothing," he sighs, giving me a crooked smile. "And, honey, my best friend is a fourteen-year-old mad scientist who doesn't just make moonshine — I know how to keep my mouth shut."

"As long as Rey isn't cooking up something dangerous," I tease, knowing he wouldn't tell me if Rey was planning to bomb the Big Three buildings.

"Yeah." His smile stretches to the other side of his mouth, and I think Johnny, with a spear in his hand and a sword by his side, looks the most comfortable I have seen him in a very long time. Still, I don't know how well he can defend himself with those when we are getting fired at from a distance.

"I miss 'em, you know." Johnny sighs, his shoulders slumping as we make our way back to the camp.

"What?" I pull Ace's shirt over my head, deciding to keep it because I'm running low on clothes that don't have holes in them.

"My gang. We may have a bad reputation for being misfits and dysfunctional, but we're family. Also I'm scared they've set the town on fire by now," he jokes, letting out an empty laugh — another pang of guilt seizing my heart.

"I'm sorry," I say, placing my hand on his arm, pulling him closer to my side as we walk.

"No." He puts his arm around my shoulder, hugging me, comforting me. He's warm and smells of dirt and moss. His closeness takes my attention away from the vision. "I didn't mean to make you feel bad. You asked for help and since you basically brought me back to life a year ago, Buckey and I figured this would be a small step toward paying you back." He holds me a bit longer, finding comfort in my strength. My braided hair leaves wet marks on his shirt when he pulls away.

For a long time, I haven't thought about that day. I pushed it to the back of my mind with the other medical miracles Finn and I performed over the years. It was after the Brightly brothers' first attempt at fighting a Big Three gang. Johnny got the worst of it. Someone from the other gang had a knife and stabbed Johnny four times. He lost so much blood that Buckey had to be Johnny's personal blood bag. Johnny wouldn't have made it if that weren't the first time a voice came into my head telling me what to do. I thought it was my own at the time. We lost his pulse twice; the last time, I felt a tugging sensation in my chest and pins and needles in my fingers, like I was giving Johnny a piece of my life. It kept him alive.

"You don't owe me anything," I say, shaking my head. He makes a grunting noise, stopping at the hut entrance, giving my arm a squeeze.

"Jimmy put new clothes on your bed. Come to the armoury when you're done and we'll all go to dinner from there," he smiles slightly, leaving, not interested in having a touchy-feely moment, and I'm grateful for that.

"Thank you," I call after him. He waves me off, running over to where Rey stands behind a barrel, handing out cups of clear liquid. "Great," I mutter, "we'll all be drunk before we leave."

As I get in the hut, I barely make it to the bed before my knees give out and my hands start to shake. *Sort your thoughts*, I tell myself, turning to the wall where one through seven are carved, still with question marks and little lines from where Ace's thoughts start and end. My snake dagger sits beside a neatly folded pile of clothes, the same ones I wore yesterday, patches of blood still on the pants.

Jimmy didn't leave these for me. Até did, as a statement that I am under her command. I close my eyes, the air seeming thinner. The scaly handle makes its way to my hand, helping me carve every idea I've ever had into the crisp wood, knowing anyone could walk in and see it, but I figure, if I can't understand it, then how could anyone else?

I start with the seven's abilities. One obviously is power. Two is healing. Three, future. Four is some type of fighting, battling ability. Five is peace. Six must be intelligence or wisdom, given the sound of its voice. Seven is still a question mark, and for some reason, I have this high-pitched voice who is the creator of the seven and shouldn't be in there at all. He did something that made the seven unable to be killed by power-hungry leaders, a gift that I've inherited. It's the reason I didn't die yesterday. He also wants to destroy the seven, me, and my bloodline, and I dread that he might find a way to succeed.

I know now that the leaders of the Big Three can't hurt me or order anyone to kill me because even if it weren't a leader pulling the trigger, it still would be an act of seeking more power. I don't understand why they need me in their clutches. What are they going to do with me since execution is not on the table? Will they keep me locked up till I wither away from old age? Or wait till starvation, dehydration, and isolation drive me to do the deed myself? I groan in frustration, throwing the dagger at the wall behind me, glaring at the red snake eyes provoking me because I can't figure out the whole picture.

"The seven don't want to tell you everything right now because they are scared you might lose your mind." The squeaky, grinding voice echoes. I want to know everything, but I suppose they're right. I'm losing my mind obsessing over absolutely nothing at the moment when I should be focused on the present task.

I slide into my clothes, finding a long cloak at the bottom of the pile, its fabric black and silken. "J — focus on finding J," I mutter, pulling the dagger from the wall and reaching under the bed for a gun and an extra clip. It takes all my willpower to leave the room and the unsolved problem behind. It sure as hell isn't going anywhere. As I push the thoughts out of my brain, the cloak brushes over my pants, making a swishing noise as I walk, serving as a decent distraction. I like how deep the pockets are and how it doesn't hold in much heat. Even though the air is chilled, the hot desert feeling hasn't left my skin yet. The vision and the thoughts are harder to dissolve than usual, but I manage to dull them by thinking of Jimmy — his floppy hair, tanned skin, the scar above his eyebrow and his goofy smile that makes his teeth sparkle in the sunlight.

As I get closer to the arguing and joyful voices, a small bonfire comes into focus. It crackles in the middle of the open area, somehow giving off very little smoke as it burns. People sway and slur their words as they share food and drink and laughter, occasionally spilling the contents of their drinks on one another, yelling until they have forgotten why they were mad. Sometimes Rey amazes me. He's managed to get half of the population here drunk without Até intervening because he still stands behind the barrel doling out liquid to eager hands.

"Rey, if you're drunk, you're not joining us," I say, folding my arms over my chest, trying not to laugh. He throws his hands up, taking a couple of over-exaggerated steps back.

"Don't worry, boss, the number one rule is to never drink the product," he says with a wink, chuckling like the rest of the gang as they emerge from the armoury. They almost look like trained Hunters in their semi-matching outfits. Tequila and I are the only ones in cloaks. The gang is armed with handguns and knives, except Johnny with his spear, Tequila with a bow, and Jimmy with a sniper rifle that is way too noticeable to carry through the streets.

"How?" I start to ask.

"You can use the scope from the rooftop to see if we have company in the windows," Jimmy says, handing it to me. The black shirt he wears gives him a colder, more mysterious appearance, surprisingly handsome. The rifle's not heavy, not too different from a handgun, but I have never shot one before.

"And I'll rig it so it clips on to a strap and conceals itself in the coat. Like so," Tequila says, opening the side of her coat to reveal a wiry, fabric contraption strapped around her waist, a similar rifle dangling from her side. The whole thing doesn't look too pretty, but I know it has a lot more to it. I didn't even notice she had anything on her.

"Beautiful job as always," I say, leaning the rifle against the inside of the hut, the gun leaving an iron smell on my fingers.

"Ms. Harley," a nasally voice yells. Asteroid runs at full speed toward us, knocking over literally everyone he passes, while his glasses slide further down his nose.

"Well, that's a sign for dinner," Buckey chuckles, leading Tequila to a wide table where heaps of sweet potatoes, carrots, cabbage and slabs of meat lie. Steam rises from the foods, the faint breeze carrying the rich, savoury scent around us. My stomach begs me to move toward the table, wanting anything other than itself to eat — but I wait, grabbing both Jimmy and Ace's arms. Luke skulks behind us and forces a smile as Asteroid skids to a stop.

"I have the information on the prison," he says between breaths, pushing the sweat from his forehead into his greasy hair.

"Let's get food and we can talk while we eat," I offer, almost drifting toward the aroma, not waiting for his answer. I know I should show more gratitude toward him, but at the moment, it's not something I can help.

Everyone piles as many veggies as they want on their plate, but we're only allowed two slabs of meat, which isn't a problem because each cut is bigger than my hand. Ace bumps me with his elbow, grinning, both of us almost giddy from hunger. I've been hungry before, always giving my food to J or the sick people on the streets, keeping enough for myself to stay fueled, but I have never not eaten for almost two days. That, on top of running across town, taking a beating and having that vision, makes my stomach beyond the point of hollowness. We squeeze onto splintery logs, far enough from the fire that the heat doesn't irritate Jimmy's and my skin. With no fancy cutlery, just misshapen wooden plates, I shovel in the food with my fingers. Jimmy's hand moves to my thigh, urging me to slow down, but even when he realizes that won't happen, he keeps it there, forcing himself to eat with his left hand, a lot of the food landing on his shirt rather than in his mouth.

"Okay, this is what I found," Asteroid says, squeezing between Ace and me, with no dinner in his hands. "The prison is where they keep what they call 'not so VIP' prisoners. Not important enough to keep in the secret prison but too important to keep in the local one."

"Don't we know this already?" Luke grunts, dragging his food around his plate, propping his head up with his hand. An assortment of knives is strapped to his chest, his appearance reserved and closed off.

"Let him talk," I say, trying to recall what he claims we know about the VIP prison. When his eyes meet mine, the guilt sparkling in them with the firelight startles me, his focus quickly falling back to his mushy food.

"It has two entrances at either end of the section. Two ways in, two ways out. All guarded by three Hunters, with two extras in the middle patrolling the prisoners, who are on either side of the hall."

"Cameras?" I ask, looking at Uri, making sure he's paying attention because I am getting more anxious as the information is piled on to us. I can tell by the change in atmosphere, the same goes for everyone else.

"We have people on the inside. They say the stairs have none, but every inch of the prison section does, not one blind spot," Asteroid states, showing me his scribbled drawing. He looks at us with wild, intelligent eyes. His black clothing is that of a neat and tidy person, but his smudged glasses and the blue tie around his neck say otherwise.

"Since one of Até's men on the inside is letting us in and disabling the alarm system for a couple minutes, that means as soon as we reach the prison floor the Hunters will see us on surveillance?" Jimmy asks, leaning closer, his hair smelling of grass and river, the slightest scent of grapefruit still lingering on his skin. Tequila raises her eyebrows, silently asking me if she has to remove Jimmy from my side. I fight down a round of bubbling laughter in my throat as I shake my head.

"Supposedly, yes, but if one or two of our inside people can get into the surveillance room seconds before we reach the floor then we should gain ten extra minutes because they would be the only ones watching the cameras. I acknowledge that is a big if," Asteroid shrugs, wiping his glasses on his tie, making them impossible to see through. I lift the last mouthful of food to my lips just as someone taps my shoulder, startling me and causing Jimmy to spring to his feet, dumping his plate onto the ground.

"Whoa kiddo, only here to tell you it's time to go." I get to my feet and fling myself into Malick's arms, overcome with relief that they were able to patch him up. "Glad we feel the same way about each other's health," he laughs, his words ruffling against my ear, his muscular arms pinching my side as he sets me down. I blush a little when I realize how out of character that was for me and that Jimmy is pursing his lips at my side. Uri moves to Malick, patting him on the back.

"No hard feelings," Uri offers.

"None at all, and Jasper says the same," Malick says, shaking Uri's hand and ignoring the rest of the gang's burning stares as they size him up.

"Ready?" he asks, pulling me forward. He keeps his easy demeanour, not waiting for the gang to introduce themselves. I suppose Até gave him that information already. I run over to the armoury, grab the rifle, and allow Tequila to strap it to my side, tying a string around the barrel so it can't swing freely against my leg. It serves as a kind of crutch as I run back to Malick.

"Ready!" The rifle's weight plus the dagger and the handgun don't affect me one bit; everything safely hidden under the coat. I feel stronger but keep waiting for helplessness and fatigue to bury me like in the vision.

A couple feet away, Até, Anna and Em, I think the guard's name is, stand around stacked-up crates. Até doesn't acknowledge us when we gather around, and Anna greets me with an awkward held-back smile. I move beside Jimmy out of habit and feel his hand slip into mine, and as much as I'm not completely happy with him, I'm grateful for the calming effect he has on my nerves.

"Okay, this is how it's going to go," Até barks, moving so we can see the map. Her hair lies loosely on her shoulders, something like makeup covering her tattoo, and for the first time, she isn't wearing her wolf skin, instead matching me by wearing a long cloak. "Four guards are waiting at the tree line. The rest of you will be stationed with them, either on the ground watching the streets or on a platform in the trees, watching the buildings." She focuses her glare at Rey and Johnny. "Do not leave the tree line or make any noise above a whisper. To ensure that you follow my wishes you both will have your own guards, Liam and Eddy, and you will be stationed at opposite ends to put the most distance possible between you two."

"What did we do?" Johnny protests.

"When you were meant to be picking your weapons from the armoury, you decided to fool around and damage three guns. On top of that you managed to get the majority of my people drunk when you decided to make moonshine," she growls, her blue eyes piercing holes into their skin, "And there's probably more that I haven't heard about yet."

"Yep, that is completely fair, your majesty," Rey says, cowering in a sarcastic way.

"Our two groups will move up these two streets and climb onto these two buildings." She points to medium-sized apartment buildings that look directly at the portions of the prison where the glass isn't one-way. "These streets have the lowest number of Hunters but have gang fights on every other alley. Do not engage with the people and blend in as best you can."

"And if they engage with us?" Ace asks, counting his fingers.

"Then you'd better be a fast runner or a very skilled fighter." She smirks, folding the map and handing it to Malick, who slips it in his jacket, fixing his stare at me, looking almost protective. Asteroid, already sweating through his black shirt, gives the boys grey and green jackets.

"Here are your walkies." Finn hands one to Ace, Luke and Uri, clipping the other to his pants pocket. He looks somewhat relieved that he gets to stay behind. "See you when you get back," he says, doing his handshake with Rey and hugging me tightly.

"Learn something new while we're gone." I kiss his cheek, and he blushes, walking away with Anna.

"And take a nap. You look about fifty years older than you should," Rey laughs, running forward.

"Ten years better than Harley," Johnny adds, he and Rey getting all their kinetic energy out before they have to be completely still for who knows how long.

"Let's move out," Até orders, leading us through the trees, leaving the camp behind.

CHAPTER 21
(HARLEY)

The little light we had seeping through the holes in the foliage disappears, the sun setting as night falls across the horizon. Dampness clings to the air, threatening rain even as the temperature drops. Uri's heavy, weary breaths are expelled faster than my own, curling into smoke as they touch the gentle frosty winds. He shouldn't have come. I should have ordered him to stay back and listen from afar like Finn, but he wouldn't allow that for obvious reasons. He groans with every forceful step, holding his ribs, refusing to let anyone help him. I flinch every time he steps over a fallen log, trudges through the rapidly flowing river or gets scolded by Até for being annoying.

"A couple more minutes, kiddo," Malick encourages, dropping back to walk at my pace.

"You said that twenty minutes ago," Uri grumbles, echoing my thoughts. His pupils are dilated, a sheen of sweat drenching him. I wish I could give him my strength. Watching him in this much pain is killing me.

"You know she doesn't hate you," Malick whispers, bumping into my shoulder. His expression is solid and serious, throwing me off guard for a step. I frown at him, his steady smile truthful, the scar over the brim of his nose and the blossomed bruise under his chin reminding me he's not the type of person to play games. It must seem unfair that Uri, Malick and

Jasper all have injuries and scars from that fight while I go unscathed, but it doesn't appear to bother him.

"No?" I question, watching Jimmy volley ideas back and forth with Tequila, most likely talking tech because Tequila's cheeks are red with frustration. Jimmy doesn't understand machines the way she does.

"No. Até respects you a little, admires you even, but it's not easy for her to make allies." His voice is soothing, talking about Até like he is her mentor, proud to be as the edges of his mouth curl up with every word. I don't feel sorry for Até though, for not having the ability to play nice. She is the second person to show me this type of hatred, the other being Eric, and I would never have respect for a person like that.

"Well, stabbing someone in the arm doesn't scream, 'let's be a team.'"

His breathy laugh eases me. "You are very right, but, like her, I suspect you know, appearing okay and tougher than everyone around you helps you put up a shield so you are less likely to get hurt. It's easier than letting someone in and giving them a chance to show that they are trustworthy."

"You figured that out from the small details I've told you?" I ask, shoving my hands into my coat pockets, nervous that someone else will get close to me and potentially get hurt.

I notice the birds ruffling their nests and animals hunkering down for the night while nocturnal ones hoot and chatter in the dark. I allow the sounds to pull me from a conversation I don't want to have. Rey snatches night vision goggles from Asteroid's bag, weaving around trees, popping up and scaring Johnny. He becomes too cocky, pedalling backwards and slamming into Até's back. She grabs Rey's arm, flipping him to the ground. Silent chuckles ripple through the group as Johnny pulls Rey to his feet, slapping the back of his head.

"You should stop bugging her before she breaks a bone," Jimmy says, a faint smirk shining through the darkness. He pulls Rey's goggles off his face then lets go, releasing them onto Rey's nose.

"Oh, but, young student of mine, everyone knows that when a girl knocks the wind right out of your lungs it is an act of love," Rey swoons, dusting himself off and quickly going back to running aimlessly through the darkness, occasionally losing his footing and slamming into the ground.

"Then Harley must really love me," Jimmy remarks, walking back to Tequila, whose hand is locked with Buckey's. I wait for Luke to make a sarcastic comment, but he stays quiet; he's been so quiet I'm not sure if he is still with us.

"I can tell by the way your friends treat you and how you treat the people around you," Malick says, startling me. I forgot he was beside me. He moves so effortlessly over the crunchy earth that his tread hardly makes a sound. "You aren't as drastic as Até, but when you meet someone for the first time you are closed off until they show you they are trustworthy. As you did to Jasper and me. Your friends always look to you first, wait for you to speak, like you hold all the answers. They see you as their toughest warrior, their most valuable asset because you know how to make them feel strong even when they are weak." He pulls out a small wooden carving, a circle with a howling wolf in the centre. He rubs his thumb over the smooth surface, handing it to me. It's tiny, fitting in the middle of my palm. He pulls his necklace from his shirt, revealing he has the same one. "Jasper and I thought you should have this. It is a symbol of the guard. The protectors of the pack."

"Thank you," I say, no other words coming to my mind. Malick has made me a part of his community. He thinks that I am good enough to be one of them.

"We don't expect you to join us. I know you have your own pack, and your loyalty lies with them — that is also why Até fights you so much. She is the Alpha of her pack and you are the Alpha of yours. Your appearance has threatened her position of power. You both would kill to protect your people, but the biggest difference in your leadership is that your pack found you. It was formed through a bond, whereas hers was passed to her because it was her duty to take on the responsibility of leadership. She is afraid you will take that from her."

"But I don't want her power," I say, his words hitting me out of nowhere. I've never viewed my gang as a pack where I am the Alpha. I don't control them; we see each other as equals, and I don't consider my presence as a threat to Até's leadership.

"People follow rulers more easily if they are not greedy for power," the dominant, important voice points out. I know what Malick and the dominant voice mean.

When Até challenged me at the fight because I had won, I backed down and allowed her to have power over me if she wanted it. Her people saw how close she was to killing me for control. Até saw how much that scared them and how much they valued my life.

"I know that, and she knows that, but it doesn't mean she won't be worried about losing something she almost died for — my point is, Até is not only tough and cruel, but she is young like you and scared because you, my friend, have the ability to win people over without much effort." He squeezes the back of my neck, walking over to Até, who is tense as she speed-walks to the five figures ahead.

I don't know what to make of what Malick said. Either it was a warning to watch my back because Até would kill to be in control, or he was trying to get me to see that a person always has a reason for the way they act, and her reason is fear. Fear of losing power.

"He's right, you know," Ace says, flinging his walkie talkie into the air, trying to catch it behind his back. I shove the carving into my pocket, hiding the shock on my face. It's annoying how good Ace is at maneuvering to eavesdrop on personal conversations.

"Yeah," I mutter, thankful that we are at the tree line, and I will have something chaotic to distract myself with.

Waiting for us are five guards dressed in outfits similar to ours. Two burly men, one with tattoos on the side of his face and the other with a large ring in the middle of his nose, stand beside three fierce-looking women, all with floppy hoods covering their heads and coats most likely covering extra weapons. They don't reveal their faces or speak as we come to a stop.

They stay motionless, hands remaining behind their backs as they wait for their commands.

"Rey with Eddy, Johnny with Liam." Até points. The one named Eddy is twice Rey's size and looks like he crushes rocks with his bare hands in his spare time. "Eddy to the left on the tree platform and Liam to the right on the other." Malick hands his bow and arrows to Eddy, who shoulders them and grabs Rey, dragging him away.

"If you don't see me again, I was eaten," he squeaks, digging his heels into the ground and disappearing into the darkness.

"I forgot to mention I'm scared of heights," Johnny mutters, trying to move slowly away from Liam, who has a tattoo of a smiling teddy bear on his neck. Liam grunts, grabbing Johnny by the hood and pulling him away. "You're right, I'm not — just scared of you," Johnny's voice echoes in the distance. Buckey bites his fist, holding back laughter at his brother's expense.

"Uri, Buckey, Tequila, you're with the girls, they'll tell you where you're stationed. Uri, you will have to be further back so your voice and the walkie's sound don't carry." Até takes the knives out of her coat pockets, stuffing them in her boots and pants, loading her gun and tucking it in her right top pocket.

"Tequila, if you can't sit still go to Uri and move around — here," I interrupt, passing her a long piece of wire. Not much, but it will keep her hands busy. Tequila thanks me, checking my strapped-in rifle one last time before they move away, scattering throughout the tree line, blending with the leaves effortlessly. "Okay, let's group up," I say. Malick, Luke and Em move to Até. Ace and Jimmy move to me as well as Asteroid, who smacks his face against my arm, too busy staring at the map. He's distracting himself from the fact that he's walking right back into the nightmare he was banished from.

"Luke will walkie you when we get to the roof and when we are set to leave. Remember, don't engage with the people." Até pulls her hood up, moving her hair to the front, covering most of her face. I pull my hood up, scolding myself for deciding to keep the braid, but maybe this way, people won't recognize me as fast. In the wanted poster, my hair was down.

"You're fooling yourself," the wise voice scoffs. I can feel her rolling her eyes and looking down at me with disapproval.

"Yeah, yeah. I know. Humor me, will you?" I think.

"No."

"Ready?" Até asks, shaking me out of my thoughts. She holds her hand out to me. I hesitate, wondering if she'll grab me and flip me, but I'm loaded with bullets and two guns, so that wouldn't be her smartest move. I take it, squeezing as hard as she does.

"Ready," I confirm, and we move out of the tree line. Leaves sweep over my face as we step into an alley dusted and broken from time, old cars and unwanted items piled in one corner. Luke gives me one last sad look before we branch off, moving down neighbouring streets.

The city is much more compact than I had imagined. From blocks away, you can see groups of people, and even from this distance, the entrance to AC's building is small but visible.

Asteroid tells me that the Big Three cities are actually one city separated into sections so the brothers won't kill each other, ruling as one.

"Uri, why didn't you tell us the Big Three was one city," Ace asks through the walkie as we step out of the alley.

"Honestly, I thought you saying 'cities' was just a figure of speech," Ace scoffs at Uri's reply.

I feel dumbfounded for not knowing this obvious fact. No one ever told us the Big Three were different cities, but I suppose it's implied in the name. It was also implied that the Big Three were better and more luxurious than the towns, but the dim light casts ugly shadows on the houses, the street lamps either flickering or smashed in, their glass scattered on the potholed, cracked cement. The apartment buildings and houses look almost the same as the ones in The Sticks. The windows are cracked, their shutters holding on to the frames with one hinge.

The further we move into the city, the nicer the atmosphere becomes, and the more technology appears on the upgraded buildings. Solar panels reflect neon signs, and floating billboards hang in the air, flashing 'Respect us and we will respect you.' Ironic, given the amount of garbage scattered over the streets, spray paint curling around walls and shoes hanging from the electrical wires between apartments. At the heart of the city are the three identical glass skyscrapers, large spotlights making them glow and shimmer. You can see the tops of them over the trees in The Sticks, but I never knew how wide and tall they were until standing only blocks away.

I feel like a kid seeing the world for the first time, intrigued by anything and everything that moves. Unfortunately, I don't have much time to take in the idea of it all. Five minutes in, we run into hordes of people. Sounds of flesh hitting flesh, metal hitting cement and enthusiastic cheers sing in the alleys. People ranging from young to middle age break bottles over each other's heads, using knives and chains to beat already unconscious people sprawled across the ground. Bystanders watch from broken down rusted cars and metal crates, holding out money to bet on outcomes, calling for more blood. For death.

"This is disgusting," Ace mutters, tucking his walkie into his sleeve, relaying back to Uri the number of people, how many steps we've taken and how many buildings look empty.

"Not all sunshine and rainbows," Jimmy agrees, raking his fingers through his hair. He moves his other hand to his pocket, securely grasping the handle of his gun.

I say nothing — no words popping into my head to help me describe the scene playing out in front of me. Everyone in the towns grew up wishing to live where the houses were big and shiny, food always filled the cupboards, and Hunters paid little attention to you. It was all propaganda, to make the towns fight to be in the Big Three's good graces, doing their dirty work for a chance to live a better life.

It's clearly a lie as I see children curled up against walls, their cheeks caved in, eyes motionless. People look half-starved from never having enough, or filled out and nourished from stealing from anyone weaker than themselves. Although they may not have Hunters following their shadows all the time, they have their neighbours, friends and even gang members, who would jump at the chance to beat someone up.

"Is it like this everywhere?" My words are barely audible against the yelling. I look at Asteroid, whose eyes are trained on his shoes, zipping his jacket to hide the sky-blue tie.

"Yes, but the further you move in, the fewer fights there are. Mostly, government workers and Hunters live in that area. The gangs that do live there, however, are the cruelest, richest and the ones that fight in the stadium. They're the top picks of the leaders and their entertainment." His voice dies off as more people swarm around us.

Some snarl, empty bottles swaying in their hands, but most let us pass easily, ignoring our presence. We are all dressed the same as the people here, women wearing cloaks, men in jackets, same pants and shirts underneath. We try to copy their movements, chests puffed out, arms swinging, faces cold, attempting to look meaner and stronger than the person next to them, grunting as unwelcome gangs pass by. It serves as a warning shield for the bigger kids, warding off challengers, but for the twiggy, smaller ones, it puts a target on their back.

There are no rules in place, like the ones in our Warehouse. Anyone is free to challenge whoever they want, even if it is not their night to fight. We pass the injured who are just left on the streets propped against apartment walls, fires from trash cans keeping them warm. A handful of healers rush around the seemingly endless clusters of patients. They whisper reassurances that they will make it to sunrise, and for those too far gone, they give a shot of painkillers and murmur a final goodbye.

"If Finn were here, we would have lost him two minutes ago," Jimmy mutters, dodging bodies and shielding me from catcalling strangers, but I can't hear them. All I hear are the cries and groans of the dying.

How could the Big Three let this happen? Hundreds of people must die every day if this is what it's like in all three sections. Suddenly, I'm grateful to my dad for having the smarts to leave. I don't even want to think about the type of person I'd be if I grew up here.

I scan the faces around me, noticing the fervour that burns through them. They are raised to think this is right, fun, the only way of surviving in a place that would eat you alive. I remember Até warning to keep our heads down, when green eyes lock with mine, and too late, I look away from the boy. I pick up the pace, shoving my hands into my coat pockets, trying to blend.

"Turn it off." I nudge Ace, feeling the boy's eyes following us. Ace shuts the walkie off without question, not looking shocked or scared. He keeps his steady stride, swinging his arms at his side. I turn to tell Jimmy that I've blown our cover when a deep voice calls after us.

"Hey, what gang you with?"

My heartbeat quickens as I hear footsteps running toward us. Shuffling and misplaced steps tell me the boy and whoever he's with aren't completely sober.

"Keep moving," Jimmy whispers, pushing Asteroid to the front, keeping him far enough from what's to come.

"Hey, pretty lady, I'm talking to you." The distinct sound of a bullet sliding into place clicks behind us, stopping me in my tracks. Jimmy reaches for my arm, but I push it aside, not wanting to show my connection to him.

"Oh, you were talking to me?" I chirp, spinning toward them, making myself sound clueless and innocent. "It's hard to tell with all this noise. Ya know?"

The green-eyed boy is heavily tattooed, his hair buzzed to his skin, giving it a different shade from his eyebrows. His curled smile and the slash across his eye make the gun seem more threatening than it is. "Answer my question," he presses, voice teasing, purring as he steps closer to me, swaying.

Two boys appear at his side. The first one is like the green-eyed boy holding the gun. He's happy he has a new person to threaten, but the second seems timid, begging me to stay calm, to do as his boss says, as though he watches people go through this all the time and is tired of it.

"I'm sorry, love, but I didn't hear your question." I plaster on my best smile, giggling like the girls back home when they're trying to get a boy to like them. His gun drops an inch, touching my collar bone while Ace and Jimmy shift at my side. I shake my head slightly, signaling them to back down, and reluctantly they do.

"I asked what gang you were from, because I'm certain if you were from here I wouldn't forget a face like yours." He drags the cold barrel up to my chin. If he's relatively sober and looks too close, he might start putting the pieces together and connect me to the wanted posters.

"But you have seen me around, because I remember you," I say, lifting my hand to the metal and slowly moving it away from me, keeping my bubbly appearance and hoping his men don't come to his aid. By the look of the second boy, I know he won't help kill me.

The green-eyed boy moves closer to my face. He cocks his head, confused as to why he's letting me push the gun toward him.

"I said I'd remember a pretty face like yours." He moves his other hand to my side, just missing the end of the rifle. I grab it, then bat my eyes, recovering by placing his rough palm to my cheek. Jimmy takes a step toward me, but Ace moves to his side, stepping in front of him, shielding me from the crowd on my left side.

"Shall I remind you?" I bring my lips to his ear, lightheaded and disgusted by his perfume of stale liquor and blood. The second boy smirks approvingly, turning away to find another kid to torment, but the third stays, his brown eyes staring me down. I guide the green-eyed boy's hand to my pants pocket. He releases a heavy exhale making my face scrunch up, and my body physically recoils. He's about to try something that would earn him a broken nose, but he freezes when his hand touches metal. "This is my dagger, freshly sharpened last time I checked." He pulls back, but I grip harder, running his fingers over the scales then guiding it down.

"What the—"

"And this is my gun, pretty thing and fully loaded. The men beside me have one too, and they've been itching for target practice — oh, and this." I grip his gun hand as he becomes distracted with trying to break free, blocking the trigger with my thumb and index finger. I press the barrel to his side. He freezes, holding his breath, sweat ripening his smell. "This is your gun, pressed to where I know I have a clear shot at your heart. And I'm not known for missing." I pull back, hating myself for doing this, but I had no other choice. I giggle, pretending like he told me something worthy of a laugh. The second boy continues to stare, not moving to help as recognition flashes across his face.

"Okay," green eyes says, his chest shaking as he stutters, eyes glossing over, not so tough when the bullet is pointed in his direction.

"Now go back to your drinking and forget about us. Don't think about telling your friends, because I have connections and you may not know me, but I know you."

"No, you don't," he complains, gaining the grip back on his gun, but he seems unsure whether to believe me or not. I look to the second boy, hoping my assessment of his loyalty toward his gang leader is right. His brown eyes memorize every inch of my face, and I feel my hand start to lose control of the gun, the gap between the barrel and the boy's chest widening. I'm seconds from abandoning this stupid plan of mine when the boy mouths the words, 'Jared Megreger.'

"You could find out the hard way and have every Hunter at your door by morning, Jared Megreger, or you could be a smart boy and listen to me," I say, his grip leaving the gun altogether. I step back, Jared's eyes bugging as he quivers. He nods quickly, gesturing to the boy to follow him, but he stops.

"Can I have my gun?" Jared turns back, a scared little boy replacing the tough guy that challenged me.

"Of course." I remove the clip, placing it beside the one in my pocket, emptying the chamber and tossing the gun at his feet. He picks it up, puffing his chest out and rolling his sleeves before he hurries off. I mouth, 'thank you,' to the second boy before they both disappear into the crowd.

I move forward, having no emotions about what I did. Ace walks backward, making sure Jared doesn't come back with an army, but I know he won't. The second boy will make sure of that. I cringe because I think I set women back a thousand years and degraded myself in ten different ways. Awesome.

"That boy who stayed by Jared knew who I was and didn't say anything," I exhale, feeling an unpleasant sensation in my chest almost like joy, triumph.

"Why?" Jimmy asks, moving closer to me. I shrug, unsure why the boy wouldn't give me up, if not to help his friend, then for the reward.

"I'm sorry," I whisper, grasping Jimmy's hand tightly, knowing he had to stand there and watch me do that.

"I knew what you were doing — I wanted to rip his fucking head off but I knew you had it covered." He checks over his shoulder. "I'm sorry, now I know how you felt at the river. You should be way more hateful toward me," he squeezes my hand, letting go to switch spots with Ace so he can continue feeding information through the walkie.

"Well, the day's not over," I tease, steadying my heart as he lets out a real laugh that helps me breathe. *Focus*, I think, resting my hand on Asteroid's shoulder. "You okay?" I ask as he loosens his tie.

"Yeah, I thought him coming over was my fault because maybe he recognized me or something, but no one ever does." His shoulders slump forward, his hand making a fist crumpling his map, the other tightening around his gun handle.

"I will." I rest my arm over his shoulders, "I picked you because of the impression you made. It's one that I won't forget." He nods, wiping under his eyes. I feel bad for putting him in this situation, but I know he's important, and he'll be stronger because of it. "You okay?" I repeat, squeezing his shoulders. He straightens, unwrinkling his map with a new determination and purpose in his walk.

"Yeah — and that was the coolest and most subtle way of disarming someone I've ever seen. I think he wet his pants." He looks up at me, curious, his blue eyes foggy through his glasses, "How did you know he wouldn't shoot, or that he's not going to tell?"

"Intuition — I'm good at reading people."

"Yeah, It's pretty annoying, especially when you're trying to surprise her," Jimmy adds, moving back to my side.

The gangs turn to specks in the distance as we reach our building. The rails of the ladder leading up to the roof sting my fingers as we climb — frost wrapping around the metal, sparkling, so simple and peaceful. The city unravels all around us, a maze of flat-topped and slanted roofs, the grey and brown tiles spotted with moss, left to weather and cave in. Light from small fires brightens the landscape, highlighting the alleys where people continue to fight. The rest of the streets are empty, except for the stragglers running home or crowding around a popular fight. Clouds hang overhead, boxing us in, showing how trapped and ignored we are.

We stretch out on the scratchy, dark grey surface. Ace is already starting to shiver as he becomes still, and it will only get colder as the night goes on. I unstrap the rifle from my side, the metal warmed by my body, and prop it on the ledge, adjusting the scope to point directly at the middle strip of glass that isn't one way.

"Luke says they're on the roof," Ace chatters, pulling his knees to his chest. This kid could bask in the sun all day without breaking a sweat, but when the air begins to chill only slightly, he acts as if he might freeze to death. I peel off my jacket, balling it up and tossing it at his face, leaving me in a thin shirt. Ace tries to object but already has his hands through the sleeves. Jimmy presses closer, lending me his warmth.

"Won't they be able to see us?" I ask, spotting the two Hunters in the window, taser-like guns in their hands.

"Well, if they look hard enough, yes, but we blend in relatively well. The lights shining on the buildings make it harder to see out and we've done this for years and haven't been caught. Plus the Hunters in there have bigger things to worry about than what lurks on the streets." Asteroid rests his back against an air filtration unit in the middle of the roof, scribbling on his map, fidgeting with his tie.

"Do you see anything in the neighbouring windows?" Jimmy asks, his voice hushed as the streets grow louder. He carves his initials into the ledge, already losing interest with nothing to occupy him. Asteroid tosses night vision goggles at him.

"What are these going to do besides help me see in the dark?"

"I tweaked them so you can use them like the scope on Harley's rifle." Asteroid hands a pair to Ace, who is currently counting the number of windows that aren't one-way. I can feel Uri groaning, hunkering down for a long night. Uri can't tell Ace to speak with less detail because, mentally, Ace can't do that, and if he does, he might start stressing out and shut down altogether.

"So, I didn't need to carry this?" I complain, gesturing to my rifle.

"We need you to protect us," Jimmy smiles, the goggles making him look like a bug as he scans the apartment windows. "Wait, so if they see us, we'll be sitting ducks?" he guesses, pressing himself further into the tiles.

"Yes," Asteroid agrees almost cheerfully.

"Great."

"Ms. Harley, what kind of weapons do the Hunters have?" I adjust the scope, making the image less grainy, waiting for the Hunters to pass by.

"They look like taser guns or batons maybe, I've seen the Hunters use them a couple of times back home," I explain. Ace echoes my words, his voice a little warmer now.

"Interesting," Asteroid mutters, recording my findings. Every two minutes, the Hunters pass by the middle window, either straight-faced or telling a joke to their partner, switching places with the Hunters at the entrances every so often.

"Do they switch the types of weapons they carry?" Ace asks, pulling the walkie out of his sleeve, cupping it in his hands like a heater, holding it inches from his face.

"Occasionally, yes, but they mostly use tasers, sometimes paintball guns when they want to have fun," Asteroid says, so dryly it unnerves me.

I scan the line of windows, wondering if the prisoners can see out or if something is blocking their view, or if they have to sit there watching the leaves change colour, the sunrise and fall, and the people going about their day so oblivious of the pain behind the shiny pieces of glass.

"Being prisoner in there — it would be torture," Jimmy whispers, finishing my thought. He removes the goggles, putting a warm protective arm across my back, making it hard to position myself comfortably while looking through the scope, but I don't make him move.

We relay information back and forth. How often the Hunters switch posts, how many people tend to lurk around AC's building entrance, only to get shooed off and occasionally beaten when they don't leave quickly enough. To pass time, we toss scenarios in the air, trying to solve them, but the hours drag on. The metal rifle absorbs all the cold, my fingers becoming so numb that I have to hold them in my armpits. Our joints stiffen, no one having the voice to complain while we watch a prison full of tortured people who could be innocent.

The longer we sit, the bigger the unsettling feeling in my chest grows. Ace's voice no longer breaks through the angry shouts below as he runs out of things to say. The Hunters begin to move slower as well, taking five minutes to reach the middle rather than two, and I swear their stares turn to us every so often as they move past. Jimmy becomes restless, shaking his arms and legs, waking them up.

"We should—" My voice dies in the air as two Hunters drag a figure to the middle piece of glass, kicking the backs of the boy's legs, forcing him to his knees. Bloody hands press to the window, leaving streaks on the clear glass. I don't want to look into the scope, but I force myself to, a small cry of pain exhaling from my body as filthy blonde hair comes into focus. I see cuts along his face, one eye puffy and bruised, his glasses absent from his hollow, pale face.

"J," Jimmy breathes, his voice hoarse and weak as he watches, helpless and paralyzed like me. Ace moves to my side to see what makes my heart stop, shatter, cry and burn with anger all at once. "He's doing something with his hand," Jimmy whispers, copying the way J's finger taps slightly against the window, appearing as a nervous twitch to the Hunters, but to Jimmy and me, it's Morse Code. Jimmy and I took a class on it for fun to have a way of communicating with no one understanding, but it turned into my way of checking on J through the wall when we were trapped in our rooms. "R–U–N," Jimmy deciphers, hurrying to pack up his things, yelling at Ace and Asteroid to move and relaying the information to Luke.

I don't twitch or breathe, my eyes staying fixed on J. I take in his possible broken nose, long burn marks on his arm, blood and rips in his clothes. His finger taps out, 'I love you.' Stray tears run down my cheeks as I lose myself in the pain, my longing to hold him in my arms and to hear his gentle laugh before I find the courage to tap out, 'I'm sorry. I love you.' Because I need him to know, even though he can't see it.

Then quickly, I grab my coat from Ace and clip my rifle to my side. Jimmy urges me forward. I reach the edge of the roof, peering down at the ten-story drop, when a ripping, nail on chalkboard sensation screeches deep in my brain.

I clasp my hands over my ears, biting down on my tongue and fighting to stay balanced as images of blood pooling on granite and streaking the floor where J was dragged to his cell, and Hunters readying massive guns on a roof flash all around me. When I realize it's a vision of what will happen seconds from now, I panic, shoving Ace and Jimmy forward, forcing them onto the ladder, nearly making them fall. Asteroid's already safely on the ground, peering around the wall of the building. I swing myself over the ledge, my hand hitting the second rung when the first wave of bullets showers the roof — both roofs.

CHAPTER 22

(HARLEY)

Bullets spray the rooftop, sounding like rain pattering against my house when the nights are noiseless. Confused screams pack the empty spaces in the building as people wake to bullets stabbing through their ceilings. Ace and Jimmy hit the ground, moving to where Asteroid stands, huddling around the map, devising a plan on the go.

The second wave is released, aimed now at the bricks, loosening them and shattering the windows. I keep my head down, letting the shards of glass scratch my skin, the sensation only stinging. My foot reaches the third-to-last rung when a stray bullet slams into my calf, the force throwing me off balance. My tailbone takes the full force of my fall, screaming-hot pain vibrating up to my chest, disappearing as soon as Jimmy pulls me up.

"You're okay," he tells me, looking at the hole in the back of my pants for a second before remembering we're getting shot at and pushing Ace and Asteroid forward.

I bring up the rear, using my body as a shield. I'm the only one who can't die in this attack, I hope. I don't have time to wrap the wound to prevent leaving a blood trail, but I can already feel the healing tissue moulding around the bullet. Asteroid veers to the right down a side alley, taking us to the street Luke should be on. We weave through the panicking people running in every direction and those who calmly remained in place, watching the ongoing fights as if this is an everyday occurrence. The panic serves as a good diversion, to give us an excuse to run toward the trees. A final round of bullets pops in the distance, most likely killing innocent people on the first couple of floors, dead because of me. So many dead because of me.

Through the chaos, I get separated from the group. Jimmy's fluffy hair is taken by the current. A whirlpool of limbs carries me in the other direction, trapping me as I hit them with my elbows, but there are too many to go against. They begin to pull me to the ground as people stomp on my feet. Then hands grab the back of my shirt and push me forward, and when I look behind me, Luke's blond hair flops as he runs. Até and Malick shove people away from us. Em's right behind them.

Blood streams down Até's face from a gash in her hairline, spilling into her eye, and by the look of Em's limp, I think she was shot, but other than that, everyone's okay. Relief washes over me, as much relief as I can allow myself to have. Luke yanks me down a different alley where Jimmy, Ace and Asteroid wait.

"Oh thank fuck," Jimmy blurts, cupping my face in his hands, relieved even though we aren't out yet. Then he makes us press against the wall as anxious bodies sprint by. I feel so disoriented, as if everyone is doing my job for me. My mind is so full — my thoughts are in disarray.

"Wait here." Até holds a fist up, moving into the open area, stopping at a pile of forgotten objects before slowly proceeding to where Buckey stands. "Clear."

One at a time, we move into the open area. Malick goes first, pulling Asteroid along with him, his face as pale as milk and his legs shaking. I make everyone else go ahead while Em and I point our guns down the alley where people and Hunters chase each other. They run past, not noticing anything other than the people in front of them.

"Let's go," Em says as Luke makes it safely across the open area. This is the first time I've heard her speak, her voice gentle and youthful. It's the first time I've gotten a good look at her without other people to focus on. Auburn hair sits in ringlets reaching below her small ears, a button nose surrounded by acne-spotted skin, her build slim and willowy. Up close, she looks a lot younger but just as much a guard as the rest.

We step into the open area. Everything seems fine. Fifteen of our people in the trees confirm they see no Hunters in the two buildings closest to us. The air becomes still, as if the leaves are holding their breath as the two of us walk back to back slowly, not making any abrupt movements.

How did they know we'd be on those two roofs? I think, unclipping my rifle to reassure myself. I know they could have spotted us from afar, but even then, it was exactly like the ambush in Dead Man's Hill. The Hunters couldn't have set up those types of heavy rifles so fast, like I saw in the vision. It looked like they didn't have a pin on our position until seconds before they shot. They also had to make sure it was us and not some stragglers spending the night on the roof. That's why they brought J to the window, to get a reaction out of us, and once Jimmy moved, they got in position. They knew that if they could kill the people around me, I would have nothing left. We have a mole in our ranks — someone feeding information to the leaders.

Steps away from safety, images appear in my vision again, the screeching in my head not as violent. A window with green trim slowly opens, the hinges squeaking from the rust and lack of use. A breeze ruffles brown sheets acting as curtains. I hear the sound of metal settling on wood, a scope being adjusted, a marksman breathing out, relaxing his muscles the way I do.

I scan the windows, all outlined in green, all with curtains blocking prying eyes from spying in. Starting from level one and moving up, I scrutinize each window, trusting Em to guide me, and finally, on the top floor in the corner window, I spot a slight movement. A finger scratching a nose, somehow out of place, but no one shoots, and we make it safely past the branches.

Até watches me, feeling the same discomfort as I do. No one moves. I point to the building, then my rifle. Everyone around me gets the meaning, knowing not to talk. Big Three snipers have earpieces that receive information from their leaders and, when adjusted, can pick up vibrations from voices and have a rifle scope pinpoint them. Até and I mouth ideas to each other about how to attack this when Em walks toward me. She's facing the other way and doesn't see my warning. I move my finger slowly to my lips to tell her to stay quiet, but it's too late.

"Everything's clear," she says, and as soon as the words leave her lips, the first shot finds her back. Her eyes widen as she looks toward the red seeping into her dark shirt, bringing her fingers to the slowly trickling stream starting from her mouth.

I signal for everyone to get down. They move behind trees and flatten to the ground. One of the women tries to reach out for Em, who crumples to her knees, cupping her wound, but Uri pulls the woman back, holding his hand to her mouth.

"Help," Em croaks, crawling to Uri. A second bullet buries itself in her spine, her body falling limp, her spinal cord severed, her breath shaking.

It takes all of my strength not to rush to her side when her face falls to the dirt. None of us can move to her until the sniper is taken out. I look around for a vantage point, spotting the platform in the tree about three yards down. I'm fast, so if the sniper is distracted, I can get there before he spots me. Jimmy lies five feet away from me, shielding Tequila with his body. Liam and Eddy do the same for Rey, Johnny and Buckey. Malick has no bow, and he's busy trying to keep the other two women from running into the open. I can't see Asteroid, Luke or Ace. Até lies to my left, trying to spot where the shooter is.

"Hey," I hiss, taking my chances with another bullet. Até's teary stare burns into me, frustration sliding down her cheeks. I point to the platform in the tree, making a 'cover me' gesture by slowly moving my hands over my head. She nods, inching her hand to her gun. I mouth, "One, two, three."

She shoots into the dusty ground, drawing the sniper's attention as I sprint to the tree, climbing as fast as I can before Até empties her clip and rolls to the side as the sniper pinpoints her location. I can't see if she was hit or not, but she did a good job. I stretch out on my belly, unnoticed, the platform at the same level as the window. Adjusting my scope, I lock in my target, who is scanning the foliage. I rest my finger on the trigger, taking a breath in and out, in and out. The Hunter notices me too late. My shot hits him dead center between his eyebrows. His hands release the rifle, body falling to the side. I close my eyes and lower my head, listening to the Hunter's body fall from his position before I move to the ground, slowly walking to Até, who is unscathed.

I let out a low whistle, making sure there isn't another sniper and no one returns fire. "Clear," I say, running over to Em, who lies with her mouth open, breathing in shreds of wood and leaves, unable to do otherwise as her blood waters the soil. I press my ear to her back, listening for proper lung sounds, but I only hear faint wheezing on one side and nothing on the other. Ace kneels at her side, putting pressure on both wounds, but he doesn't know one of the bullets went all the way through. Even if the blood is stopped on one side, it will always find another way to exit.

"Help me turn her on her back," I say, gripping one of her shoulders and supporting her neck.

"Won't that damage her spine more?" Ace asks, but as soon as he looks at me, he knows it's as damaged as it can get, and there's nothing that Finn, Anna or I could do. We roll Em onto her back. I slip her head onto my thighs, stroking her hair, wiping the dirt and blood from her face.

"Talk to me, Harley," Finn's voice crackles over the walkie as Luke holds it to my ear. Loud breaths emit from the walkie as he sprints to Em's aid. Jimmy stands at my back, Luke handing the walkie to him so he can patrol with Até. The women stand over Em, saying some type of prayer. Someone found Asteroid, who is now watching me with the rest. Amongst all the chaos, all I can focus on is Em's eyes locked on my face, smiling up at me, not begging or in pain. She knows this is how she will die.

"Two bullet wounds," I keep my voice steady for Em's sake as I speak into the walkie. "The first bullet entered through the back and exited through the front, possibly hitting her spleen and the bottom of her left lung. The second hit her ninth thoracic vertebra, severing her spinal cord, affecting her intercostal and abdominal muscles," I declare. Even though I have no technology to confirm my observations, I know I'm not far off. No answer comes from Finn. He has no ideas, no advice to give me, nothing that can save her.

If we did get her back to the camp, alive, we wouldn't have the right technology to help keep her breathing. Not even the healing voice in my head has anything to say. All I can do is make her comfortable and keep myself from falling apart.

"I'm dying," she wheezes, tears rolling out of the corners of her eyes, her breath shallow and watery as her nerves start to die and the muscles in her chest shut down. Ace sits back, his hands stained with blood, making space for Até to lean next to Em's head and hold her hand, though she can't feel it.

"Yes," I whisper, pushing her hair from her face and holding back my tears. I don't want to lie to Em like I did to the dying young boy in the school fire. He was young and knew nothing of death, but Em has seen it her whole life. She's not naive and I asked for her instead of Jasper. I owe her the truth. "Em."

"Emerson," she corrects me, "I don't know why Em stuck." She starts to cough up dark red clots that roll from the corners of her mouth. I wipe the blood away with my sleeve, wondering if she has parents, a partner, siblings at home who are about to start their mornings expecting Emerson to be at the breakfast table, to smile at them while she shares her adventures.

"Emerson, I like that," I whisper, trying to return the smile she gives me. Anna and Finn's footsteps arrive, but I don't look up, and they don't come forward.

"I — I've always wanted to meet you, because of your dad," she chokes on the words as they struggle against the blood and carbon dioxide to have a place in the air. "I want — you to have — my silver angel — on my necklace." She pushes a forceful breath from her nose. In seconds her lungs will fail.

"What about your family?" I ask quickly.

"It's only me here, I made it and my family didn't. I want you to have it. To protect you and serve as a reminder of why you're fighting so hard to get your brother back." She starts to gasp, more blood escaping through her mouth and nose. Her belly swells as she hemorrhages from her ruptured spleen. Her fingers and her toes twitch. I feel the hope circulating through the people around me, but the twitch was only a reflex that couldn't be controlled. Her face becomes slack as she drowns from the inside, no more signs of life in her eyes, no pulse thumping.

"You're safe now, you did your job," I manage, holding her until her body stops fighting and her mind sees nothing. I lean down, shutting her eyes, whispering the words we utter to friends and family members found lifeless on the streets. "May your soul reach the heavens and your heart have all my love, we shall meet again." I kiss her forehead, moving my legs out from under her, using my cloak to cover her body. Até stops me, removing Emerson's necklace, and hands me the silver angel. I don't look at it before I slip it into my pocket.

We both blanket her in our cloaks, wrapping them around her limp body, preparing her to be carried. I close my eyes, and for a second, I almost believe she is sleeping, and at any minute, she'll open her eyes. *No*, I tell myself, not waiting for the voices to tell me I'm foolish.

"Harley?"

The hole in my heart is growing bigger and bigger every fucking time I wake up and let people die for my cause, and I am so sick of it. The high-pitched voice was right. I will continue to add bodies to the pile.

From the inside, I am breaking into nothingness like the day my father went missing. He might not even be dead; he could have just left. Left me so he didn't have to experience the horrible things I have done. My mind, my soul aren't even my own — they never were. My presence has killed so many people and hurt even more.

"We need to carry her back," I mumble, reaching down, but Malick stops me, his face showing no emotion. Nothing to indicate his grief or closeness to Emerson, but I think he's waiting until he has his wife and friends to grieve with. He nods toward the other guards, who all take hold of Emerson. Some with shiny cheeks, and some blank, like Malick. Até and Anna walk beside Malick like they're carrying a casket to an empty pit. I pull Ace up, keeping close to him as we walk, waiting for him to break.

"After we rescue J—" he starts, his voice hollow and hushed. I press to the curves of his body, making his weight mine and my weight his, moving as one — the two closest to Emerson's death, the ones who saw a spirit freed from its home.

"We stop this endless cycle of the Big Three killing whoever they want," I end his sentence, knowing that I, the last soul ruler, am the one who has to stop this, and I can only think of one way to do so.

CHAPTER 23

(JIMMY)

If any of us had a word floating around in our heads to disrupt the dread holding us by the necks, Rey and Johnny would be the ones but not even they uttered a whisper.

We're stunned. I watched Em–Emerson jerk as the bullet tore through her flesh, not once but twice. I saw the shock on her face when she realized what had happened. All any of us could do was lie still and watch as she called for help, expecting her people to come to her aid. Then the second bullet hit, and she tried to move, only to find she no longer had control over her muscles. In front of me, it felt like a slow-motion nightmare, minutes turning into hours, then everything lurching into overdrive when Harley took out the sniper.

It had a dizzying effect on my body because all I could see were my parents in Emerson's place — their cries for help, their shaky last breaths, their bodies falling limp. I stayed frozen even when Harley gave us the all-clear, remaining on my stomach and watching the colour of the ground change as blood pooled around her body. I couldn't get to my feet until Asteroid tripped over me, jamming his bony knee into my shoulder blade. I had to stand to get him to stop running around aimlessly. Then I forced myself to stand at Harley's back, watching as she held Emerson until her chest fell and did not rise.

Anna leaves Até's side, running ahead, and as we enter the camp, we are led to a quickly thrown-together funeral with everyone in attendance. For the first half, people share memories of Emerson, how she fought ruthlessly with the guards, sacrificing everything to keep them safe. They speak of how kind and well respected she was — how, even though just a year had passed since she found her way to No Man's Land, she, at sixteen, was more mature and skilled than her greatest opponents. They bury her alongside twenty-two protruding piles of earth. Some have grave decorations, woven with leaves and flowers made to resemble a wolf with its head bowed, no longer able to howl. Malick says they've lost more than twenty-two people during the time they have spent here, but some could not be brought back to camp for burial.

The second half is more of an upbeat commemoration of life than a time to cry. Moonshine is passed around, spirits lifted through memories and food. I even see Até with a cup, her cheeks becoming flushed the more she drinks. People dance, sing, and laugh till they cry, showing the world Emerson's spirit will never be forgotten, celebrated till the world is dead itself. Not one person does their chores for the day or leaves until night falls again.

Até tells us to go to bed and sleep for as long as we like because we are moving out tomorrow night. She slurs her words a little when she says this, implying that not even she will have an undisrupted sleep. Her nose is red, her cheeks wet. Someone told me Emerson was one of Até's top guards, fifth to Jasper and Malick. More of a little sister to Até than anything else.

Jasper and Malick have been sitting with the other guards the whole day. Jasper's face is multi-coloured and swollen in the firelight and Malick's wife hasn't let go of her husband since we returned. Our gang didn't know Emerson as long, but the effect is just the same. Rey hands out drinks in order to cope, telling jokes that don't make sense. "How are grapes and elephants the same — they're both purple."

To occupy their minds, Finn and Anna escape to the medical shack. Johnny sticks by Rey's side, making sure he doesn't insult anyone. Buckey and Tequila stay until the first person leaves, then retire to the hut, unable to hold it together much longer. Uri finds mourning women to comfort. As dusk creeps through the curtain of leaves overhead, the mood of the crowd shifts to quiet acceptance, leaving the remaining Nomads with their thoughts.

Ace, Luke and I stay by Harley as she stares into the firelight, the heat making her skin red. She didn't look at a soul the whole celebration or even acknowledge Ace and me when we tried to give her water, food, clean the blood from her skin or get her leg checked. She just sat there, letting her mind run rampant while she did nothing on the outside.

Eventually, Luke gets sick of us trying to lure her back to the hut with gentle whispers, tiptoeing around her, as if at any moment she'd lash out. He crouches in front of her, removing the rifle from her lap and the guns from her pocket, leaving the dagger clenched in her hand because she has a death grip on it. He pulls her arm around his neck, lifts her into his arms, and carries her to the hut, laying her on the bed. He stares at her for a moment, worry creasing his forehead, before he storms back out.

I close the sheet separating the room, slide the two clips from her pocket, pry the dagger from her fingers and pull the wooden carving and silver angel from her pocket, ensuring their safety on the table. I know she's not dazed or disoriented from trauma; that doesn't happen to her, no matter what or how much she sees. She's stuck in her thoughts, checking and rechecking what she could have done differently.

"I shot the sniper without even giving it a second thought." She presses her palms to her head, dull eyes with dark bags under them following me as I change into shorts and set a pile of clothes on her chest. I grab one of my shirts and pour water on it, scrubbing the blood from her hands and neck where scratches are already scabbing over. She stands, leaving blood on the sheets, and removes her pants, revealing the hole in her calf, pulsing as it tries to push the bullet out.

Harley follows my gaze, leaning down to dig it out with her nails, allowing me to wipe away the dried blood and place a piece of thick cloth over the hole. She yanks on sweatpants, turning to face the wall, changing out of her bloody, torn shirt and rainbow sports bra.

"Harley," I sigh solemnly. Her arms and back are covered in more cuts, and small shards of glass from the shattered apartment windows protrude from her skin. Ace and I only saw the glass fall because she made us go before her to shield us. "By killing the sniper you saved all of us," I say, moving over to her, closing my eyes once I remove the glass and help her into my shirt, so long and baggy on her slim, muscular figure.

Harley slides into the sheets, silent tears dripping onto her pillow. Over the past couple of days, she hasn't stopped fighting or slowed down to notice what needs repairing inside. Now she has no choice but to let all her sorrows seep from her and drift away. I crawl beside her, curling my body around hers, kissing her cheek and running my hands over her bumpy hair. She rolls over and wraps me in her arms, nuzzling her face into the nape of my neck. Her chin rests on my collar bone, her hot breath mixes with salty tears on my bare skin.

"What if—" she starts, her voice so weak it reminds me of when we were eleven, and I found her for the first time in the alley, beaten senseless and talking nonsense. My heart breaks now just as much as it did that night.

"J's okay," I whisper, putting a finger to her lips. "We'll find him tomorrow, and he'll be with us again, and we can run far away from here with whoever wants to come. We can start a new life," I say. She nods into my chest, and as the rest of the gang piles into the hut, she breathes more evenly. I don't know if she is doing this to shut me up, because she doesn't want them to hear her cry, or she really found sleep in all her distress.

I doubt she will be lucky enough to catch two minutes. With the comfort of her beside me and the movements of her breathing, I let my exhaustion take over and seal my eyelids shut.

Swish — thud — swish — thud. I tilt my head back, rubbing the crusty sleep from my eyes. I stretch, reaching for Harley, but her spot is vacant, only dried blood remaining. *What's she doing now?* I change from shorts to sweatpants, zipping a jacket up to my chin. The cracks in the hut let the wind rush through too easily, and the open window doesn't help.

Swish — thud — swish — thud — I tiptoe over still bodies. Rey mumbles in his sleep about some sort of science experiment and Tequila snores louder than any of the boys, Buckey sleeping so peacefully at her side, an unconscious smile on his lips.

"Gross," I mutter, pushing the squeaky door open. The cold stings my face as I step onto the frozen ground, soaking my socks.

"She's been doing this for two hours." Ace's muffled voice comes from beside me where he sits against the hut, bundled in two jackets, a blanket and layers of socks. Beside him, Luke carves into a slab of wood with his switchblade, tongue sticking out of the side of his mouth in concentration, not looking up at me.

"And you've been keeping an eye on her?" I question, spotting Harley, who stands in the distance.

"More like distracting myself while making sure she doesn't try something stupid," Ace says, pulling the blanket tighter around him, only showing his nose and amber eyes. It doesn't surprise me that these three are the ones who will not sleep. Luke has kept an eye on Harley since we left The Sticks. Ace was as close to Emerson as Harley was; he carried her blood on his hands back to camp, and Harley found out how much Emerson trusted her and cared for her, even though she had never talked to Harley until she was dying.

"And you?" I ask Luke, taking a seat next to Ace, blowing hot air into my cupped hands. Luke looks up at Harley for a long while before going back to scratching into the wood.

"Watching out for her and making sure she doesn't leave," he confirms, not saying it to best me or imply that he's still pining for her. He's sincere, genuinely meaning it, and I trust him. So far, he has.

Harley moves to the tree, yanking the blades from the bark. She stops when she sees me. Her mouth is drawn in a firm line, and the scabs on her arms are now faint marks or gone altogether.

"May I have one?" I explore, sticking my hand out to her, wondering if she might just throw it at me. She spins back to the tree, throwing three knives in a straight line, one directly under the other. She slaps the fourth into my open palm, expecting me to throw it, but instead, I bury it into the ground at my feet. She takes a heavy seat in front of me and beckons to Luke, who hands her the slab of wood. He leans back, closing his switchblade and shutting his eyes.

"You didn't write anything," she complains, chucking the wood away, rubbing her hands across her face.

"I think I carved a pretty good flower. Considering I've never done it before," he snorts, not giving in to her irritation and whatever she's trying to get him to do. He's good at that, making her understand that the past cannot be changed, so it shouldn't be stressed over.

"Harley, come here," Ace offers, patting the spot in front of him and moving the blanket from his upper body.

She looks pale and icy, her skin covered in goosebumps, but her stress keeps her bare feet from becoming numb. She rolls her eyes, giving in and settling for a spot in between Ace and me, her back against the side of his legs and her feet propped up on my thighs. I wipe the excess dirt off them before pulling them toward me, tucking them under my jacket. She smirks at me when I shiver from her cold toes touching my flesh.

"This braid is too tight, it's squeezing your brain." Ace's fingers dance as they undo the tangles of frizzy and messy waves. Harley leans into Ace's hands, sighing as tears escape from her eyes.

"I could have done something to help Emerson."

"You did everything," I say, scooting closer, tugging Ace's blanket, pulling it across her, warming her because it's the only thing I can think of doing to help.

"You asked me to write down anything that you could have done differently. I put nothing. I'm no healer, but it doesn't take years of healing practice to know this place doesn't have the equipment that she would have required. Finn and Anna would tell you the same thing," Luke says, moving to sit in front of her, leaning in to wipe at her tears.

Normally seeing them do this would get me steaming and ready to smack Luke silly and maybe give Ace a shiner, but oddly it doesn't. Nor does it make me feel like I can't comfort her on my own. It reminds me that if I were to drop dead tomorrow or get separated from her, I wouldn't have to worry. Not that I would need to because she's gotten a lot stronger and sharpened her skills. I would just know she has an army of people around her who would make sure she stays alive.

"You did the one thing any dying person could wish for. You stayed with her, comforted her, accepted her gift and held her until she died. She wasn't scared and wasn't alone." Luke's voice catches on his last words, tears brimming from his eyes. Ace's eyes are puffy and red, all cried out. If I let myself cry, there's no telling if I'd ever stop because every time I think of Emerson, lying in a pool of blood, not only do my parents show up in her place but so does Tequila. So does Harley.

"J's dying," she whispers to herself bluntly, keeping her eyes shut. Her chest sinks as she pushes all the air from her lungs to prevent herself from falling apart.

None of us say anything, not knowing how to comfort her without lying. J must be close to the edge from physical exhaustion, the infections and untreated wounds that won't let go of him until he's past saving. I saw the same thing she did. How pale he looked, the light beaten out of him, his eyes dull and lifeless. He's been there for so long that if he does survive, the boy Harley tried to protect from the bad in the world, the boy who loved school and went on his first date just weeks ago will be gone. That boy will be dead.

"Harley, do you remember the story I told you when we were in your alley for the first time?" Ace asks, breaking the silence and smoothing down Harley's curly hair. A slight smile, gentle on his lips.

"Yeah. I was half alive and wouldn't let you take me to Finn so you told me the story, and waited till I passed out," Harley retorts, acting like it doesn't bother her, but it does.

I remember that night. The whole town's power went out, so I decided to check The Shed and her usual places because I figured Eric wouldn't be too happy. I peered into her house first to make sure she wasn't there and saw Eric hammered, knuckles dripping with blood, yelling at her mom. So I ran and almost slammed into Ace, who was walking down the street, trying to go unnoticed with Harley lifeless in his arms. It was the worst beating she had ever received and the most terrified I had ever been.

"Yeah," Ace cringes. "But do you remember the story?"

"Parts."

"It was the one about the stars," he says, not waiting for her to nod before he jumps right into his story. "I went to your window that night, to drag you out of bed and make you stargaze with me so I could unload my ideas on you — whether you wanted to hear them or not — but you were gone. So I went tiptoeing through the streets, dodging Hunters left, right and centre. Like a superhero. Then I came across your alley for the first time and saw your hand hanging over that old mouldy couch."

Harley laughs through her nose, probably imagining how squirmy Ace must have been when he forced himself to lie on it with her.

"I was about ready to unleash all my wrath on some Hunters when you grabbed my pant leg. Your grip was really weak as you told me to lie beside you. I begged you to let me take you to Finn, but you, being the stubborn person you are, convinced me not to. I couldn't leave you so I had to trust you not to die and wait for you to pass out. I thought, what better way to do that then tell you a story."

"Ace, I'll be dead by the time you get to the point," Luke mumbles, but he gets comfortable anyway, leaning on his hands and stretching his legs out.

"Patience. Anyway, I said, 'Harley, you see those stars up there? When I die I want to be a star. Reborn into something that shines through the thick darkness from light years away, where it's so quiet I'll always be able to hear my thoughts, instead of neighbouring screams. And for once in my many years of life I'd know what it's like to be at peace. Something none of us have ever had.'" He pauses, all of us clinging to his words. Even the wakeful breaths of the gang listen, maybe even the whole village. "Maybe Emerson is now a star at peace and protecting us, or a bird soaring through the softest breeze, or an angel. One that walks among lost souls freeing them from their broken lives. I believe that whatever or wherever she is, she is safe and at peace."

I feel as if all the blood has rushed from my arteries, leaving me colder than the air did, but somehow, what he said makes me feel better, and I can tell the others feel the same. He's given us something to hold on to, that somewhere Emerson and my parents are happier than they were before they died. Luke almost looks shocked himself.

"How are we going to make sure we go unnoticed tomorrow?" Harley asks, not wanting to linger in her thoughts any longer, not wanting to imagine her brother as a peaceful faraway star.

Scuffling feet hurry to the door. Rey and Johnny stumble over each other as they fight to get through the frame, ending up on the ground. They prop their heads up with their hands, grinning with all their slightly yellow teeth.

"We thought you would never ask," Johnny says, pushing Rey's head and jumping to his feet.

"Over the hours of being left to our own devices after the fight, while you were knocked out, and doing god knows what at the river, I—"

"We," Johnny interrupts.

"We," Rey grudgingly adds, "created a disorienting explosive that, when activated, knocks the target out for—"

"Ten minutes," Buckey complains, dragging Tequila out of the hut with him. Uri and Finn close behind. "I was the test subject."

"So was I," says Uri, his face looking better, not groaning or limping as much when he walks. "They did a good job. Even after waking up, it still makes it hard to focus and move for a bit."

"We figured if we used it on the Hunters it could give us more time."

We all look to Harley, who twirls her hair, eyes focused on the knife in the ground. I never really thought about how hard it must be for her to take on all the responsibility, be the one we look to for every decision that has to be made. That's why she blames herself for all the deaths. She takes on the weight of everything that goes wrong.

"What about the prisoners?" I ask.

"It would knock them out as well and make it easier to carry J back to the camp without him yelling in pain or moving around," Finn reassures us, his eyes so dead and tired that he looks ghost-like with his pale skin and blonde hair.

"And I, the queen of technology who hasn't been able to wear makeup or dress up in a long time…" Tequila stretches out on the ground, her hair sticking up on one side, "… but don't fret; that hasn't affected my ability to make masks from some plastic and stuff I found. Masks that will stop us from passing out with the Hunters." She smirks proudly.

"Are you just going to throw them in the door and expect them to not run out the other exit?" Luke grunts, getting to his feet.

"Well, you little non-scientific and architectural fool," Rey laughs. Luke makes a fist at Rey, who flinches slightly before recovering. "Asteroid showed us his blueprint of the building. There are vents in the stairway that lead right over the prison so, if we are right, Johnny and I can crawl through them and drop our masterpieces."

"Okay," Harley interrupts us, only looking at me. No more tears in her eyes, no more pain on her face. Numb and emotionless. "Now let's go through the whole plan."

CHAPTER 24

(HARLEY)

One. One death. One sacrifice. One loss. That's all I will allow on this rescue mission, even if that means only holding my brother once more, kissing Jimmy once more, or watching my gang — my family — smile for the last time. I will be that sacrifice and hand myself over to the leaders if it means they will live.

When Rey and Johnny explained their creations to me, I was pleasantly surprised. The small, silver cartridges are made from a table that they stole. They fit in a pocket and are filled with a mixture of dream root and medical supplies Finn unwillingly gave to them. They're activated by four light touches to the centre. Johnny informed me that four touches were a must because while a silver cartridge was in his pocket, he bumped it, knocking Rey and him out while they were out in the woods. Overall, everything about their creation, as well as their plan to go through the air ducts and drop the cartridges on the Hunters, was well thought out, easing me a little. They made me proud and brought our whole plan together.

We talked until the sun rose again, and Luke told me to stop being so uptight and let them go to sleep. All around me, they drifted off at some point, even Luke, who showed his morose side during the talk and grumbled to himself as he passed outside before he crawled into bed. I listened to their sleep sounds, ruffling sheets, snores and whispers, while Jimmy's head rested on my chest. I teased his silky hair and traced every curve, indent and imperfection of his face, making sure to remember all of him.

I watch the wall where the numbers one through seven, accompanied by question marks, sit unchanged. No more of my ideas fill the empty places. I wait for a vision to pop into my mind, but nothing comes. No voices reassure me or warn me. I am alone with my thoughts for a whole day — until Até comes storming into the hut, yelling rather than telling us it is time to go.

It's harder to wake the gang than it was for them to fall asleep. Jimmy took some coaxing, shaking, and kissing before he fully got up. Até nudged everyone with her foot and slapped Rey so hard that, even now, as we walk to AC's building, a hand imprint is still visible on his cheek. He still thinks Até does this out of love, but all of us know it's because he won't bite back. No one can bear to break his crazy little heart, out of precaution rather than sympathy because he's capable of making more dangerous things than a smoke bomb.

Before we left, Até informed us that she found our plan 'decently constructed,' and she will not be accompanying us on this mission, for she could not leave her people again. Asteroid will be remaining at the camp with Finn, communicating over the walkie if we run into trouble. Also, Malick and Jasper will be stationed with Buckey and Tequila in the trees, making sure the sniper situation doesn't happen again. Até claimed it was because she couldn't risk losing her two best guards and the only one who knew how to make the map, but she really meant that she didn't want them to be a part of a suicide mission.

Now we walk in near silence. The only sounds are my racing heart and the breaths of the people brave enough and loyal enough to walk by my side. The streets are all empty besides the staggering drunks and drug dealers standing in door frames. It happens to be a holiday, MC's birthday, and he was kind enough to ban all fighting on this day. He most likely spent months arguing with JC, his twin brother, to make this happen.

Every so often, a Hunter will pass by, and my heart will stop, thinking that they will know instantly that we are not one of them. We wear the same grey and green Hunter uniforms and hats that Até stole for us. I think maybe our disguises work, but when I get a closer look at the Hunters, I notice the hint of a tattoo peeking from a woman's collar and, on another, the symbol of the howling wolf just behind a man's ear. One Hunter even winks at me. Até must have more people on the inside than I thought, or she killed Hunters and made her guards take their uniforms. It wouldn't surprise me at this point.

My hair tickles my nose, and my feet tingle as the borrowed boots pinch my toes.

"The walk should be thirty minutes to the middle, since it takes just over an hour to walk from one side of the city to the other," Uri mutters. He and Ace follow close to Rey and Johnny, who are trying their hardest to act like Hunters, their backs straight, arms stiff, but I can tell they're getting restless. "That means a fifteen-minute run back, or ten if we sprint the whole way."

We nod, but no one says anything as AC's building gets closer. We're moving down a different street from the one we were on the night before, but I can sense that we have just passed the bullet-filled buildings.

"What if—"

"It will work," Jimmy interrupts, squeezing my hand but quickly letting go, his eyes fixed on the Hunters waiting for us at our entry point. One is meant to let us in, and the other is meant to lead us to the prison. I find it hard to believe that out of the hundreds of Hunters, Até was able to get both her guards on this shift tonight. No one talks inside my head, and I feel the uneasiness radiating through all of the voices, as if they want to warn me but don't know what it is they need to warn me about.

We slow a little as we reach the door, not wanting to draw more attention to our group than we probably already have. The Hunters lift their guns, not enough to make it evident that we don't belong but enough to warn us. One of them is no taller than me, his face scattered with freckles, his eyes hooded. The other has a long nose and tattoos peeking over the edge of her uniform. I place my gun in my pocket, slowly removing my wooden carving from under my shirt. It hangs on a woven necklace alongside the silver angel Emerson gave me. The Hunters relax, the freckled one smiling.

"Sorry, we knew it was you," he admits, "But Até gave us strict orders only to let through the group who showed the silver angel. Can't trust anyone these days," he jokes as the other Hunter turns to a reinforced metal door and types in a code, letting us in and shutting the door behind us.

My eyes burn along with my nose as lights bounce off the white, dust-free granite. The room's warmth makes it reek of fresh bleach and the scent of flowers, probably meant to cover up the first smell, only to make it worse. My eyes adjust, and I'm almost certain that AC stole an entire quarry of granite, only the ceiling and stairwell aren't covered in the stuff.

"Angel?" I question, not sure why the wooden carving alongside my face wouldn't be enough to get us in.

"The one from your necklace?" He frowns, narrowing his eyes before carrying on. "This is where two of you enter," he says, pointing to a shiny vent blowing cold air onto us, not a speck of dust dangling from it.

Luke and Uri move under it, crossing their arms and locking their hands together. Rey climbs on first, his uniform bunching at his ankles and sliding down his arms as he reaches up, unscrewing the vent.

He forgets that he has to hold on to it, letting it drop and clatter so loudly on the ground it makes all of us jump as the sound carries. Ace and I peer up the spiralling stairwell, anticipating hordes of Hunters running toward the sound, but the stairs remain empty.

"You'd better learn to be quiet while you're in there or I'll kick your ass," Jimmy grimaces, pushing Johnny toward Luke and Uri.

Rey pulls himself in, then hoists Johnny, who hits his head hard on the metal. Jimmy rolls his eyes, running his fingers through his hair. They turn themselves around and poke their faces out, smiling, sticking their tongues out at Jimmy because he can't reach them.

"You know the plan?" Reassured by the Hunter that no one will be coming, I move back under the vent, taking care to avoid being within spitting distance of the boys.

"We listen to Asteroid and every direction he gives us, even though he can't actually see what we're doing," Johnny recites with a sigh. I narrow my eyes at him, having half a mind to pull them out and send someone else in their place. I don't even know why I let both of them go; the job only needs one.

"We listen to everything he says, wear our masks, drop our brilliant creations and leave right away, not stopping for anything until we get back to Buckey and Tequila," Rey quickly says. His smile fades as he focuses on me, just now realizing how serious this all is. "Be safe, okay," he says, his voice becoming small as they shimmy away. Already beginning to bicker, their voices crackle over the walkie in Uri's hand.

"Stop kicking my face."

"Stop putting your face there."

"No, your other left, you dunce."

"Oh right you, umm -- pipsqueak."

Uri dials down the walkie's volume as Asteroid's voice tries to be heard over theirs. The Hunter beckons to us, starting up the stairs, his gun secure in its holster. We clear every turn, with no one in sight. Not a soul passes through the hallways as we peer through all the doors. Lucky for us, the stairwell walls aren't made of one-way glass like the rest of the building. It's less likely we will be seen. We reach the second landing. The Hunter wishes us luck and carries on, his footsteps echoing in our ears.

We press against the walls, moving to the metal door as I peer through the small window. A short, dark hall sits between us and the second door, not more than ten steps away. A Hunter's back blocks my view into the prison, making it impossible to tell what waits for us.

"Jimmy, stand inside this door and watch the stairs until I call you. Uri, as soon as we get in you watch the other entrance while Ace, Luke and I get J," I order, my stomach twisting, my instincts warning me of something.

"*What do you notice?*" the wise voice whispers.

I scan everything in sight. *If I were a Big Three leader and I had angry gangs all around me, people who are starving, knowing food is in these buildings, I'd make sure every entrance was guarded, every inch of the building was surveyed, and I would even put a Hunter at each door inside and out at all times. So why is this not the case?*

"Are you in position?" Uri asks, his lips dried and cracked, inches from the walkie. His gun looks so heavy in his hands, and the tired look on his face makes me question his being here, but it's too late for that.

"We are in position, big man," Rey breathes back.

"Drop the smoke bomb," Uri orders. We pull on our masks which smell of garbage and rust. They must have found the material on the trash pile past the tree line. My grip tightens around the gold door handle.

"It's not called a smoke bomb, you great idiotic chicken, it's a streaker."

"I don't know if I should be offended by that or not," Uri mutters, "It doesn't even make sense."

"You just don't—"

"Rey, drop the damn thing," I say harshly, interrupting him. The urge to kill the Hunters consumes me, the ones that will be knocked out on the other side of this door, the ones who beat my brother. The cold part of me surfaces only to be pushed down by the happier thought of seeing J again.

"Right," Rey laughs nervously. They fall quiet for only a second, shuffling around.

"Put on your mask," Johnny orders.

A sizzling sound comes through the walkie as they detonate the streaker, the sound fading as it falls. As soon as it finds its target, we hear coughing and gasping and then nothing.

"Done," Rey chirps as if he doesn't hear the sound of the bodies falling below him.

"Now get out," I tell them as I twist the handle and apprehensively move down the hall before bursting into the prison. It takes a minute for the thick grey clouds of smoke to clear. Prisoners are knocked out in their cells, and Hunters lie in heaps on the floor, their limbs bending at weird angles, their mouths drawn open, but our masks keep us standing.

The fact that only four Hunters, instead of eight, lie on the floor isn't the only thing that throws me off as we move further in. J sits slumped over in a rusted metal chair, placed in the middle of the room, his wrists and ankles not bound to anything. Waves of longing, relief and apprehension wash over me.

"It could be a trap," Uri says, his voice muffled as his tall frame moves along the glass cells. Reaching the other side safely, he holds his gun out and around the corner, watching the opposite entrance.

"Probably, but it's too late," Ace says, keeping his eyes away from J.

No one else can bear to look at him, but I do. Along J's face and neck are green bruises in the recovery phase, and I can see new, bloody purple and blue ones layered over them. His nose is broken, the cut on the bridge of it infected, and his arms are covered in long bubbling burns, oozing orange pus. His ankle is either sprained or broken, and that's only what I can see on the outside. Under his blood-spotted t-shirt and pants, there has to be worse. I forget Luke and Ace at my side and the Hunters on the floor as I move forward to cup J's hollow, child-like face in my hands, kissing his forehead.

"I'm so sorry," I whisper, even though he can't hear me. I run my hand over his blonde hair, blanketed with knots and dried blood. "I love you."

"Harley, we have to go. I can hear people," Uri calls, running back to us, averting his eyes from J as well. It hurts — it hurts everyone too damn much to see J so disfigured.

"Jimmy." I stand, pulling myself together, removing my gun from my pocket. I run my fingertips over the dagger handle, thinking. Jimmy leaves his post, running to my side but hesitating at the sight of J. "I need you to take him." I take Jimmy's gun from his clenched fingers, sliding it into his pocket. He grabs my arm, trying to object, hardening his jaw because he doesn't want to leave me again. "It's non-negotiable. I have to be able to shoot, and Uri can't carry him, and I trust that you won't stop running for anything until he's safe."

Jimmy bites his tongue, holding back his argument. "Okay," he whispers, scooping J into his arms easily, even though J is dead weight. He is now only flesh and bones, a light feather that could be carried by the wind.

"We have to go, now," Uri orders, as footsteps thunder into the room.

"Okay, Jimmy, go. Uri, stay at his back. We will be minutes behind you, only stopping if any Hunters try to follow — and remember, just keep running." I press my lips to Jimmy's, the connection feeling rushed and warm — fearful. "Promise me," I demand, moving them out the door.

He holds me with his crystal eyes like he has done my whole life. "I promise on the sun," he whispers. He and Uri sprint out the doors and down the stairs.

I grab a couple of clips from the Hunters and am about to run out the door, sure Ace and Luke are close behind, when I freeze. A reflection in the window of the steel door catches my eye, and the gold doorknob just brushes against my fingertips.

"Harles," the only person who is ever allowed to call me that says, his voice strained. In the window, Ace stands with Luke's gun pressed to his temple.

I knew this whole mission was too easy — fewer Hunters than expected in the prison, no cameras where there should have been the most, and J readied for us. Luke is the mole in our rank. He has been since day one.

My mind floods with the memories, the hints, and the now clear explanation as to why Luke was so compliant and willing to help us get J. This — him leading me straight into the arms of the leaders, is the reason he's here, the reason he let us stay at Emma's. It all makes sense now. I bet he even waited around at the school fire — might have even been responsible for the explosion. He knew I would go in to save J. He knew we would need help. He waited with his car, ensuring he would be on this rescue mission. I feel so stupid.

A small part of me buried under a deep layer of disgust and mortification is surprised, pained even, that someone who I had trusted and had started to care about would betray me. Though every other inch of my being knew he was capable of far worse things than this.

"Harley, I need you to listen to everything I tell you to do or I'll put a bullet in his head and make you watch him bleed. Now drop your gun and empty your pockets of your dagger and knives," Luke demands, manipulating his voice to disguise himself as strong and confident. But his pause between each word tells me he's just as scared as Ace.

I comply, dropping my gun, dagger and two knives, kicking them away and inching toward Luke, noticing the twitching limbs of the unconscious.

"Luke, what are you doing?" My voice is steady, even though I feel far from that. I move toward them as slowly as my body will allow, treating Luke like a scared, beaten victim who is ready to jump at any unfamiliar movement or noise.

"Under the order of the leaders, I am to get you to willingly surrender yourself to them in any way necessary," Luke says, moving his finger closer to the trigger with every step I take. So I still, barely breathing. I scan the room for anything I can use to stop this, but I figure there are more people than just him with orders to keep me in this prison. The footsteps that we heard coming through the other entrance have stopped, no one storming into the prison. They're waiting for him to fail and for me to run.

"You don't have to do this," I say, willing my voice to be persuasive. "You can put the gun down, and we can all leave here safely and figure something out when we—"

"Stop!" He screams, pushing the gun harder into the side of Ace's head. The veins in Luke's neck pop and his face reddens as he begins to lose control. "Your voice doesn't have the same effect on me."

He pushes Ace to his knees. Ace shuts his eyes, counting his fingers at his side, accepting what he thinks is to come, but I will not. "It's okay, Harles, don't listen to him, I'm okay. Go see your brother. A star isn't so bad," he whispers, tears floating down his cheeks into his mouth, reminding me of his desire to be at peace. By protecting me, he's thanking me for saving him and making him feel loved.

"Ace, I love you, but this is not the time to be stubborn. You don't get to leave me this easily," I say, my voice breaking as I move closer to Luke, who moves Ace closer to me.

"Say it, then," Luke presses, his eyes wild and tired, no longer anticipating this moment, no longer fighting with himself about whether or not he could do this to me.

"It's not really a willing surrender if you force her to do it," Ace snarls, his old fight resurfacing for a moment. Luke considers this, then places his finger over the trigger, his arms flexing.

"No!" I beg, taking a deep breath, asking the cold voice for anything that will help, but I have no time to wait and see if she will respond. "Willingly, I surrender. Now let him go," I say, staring him down.

Luke releases Ace into my arms. Ace grabs hold of me, not caring that Luke still has a gun pointed at him. He cries into my hair, gripping my shirt, forcing all the air between us away. I wipe my face on his sleeve, the smell of grass soaked in dew engulfing me. "You have to go," I demand, but I hold him as tight as possible.

"Harles, we could—"

"No." I pry him off, holding his shoulders, turning him in the direction of the door, moving him toward it. We can't fight back when it could mean Ace's death and my survival. He is my person, the one I can tell everything to, including things about Jimmy. He is purer and more human than any of us, even Finn. If I let him die I ... "You have to run, please, make sure J is okay and that Jimmy doesn't come back. I'm a survivor, right? I'll see you again," I say, managing what I think is a smile as my throat tightens and tears threaten to flood my eyes.

He continues to count his fingers, silently pleading with me to come with him, but I can't. Luke is growing impatient, and at any minute, he might change his mind and shoot Ace. I push Ace out the door.

"Promise," he cries, running down the hall, "that you'll come back." His strangled words kill me, making this moment feel endless, as if it's been longer than a couple minutes.

"I promise," I say, hearing his footsteps fade, his curly black hair and a glint of his birthmark the last thing I see.

"Promise is a strong word," Luke whispers behind me, handcuffs jingling as he pulls them from his pocket.

"Leave, you idiot. You can outrun him," the cold voice screams, working to move my legs, but I don't allow it, even though it's the only thing I want.

"For once I agree with her," the powerful voice says.

No, I think, my throat tying itself into knots, my body finally giving in to the human parts of me — so tired and in pain.

"If she does, they will all die," the wise voice states, throwing me off guard for a moment. Not because she's right, but because there are three of them with me at the same time. I can feel it.

"Come on." Luke's hand falls on my shoulder. Hunters and prisoners start to move, still appearing groggy.

The ten minutes must be up. That means Rey and Johnny have to be close to the tree line, and Jimmy and Uri aren't far behind. Ace is fast; it won't be long till he's there as well. Close to safety. At this moment, I decide I will not go quietly.

I throw my elbow over my shoulder, hitting Luke in the eye, then the nose, drawing blood. I spin and kick, knocking his gun from his hand and tackling him with all my force to the ground. I rip his mask off, but all the smoke is gone. He pulls mine off, too, scratching my face, grabbing a fistful of my hair. He flips us, knocking my head hard on the granite floor, pinning my arms and legs down. His weight is far greater than mine. He grips both my wrists in one of his massive hands, throwing punches with his other. Squirming, I make him miss every time. His knuckles collide with the floor, blood dripping onto my face. I lurch up and bite his arm, the taste of iron streaming down my throat. I manage to free my leg, driving my knee hard into his groin, making him fall to the side, crying out.

I crawl for the door, the Hunters stumbling around and past me. I get to my feet, dazed, my head ringing, my breaths unnaturally forced. My hand opens the cold door when a low voice booms behind me, a voice I recognize from years of listening to mandatory speeches.

"You're leaving the party so soon? I cleaned the whole place for you," he says malevolently, his shoes clicking on the floor. "Besides, I wouldn't run if I were you. I have Hunters everywhere, even around the banished in No Man's Land, since Luke has given me their location." His words seem liquid, smacking against his saliva-soaked lips. "If you leave, I will kill your beloved gang and more, not just Ace."

Stand down," the cold voice whispers. Even she knows when a battle can't be won.

I don't turn around when I fall to my knees, raising my hands to the back of my head. All my fight has vanished, exhaustion and emptiness taking over. Again.

"Good girl," he chirps. Hunters grab my arms, shoving my face to the granite, cuffing my wrists behind my back too tightly. They place a bag over my head, so all I see is pitch black when they drag me up and forward.

I struggle against their grip until someone slams the handle of his heavy gun into my stomach, knocking the air out of me, making it hard to gain it back through the tightly woven fabric.

"Sorry, sir," Luke says, his voice strained, following me. The fact that he called him 'sir' makes me struggle against the Hunters again. Another blow to the stomach makes it so hard to breathe, my head hurts.

"Stop doing that, we don't want her to suffocate. If she does, I'll die," the leader intervenes loudly, hinting at his anger and fear. "And no. You did your best, but now you will be her guard and stay with her until the end. I believe this will be a sufficient punishment for almost letting her go. It will hurt you as much as it hurts her," he says to Luke.

I imagine the leader in a long silver coat, with his hair slicked back, his lips pursed and hands held behind his back as he walks at Luke's side. I feel his eyes on me as they drag me to my death.

CHAPTER 25
(JIMMY)

I promised on the fucking sun. I wish that promise wasn't so serious to us, but it is, so I couldn't stop running. Not when the blood circulating through my legs consisted only of lactic acid. Not when it felt like bleach burned into my chest and leaked into my stomach or when Tequila told me it was okay to stop.

"Jimmy, it hurts," J whimpers as he starts gaining consciousness. His face is barely even surprised when he sees me. He started groaning a couple of blocks back, his broken, burning body hitting mine with each careless step. It took all my willpower not to stop because even though I knew how much pain he was in, his inability to scream in pain made it worse.

I shield him the best I can from the lashing branches and leaves, but they still slash at his delicate, inflamed skin. I lay him down in the medical hut, noticing for the first time how hollowed out his cheeks are. When they cut off his shirt, I can count all his ribs, and only small portions of his skin are free of any wounds. Finn and Anna push me out as I pace, thinking the worst. His body falls limp as I watch through the piece of plastic, my own circulating pain causing my knees to almost buckle under my weight before a heart monitor beeps to life, lines showing the faint rhythm.

I relax for only a second before I tense again. Harley should have been right behind us; she should be here. I look frantically through the gang for her wavy brown hair, for her golden eyes. Rey and Johnny lie on the ground, their smoke bombs and weapons strewn around them as they argue. Uri sits, holding his ribs as a person I've never seen before wraps him in cloth. Tequila and Buckey must have run after me because Tequila's nimble fingers lock around my forearm, and Buckey belly flops on his brother. Even Até is moving toward us, but there's still no Harley, Ace or Luke.

"You okay?" Tequila asks, leading me to a log, forcing me to sit and catch my breath.

People come toward us, some trying to help clean us up and check if we are injured. I wave them away. The others sit singing around the fire or have retired to bed.

"Yeah," I mutter, removing my weapons from my pockets and pulling my jacket off because I'm burning up. "J's not doing too well, but he's a Hudson, tough like Harley. He'll be okay," I say firmly, mostly to myself, my chest loosening and the pain of my overworked legs disappearing as my breathing steadies. "Harley should be back by now."

I know she didn't need to sprint like I did; there could be so many reasons why she's delayed. Knowing her, she could have tried to help the other prisoners escape. I'm filled with dread, though, I can't even check on her. Rey, Uri and Buckey were the only ones with walkie talkies.

"She might be caught up saving some people," Tequila reassures me, repeating my thoughts, "Besides, Harley's not alone. She has Ace and Luke, and Malick and Jasper are waiting for them at the tree line."

"That's what I'm worried about," I mutter, running my fingers through my sweat-soaked hair, my heart beating as fast as my knee bounces. I trust Ace, but he and Harley can't take on all the Hunters alone. And though Luke has shown how much he wants to protect Harley, I still can't find a reason to believe he won't save himself instead of her.

As if on cue, Ace walks into the clearing, Malick and Jasper walking solemnly at his side, their heads hanging. No Harley. No Luke. It takes me a minute to get to my feet and put all the pieces together. I notice Ace's tear-soaked face, his eyes locked on the dirt, droplets falling past his nose.

Tequila's hand leaves my arm to cover her open mouth. Ace pulls at his fingers, mumbling as he counts.

"Where is she?" I first whisper, then demand as heat rushes to my cheeks. But he only shakes his head, sniffling.

"I tried to — but — she wouldn't let me die." His words throw me off.

Let him die? I don't know whether to scream at him for leaving her or comfort him because he was close to death. Harley would never choose herself over him, over any of us. Obviously, anyone with eyes can see Ace is her person. She would sacrifice her own life rather than let him die.

"What happened?" I breathe, stopping myself from jumping to conclusions and losing myself in rage toward the wrong person. I unclench my fists, his puffy, glossy eyes finally meeting mine. He's barely holding himself together, working hard to hold back the waterfall of tears pressing against the dam he has hurriedly built for our sakes.

"Luke waited till you and Uri left. Until Harley and I were alone with him. He grabbed me and put a gun to my head." As he talks, I grab at my hair, trying to pull myself out of this nightmare because it's the only sensible explanation for all of this. A nightmare. "He told her to surrender herself willingly to the Big Three or he'd put a bullet in my head and make her watch me bleed." His voice starts to shake. The gang and other people close in around us, making me feel boxed in, claustrophobic. "I told her to leave, that it was okay, but she wouldn't. They took her, and I couldn't do anything." His voice breaks, and he starts to hiccup. Uri moves to Ace's side, supporting him as hesitant tears return.

Faces look to me, mouths moving, but my whole universe has gone quiet. My biggest fear takes hold of my tough exterior and places its rough, scaly hands over my eyes. I've worked so long and hard to protect her, to have her in my arms, and once I finally did, I wasn't able to put myself in front of her. To do what she has done for me for fourteen years, never asking for anything, not even a thank you. I could have saved her, made Uri or Ace take J, stayed with her the whole way, but I listened to her. I believed she would be okay.

"Jimmy?" Tequila cautiously reaches for my arm, but I rip it away.

"We have to go back." I start forward, my heart pressing into my airway. Ace doesn't think twice before stepping in front of me, blocking my path.

"You can't. They've probably moved her already. She made me promise not to let you go back. Not now, anyway." He frantically pushes against my shoulders, but I shove him aside effortlessly. He may be more muscular than me, but I am more aggressive and ruthless when driven by anger, by the need to get to her.

"You could have stayed by the building, waited till they moved her, followed them."

"I had no way of knowing which exit they would take her through, and once you left more Hunters showed up. They would have shot me. I almost didn't make it here without being seen." He moves back in front of me, not backing down. Malick, Jasper and Uri all assist him now.

"You were scared of being seen and shot?" I spit, my mind racing, my neck muscles flexing. "She got taken to save you, and she might die—" I stop my words before impulse takes over and I put all the blame on him.

He couldn't have done anything alone, and he was willing to die so she could live. Ace drops his eyes for only a second, and I see my chance. I spring forward, moving a couple of feet before hands grab at my legs, pulling me down.

My chest tightens, lungs gripped by grief, struggling to help me live. My eyes turn to ice, shattering as tears blur the world. My jaw seals itself shut as I scream through gritted teeth, my head pounding like an orchestra playing fifty different songs at once, all off-key. I grab at roots and branches, crawling, pulling, fighting forward, but four bodies land heavily on mine. Too much weight for me to fight against, as they eventually secure my arms and push my cheek into the dirt.

"I need to—" I cry at the top of my lungs, jerking and flailing, hitting limbs and solid objects.

"Jimmy, stop!" Tequila yells. Her words reach me through the chaos, her tone almost sounding like it did the day she found my stash of drugs. She repeats her plea for me to stop, her agony piercing my eardrums, and I break.

I let them hold me down, having no more strength to fight against them, but the urge to get to Harley only grows, fuelled by fragmented pieces of my heart, the feeling so powerful that I forget what used to occupy the space before. Nothing around me matters as I imagine what might be happening to her.

"Let me go!" I scream, inhaling dust and splintered pieces of earth, letting them scrape my throat. "Please, just let me go," I repeat. This time my voice leaves me, along with my common sense and my consciousness. I am weak.

If our roles were reversed and I were taken, Harley wouldn't be breaking down. She would stay strong for everyone around her, quickly making a plan to get me back, but she is the stable one. I am not. For her, I am forever vulnerable when she is not around. She is what makes me strong. I let her down.

Bodies slowly release me as I stop fighting. They're testing me, but I don't spring forward. I only move my fingers through my hair and use my shirt to help wipe my tears — the shirt she wore yesterday, her beautiful scent like perfume lingering on the fabric.

I lie still, staring at the small bugs crawling over fallen leaves, wishing to be like them, aimlessly wandering.

Até's face appears as she sprawls out beside me, sparking irritation through every inch of my body because that's what Harley does when I'm in one of my moods and she needs to talk to me. That feeling quickly turns to pain when I see Até's face. It almost looks like her eyes are watering, like she has recently been crying. Actually sympathetic. The last person I would expect to comfort me.

"Jimmy," she whispers, her pack swaying to one side. "We're going to get her back. I promise. But right now Luke has most likely shared our location with the Big Three. We have to move camp. We sent guards to find out if there are Hunters spying on us." She pushes herself up now, kneeling, stretching her hand out to me.

Her braids are rushed, and the wolf skin sits crooked on her shoulders. I push myself up, ignoring her hand as I slowly make my way to the hut to pack up Harley's and my things and to give away Luke's.

"What about J?" I ask, remembering there's a new person I must take care of, someone I can't let die or get retaken. I don't want to think about the fact that if Harley never comes back, J will be all I have left of her, constantly there to remind me of how useless I am. *Stop,* I scold myself.

"We're moving him first, along with the medical supplies. Anna and Finn just got him stabilized. Malick, Jasper and four other guards are going with them," she says. Malick and Jasper instantly leave my side, going to J's. That eases me a little.

"I'm going with him too," I say firmly, wiping the dirt from my clothes, finding a task to distract myself with for the moment.

"Very well," Até nods, standing in place as the gang runs off, rushing to gather their stuff. She stays with me, waiting for me to say more.

"What about the huts?" I ask.

"What about them?"

"Are you going to leave them for the Hunters to take over? To find stuff they shouldn't? Why run when you can fight, for what might be the only bright place in this miserable forest?"

"It would be idiotic to stay," she snorts. "If we stay and fight and by some miracle win, they will never stop sending more and more Hunters until we are no longer here. I would rather have all my people live than watch them die." Her muscles tense, a silver breastplate glinting through her jacket as the sun hits it. I sniffle, wiping my nose, making her relax again. "I know you're concerned we'll be moving farther away from her. I know you're not thinking straight, and I know you think I'd rather let her die than save her because I've been dreaming of that since the first day she showed up. But for some reason I can't let her die. I don't think I could live with myself if I did." She touches my arm softly before moving on to help the others hurry along.

I don't know if she's changed her mind about Harley because she's seen how the gang relies on her or because of the way Harley held Emerson when she was dying. I never thought Até would ever feel that way about her. It would be as unlikely as Rey sitting in silence.

"We found some," a guard yells. He and four other guards move into the clearing, pushing three Hunters in front of them, their hands bound behind their backs. The first Hunter's uniform has blood blossoming over his stomach, his face pale. The second is badly beaten, his face swollen, and the third is unscathed.

Até appears at my side again, removing her bag and pulling out her dagger. "How many of you are there?" she demands.

"They're not talking, but these three are all we found close to the camp," says a guard as he pushes the Hunters to their knees. Até pauses in front of the Hunter with the bullet wound, pursing her lips. I gravitate toward them, feeling my heart slow. Até steps aside, letting me take over, knowing what I intend to do.

"How many more are there?" I grunt, choosing the Hunter who is unscathed. He's smart enough not to get hurt and selfish enough not to put himself in danger. He smirks as though he would never expect someone like me to do anything rash. He hasn't seen me in a fight; he hasn't seen what I do to people who threaten my gang, my family. "I'll ask you one more time — how many are there?"

He shrugs, his ugly, dull green eyes taunting me. I punch him hard in the stomach; he grunts and keels over, low enough for me to kick up and connect with his face. He looks back up, shrugging. My knuckles connect with his eye. His jaw. His nose. I punch and punch until the Hunter is on the ground, groaning. I swing back my foot.

"Stop," the Hunter with the bullet wound yells. "It's only us," he sighs.

I turn to him, raising my hand. No more tears, no more weakness.

"How do I know you're not lying?"

He flinches, the bullet wound dripping blood down onto his pants. "I have a map in my breast pocket."

"Steve…" another Hunter tries to object, but the man he called Steve glares back at him.

"It shows the position of every Hunter, in the city and towns," Steve says, his eyes focused on the ground now. Até reaches into the man's pocket, pulling out a small gold coin. She turns it over in her hand, seeing no button to activate it. "It's face activated," Steve says, offering his face to her.

Até points it toward him, and a holographic map pops up, with green dots moving about the streets and in the buildings. Only three of them are in No Man's Land. Até calls Asteroid, handing the gold coin off to him to copy or hack into. She pulls her gun, pointing it at Steve. The second badly beaten one starts to panic.

"We gave you the information you asked for. We aren't loyal to the Big Three, Steve and I. They killed our families and forced us to become Hunters because we had potential. If you let us live, we'll work for you. We have trackers in the back of our necks. If you leave them here it will give you a head start, throw the Big Three off your trail for a bit."

Até considers this. Steve shows no objection to what his friend said. The other Hunter pushes himself up, looking more surprised than the guards.

"Very well. You two," Até says, lowering her gun, gesturing to two of her guards. "Remove their trackers and then take them to Anna or any other healer to be treated."

Steve and the other Hunter look grateful as the guards drag them away, but the one still kneeling in front of me smiles. "You will not go unnoticed for long. They will find you and torture you, the same way they will torture Harley," he snarls, his words feeling like acid. "They will kill her and all of you for being traitors," he crouches and laughs, spitting blood at my feet.

I stare at him, not moving, watching his mouth twitch with hysteria. The fiery pit in my stomach flares up into my throat. Into my eyes. Até flips the gun, presenting the handle to me.

"Will you do the honours?" She asks so plainly that I expect her to smile, but when I look at her, she appears distressed. His words hurt her like they hurt me.

I grip the gun, pressing it to the Hunter's forehead. His eyes stay locked on mine, showing traces of fear as he braces himself for the impact. My hands don't shake and my mind becomes blank till I see the Hunters who killed my parents. The Hunters who jumped me for the first time. The Hunters who took the woman I have loved since I was four. I do not feel my humanity trying to sway me. I feel it cheering me on.

"Jimmy," Tequila gasps, emerging from the hut, holding her bag and my own, dropping them as she sees me. She moves slowly toward me while the rest of the gang emerges from the hut. Some stare at me with blank expressions, not knowing what to feel, some encouraging me. "She wouldn't want you to do this, not for her," she says softly.

She's right. Harley wouldn't want me to do this. Kill for her. But this isn't for her. I have been waiting for this moment, to silence the voices and the nightmares, ever since my parents were killed. To stop my depression from holding me down and clamping onto my wrist with its fanged teeth. This person kneeling in front of me has beaten thousands of people and killed hundreds. He is not human — he is a puppet who can't think for himself.

"May your soul find the heavens," I whisper, and pull the trigger.

CHAPTER 26
(JIMMY)

I was a child when I started to understand why we got a certain amount of food each day, why gang fights were more important than learning, and why people in uniforms were enemies, not friends. There were two things, though, that I couldn't grasp. I couldn't quite understand why drugs were more abundant even than food and why people ruined their lives to get a small dose of whatever they could afford. I never understood — until my parents died, that is.

Rage, vengeance and depression left the dying soul of a druggie and crawled into my body, seeking refuge in my insecurities, my pain, enhancing them. I woke to find my imagination and memories filled with darkness until I knew nothing of what it was like to be happy.

When I looked in the mirror, I saw only the pieces of my mind and body that I despised the most. When I was with my friends, all of them laughing, joking, talking about whatever crossed their minds, I felt alone and empty, tiredness clinging to me like wet clothes in a storm. I felt heavy, so heavy that holding my head up without resting it against a wall was my biggest accomplishment of the day. I was a burden to Harley, who dragged me along so I wouldn't be left behind.

Then I came across ecstasy. Eric gave it to me, told me to try, that it would help with the nightmares and dark thoughts. It did, and I understood why addicts choose drugs over food. It made everything disappear. Suddenly the whole world was in colour when I was so used to seeing dark greys. I was free from everything that pulled me down, though it never lasted. After that first time, I tried to replicate the first euphoric experience, but I never could. It only got worse, yet I couldn't stop.

I thought killing that Hunter would give me the same feeling as my first taste of ecstasy. I was foolish to believe it would. Revenge wouldn't dull the demons throwing parties in my nightmares. It would only add new ones to the mix. Killing the Hunter wouldn't bring my parents back. I became the thing haunting me, the worst demon of them all, the one who killed that Hunter with not a trace of mercy or remorse, a Hunter who was brainwashed to follow orders. I became the exact person who started my downward spiral. I was exactly like the Hunter who killed my parents.

On the outside, I sculpt a mask resembling the guard's expressions to appear unaffected as I walk at J's side through the woods. I act like I kill people for a living, not like my first kill will live with me forever. On the inside, I watch a version of myself screaming at the top of his lungs, pounding at the walls of my glass heart, suffocating as I steal all his air.

"It gets easier," Malick reassured me, walking at my heels, but the look on his face told me it only gets easier to forget the bodies for a second before being reminded of their faces. Tequila didn't look at me or speak to me as we found and set up our new camp on the border of AC's and MC's city. She may never talk to me again. She thinks I'm cold and inhuman because I shot the Hunter for revenge, not to protect myself or anyone around me. Maybe she's right, but I wish she could see how much I want to go back in time and not take the gun. I wish she could see how much weight and pain I've added to my shoulders … see how much I wish it were me and not the Hunter.

At camp, I went with Áte to talk to the Hunters, Steve and Amar, but I didn't speak. They don't hate me for killing their friend. They're glad, which makes things worse.

"He was a cruel man," Amar says, twisting his lip ring with his teeth. His eyes are lighter and happier because, in addition to extracting the trackers, Anna and Finn found a way to remove their earpieces by deactivating them with magnets, pulling them out carefully without pushing them further into the ear where they could damage the eardrum. They don't have to be controlled anymore.

"He had the highest number of kills out of all the Hunters. You took a very bad man off the streets," Steve said, his voice bolder, his wounds stitched, bloodied clothes replaced with raggedy patched-up ones.

We learn that the Hunters have been divided over the years into two groups. One group believes the leaders care about them, and therefore they do everything asked of them and more, trying to impress them. The Hunters in the second group, who don't think killing and hunting innocent people is right, ignore what orders they can. These Hunters divert the innocent from the cruel Hunters, giving people extra food and warm clothes. We decide to trust Steve and Amar, removing their handcuffs, allowing them to build themselves sleeping areas and wander around with one guard. They cause no trouble.

I do what I can to help people settle in, building moss beds, learning how to weave hammocks until Asteroid pulls me into a strategy meeting. I sit there at the edge of the group, playing with my hair while everyone goes on about where the leaders could have taken Harley. There is the occasional comment about Luke being a snake and worse and I don't chime in. I know there's only one way to handle this, and it is too dangerous to involve the others. I keep my mouth shut, avoiding Ace's knowing eyes.

As soon as the meeting ends, I make a beeline to where all the weapons and clothes are piled, stealing a jacket, two knives and a gun, then wait for Tequila to take her mid-day nap like she always does.

"Where the hell do you think you're going?" Ace asks, appearing at my side, where I sit waiting peacefully behind a tree, sharpening my knife with a rock. An exaggerated sigh escapes from my mouth.

Harley could have picked Rey or Johnny to promise to make sure I didn't do anything stupid. At least they would forget and busy themselves with an even dumber task. But not Ace. Oh no, that kid takes promises almost as seriously as I do, and he would do anything to make sure he didn't break one to Harley.

"I'm not going to the Big Three," I grumble, watching Tequila finally settle her head on a pillow she carried from the camp, the only one smart enough to do so.

"Then where?" he presses, watching with me, his voice growing more unbearable to listen to with every word.

"You're not my babysitter," I huff, facing him.

His appearance is relatively back to normal, but you can tell by his slightly slumped shoulders and his distracted gaze that he's in as much distress as I am. He loves Harley in the same way I do. I guess that type of love never truly goes away.

"Ryker's," I sigh, giving in. "She'll know where Harley is," I say, knowing as well as everyone else that Ryker is the only one able to pinpoint Harley's exact location. I am reckless enough to even consider going back to Dead Man's Hill and walking into her territory where she played with my life. I expect Ace to tell me how stupid I am, but to my surprise, he doesn't object to my plan and doesn't argue about it; he smiles.

"I'm coming with you." He straightens, causing me to notice two knives poking from his pocket and a gun in his waistband. I nod, having no energy to debate with him, and it would be nice to have a second pair of eyes.

"I just have to tell Tequila first." I move from behind the tree, hoping she's asleep by now.

"But she's—" Ace objects. I quicken my pace so I don't have to explain what I'm doing and why I'm talking to her when she can't hear me or reply.

Since Tequila avoided me all day, I figured she wouldn't stick around long enough to let me get in two words. I have to tell her what I'm doing. So while she's sleeping is a good time and might even be better for me, since she won't be able to burn me with her stare, talk circles around me or forgive me. I don't deserve it.

I crouch next to her. Her breathing flows evenly, muscles twitching every so often as her mind drifts off.

"Tequila?" I whisper, tapping her arm lightly and waving my hand across her face. "You awake?" She doesn't move or answer. I look around us, making sure people are out of earshot, but everyone is too caught up with settling in to hear my whispers. "I'm going to Ryker's — or the Flame, as you like to call her. She'll know where Harley is, and don't worry, I'm not going alone. Ace has insisted on following me around — perfectionists follow orders to the T, what can I say?" I laugh softly, anxious she might wake up.

I'm scared she'll never be my sister again. "I know you may hate me. May never talk to me, and you shouldn't. What I did was selfish, beyond wrong. I thought it would help silence everything in my head. I thought it would be payback for what they did to Mom and Dad. But It only killed me more and made me the person I have spent my whole life hating and running from. I'm so sorry." I feel my voice shake as I push my fingers through my hair. "I'm so sorry I've been a burden, that I never tried to fix myself. I figured I was too broken. I'm sorry I never lived up to the person you knew I could be," I sigh as she rolls to the side, beginning to snore. "I'll be back. I love you." I stand quickly, making my way back to Ace. My mind is jumbled, frantic, wanting to run from itself.

"You know she won't be mad at you forever. She's in shock," Ace says, trailing behind me. I know he's right, but every time I do something drastic, I fear she'll stop seeing me as her little brother and start seeing me as an unstable bomb.

When we finally make it to the edge of Dead Man's Hill, sweat and dew slide from our hair, exhausted breaths forming like clouds. It took ten times longer to find our way, which is worrying because the pale blue sky is slowly becoming bruised with night. I don't want hordes of people snooping around while trying to convince Ryker to help me.

"Did you hear that?" Ace whips around, nudging me with his shoulder. I turn my head and point my ear to the trees, closing my eyes to listen. The footsteps sprinting across the forest floor would be almost too quiet to hear if it weren't for curse words occasionally surfacing and the snapping brittle twigs, invisible in the dull light.

"Don't shoot." I relax a bit, a smile pulling at the corners of my mouth as Tequila appears, batting at her toque and clothes.

"Stupid spiders and bugs." She shivers, not even out of breath. "Oh, hey." She folds me into her arms, her head hitting my chest. "Don't you ever say or even think that I hate you or that you're a burden. I could never hate you, idiot. You're my brother. My blood. You could bomb the city and I would still love you — I might not like you all that much if you did, but I could never hate you — and don't bomb anything. Okay?" She punches me, her bony knuckles pinching my muscles, but her speech makes it hurt less, and as she smiles a layer of depression encasing my heart slides away.

"So you weren't sleeping."

"No. I knew since I avoided you all day, you would only talk to me when I was unable to say anything back — I mean you do that a lot. Also I had to let you soak everything in for a bit," she says, moving over to Ace, pulling up his hood and tucking his hair back, hiding his curls.

"Okay, you can come, but you and Ace have to keep watch at the tunnel entrance. I want to talk to Ryker alone—" I start, but Tequila whips back around, glaring at me, crossing her arms.

"Oh, no, no, no. You think I'm missing my chance to see the great and powerful Flame? Ace will be fine by himself. Right?"

"Yeah," Ace hesitates, nodding quickly, not wanting her intimidating stare to be directed at him. Ace isn't scared of much, but for some reason, he goes out of his way to make sure Tequila is never disappointed in him.

"Fine, but I'm doing the talking," I sigh.

"Yeah, okay," she says with sarcasm, raising her hands in defence, moving past the tree line and taking the lead, forcing us to follow.

The streets of Dead Man's Hill are scattered in mellow orange and deep red autumn leaves, almost empty as people punch their work slips, signalling the end of a dull, repetitive day. The exhausted citizens who linger wear heavy jackets as the temperature drops with the disappearing rays of sun. Sizeable hoods shadow their faces, allowing us to do the same without looking suspicious.

Flickering street lights click on, creating shadows in our wake. Every turn we take, my breath catches in my throat as we see more Hunters than usual patrolling the streets, the lights playing tricks with their expressions. They knock over easy targets, ripping warm clothes from skeletal bodies, leaving the defenceless to shiver in their homes. We make ourselves look bigger and wider, but not so much that they'd want to challenge us, even though I'd like them to try. After passing twenty or so hungry, snarling Hunters, we somehow make it to the trap door.

I can feel my heartbeat in every part of my body, even my toes, as Ace settles into the shadows of a neighbouring alley and Tequila unlatches the door, gesturing for me to enter into the place that occupies my nightmares. I'm guiding us through the tunnels based on instinct. My memory isn't as good as Ace or Uri's, and I was passed out half the time we were down here. I could be leading us into a different town for all I know.

"Do you even know where we're going?" Tequila asks, her voice apprehensive, pointing her flashlight at me instead of in front of her. I wonder if she can hear my lungs rattle as they force out air, or my thoughts run through a list of how many drugs could be down here.

"We'll see," I answer, trying to make my voice stronger, but I can't. I point my gun out, positioning my flashlight on my arm. The thin strip of light is daunting, even with Tequila at my side. It only shows me what isn't hiding from the light, not which creatures might be following us or lurking at our sides.

I'm not scared of the dark. In The Sticks, you can't afford to be. If you're too caught up guessing what might be around you, you don't hear or notice what is. This, however, is a different type of darkness, thicker, grimmer.

"Creepy," I mumble, giving myself *déjà vu*, shifting the light from side to side. I ignore my racing heart while I listen for Tequila's breath and watch her light sway, confirming she hasn't wandered off.

"Yep, this is where the ghosts who hate homework and tests come to live while they're not haunting the school," Tequila says in a gravel-filled voice.

"Shut up."

"They have fun down here though, waiting for drunk partiers in the rocks, poking their heads out when they hear laughter and whispers echoing down the tunnels."

"Tequila, it's not funny." My voice quivers as I reach for her arm, but I only grab air. She's not anywhere around me, her light gone. She's vanished into thin air. "Tequila," I hiss, continuing forward, trying not to think of ghost heads poking from the thick rock, laughing at me for believing her. I lower my gun, making sure I won't accidentally shoot her if she tries to scare me.

"Boo!" She springs up in front of me, the light from her flashlight shining under her chin. I jump back, covering up my manly squeal with a forced cough.

"Dude, I could have shot you!" I yell, pushing her aside.

"Yeah, but you didn't — relax," she chirps, skipping behind me.

I trudge forward, pretending to be furious but end up bumping into a wall, which only makes her burst into laughter.

"Wait," I hush her, running my fingers over the chilling word 'Ryker's' carved into the metal. "We're here. Now don't be stupid, don't touch anything, and let me do the talking, okay?" I order, feeling around for a handle, but it opens when I push on the door, no one there to let us in like the last time.

The lights flicker from purple to white, not as bright as before. Soft piano music plays instead of loud jazz. A bleachy synthetic smell seeps out of every crack and piece of fabric, clinging to our skin. Ryker's bodyguards ignore us as they drag lifeless Hunters from the room, leaving lines of blood behind.

"I would say we are closed for the night, but I am assuming you aren't here for a drink." Ryker emerges from behind the ruby curtain shield, the spot where I dropped to the floor, losing all control. She wears a full red leather suit, along with a fluffy black coat. Her lips are painted the same colour as the leather, her cheeks rouged, her eyes a sickly yellow. She stops, kicking off her heels, wiping blood from her knife, the smeared red on her face no longer appearing as blush.

"I need information on Harley," I announce, shocked by the scene, her flame tattoo the only thing normal in the room.

"Please," Tequila adds, her mouth forming a slight O as she processes this room's beauty and evil.

Bodyguards, dressed in janitor uniforms, start mopping the floor, spreading around the red, dirty mop water. All evidence of the dead bodies vanishes as if it was only ever in my imagination.

"What happened?" Tequila questions, her voice teeming with interest.

Ryker slides into one of the booths, the tablecloth purple, the candlelight flickering grey instead of yellow. Her knife settles against the wood as she tucks a red cloth into her coat pocket, her firm-lined lips changing as one side gets pulled in by her teeth.

"Hunters aren't allowed in my tunnels, nor are they allowed to set foot in my place of business. They decided to do both today. They knew the consequences."

"Why did they?" Tequila blurts, pulling herself onto a bar stool, her wide eyes never leaving Ryker's.

"Tequila," I hiss, sitting two stools away from her. I should have known she wouldn't keep her mouth shut; she doesn't know how.

"You ask a lot of questions." Ryker points, snapping her fingers. A bodyguard appears in seconds with a crystal glass layered with liquid: the bottom blood red, the top soft pink.

"Sorry." Tequila shrinks into her coat, biting her nails.

"What do you want, Jimmy?" Ryker asks. She crosses her legs, using her long-pointed fingernails with cat eyes painted on the surface to mix her drink, and as she does the colour changes to a bright orange.

"I need your help finding Harley. She was—"

"Taken by the Big Three — pity, I liked her," she interrupts, tightening her unbelievably long braids. Her breathy voice floats around our heads and back down her throat. "She almost got away — though, I heard she stayed to save your little group. See, that's where we're different. I would have let you die," she laughs. Her bodyguards instantly play along, doing the same.

Harley could have gotten away. She could have been safe, I think, pulling my gun out, placing it on the bar, making sure Ryker is forced to stare down the barrel.

"Tell me, Jimmy, why would I help you?" she snorts.

Irritation prickles into my limbs, replacing the dread. "You owe me a favour," I fume, forcing myself to remain seated. Ryker raises her eyebrows and stands, her throat grumbling as her long legs strut over, engulfing the space between us. She sits as close as possible, moving my gun, so it continues to point at her.

"I owe you no favours."

"You almost killed me."

"I saved you with the antidote and helped you find J." Her voice grows firm as she sets her eyes in such a way it almost appears like she is smiling, though her mouth stays in a line. I narrow mine at her. Tequila's hand presses down on my shoulder as I lean toward Ryker.

"How do I know you didn't set up her capture?" I counter, pleased when she leans back, feigning surprise. Her glass shatters under the pressure of her claw-like fingers, the liquid splashing both her and me.

"Don't you dare accuse me of that! I take orders from one person, and he does not want Harley dead," she spits, losing her cool for the first time, her yellow eyes and ghost-like breath distracting me from her words. Tequila moves beside us, breaking our death glare.

"Ryker, Jimmy didn't mean to insult you. He's not thinking straight," she says, pinching my traps too hard. "Love makes people jump to conclusions. We're only wondering if you have any information on the whereabouts of Harley and, if you have, could you be so kind as to share it with us?" Tequila inquires, her voice calming, managing to loosen up Ryker a little.

"I don't know where she is, but I can find out," she says, slowly unclenching her fist, adding more blood to the hardwood floor, the cuts on her hand fairly deep.

"What's the catch?" I grunt, shaking Tequila's hand from me and pushing my fingers through my hair, finding I'm sweating.

"You take me to No Man's Land with you. If I help you once more, my connection can no longer keep me hidden — no longer protect me from, well, you know," she explains. She waves over a bodyguard, who pulls up a chair, cleaning and stitching her cuts. Another one slides her a glass, half full of a clear liquid that I doubt is water. She takes the whole thing in one gulp, grimacing, either from that or the needle weaving through her skin.

I laugh, only to realize she's dead serious. "No way," I object, shaking my head fiercely, waving my hands in front of me, making it overly apparent that I would rather ask the Big Three where Harley is than take Ryker with us.

"Then I guess you'll never find your girlfriend." She winces as the man finishes the last stitch, pours white liquor over it and wraps it in red gauze.

"Jimmy, can I talk to you for a second?" Tequila sing-songs, pulling me to the side out of earshot right when I'm about to blurt, 'fine, who needs you anyway, Ryker, I'll form my own connections and do it myself.'

"Jimmy, I understand you are somewhat hard-headed and stubborn — not somewhat, you are, but even Harley and I wouldn't leave Ryker here if it meant we could save you, and Harley is almost as stubborn as you are." I consider this, messing with my hair.

"I don't trust Ryker, or believe a word she says. She almost killed me, for fuck sakes. For fun," I proclaim, but I know Tequila's right. We know of no one else who could find Harley's location.

"You love Harley, right?" she asks. I nod instantly. What kind of stupid question is that? What I feel is stronger than love. "Then put your ego aside, and let Ryker come with us. She'd be a good person to have on our side, plus she knows a lot about the Big Three." Tequila holds my arm, looking at me like I'm unstable. I don't want her to see me like that.

"Fine, you can come. I just have one more request," I yell over Tequila's shoulder, retreating to the metal door, wanting to breathe in air that doesn't reek of blood. I pull at my hair, forcing myself not to rip it all out. I play with my hair so much I'll go bald by the time I turn twenty.

"And that is?"

"I'm guessing if you help us and you are no longer safe, that means the people we love won't be either. Correct?" I inquire. She tilts her head, narrowing her eyes. I stand taller.

"I suppose that is true."

"If I let you come, you have to get the people we want out of the Sticks and take them to No Man's Land," I demand, making my voice firm and careless like hers, watching her play with something on the inside of her coat.

"Very well," she sings, slipping on her heels, appearing at my side with a small bag pressed against her fluffy coat. I look her up and down, my head almost hurting from her bright clothes.

"You're not going to change?"

"What is the point of living if not to be noticed?" She yanks open the door, leading us down the tunnel, no light needed to guide her since she's lived underground for so long. I click on my light, watching her twiggy figure saran-wrapped in tight clothes that swish every time she takes a step. The sound mixes with the clicking of her heels on the rock floor, filling the emptiness.

I hope Ryker can get everyone the gang loves and needs out of the home that will soon become hell once we get Harley, who will be the most hunted person in the world.

Ryker looks over her shoulder, her eyes glowing in the light. "My guards and I have watches that we communicate with. When we get to No Man's Land, your friends can tell me the names of the people they want to save, and I'll get my guards to retrieve them — does that suit your demands?" she taunts and hisses. If I were to turn the light off, I could mistake Ryker's movements and voice for a stealthy underground creature, clicking around in the inky darkness.

"Yes, thank you," Tequila says, clinging to my arm.

"What about the information from your connection?"

Ryker snorts. I can almost hear her thoughts call me an idiot in ten different ways. "My connection has a watch too. Only two people in the Big Three have my watches so it's secure enough to communicate without getting found out," she says, finding the stairs before the light does. She drops her coat and, reaching into her tiny bag, pulls out a very long white cloak, slipping it on. It covers the red but doesn't make her any less noticeable.

As we emerge into the chilled air, Ace springs from the alley, raising his gun to Ryker's head. His eyes jump back and forth, switching between confusion and rage.

"It's okay, she's coming with us," Tequila says, grabbing his gun, moving it back to his side.

"Why?" He looks to me for help, but I don't fully understand why I'm letting her come without putting up more of a fight. I shrug, rolling my eyes and stuffing my hands into my pockets.

"She's going to help us, and we are going to help her. It's a 'scratch my back and I'll scratch yours' type of situation." Tequila reassures him, helping with his hood, always fixing his hair. Ace smiles slightly at the reference but starts pulling at his fingers. She gently takes his hands. "She's going to help get your brother out of the Sticks, Ace."

He stills, looking at me, then Ryker, his face saddening. He drops his head. "He won't leave the gang," Ace sighs.

"Then we'll bring them all," Tequila adds, getting ahead of herself. Ryker moves her lips to say it would be practically impossible to do so, but I stop her.

We can't get Ace all sad and frantic now when we have to move back through the Hunter-filled streets with the most noticeable person in the world at our sides. Ryker plucks at her eyes, removing her contacts, revealing soft grey irises.

Not what I was expecting.

"I'll get to see him again?" Ace brightens, pulling Tequila into a suffocating hug. He beams at me and, releasing Tequila, takes Ryker's hand, shaking it too aggressively.

"Yes, now shall we go before the Hunters bump into us and we have to shoot our way out of here?" Ryker grimaces, peeling Ace's hand from hers and moving to take up the lead with Tequila as we walk.

"Do you trust her?" Ace whispers, sticking close to the wall. He counts every Hunter and civilian that walks past us, all too distracted to care. I genuinely don't understand how he can focus on so many things while holding a conversation and thinking.

"No, but she can help find Harley, and I believe she won't betray us. Like Até, she respects Harley. I don't know why they've changed their minds all of a sudden," I add, thinking back to when Ryker tried to make Harley take the drug that almost killed me and to when Até almost killed Harley because she threatened her power.

Ace laughs for a breath, looking at me like I should know. "It's because Harley's different from anyone else. She's kind, yet fierce. She's intelligent, yet able to say things in a way that registers with everyone. She sacrifices herself for people she's never even met—" Ace stops abruptly, pushing all of us into a narrow alley as six meaty Hunters thunder past, holding automatic rifles. As soon as they're out of sight, we go through the other end of the alley, sprinting to the tree line till bushes and darkness shield us. Ryker and Tequila continue ahead, their heads close, discussing something that makes them frown and chuckle.

I turn to Ace. "What do you mean?" I ask, struggling to process his words in the part of my brain that can understand. I know Harley is special and unique. Since day one, I knew she was, but what does that have to do with getting people to respect her after they've decided to hate her?

"She's a born leader. I think that has something to do with the voices in her head. People gravitate toward her, people who still have good in them and share the same qualities and values under their gritty rough shells," he says, remembering her as if she were never coming back. "They learn to respect her because she gives them what no one can give themselves anymore. She gives them hope and shows them they can be better, that they can change. She takes their ugly pieces, presenting them as beautiful — that's what she did for me anyways. Maybe even for you too." He locks his fingers around the corner of his jacket, surely trying not to beat himself up further for leaving her behind. He is seriously smart for his age and for the life he lives.

"Ace, you—"

"Ryker, where the hell do you think you're going?" A gruff voice interrupts me. The six meaty Hunters we saw before push their way through the bushes, creating a daunting wall with their bodies. All of them wear green masks with slits for their eyes and noses, and deep red paint dripping from a jagged smile. They hold their rifles out, red dots of light shining onto all four of our chests.

"Paid vacation time," Ryker drawls, removing her cloak, revealing two gold-plated guns hanging at her sides. They're held there by white leather holsters, straps fitting around her shoulders. "Though I guess your leaders don't pay you or give you days off."

"Criminals don't get vacations," one of them laughs, the mask making the words muffled, almost robotic. All six step closer, but Ryker doesn't reach for her guns or stray from her high and mighty appearance. So we remain still as well.

"Criminal," she snorts, cautiously sliding her feet from her shoes.

"So brainwashed playthings do know how to joke. Thought they took your humour along with your free will," Tequila yells, but Ryker places a hand on her shoulder, moving Tequila behind her and out of harm's way.

"Don't worry, they are simply vexed with me for never providing alcohol to numb their pain," Ryker chuckles.

"We have no pain — they saved us," one of the Hunters yells, jerking forward, only to be stopped by the biggest Hunter.

"Don't engage with her. She'll pull you into her hurricane of crazy. She knowingly worked with a wanted criminal, so we can take her in."

"She's not a criminal," I bark, knowing they're referring to Harley. I grip the handle of my gun; rage and vengeance gripping me like a vise again.

Ryker moves closer at their words, the rest of us following at her back. Even Ace manages a hateful glare. I've been itching for a fight to release every damn feeling I've felt in the past twenty-four hours ever since we stepped into Dead Man's Hill.

"Come with us," one Hunter says, a woman's voice. She reaches her hand out to Ryker. I'm ready to pounce when Ryker raises her hands, bending down to retrieve her shoes.

"Okay, but I'm not leaving my one-of-a-kind flame shoes behind," Ryker grunts, stunning all of us, even the Hunters, by walking toward them, putting up no fight, not even with her words.

I stutter, trying to object, when she turns, winking in my direction, and that's when it happens. Only for a second, the Hunters hesitate, lowering their guns, sharing confused looks — rookie mistake.

Ryker jams the points of her heels into the necks of the Hunters closest to her, then pulls her guns and shoots them, leaving smoking holes in their green masks before the other Hunters can react. Ryker waits till they have their fingers on the triggers before springing up, grabbing hold of a low-hanging branch and swinging herself up and out of range. The Hunters react too slowly, not moving their guns up in time before they fire, lodging bullets into each other's chests, all falling to the ground.

The three of us stand with our mouths hanging open, not sure if what we witnessed was real or if we inhaled some dream root by accident. Ryker drops down, landing in a crouching position. She retrieves her heels, then drops them, rendering them useless as they drip with blood. Ryker approaches the last twitching Hunter, who wheezes, trying to crawl away. She kneels to remove the woman's mask, stroking her scarred face and touching her lips to the woman's ear.

"No," The woman cries. A popping sound comes from her open lips. Her pupils explode, and blood slithers from her ears, nose and mouth, her head falling to the side. She could have just killed the woman like she did the others, but I guess she wanted her to know she's on the inside. She knows everything about the Hunters; she knows their most fatal weakness.

"What the—" Ace's words catch in the air, not knowing what else to think, let alone say. He slips his gun into his waistband. Tequila does the same, but I keep mine in my hand, ready. My mind races, adrenaline taking over the places in my blood meant for oxygen.

"All earpieces have a kill switch in case of capture so the Hunters can use it to prevent being tortured and revealing secrets — the leaders don't control it, otherwise all the Hunters would be dead by now, 'cause they're so stupid," she says, moving past us, striding ahead like she didn't go all ninja on us.

"No, I mean where did you learn to fight like that?" Ace gawks, running after her, stumbling over his feet.

"Oh, sweets, you should know by now that in order to survive in this world you have to be the best problem-solver and fighter out there.

Besides I was raised to be a Hunter, but they said no creating, selling or using drugs. I had to escape and move underground. It was the best decision I could have made," she says lightly.

"I think she'd be a good role model." Tequila nudges me, holding six new types of knives and chucking the rifles into the bushes.

"You're joking," I huff, finally getting my feet to move forward, recovering from the shock. Ryker would be the worst person to be a role model, but she would make a good fighting instructor, I suppose.

"We have to keep Rey away from Ryker, though. We can't let him learn more chemical experiments," she laughs, and I become lost in the idea of Rey turning his smoke bombs into something else.

"Até won't like her — or, worse, she will," I say, imagining the two of them sitting side by side in fur-covered chairs, firelight enhancing their dramatic dripping makeup as they bond over gory fights.

"We shall find out." Tequila points to a scowling Até. Her hair is slicked back into a high ponytail, wolf skin pinned together at her chest, acting like a parka, dagger shining in the light of the torches held by the guards. The two stand face-to-face, looking over one another, mirroring anger. Ryker holsters her guns.

"Thought you'd be here earlier," Até scoffs, her face breaking, relaxing as she pulls Ryker into a hug.

A HUG.

"Would have, but something got in the way, and I lost my shoes," Ryker laughs.

"Guards told me you took down six Hunters," Até praises, pulling away. She holds Ryker's shoulder, smiling with all her teeth as they look each other over again. Ryker shrugs as if it was no big deal.

"You're joking. You're friends?" I groan, pressing my fingers to my temples. This shit is more mind-boggling than Harley telling me she has six different voices that talk to her. Craziness overload.

"Jimmy, the most drastic and dominant women are usually connected in some way. Besides, where do you think I get my drug ingredients and guards?" Ryker winks, scrunching her toes, tossing her bag to one of the guards.

"And where do you think I get my supplies?" Até laughs, a real genuine laugh that sounds more like coughing.

"I think my head might explode one day," I grumble, plopping down onto a rock, wondering what new and mind-shattering stories wait for me when Harley is back in my arms. I sadden at the thought.

"Ryker!" Anna squeals, running into Ryker's outstretched arms, spinning around. The rest of the gang follows. Rey bounces over to Ryker, but Ace grabs him by the waist, turning him toward me, not excited about the moment those two minds will come together either.

"What the hell is she doing here?" Uri grunts, nostrils flaring, gripping his knife's silver handle so hard he's probably leaving dents in the metal.

"It's okay, man, she's here to help find Harley — though she hasn't apologized for almost killing me, but it's fine." I roll my eyes, glaring at Ryker, who struts toward me, grinning and leaning down.

"I am very sorry ..." She licks her lips. "... that I almost killed you, most likely reactivated your addiction and saved your life twice — but wasn't the vision my creation gave you beautiful?" she whispers, tracing her fingernail along my jawline.

"Apology accepted." I slap her hand away quickly. The vision automatically resurfaces as I sweep my fingers through my hair and move to Tequila's side.

"So you like flames?" Johnny asks. He, Rey, Buckey and Finn all stare intensely at her tattoo.

"You could say that," Ryker replies, taking a seat beside Até on a stool a guard brings forward. She crosses her legs, the bottom of her feet are caked in mud, cut up and bleeding, along with her hand, the cloth stained a deeper red, the stitches surely torn.

"Heard you had red eyes." Rey leans closer to her, clasping his hands behind his back, staring with intense interest in keeping with his scientist nature, as if she's a new experiment.

"I heard you were funnier."

"You heard about me." He smiles, turning to all of us, his eyes beaming with pride, taking a step back to high five Johnny.

"No," Ryker says bluntly, picking her nail. Rey stops mid-high-five, his face falling. Guess Rey has another person to push him around.

"Do you know where Harley is or not?" Uri demands, irritated, the only one who hasn't accepted that Ryker can help. He stands with his arms folded, biceps pushed up to appear bigger, though he doesn't need to; he's already much bigger than her. He stands at Tequila's side so she can ground him, stopping him from doing anything rash.

Ryker pushes her sleeve back, taking her time as she checks her watch. She casually leans forward, pressing her elbows into her thighs and propping her head up with her fist. She acts like she is posing for a picture, enjoying the anticipation building in our chests. Something lodges itself in my throat, waiting for her answer, igniting the pit of fire, the smoke burning my tear ducts.

"Yes."

CHAPTER 27

(HARLEY)

I've lost track of time — my senses disoriented by the thick dark fabric placed over my head. They put me in a car and drove me around in circles for what felt like forever, blasting classical music, so that I couldn't figure out where they were taking me. I couldn't hear the car sliding on asphalt or the fighting in the alleys. I couldn't smell trees, dust or metal. I couldn't focus.

They led me up flights of stairs. It became evident that the small irritations brought on by their careless movements wouldn't fade away quickly, like the tiny bruises they left on my arms, the stiffness in my shoulders from being yanked back and forth and the handcuffs pinching at my wrist. That type of pain never fades.

No one talked as they shoved me into a heated room and sat me in an icy metal chair. They chained my hands to a wooden table, its splinters burying themselves in my arms.

The Hunters shuffled out of the room, grumbling about the scratches and lumps I left on their bodies, but I knew I wasn't left alone. I could sense someone's eyes clinging to me, the faint smell of firewood seeping through the fabric. Luke was watching me, ordered to be by my side till the end. I didn't want to think he could sit there, witnessing all of this unfold and not feel one shred of guilt.

I link my fingers together, chains jingling on solid metal as I shift. I can't lift my hands above my chest. *Where am I?* I ask myself, forcing shallow breaths. Questions whirl around my head, trying to fill the silence. *Did Ace make it back? Did he make sure Jimmy didn't try anything stupid? Is J alive? What did I do?*

I sigh, nearly giving in to my last resort, Luke's name, at the tip of my tongue when a door squeaks open. Three sets of footsteps saunter in. Chair legs screech across the floor, moving in front of me. The door clicks as it locks me away from the world in a strange place where I prepare to face the men who want me dead.

"Luke," the leader I'm already acquainted with, barks.

I'm startled by a harsh ripping sound as the bag leaves my head, my hair falling into my eyes and mouth. Luke carelessly pushes the strands away, not quite looking at me as he returns to his seat in the corner. I pinch my lips together, my new reality coming into focus.

Jackson Clarke, the dominant of the three, sits directly in front of me, his dark hair freshly cut and styled. His eyebrows sit in uniform arches above his menacing eyes, a bold black ring around his brown irises. His skin is flawless and clean, no trace of a beard. He mirrors my expression: lips pinched, eyes careless yet directed, intimidating. Unlike his brothers, he dresses in all black, seeming to be above them, too perfect to be human.

Sitting to JC's right is Aron Clarke, who snarls at me, his silver button-up shirt glinting with the light, illuminating his young face. His ruffled blonde hair and grey eyes are so different from the twins. He's bulkier, scarred and worn, rough around the edges from doing all the grunt work. His merciless personality was strategically sculpted by his half-brother JC and the fact that he rose to power at such a young age.

Then there's Maddick Clarke, JC's twin. Not identical but close enough. MC has floppier, uncared-for hair and a prickly beard that hides his pores but not the freckles that start at his cheeks, migrating and scattering over his nose. He sits behind a small pop-up desk in the corner opposite Luke, jotting notes on a piece of paper, a slight smile on his lips. He's reticent, not one to back his brothers or share the same thoughts. I can't see his eyes, but I sense they are light and calm, like Anna's.

"Do I have to be the one held prisoner *and* the one to start this conversation?" I snort. I run my tongue over my teeth, leaning back like I don't care, and I don't think I do. For some reason, they don't scare me at all. Maybe Eric was preparing me for more than dealing with Hunters. The thought makes bile rise from my stomach.

Luke begins to clean his gun with a grease-stained cloth as JC's lips peel apart, displaying a mocking sinister smile.

"It is the polite thing to do as our guest," AC snorts, his hands resting on the table while his eyes undress me. I resist the urge to attempt to cross my arms over my chest.

"Yeah. A guest you captured and chained to a table—"

"No," JC interrupts, his voice unpleasantly similar to the high-pitched one in my head. "You, my sweet girl, surrendered willingly to us. You chose this yourself. You could have run, but you knew better." His smile grows, never reaching his eyes, giving the impression that at any moment, his face might split down the middle and show the gears and machinery that allow him to function with no heart. No soul. No human empathy.

"He has a point," the cold, warrior voice scoffs, still mad at me for not running when I had the chance.

"He's an arrogant, egotistical bastard who knows nothing about leadership," the dominant voice hisses to the cold one.

"He's disgustingly dreamy," the rose-like voice chimes in, trying to agree with the others, but I feel all of them groan at her. I almost laugh at the thought, which makes me feel lighter, more in control.

I don't argue that the leaders threatened to kill everyone I loved if I didn't hand myself over. I don't want JC to have the satisfaction of watching me fight when I am not in a position to win.

"You have been a tough girl to find. Took us ten years to figure out who you were and eight more to find a safe way to bring you in."

"Eighteen years of your ineptitude," I retort, disturbed by the fact that they have been watching me for most of my life. Everything I've done, every beating and fight, even every boy I've kissed. "Why am I here?" I ask, surprising even myself when my words come out almost bored.

"You are the last soul ruler, my dear, the only person who could ruin our ability to rule, and the one who can help us gain full control of our people," JC says, crossing his legs, elegantly folding his hands over the top of his knee.

"Couldn't you just be a better, less psychotic ruler?"

"Oh, she's a funny one," AC says evenly, his voice flat and unimpressed.

Out of the corner of my eye, I swear, for a second, I see MC smile for only a moment before his face becomes neutral once more. He isn't known for torturing people or being cruel, and he doesn't participate or engage with his brothers' drastic actions. He's calm and hasn't looked at me since they all walked in, and hasn't acknowledged his brother's words either.

"It's too late for that. Once you decrease the food rations and allow Hunters to kill anyone they want, people don't have the desire to follow you willingly," JC shrugs, smirking as he taps his lips with his fingertip, treating me like I'm beneath him — a stupid girl who knows nothing.

"I wonder why they need help ruling," the dominant voice snorts, her feelings giving me the strong urge to lunge forward and gouge JC's eyes out.

"Would all of you calm down and stop playing with my emotions?" I demand, and instantly, control belongs to me. Peace washes over the voices and me, although the dominant voice manages to leave a little bit of rage to help me appear superior.

"That's the main reason you are here," JC continues, leaning forward, placing his elbows on his thighs. "You can make things easier by saying you wish to willingly lead at our sides, which would then give us pieces of your abilities."

"Not a fucking chance," I object, pulling at my chains, making AC flinch, but JC doesn't even blink.

"I suspected that would be your answer," JC says, feigning annoyance. He attempts to frown, but his lips only manage a straight line, his muscles not allowing them to stretch further. "Then we will do this the hard way. Tests will be run on you starting tomorrow to determine whether the soul ruler gene can be placed into our DNA." He straightens, dramatically pausing before he delivers the last words. "If it does work — and even if it doesn't — we will execute you in four days. We've been working on finding a loophole that will ensure your death without endangering ourselves, and we are close."

His words almost float over my head — so foreign and alien to me because I thought I couldn't die by their hands. I thought I was safe, invincible. I can't mask the shock that finds my face. "Executed," I echo, "in four days." My mouth is dry. I can't swallow, I can't—

AC echoes his brother's amusement. He stands, kicking his chair back, the sound of the metal clattering on the slick tile floor hardly registering. "Today is the first of November," he laughs, towering over me, my emotions sinking lower than humanly possible.

"Executed, on my birthday," I mutter, my eyes drifting to Luke, who is realizing the same thing. His hands freeze, then hurriedly go back to their task, making sure the leaders don't see his fear. I squeeze my hands tighter together as they threaten to shake, then pull myself up straighter.

"They won't figure it out," one of the voices says, but I don't want to listen. *"They'll die if they kill you."*

I'm not sure she's right. I don't understand what a soul ruler even is. How am I supposed to believe there isn't a loophole to my demise? I swallow hard, rubbing my handcuffs over my skin, automatically attempting to form a plan to escape, but is that even possible?

"Are you at least going to tell me where I am or are you going to make me guess?" I blurt as the leaders start to move toward the door. JC continues on, but AC gets pulled in by my question, spinning on his heel, marching back over to me and slamming his hands on the desk.

"You could never figure it out. We drove you around in circles, messed with your senses, built this whole damn room just so you would never know where you were." His words smack from his saliva-soaked lips, sprinkling my face.

The way he gestures around makes me think this part of my capture was his idea, probably his only role. He's right; I couldn't listen or count the seconds and turns like Ace taught me, but AC is also arrogant and careless. He believes he is the smartest in the room, and when a person believes that, they always make mistakes.

I look around, taking in the room for the first time. It's no bigger than my bedroom at home, and they did a good job of making sure everything was generic. The tile floors are cheap, and the beige paint isn't something the leaders would have in their buildings. No windows line the walls, the chairs are simple, and the silver door handle is shaped like the ones at school.

AC drips with confidence, waiting for a response, when something at the corner of MC's desk catches my eye. It's a small detail not very many people would think to consider as anything but a brand. The letters MC are engraved in the top right-hand corner of the desk. He could have brought it from his building, but why? I hide my smile as I look into AC's grey eyes, his cockiness fading the longer I stare.

"Is that so?" I ask, leaning forward, almost choking on his garlic-scented breath. "Next time don't use custom furniture, engraved with initials." I mimic their slithering voices and look at MC, whose faint smile has returned. He packs up, a small slip of paper trapped between his fingers. "I've always thought Maddick's building was the nicest of the three."

AC screams in frustration. His palm collides with my cheek, and his foot connects with my table, pushing it further into my rib. "Fuck! How did you know," he yells.

"I didn't," I smirk, leaning back, "You just told me."

AC's eyes lock onto the pop-up desk. He starts toward MC, who keeps his eyes on the wall, not attempting even to move. JC grabs his brother's arm, shoving AC to the side, his shoulder slamming into the door before his fists have a chance to connect with MC.

"Stop it, brother, you knew she would figure it out when she got to the cell — anyway, she has no way of telling her simple-minded gang where she is," JC scolds, trying to stay unaffected by his brother's mistake. I know he is hiding his anger because I'm here and will take it out on AC once they leave. AC frowns, flinging the door open and storming out, mumbling obscenities as he goes.

"Luke will escort you to your cell. It was a pleasure finally meeting you, Harley," JC says, leaving, his voice making me hate my own name.

"Mr. Clarke, do you have a key?" Luke asks, slipping his gun into his holster, taking a deep breath as he gets to his feet. He looks less worn, less tired, having had time to convince himself that what he did was right.

MC nods, crossing the room, looking straight into my eyes for the first time. He doesn't smile, purse his lips or jab at me with his words. He says nothing as he fumbles around for his key, slipping it into the lock. He looks at me like I'm an old friend, reuniting with him after years of being apart. He removes the chain from my handcuffs, his hand brushing over mine so quickly I might not have thought anything of it, if it weren't for the shadow left on my skin and the small piece of paper pressed into my hand. I look up, his gentle brown eyes urging me not to look at the paper with Luke so close. I clench it tighter as MC passes me off to Luke, letting him lead me out the door.

Luke tugs me through halls with simple black tile floors and hardwood covering the walls, the glass windows shimmering in the sunlight. The lights look almost natural, and the air smells of sweet lemongrass and pine instead of bleach and sickly sweet flowers. Workers pass us with no interest as they happily gossip to their co-workers. This place could be almost pleasant if I weren't walking to my holding cell and Luke's grey eyes weren't drilling into my back.

"Don't do it," the wise voice says nonchalantly, her tone almost sing-song and taunting. *"It won't end well."*

I want to listen to her, to keep my lips sealed, to not engage or ask for an explanation from this brooding, brainwashed boy. But I barely take my own advice, so why should I take hers?

Luke shoves me forward, sticking his gun between my shoulder blades, the cold touch of the metal foreign to my flesh.

"Why?" I ask, quickening my pace to put space between him and me, but he only grabs my shoulder, yanking me back. He stays silent, and I press on. "Did you even mean any of it?"

"Any of what?" he snorts, taking his gun from my back, dropping it to his side.

The voices start to scream, fighting with Luke. I push them away, back behind their wall so I can be alone with the boy who was once my friend, who I could have loved.

"What you said at the speakeasy. How I made you feel wanted and—"

"Yes," he chokes out, his muscles hardening, his breath tightening.

"Then why did you do this?" I don't even know why I'm asking. I want to appear strong, as though I hate him for what he did, but I only feel pity. I should hate him, kill him with the silent treatment, but I want closure. I want to know what I did to make him feel like this was the only option.

"To finally do something good in my life—"

"Good?" I interrupt. "How is any of this good? They starve people, kill people, turn friends and families against each other for their own entertainment. They're trying to take away the people's choice in order to support the leaders' insanity," I say, trying to look at him, but he keeps me facing forward, his nails digging deeper into my flesh.

"Some people don't get to choose to follow you either. Your abilities allow you to control them—" He bites his tongue, saying too much. What the hell is he talking about? I don't control people. I jerk my arms forward, but he only grips harder, moving me closer to him. His shoe touches mine, and his breath parts my hair, raising goosebumps. "They're doing a good thing, Harley," he sighs. "They're going to get rid of the fighting and the Hunters once you help them."

"Luke, don't you see they're brainwashing you?" I yell this time, turning heads and stopping feet in their tracks. He pulls me through a door reading, 'Storage do not enter,' slamming my back against a wall once it shuts.

"You want to know why I did this?" he asks, clenching his jaw, his eyes becoming wild. "I did it because they made me feel wanted. I tried so hard, Harley. So hard to give you the benefit of the doubt, for you to show me that you still cared, that you wouldn't leave me, but you chose him. In every situation you chose him," he fumes, moving closer, driving his palms hard against my shoulders, irritating my muscles.

"I didn't—"

"Yes you did. You never felt the way I felt about you. You never once cared. I was just a distraction from your life, when you were what made me want to live. You were the only person in my life who wanted to be around me," he says, and it's then that I see all the pain, all the tortured pieces — but we're all broken by another person at some point in our lives, so why should this justify his actions?

"My intentions weren't to break you," I whisper, trying to raise my hands out of habit, only to remember that they're cuffed. He steps away, still holding me with his tormented stare.

"My whole life I've been ignored. My parents never talked to me, I lost my best friend and then you. The leaders — they care about me. They want me to be around," he sighs, reaching behind me, unlocking a door I wouldn't expect to be anything but a closet. He jerks me forward, forcing me to stumble and struggle to keep up with his long stride.

"No one's parents like them," I mutter under my breath.

He doesn't say anything else, so I focus on this new room. It's long and narrow, everything white, not one speck of colour or furniture anywhere. The lights are dull, so I can look around without my eyes stinging. At the very back of the room, a row of white metal bars stretches from wall to wall, holding four bunk beds, two of them occupied by a man and a woman. They don't acknowledge Luke as he unlocks the cell and my cuffs, shoving me in. I lose my balance, the man managing to grab me before my face hits the ground.

"I'll be back for you in the morning," Luke sneers, walking back out the door.

"Welcome to the VIP prison. So exclusive there's now only three of us." The man smiles, helping me to my feet.

When I look at him, I almost lose my voice. He seems so familiar. He has bushy coal-black hair, traces of a beard on his dark skin and is not much taller or more muscular than me. His smile is what pulls at my heart, though, the way his lips turn up naturally like he was born to show his smile to the world and how tiny flecks of gold dance around in his sweet hazel eyes. He's almost too similar to Uri. But he can't be. Uri said everyone he loved is dead.

"Thank you," I say, rubbing my wrists, "I'm Harley — Hudson." I stretch my hand to him.

"We aren't supposed to use our real names," he frowns, observing my hand. I draw it away, scolding myself for being so foolish, but he pulls me into a hug before I can fully retreat.

"I'm joking," he laughs, the sound so musical and human, playing with the empty spaces in the prison. "Besides, everyone knows who you are, even if they haven't seen the light in years. I'm Levi Winston, and this is Mary — who's never actually told me her last name, or anything about her really." He points to a woman stretched out on the bed across from us, her arms folded over her face.

Winston. I think. That can't be a coincidence.

I remember the note in my hand, promising to focus on Levi after I find out what MC wants me to know. I uncrumple it, finding Mary's name displayed in bold letters.

"Mary?" I question, taking a seat beside Levi on the bed.

The older woman looks up in my direction but not at me. The colour of her eyes is faded and clouded over, grey roots conquering her thinning blonde hair. When she pulls herself up, I notice the severity of their condition. Both wear clothes that are torn and dirty. Mary's face is bruised and scarred, her right arm has an irritated cut running down it, infected and poorly stitched up, the sutures jagged and rushed. Levi is the worse of the two, cuts and bruises covering most of his skin, and the way he sits looks almost too painful. He's been taking the beating for them both.

"Yes," she croaks, adjusting her stiff body.

"MC told me to talk to you," I continue, making a mental note to ask Luke for supplies.

"Did that bastard tell you to look for the old lady, because I'm not old — mind you I'm not going to tell you my age, like I haven't told this kid my last name, but I'm not old," she grumbles. "What does he want me to tell you?" she snorts, her voice husky as if she hasn't had anything to drink in days. Levi's hand moves to his knee, displaying a finger bent at a worrying angle.

"Sorry, one second," I say to Mary, who leans against the bedpost, shrugging her shoulders. "How long has your finger been like that?" I lift Levi's hand, gently moving it to my leg. He looks at it like it's his first time noticing anything unusual about it.

"Maybe a day. It's hard to keep track of time here — don't worry, I'm getting used to the pain." He flinches as I move to tear a strip of fabric from my sleeve.

"I'm going to reset it. We don't have any pain killers, so I'm not going to lie to you and say it won't hurt." I look over at Mary, who seems pleased with me as she smiles at the wall.

"Are you sure you know how to do this?" Levi asks, bracing himself, gripping the mattress, trusting me as he looks away.

"Let's just say my mentor has a lot of experience, and her voice is always with me," I breathe nervously as Mary mumbles something to herself. "On three?" I offer, and he nods. "Okay, one…" A loud crunch replaces my words. Levi groans as I wrap his two fingers together.

"Fuck — wait, actually that hurt surprisingly less than it did before," he beams, hugging me again, thanking me through gritted teeth.

"So you're a soul ruler," Mary presumes, more telling me than asking, playing with a gold band on her ring finger. Excitement bubbles up in me. She knows, but how?

"A what?" Levi mumbles.

"How could you tell?"

"You give off the same energy the others did, and I'm guessing that little mentor of yours lives in your head and talks to you, giving you the power to heal."

"But—" I stutter, looking for something to ask but all my questions are fighting to get out at once, leaving me speechless.

"Sometimes the rulers in your bloodline are forgotten by their parents. Not on purpose, but because they are too busy maintaining the laws and keeping people in order, or they get separated from each other by leaders like ours. People like me are used as guides, teachers, but we still know very little about the soul rulers. My mother was a mentor, I was one, and my daughter was supposed to be one too," she sighs mournfully, her fingers rubbing over a silver necklace. "That's why I'm here. I was searching for any soul rulers who had survived the toxic gas. But before I could find any, a Hunter found out what I was doing, and the leaders took me. I've been here for twenty years. They didn't want me threatening their power and making their lives more difficult — I heard they had a hard time finding you, though," she laughs, causing Levi to look nervously at me.

I continue to stare in awe at her, a person to teach a soul ruler who they are, where they come from and why this is all happening in the first place.

"Can you tell me what this all means? Why are the voices in my head? How can I stop the leaders?" I babble, accidentally squeezing Levi's thigh, but he doesn't care. He's more captivated by Mary's words than I am.

"Slow down, child. Let me tell you the history of it all — how and why a soul ruler was created and needed in the first place." She settles herself in, getting comfortable as she closes her eyes.

Levi and I follow her lead, pushing ourselves further onto the hard, narrow bed, resting our backs against the frames. We face each other, placing our legs one over the other's, despite having just met, but we're both too distracted by her voice to care.

"Centuries ago, an evil dictator ruled the world, killing millions and capturing more. Rulers from every kingdom were drawn to follow a worthy king named Lex, and together, they teamed up with him to defeat the tyrant. They were successful. After the war, they took precautions and formed a plan. Lex called upon a witch who granted each of his daughters a gift to help them lead fairly and prevent them from being killed by evil, power-hungry dictators.

Soon seven sisters ruled the world together, alongside their father. Each sister was named after the gift they were given at birth.

The eldest child, Imperium, was named for the power given to her to rule and to influence her followers, granting them strength.

Sapientiae was named for her wisdom in rulemaking and life decisions, able to see any side of any problem, devising plans and executing them flawlessly.

Medicus was named for her gift of healing, able to heal faster than humanly possible. She could give a piece of her gift to aid in healing the most far-gone patients, as long as they had a flicker of life left in their hearts.

Pulchritudo was named for her beauty and the beauty she held in her soul. She felt people's pain, not judging it, willing to do anything to fix it. She saw the ugliness in humanity and gave it beauty.

The twins Bellum and Pax were made opposites. Bellum was named for her skills in fights and wars, seeing and hearing everything, finding people's weaknesses and exploiting them. Pax was named for the peace she brought after war to ease the suffering, and the calm she gave to the warriors before a battle, trying to minimize pain and destruction. She was kind and gentle, making even her twin feel happy and calm.

The youngest, Futurae, was named for her ability to prophesize, warning people of life-threatening consequences, and of wars and pain. Still, she could never see her own future, and her visions were never clear enough to be reliable, to save everyone.

They all complemented each other's abilities, more powerful together.

The seven sisters lived atop a mountain far out of sight, forbidden to have any contact with the commoners in the town or servants in their castle. Lex was protective of his children and wanted their blood to remain pure and royal. He made the sisters promise to abide by his rules, for he was a man who took trust and promises very seriously.

The girls listened and lived in fear of their father, but one day Pax met a man who worked in her favourite rose garden, and they ended up falling in love. For years they lived in secret, meeting in the night and among crowds in disguise.

Eventually, they married in the presence of her six sisters, the ceremony officiated by Sapientiae atop a snow-covered hill, and soon after this day, their daughter was born. Pax hid her daughter with the help of her sisters. They knew if Lex were to find out Pax's secret, all of them would be punished, even if only one did break the rules.

One day the sisters got careless, meeting openly, thinking their father was otherwise occupied. Pax handed her baby to Imperium, and a servant saw. The servant ran through the hallways and up one hundred stairs to Lex's quarters, telling him of all that had unfolded in front of his eyes.

Lex did not believe him at first, for his girls were not stupid. They obeyed every rule he made and never once broke them. So, he followed his children, waiting for them to reveal their secret. He hid in the bushes, behind walls and on roofs, until one day he saw a cloaked man kiss Pax and the forehead of a small giggling baby girl.

At first, Lex was heartbroken, then he was enraged. He called the seven sisters to his quarters that same day. He yelled and threw things; he cried and hugged them. He told them he loved them, then killed every last one. He waited hopelessly for his actions to kill him, though he knew he would not die, for his actions were not to gain power. He was so ashamed of allowing rage to envelop his soul that Lex devised a plan. He yelled for the nearest servant and sent him to kill the child and Pax's husband, who Lex blamed for unleashing the rage that made him kill the only people who loved him.

Then Lex shot himself, thinking the soul ruler line would be destroyed. He wanted no one else to have his daughters' abilities, especially not a child born from a broken promise.

While their bodies lay still in Lex's royal quarters, the seven sisters' hands intertwined. The servant who the king had called to kill the baby, no longer needing to hide his identity as Pax's husband, ran out of the castle, down to a small hut where the baby was rumoured to be hidden. He swung open the door and walked over to the crib that held an infant girl with radiant blue eyes, just like her mother's. Instead of performing his murderous task, he put clothes in a bag and scooped up the child, speaking softly while tears ran from his eyes.

'Spe, my child you are safe. We will be safe.' He choked out the words as he whispered one last goodbye to his home, filled with memories of the women he loved. He silently promised Pax he would protect Spe with his life, for Pax had sacrificed everything so they could share their love. He left in the foggy night to find a new place for him and the child to grow up and grow old.

Lex was wrong. The child survived, and the soul ruler line was not severed. He did not know what happened in the time before he called his children to his quarters. Futurae had a dream the night before, showing her the child's terrible fate, the baby in the crib with a figure hovering over her. She knew what this meant and had to make sure it was true. She followed her father throughout the whole day, watching as his eyes finally met his first grandchild. When she saw him discover their secret, she found Sapientiae first to form a plan. Then she gathered her sisters, the child and Pax's husband.

Futurae told them what she suspected would be the child's fate, and Sapientiae told them how to prevent it. They would go to their father the minute he sent for them, but before that, they would give gifts to the child.

Each sister gave a piece of her soul to the child: power, wisdom, healing, beauty, future, peace, war, and the protection against power-hungry leaders. They gave her the seven rulers' strengths and blessed the future women in her bloodline with the same gifts and same destiny. The women of the bloodline would rule their kingdoms if that is what they wanted, or they could share their abilities with a ruler they chose and trusted.

The seven sisters gifted the child one more thing. They gave her the name Spe for the hope she would bring to her father on his most challenging days and to allow her to see the light when everyone else saw nothing. Pax gave her husband and Spe one last kiss and then was gone. Sapientiae anticipated Lex's last wishes and knew her father would be so ashamed of what he had done. He would rid himself of all reminders of his family and order someone to kill Spe. She made sure the man — Spe's father was nearest to Lex's quarters, so he would be the first to hear the order, and he could keep his baby, his last reminder of his wife, alive.

The soul ruler was meant to keep the world safe and happy, prevent vile souls from gaining more power and ruling more of the world. What Spe later found out was that it was harder for people to follow a soul ruler if they had killed someone for their own purposes, rather than out of self-defence or to save someone. This made it harder for the seven abilities to break through icy hearts, and that's how bad people like our three ugly brothers were able to gain power."

Mary takes a deep breath, rubbing her face. "Harley, you are the only soul ruler left at this time. You are the only one able to stop these dictators from destroying the world, from destroying our humanity. You are the last one able to show the people who they can be and turn them away from what the leaders are forcing them to become." Mary lies down, resting her head on the pillow, pulling the blankets up to her chin. "You have to find a way to communicate with the sisters and connect to the one you need most right now. She will guide you, and she will teach you what I cannot, because I am afraid this is all I know. I am here to repeat what I know, which is not much and to show you that you are strong," she whispers. She faces away from us, showing me she is done talking as her breaths quickly become even. Levi and I are now left to process and piece everything together.

CHAPTER 28

(HARLEY)

"So you're a soul ruler?"

"Yes."

"And you have magic powers?"

"I wouldn't call it magic."

"But you can see the future, heal things, give people strength, solve impossible problems and so on?"

"Yes, Levi," I half-heartedly groan. We've been up for hours, the time mostly spent answering Levi's questions. I was able to connect the soul ruler qualities mentioned in the story to my life an hour ago: The winning of impossible fights, how I picked up skills so quickly, saving Johnny, and not dying from Eric's beatings, but I still have questions.

Do people really not have a choice whether or not they want to follow me? Do my friends love me, or the soul ruler parts of me? Does Jimmy love me…

Since Mary's asleep, and I don't think she knows the answers to my questions, I focus on Levi. I take my time putting together the right words to help me ask him in the least weird way possible if he has a brother.

Levi nudges my knee. "Do you have voices in your head?" he asks the dark. The lights went out minutes after Mary fell asleep. We've been lying on the bed, our sides touching, talking to the bottom of the mattress above us.

"Yes," I sigh, tired, starting to feel the effects of today but knowing I won't fall asleep, not in this strange, echoey place. I don't want to wake up disoriented, thinking for a brief moment that I'm home or in the hut with Jimmy holding me. "Have you run out of questions yet?" I ask.

"Yes — can you see my future?" He taps my shin. His warmth and gentle tone are strangely comforting; it makes talking to him feel so natural.

"It doesn't work like that. I can't control it."

"That's annoying."

"You don't even know," I grunt, interlacing my fingers together, pressing them to my chest, heartbeat steady, breaths even. I'm not scared or steeped in anxiety. I'm not afraid of dying. I guess the peaceful sister, Pax, is working overtime to make sure I don't freak out or shut down. Possibly I'm too distracted by the fact that Uri's only living family member, who he thinks is dead, is lying next to me, and I'll die before I can tell Uri any of this.

"Levi, how long have you been here?" I push myself up, feeling the coolness of the bedpost through my clothes and my hair as I squint to make out his silhouette.

"Umm, four years," he hesitates, his foot twitching so vigorously the bunk beds shake.

"Can I ask you a question?" I bite the dry skin on my lips, only allowing my words to whisper, not wanting them to echo off the walls and linger in the air.

"Yeah," he says, the word filled with joy. I've noticed that about him; every word he utters is infused with a single powerful emotion that courses through his body.

"Do you have a brother?"

He inhales sharply, holding his breath before letting his chest fall again. "I did," his voice drops. I've never heard two words portray so much pain and sadness without the assistance of facial expressions.

"Was his name Uri?"

He shoots up, smacking his head on the top bunk. "How did you—"

"He showed up at our Shed when he was sixteen, beaten up so badly that he could barely breathe. We didn't know how he made it from the Big Three without collapsing," I continue, my body aching as I remember that day, remember him.

"He's alive?" Levi whispers so quietly that I wouldn't have heard him if the room weren't so empty. I nod, tears starting to well up. My throat tightens as I imagine being in his position, finding out J is alive after accepting that he is dead, mourning and moving on like both Levi and Uri did.

I nod before I remember he can't see me. "Yes."

What if Uri isn't alive? What if he didn't make it back to the tree line, and I'm getting Levi's hopes up, only so they can fall all over again. The bed squeaks as he shifts about. He pats my face softly, finding where my upper body sits, locking his arms around me. His hip rests against mine, his chin settling on my shoulder.

"He's alive," Levi breathes against my ear, his wet cheeks brushing against mine, leaving streaks of hope and sorrow on my skin.

"Yes."

My chest loosens as the first feelings of happiness and relief fill me. I let my arms fold around his waist, inhaling him, feeling safe and loved in his presence. He draws back, and I can just make out his teeth as his lips turn up.

"How is he?" Levi sits beside me, leaving space between us, but his hand finds mine, gratitude coursing through his palm.

"He's good, we — the gang — took him in. We take care of each other — we love him. He has nightmares and never talks about what he went through — and he only gets sad when he thinks no one's around. He misses the people he lost, every day."

"Good, good," he says, distant, his hand falling to rest on my leg. His breath shakes, not trying to hide his emotions. Usually, I'd move away from a stranger who's invading my personal space, but Levi hasn't been a stranger since he opened his mouth. I feel like I've known him as long as I've known Uri, like he's one of the gang.

"He's alive," he repeats, giving my leg a slight squeeze.

"What happened to you guys?" I blurt without considering the effect of the memories my question would bring up. He tenses, lifting his head.

"I'm sorry, I can't. I haven't talked about it since I got here."

"I'm sorry. I—" Levi silences me, putting an arm around me, pulling me into him.

His breaths shudder and his body shakes as he cries, but I don't say anything to comfort him because nothing could. I don't move, I just let him use my presence, my closeness to remind him he's no longer alone, and I use his, to keep the memories of the gang at bay.

We must have been sitting in silence for longer than I thought because the lights start to click on one by one, a booming sound bouncing off the walls. Levi's cheeks shine, a soft smile making his eyes seem less puffy and lost as he moves away. Mary groans, pulling her blanket over her forehead as Luke skulks toward us, twirling handcuffs around his fingers. His face is blotchy, hair damp, boots freshly polished.

"Let's go," he bellows, unlocking the cell, beckoning to me. I sweep my fingers under my eyes, wiping my face with my sleeve and rising to my feet slowly. I take my time because I don't know what waits for me, and for the first time, I don't want to find out.

"Where are you taking her?" Levi asks. He stands in front of me, almost protectively, as if he would take a beating so I wouldn't have to.

"Why would I tell you?" Luke grunts. He moves around Levi, yanking my hands forward, tightening the handcuffs until there's not a sliver of space between the metal and my flesh. Levi doesn't say anything. He only mouths, 'you're gonna be okay,' as the cell door separates us, bringing me back to reality. I'm reminded that I'm now a lab rat who will be prodded and jabbed at until I am no longer needed. I nod, turning from Levi.

We don't talk as Luke walks me to a pristine, spotless lab. He leaves me alone with masked people, every inch of their bodies covered in protective clothing, acting as if I might be toxic. They take my blood pressure, saliva samples and monitor my heart rate, writing down things, nodding every so often and whispering to each other. No one talks to me or answers my questions, but being ignored doesn't bother me. It gives me time to think, to try to connect to the seven sisters as Mary instructed, though my mind keeps circling back to what Luke said in AC's prison and what Mary said to me last night. 'Your voice doesn't have the same effect on me.' Luke knew what I was the whole time and that a person who has killed someone with a purpose doesn't follow me as willingly. Though, I can't see Luke killing someone in cold blood, even after his betrayal.

I don't feel anything the people do to me, and it seems like only minutes have gone by before Luke comes back, moving me to the first room I was in. He chains my hands to the desk and takes a seat in front of me where JC sat before.

In this light, I can see every bump and shadow on his freshly shaved face, his eyebrows feathery, thicker toward his nose. His bleached blonde hair is longer and shaggier than I have ever seen it.

"What?" he snorts, picking at the peeling skin around his nails. His eyes flicker up, lashes sweeping across the skin under his eyebrows, slight specks of blue playing tricks in his grey eyes.

"The hard drive. Did you give them information about me?" I ask. His glare falls back to his hands as he slowly shakes his head. "Then what?"

"It had information about you. The soul rulers. It's how I knew what you were — how to get you to do certain things," he mumbles.

"Like what?"

"The school fire — using J — I put the idea in Até's head to kiss Jimmy so she would drive you two apart — threatening to kill Ace so you wouldn't fight me," he admits, without any hesitation, looking back up at me, his eyes holding no regret.

I huff because I'm not shocked, and to think the answers to everything were so close. If Jimmy or Ace had told me about the hard drive earlier, it could have saved us time and a lot of pain. But even if I'd known everything, I would have ended up in this chair, in this place anyway, maybe even sooner.

I close my eyes for a second before leaning against the wooden table, putting pressure on my ribs. "Do you remember when we first met?" I ask. He keeps his thin lips in a straight line, showing me no emotion, no empathy. "You were kind to me. People were whispering about my new bruises while I walked through the hall. I wasn't with anyone from the gang so I was vulnerable, though I knew no one would touch me. Some stared, some teased, but you linked arms with me and led me down the hall away from the words, only asking about the class I was going to and my name, nothing else. I trusted you after that." I pause, waiting for him to say something as the realization dawns on me that I could never trust him again.

"I'm not the same person," he mumbles, placing his gun on the table.

"Maybe not, but that boy—"

"No Harley," he interrupts, clenching his jaw, "I'm cruel, heartless and inhuman, I..." He trails off, giving me the answer to a question I didn't know I was asking.

"You only think that because when you look in the mirror, you see your parents. Empty, unfeeling people who ignored you from the time you could walk."

"No," he whispers, his knee bouncing as my veins vibrate with anticipation.

"You know, Luke, I've learned a lot since I've come here." I narrow my eyes, sharpening my words into points, driving them with a purpose into the places I know will cause the most pain. "Yet I keep coming back to what you said — how my words don't have the same effect on you." Luke's eyes harden, muscles and tendons flexing, flaring.

"Stop." His cuticles start to bleed as he rips away the protective layers of his body, bit by bit.

"You told me you turned out exactly like your parents, though I never thought that." I rest my forearms on the table, switching our roles. Me the interrogator, him the prisoner. "You said that the same day we had that picnic — you remember that?"

"Shut up!" he yells. He slams his fist on the table, making my chains clatter. Frustrated tears break through the surface of his stone-cold appearance. A satisfied feeling rises into my chest, but I push it away.

"The same day one of your gang members died. Your best friend," I continue, making my voice harsher.

"Harley, shut the hell up," he yells again, on his feet now, but I keep pressing, intending to break him word by word.

"Beaten to death by Hunters, they said, but I saw the look on your face, the guilt, the disgust, and the hatred mixed with something like pleasure."

He shakes his head, picking under his nails, removing the memories one speck at a time. "No, that's not — I didn't," his voice breaks, heavy with his lies. I hesitate, almost feeling sorry for him. Almost.

"I saw the blood wedged under your nails, unable to be scrubbed away. At first I didn't think much of it — you could have been in a fight, but the look on your face now tells me that wasn't the case."

He grabs my chains, yanking me toward him. He raises his hand, flattening it. I brace myself, keeping my eyes on his, willing my face to be as hard as diamond.

"Do it, hit me. Show me the person everyone else sees," I spit, suffocated rage stealing all my sympathy. "Do it," I yell. He squeezes his eyelids shut, breaths burning, shaking. "You killed him, Luke — you killed him," I say, watching every hint of denial and years of lies fade from his face. His hand drops to his side as tears push their way down his cheeks. "You lost control. *You* killed him."

He lets my chain go, but I stay leaning forward, watching as he collapses back down, hands hiding him from me.

"Yes," he whimpers, "I killed him, Kale — my best friend, my only friend besides you. We were playing around, joking. He said I was turning into a monster, but I realized after — he didn't mean it the way I thought he did." He takes my hands, pressing them between his. His change in demeanour startles me. His voice is small, eyelashes clumped with salty tears, the whites of his eyes scattered with red. I've never seen him cry like this, or cry at all. Not when Kale died or when his parents kicked him out of the house. "Harley, you have to understand, I didn't mean to. I didn't. I was mad and scared, I lost control. It was an accident."

I forget what the point of me doing this was as he grows weaker — more broken. He's never had anyone to show him what kindness and love are or to teach him right from wrong. That's no excuse, but I could have turned out like him, alone in the world. At least I have J, Jimmy, Ace and the gang to keep me sane. He has no one, the ones he had didn't care, and the ones he trusted never stayed.

"We were in the garden shed I slept in after I wasn't allowed to go home." His hands start to shake mine, his appearance wild, untamed. "We were playing around and I was mad after what he said. I pushed him, and he tripped over something I left on the ground. He hit his head on a sharp piece of metal — I don't know what it was. I thought he was dead when he hit the ground — he didn't suffer like Emerson, but even more blood pooled around him. I panicked. I was scared."

"Luke," I gasp. He swallows hard, snot and saliva running with his tears, but I don't pull away.

"I was afraid the Hunters wouldn't understand. I was terrified they'd banish or kill me. I had to make it look like they did it, like he was jumped — I beat him up — his brain could have still been alive — I dragged him into an alley and left him there. I cleaned the blood, all the blood and then met with you." He drops my hands, covering his face again, his shoulders shaking as he sobs openly. "I left him. I didn't mean to kill him," he whispers, pleading with me to understand, but I sit back wide-eyed, not expecting this. Out of every emotion I imagined to surface with his confession, I'm surprised to feel sorry for the deceiving murderer I used to kiss. "I loved him. He was like my brother. I didn't mean to. You have to believe me." I stare at him for a long minute before waves of bile wash over me, followed by empathy and slight understanding, bringing me almost to tears. "And I know you may not believe me now, and I'm not saying this to change what I said yesterday, but the leaders knew what I did. They threatened to kill me and Kale's family if I didn't help, and when they told me what you were, I — what I said before wasn't a lie. You leaving me for Jimmy just gave me more of a reason to hand you over."

A loud knock at the door makes both of us jump. Luke stops, wiping his face as a Hunter enters and signals that it's time for me to move. Luke fumbles with the key, struggling to connect with the lock. I hold my hand out.

"It's okay," I whisper. Not to imply that what he did wasn't inhuman or wrong, but people have done much worse in this world. He didn't kill Kale out of vengeance, desire. He did it because he was frustrated, selfish and terrified like everyone else in this fucked-up place, in the world sculpted by the leaders. Luke drops the key into my palm, using his uniform to hide the snot and weakness drenching his face. I unlock my handcuffs from the silver braided anchor that chains me to the table and stand. "It's okay," I repeat more to myself. Now I'm filled with new anxiety and confusing feelings as I'm led to another room.

CHAPTER 29

(HARLEY)

This new lab Luke leaves me in is more private and a shoebox compared to the other. Its ceiling is manipulated to show a 3D galaxy floating and rotating slowly. The stars range in colour, brighter than stars in real life. I make patterns with them as I wait in a white leather chair that creaks every time I adjust myself. At first, I thought the stars were a sick joke to taunt prisoners and test subjects, giving them a false sense of hope — a taste of what they will never experience again. But the harder I look, the faster my emotions fade, scattering like the stars. I don't know or can't figure out what to feel anymore, so it's better not to feel at all.

None of the voices have talked to me since Mary told me about them. The war voice, Bellum, didn't even snort or comment on what Luke confessed to me. I recited all of their names to myself, but no one answered, not even the high-pitched voice who loves to try and send me over the edge.

I move my arms up and down, trying to keep my shoulders from stiffening, noticing that I've become used to the feeling of having the cuffs on. It's like a fucked-up bracelet, though Luke let me loosen them and stopped pointing his gun at my back as we walked.

I've spent years with him, not allowing myself to believe the rumors surrounding him or the warnings Jimmy gave me that I thought were based around jealousy. I can't believe that Luke could be the person who beat his best friend while he was dead or maybe even still breathing.

I push every thought, mistake, misconception, and regret aside, forcing myself to focus on the one thing I haven't allowed myself to do yet — find which ability, which sister, which piece of my soul is necessary to my survival.

Power is what got me in this situation; more of it would drag me further into the hole where I am meant to be buried. Beauty won't help, nor will wisdom, unless I'm planning to slip past hundreds of Hunters while batting my eyes and handing out compliments. War will only make me lose control and put the people I love and my new friends in danger, more danger than they're already in. Healing is always my comfort, something I take for granted. Peace has been doing her part and has been with me every step of my imprisonment. She is not needed. She is simply there. Lastly, I can't even see my own future, and if I could, I would only want to see Jimmy and J, but I don't think I could bring myself to do so. I'm scared I'll see nothing.

I slam my head back, the cushioned chair too soft to do anything but tap my brain against my skull. If I don't need any of the sisters, then what is left? Am I meant to connect with the high-pitched voice? The mere thought of that makes me gag.

I run through the story again, paraphrasing Mary's words, my thoughts slowing when they speak the silken name Spe. The word waltzes across my tongue, tasting like the chocolate cake my mom used to make.

"*Spe*," I call, wondering if it could be possible for the whole family to be in there. The thought of Spe and Pax reuniting after centuries brings a warm, bubbling sense of happiness into my heart, but still, no one answers. The longer I whisper Spe's name, ironically, the less hope I have. I connect the stars, drawing her face. A slight outline of round cheeks, long silken hair, a button nose and almond-shaped eyes that laugh with her thin lips.

"*Harley*," a small, childish voice whispers far away, fighting against currents and hurricanes to connect with me, climbing up my spinal cord.

The door flies open, the knob crashing into the wall, almost causing me to fall from my chair, but I right myself, the connection fading as the leaders file in.

"*Spe*," I call, sending boats and search parties to bring her closer, but she's gone. I'm alone once more.

"Looking good, Harley," AC notes, his liquid words seeping into my eardrums, dissolving them with acid. He fumbles around with scalpels and syringes, presenting them to me before MC snatches them away, grabbing a stool and rolling to my side.

"Maddick will be the one to run your procedure," JC says, standing over me so I can't avoid looking at him. I fantasize about slamming my fists into his stomach and head butting him as he keels over, but decide it would backfire. I would end up knocked out and unaware of what they do. "You will be given a shot to slow the effects of your healing. Luke will return you to your cell after. Hunters will be posted outside, so don't try to kill my brother." JC winks, touching his icy hand to the top of my head. I wait till his hand falls to eye level. I snap my teeth at him, but he's too fast. I miss his hand by inches. "You know, you would have made a great ruler. Tough, feisty. If you would like, you can rough Maddick up a little, get your anger out. He never fights back," JC laughs, then frowns at MC when he shows no reaction. JC collects himself, slapping MC on the back and pushing AC out the door, wishing me luck before the door clicks shut again.

MC focuses on the supplies sorted on a small silver table containing a massive syringe, a scalpel and loads of blood bags. Occasionally his eyes fall to the emerald tiled floor, searching for something else to do, avoiding me.

He looks like he was woken up seconds before coming here. His hair is pressed down at the back and messy around his forehead. He has crusty bits of sleep stuck in the corners of his eyes, light purple circles curving under them. He wears grey pyjama pants with a striped wool sweater, an off-white shirt peeking from the bottom. The only sign of his interest in coming here is his smooth, freshly shaven chin and upper lip. Even with no beard, he seems so different from his twin.

I focus on the stars, imagining The Shed's roof instead of the chair under my body. It's the spot in The Sticks where the stars shine brightest, the streetlights barely affecting the dark. Right now, if I were to close my eyes, I could feel the roof under my back and the slight pressure of Jimmy's clammy hand, folded into mine — I don't close my eyes. "Do you know what you're doing?" I ask.

MC snorts, gliding antiseptic wipes over my arm and down my thigh, tying a rubber band around my bicep. "I'll do it myself, if you don't know how," I try to tease, but my words don't reach the level of sarcasm I want. I don't know if I could stick a needle into my arm and hand over my DNA.

"I've been studying medicine since I could pick my own classes, but by all means," he offers, handing over the scalpel.

From his voice, not a vision but a memory surfaces. It's fuzzy around the edges, worn and tinted. A wooden mobile hangs over a crib. My delicate tiny hands with stubby fingers reach for the dragons and horses flying in circles. A man plucks my hand from the air, pressing his lips so softly to my fingers, his face out of focus.

"She will be tough and hard-headed like you," he whispers softly, looking away and chuckling, a deep sweet sound — his voice effortless, flowing and low.

I roll my head toward MC, struggling to match the point of his nose to the one in the memory, but the voice is unmistakably the same.

"I don't think I could live with myself if I gave you my stem cells and DNA," I say, confused as laughter rushes into my throat. I am giving it to them, and I will die. I'm doing nothing to stop them. I gave up. I let the laugh open my mouth, but it dies as soon as it meets the world.

MC's eyes flicker to mine, then to the needle in his hand, frowning at it. "I'm going to give you the shot now. It will slow the healing process down. This way I don't have to reopen your wound every time I retrieve bone marrow."

"Or you could just not take any," I huff as he flicks the needle, pushing it into my vein, forcing the clear liquid out and into my blood.

"I'm sorry," he whispers, brushing a clean cloth over the injection site, moving on to my thigh. My limbs start to ache as the liquid familiarizes itself with my body, removing whatever stops the pain and speeds up the healing from my nerve receptors. He presses another smaller needle into my leg, also rubbing numbing cream on my skin until I feel nothing in that one spot and everything everywhere else.

"Why did you tell me about Mary?" I ask, trying to focus on something other than the snake finding my trachea, slithering down and around my lungs, tightening, constricting. His head moves up suddenly, then looks back down just as quickly, his hair flopping over his eyes.

"There's a camera in the corner facing my back," he whispers, grabbing a hollow syringe. "They're watching you, observing you, they always are. They can't hear us, but you have to act like we're not talking — like you hate me." He begins to collect my bone marrow, making a small incision over my femur, sticking the long needle through my skin, sucking up thick red fluid.

"That won't be hard," I mumble, looking away, perfecting my poker face as I wait for his answer. I rest my hands on my stomach, feeling my diaphragm rise and fall.

"I wanted you to find Mary because I wanted you to understand who you are and why Jackson is so determined to have your abilities, Aron as well." He holds his breath every time he removes the needle and drives it back in. I can feel the steel burrowing down and entering my bones. I can feel all my cells drawing upon their energy to heal like they used to, my body beginning to cramp and stiffen.

"You don't want the same thing?"

"I didn't want any of this," he sighs, shocking me. I move to turn toward him before I remember I'm not supposed to engage. I pretend to flinch, to make sure his brothers don't burst in and stop MC from talking. "Harley, I apologize for all we did to you — are doing to you, and for this next part," he whispers, running stitches through the small cut. I've never had stitches before. It makes my skin feel tight and irritated.

"What part?" I ask hesitantly, managing to talk through clenched teeth. He holds up a long clear tube with a short needle connected to one end, plastic wings on the sides. He picks up a blood bag, screwing it to the other end.

"You have O negative blood — I'm sure you understand what that means."

"They can have my blood and not reject it," I say. He smiles, slightly impressed with me, then remembers what he's doing.

"I told Jackson a blood transfusion wouldn't make a difference. They don't care. They're reckless, taking lives left, right and center. I used the shot first because it will prevent me from taking all your blood, since you can't reproduce it as fast now. However, as more blood leaves your system, the effect of the shot goes with it. I'll take enough so you appear weak, and I can send you back," he says, seeming almost distressed, like he cares about me. He did say his brothers wanted this, not him, but in this room, in this moment, those words make no sense. "I'm sorry," he mumbles, pressing the needle into my arm. The action is oddly satisfying as my blood drips, then falls through the tube, expanding the bag.

I roll my head away. "Why are you helping me?"

"I—" His voice breaks. He stands, clattering around, taking his time before sitting back down, playing with something in his hands. It's probably something to take samples of my stem cells. I genuinely don't care. Take my blood, my bone marrow, my brain. The rulers live in my soul. The leaders could spend years coming up with new technology to extract it, but my soul would leave my body before they could take it.

"I knew your father as a kid," he says. I keep my head facing the wall, though I want so badly to strain toward him, to punch him or ask him questions, but I stay still. "We studied medicine together. I knew your mom too. They were the people I escaped to when my family drove me crazy. Which was all the time." He screws on a second blood bag, his body positioned to block everything he does. He rests his hand on my cuffs, inhaling deeply. "When I was seventeen, I learned Jackson and I were to start training for the position of leader. The past ones picked us. Jackson learned about the soul rulers from Boris, my umm — the old head leader. Jackson started obsessing over them, searching night and day. He knew he couldn't get everyone to follow him without the abilities, and I knew your dad had the gene." I hold my breath, calming myself, silencing my mind so as not to miss a single word. "Your mom became pregnant with you, so I banished them, changed their names and helped them build a new Identity and a life in the Sticks — I knew about the Nomads. I told your parents to seek refuge and give birth to you there so we didn't have to register you and invite scrutiny," he says, screwing on another bag. The medicine has to be starting to fade; I can feel my bones rapidly making more cells, straining to keep me from passing out, but not fast enough. I begin to feel light-headed and heavy, as if weights are glued to me.

A human can lose two litres of blood without dying, no more. I don't know if that's the same for a person with nine souls, ten including my own. "Sorry, Harley, just a bit longer." He screws on another bag, continuing to talk, and I can no longer hold my head up. It keeps falling to the side, waking me every time it jerks. "I met you when you were a baby, visited till you got to the age where you could remember."

"I remember," I croak. I feel him smile at the back of my head as he squeezes my arm.

"I kept you off the grid for as long as I could, but somehow Jackson found you." He sniffs, a couple tears hitting my skin before he stops them from pouring out. "I'm your godfather, I was supposed to keep you safe. I tried to make it harder for you to be taken, but I couldn't keep my promise to your dad."

It's getting hard to follow his words, not because they sound crazy and unrealistic. I've built up a tolerance for that shit. I'm simply too weak and dizzy. My vision shifts and tilts, the stars spinning faster, causing my stomach acid to lurch up.

"What were their real names?" I interrupt, struggling to keep my eyelids peeled back. He slides the needle from my skin, pressing a fluffy cotton ball to the doming red dot coming from the pinprick. It looks like a bunny's tail, like the stuffed bunny I used to have, but his tail was green.

"Noah and Ophelia." He leans over me, bringing my memory into focus, his gentle, kind face the same as when he was in his twenties, and for some reason, I trust him. I believe he's not lying, that he wouldn't.

"The other prisoners need medical attention," I slur. Cement joins the snake around my lungs and the weights taped to my limbs, filling my bloodstream and every empty area it can find.

"You'll be okay," Spe reassures me, the healing voice echoing her. I don't want to die like this. I don't want MC to be taken in my place.

"MC, make sure J survives. Keep him safe."

"Call me Maddick," he offers so pleasantly, I might be dreaming. "I'm not going to let you die. I'll find a way to help you survive," he says, moving my hair behind my ears, "I promise." Then he leaves my side to let Luke in.

Luke looks down at me, eyes still puffy. JC and AC crowd around, patting MC — Maddick on the back and observing me. "Good job," JC says, holding my blood to the light. Luke sweeps me into his arms, pressing my head to his chest. He smells like gingerbread, but that might be my nose betraying me. Luke carries me away without being ordered to, and I watch Maddick for as long as I can before his stripy shirt disappears.

"Harley, I—"

"It's fine," I interrupt, shutting my eyes, listening to his heart as my blood flows faster. I sway with his body as though he is gravity, and I am no longer on earth. "Do you hate me?" I mumble, not remembering when I decided I thought he did or why I wanted to ask him or why I even care. It's not like his opinion means much.

"No, Harley," he almost laughs, looking pale, dim, like all the light has gone out of him.

Luke fumbles with the cell lock while trying not to drop me. He kicks open the door, setting me on the hard floor, not wanting to risk stepping into the cell. He rests my head down gently before quickly moving away and locking the door behind him as Levi emerges from the shadows, a bottle of something clenched between his fingers.

"Oh, my god, Harley, what the hell did they do to you?" He stumbles toward me, falling to his knees, almost hitting my head. His hands float over my face, not knowing where to settle as he takes everything in.

"They took some bone marrow, blood and deep tissue for testing," Luke mumbles.

"They didn't have to take it all," Levi yells, pulling two mattresses from their frames onto the floor, making a bigger bed by pushing them together against the wall. He lays me across them. I can move my head just enough to watch him stomp back over to Luke.

"Calm down, she'll heal," Luke says dismissively, waving him off.

"She's too weak, it will take longer, they're gonna kill her, you know that. You did this to her." Levi slams his hands against the bars, trying to shake them apart. I make a wheezing sound in the back of my throat, drawing him back over to me. He cradles my body using his own as a shield from Luke even though rusted bars serve as a barrier between us.

"No, I didn't, she stayed on her own," Luke protests, but this time when he says it, there's no conviction behind his words.

"You did this to her. You're letting them drain her blood, take her bone marrow, tissue, skin for testing so your so-called leaders can have all the towns and cities locked under their thumbs. For what, so you can get a promotion, so you can be their right-hand man, so you can kill more innocent people?" Levi yells, his eyes bugging, a vein in his neck bulging.

"What do you care, you haven't known her for that long, besides the leaders..." he trails off. I catch Luke's eyes, sad and tired, before he trains them on the ground.

"She put her life at risk to be here, and she doesn't even hate you for what you did. She's a better person than any of us will ever be, how could you not care? And how the hell would you know that everything they're doing is for the better. They don't trust you with shit, you're expendable, I'm surprised they haven't fucking killed you yet — that's what they're going to do to all of us." Levi presses his back to the wall, sliding his legs under my head. I know Levi is only defending me because the soul ruler parts have a lot of influence over his feelings, but what he says still makes me feel safe.

Luke doesn't have anything to say. He falls silent, moving his fingers to his gun's trigger.

In our history books, there's a lot about wars, dictatorships, and cults. I read that people who have no ability to be a leader, to show true strength, tend to follow those who can, especially those who take advantage of them, of their loneliness and weaknesses. This is what made it easier for Luke to be brainwashed. I'm sure at first, he helped the leaders bring me in to save himself and Kale's family, but along the way, he fell under their spell and fell for their lies. Fell for their fake affection.

"That's what I thought, you're a worthless coward. Look at her. Look at her!" Levi yells, losing his easy demeanour, his words stinging my ears. *Stop yelling*, I want to say, but nothing comes out. Luke lifts his eyes, training them on me and for a second, pity, regret and sympathy cross his face. *He didn't mean to kill Kale*, I tell myself, wishing Luke wasn't here to remind me of the people I left behind. That I let down. "You're responsible for the damage they cause to her and everyone else killed or hurt because of this," Levi says, clenching his hands into fists.

I lift my hand to Levi's cheek, wincing as I pull his face down, forcing him to focus on me. He strains against me before his shiny, hypnotizing eyes lock with mine. He pinches his lips together, holding a hand toward Mary as she follows our voices, trying to figure out what all the chaos is about.

"Tell me a story," I croak, my voice breaking, scraping my throat on its way to my lips. He fights my weak hand while trying to keep his eyes on Luke disappearing down the hall. "Please."

"What do you want to hear?" he sighs, giving in to me and helping Mary settle onto the makeshift bed. She rests her fingers on my knee, looking away, though she's blind. Levi guides my arm from his face to my side, not letting go.

"Why are you here?" I ask. He busies himself with making sure I'm comfortable, checking my stitches, trying to avoid the memories and trauma he and Uri share. Mary slides down the wall, grunting, her knees cracking, her body too stiff. She says nothing as she takes my feet, massaging the blood back into them.

"I remember the smell of smoke seeping through the floorboards. Her hair, burning. Her flesh, burning. I hear her screams every time I close my eyes. I think Uri does too." Levi tightens his grip on my hand, leaning his head against the wall. "My mom. She was a great woman with a pure heart and a pure soul. Too pure for her own good. We lived in MC's city. She was a government worker who ran the agriculture wing where all the food is grown." He moves to lie beside me, placing my head on his arm and putting pressure on my stitches. I can feel the blood sliding across my waking skin. "Harley, it was beautiful there. Floor apon floor of fresh fruits and vegetables, wheat and corn and every colour of flowers. MC doesn't keep livestock and only grows crops in his building so there's more than enough food for all the cities and towns, yet the leaders keep all of it for themselves." He closes his eyes.

"Mom hated that. She would come home every day and tell us how horrible it was, how the children in the streets were starving and they wouldn't feed them. She sat us down every night before bed and told us. 'You are strong, and if you believe in yourself as I do, you can change the world.' My mom thought with all her heart that when we got older, we'd make a difference..." he trails off, stroking my hair. "She tried to change the world. She tried at the cost of her life. She never told us that she used to give food to people who would distribute food bundles, blankets and clothes to the children in the streets." He starts to tremble. I try to put my arm around him, but I still feel heavy. "She was so kind and loving. She made us feel whole and wanted, like the world wasn't broken around us. You would have loved her, Harley. She would have loved you. One day a person started following her. He appeared at our home when we went on walks or when she went to work. She thought she was careful, but she wasn't careful enough." He takes in a deep breath and keeps his eyes on mine. "One night, they decided she was dispensable. They didn't arrest her or banish her like they would anyone else. It would have made people angry because she was so respected. So, instead, they set the house on fire, making it look like an accident — we were sleeping, all of us. I woke to the smell of burning flesh, to the sound of her screaming.

I was fourteen. I wasn't in a gang yet because Uri kept me away from that. I didn't know how to handle someone being in so much pain. She shook us awake and her skin—" he chokes, flinching as he opens his eyes, to prevent the image from holding his throat shut. "Her skin was bubbling red, all her hair gone, you could see the inside of her cheek. I thought I was having a nightmare. I wished it was a nightmare. But it wasn't. She ran through a wall of fire outside our door to get to us and help us out the window—"

"You don't have to say any more," I whisper, my throat tight, trying not to cry.

"No, it's okay." He takes another deep breath, wiping his tears and taking my hand with his bloody one as Mary takes over the job of applying pressure to my stitches. "She helped us out the window, told us to run, to never stop. She told us not to be scared. We watched the flames pull at her face. At her body. We watched her mouth open so wide, unleashing nothing. I tried to fight toward her, I yelled her name, I yelled for help, but I couldn't get to her. Uri and I watched her fall to the ground, grabbing at her skin as it dissolved, as we stood helpless, until Uri pulled us away. For days we ran and hid as the Hunters tracked us down, and eventually, we found an abandoned hut in The Sticks. We stayed for a couple days. We thought we were safe, but they found us. Uri tried to fight five Hunters off, but they were too strong. They beat him unmercifully and left him to die, taking me instead. I didn't know why they needed me. All I could think about was how I failed to save the two people most important to me, how I was alone. That's why I thought Uri was dead. I hated myself every day for not fighting hard enough to save him. I'm here because they didn't know how to keep the agriculture building going without my mom. They needed me for information, for formulas and passwords and of course, I knew them. My mom made everything into a song to remember, so I did too. I'm running out of things to give them, though, so I've been waiting for them to kill me. Until you came along, that is. You've given me hope that I could see my brother again. I miss him."

"You've given all of us hope," Mary says, her voice carrying through the room.

"I wanna see my brother," I whisper, hot tears falling to Levi's arm.

I don't want to give them hope. I don't want to make them feel strong when I feel so weak. I want to go home. I want my mom. I want Jimmy. I don't want these two people, who have been here much longer than I have, to think that I can get them out, because I can't. I don't know how. I'm going to die in two days, even if the leaders don't get what they need.

"Do you want me to leave?" Levi asks, pushing my hair from my face, tears dripping from his chin. I shake my head.

"Hold me till I fall asleep, I'll be better in the morning. I need to heal," I whisper, letting him hold me and comfort me because this may be the last time for any of this — for me to feel another human's warmth.

"Okay," he agrees hesitantly, shifting so my head rests on a pillow that I didn't see before. His hand gently, cautiously moves to my side as Mary lays a blanket over us.

"You are strong, and you will change the world, I believe it," I whisper, his timid smile the only thing I see before my eyes flutter shut.

CHAPTER 30
(HARLEY)

Once again, I find myself in a field. The sky is laced with a soft orange, and every fluffy cloud is reflected by a slow-moving river so captivated by the view, it takes in every detail before it drifts away.

Two boys, different heights, sit on the riverbank in wavy grass spotted with dandelions. Their pants are bunched up at their knees so their ankles and shins can be submerged in the shimmering water.

I stand on the other side of the riverbank, facing them, though they can't see me, and I know, no matter how hard I try, I can't get them to. So instead, I watch as the smaller boy picks at the grass, piling it on his leg. His face is fuller, his skin no longer damaged, the traumas no longer visible. He wears square glasses that hug his face, not broken in the middle or held on his head by rubber bands. They brighten his light blue eyes and highlight his gentle lashes. His blonde hair has changed with age, shorter and softer in colour, making him seem more mature, though I still see him as thirteen.

The other boy is much taller and leaner than the first, and time hasn't touched him. His hair is shorter on the sides but still floppy on the top, so his hands can run through it. His skin is tanned and clear, and no tired bags curve under his eyes, yet something dims his smile. As he splashes his toes in the water, leaning back on his hands and watching the sky, I know his smile isn't real — it isn't like the one he always gave me. It's plastered on to make the smaller boy think he's okay. He smiles so he won't cry.

"I miss her," the young boy says, his voice deeper, pitching up in unexpected places as puberty changes him.

"I know, I do too, but she's not gone," the older boy says, leaning forward, ruffling his dark straight hair. Oh, I wish I had more time to play with that hair and steal kisses from those sweet lips. "She's here," he says, tapping the young boy's head, "and here," he taps the spot over his heart. "All around us," he declares, throwing his hands up, gesturing to the world, a new world I've never seen before. Tears begin to fall from the older boy's eyes, his heart breaking as it probably does every time I pop into his head. As he looks up, his eyes run over my face, looking at me as if I'm here and this is not a dream or a vision.

"*They will be safe,*" Spe whispers, her nimble fingers falling on my arm, holding me steady.

I don't want to look at her, though I may never have her this close to me again, but I can't look away from the boys. I want Spe to be right. I want my heart to stay full of love, joy and the thought that they will be okay. I want their faces to be engraved in my mind even after I wake to numbness.

"It's okay," the small boy says, reaching for the older boy's hand. "My mom and dad are waiting for her on Lullaby Mountain. They're together again."

"Lullaby Mountain," I echo, rolling the words over my tongue, trying to place the reference to the story behind it. The story I know we both share, but it's under too many pushed-down memories to find me.

"Harley," Levi's voice falls into my dream.

"*I'll find a way to talk to you,*" Spe whispers before her hand leaves my arm, and the image of the boys dissolves into dust, floating away with the imaginary wind.

"I miss you too," I whisper to the darkness, to the boys I have lost and will never see again. I watch them till nothing is around me.

I drift in and out, my head resting on Levi's arm instead of the pillow. A wet cloth patting my face. He smiles at me, and I no longer feel dizzy and lightheaded, like yesterday never happened. My stitches are gone, my wounds healed.

"You okay?" Levi asks, standing slowly, his body stiff from sleeping on the thin beds. I peer over his shoulder, looking to where Mary sleeps in her bed, a blanket pulled over her face. Levi tells me MC stopped by, treating both Mary and him as well as tending to me. Levi looks stronger, taller, some of his scars gone. Mary's arm peeks out from the sheet, displaying neat, new stitches in her skin and all traces of infection vanished.

Levi tells me nothing more of what happened after I passed out. He freezes, his features hardening as the cell door squeaks open, and I shift my gaze to where Luke stands in front of us now, keeping a safe distance from Levi.

"How are you feeling?" Luke asks, holding the bars, his voice emotionless. Today, he wears a different uniform, navy blue, with black combat boots and a gold badge over his heart. It appears to be an upgrade in his ranking, but I've never heard of a position higher than a Hunter.

"You don't get to ask her that," Levi retorts, helping me to my feet, stepping in front of me to put himself first if any danger should come.

"It's okay, Levi," I answer, louder than I thought my voice could handle. I rest my hand on his shoulder, and he moves aside, frowning.

"I'm fine," I say, ignoring the urge to cough, my throat so scratchy. I haven't drunk or eaten in two days, though I don't think my body could take any food without throwing it back up.

"Today's your last day before the execution," Luke says so plainly his words don't sting. Luke picks at the chipping paint, his eyes avoiding Levi's glaring, hateful ones. "The leaders said you could do whatever you want today — within reason. You can't leave the building or ask us to contact J, Jimmy or anyone else."

What else is there to do? I think, walking my mind through the drab halls, trying to find a cool-looking door I can visit, but I keep wandering back to the lab. That would be so completely depressing, if on my very last day, I went back to stare at the fake stars, at the place my DNA was stolen. I laugh at the thought, looking down at my ripped and tattered clothes.

"I want new clothes — for all of us. Please," I say. Luke nods, pulling a worn brown bag I didn't see before from his shoulders, tossing it to the mattresses on the floor. As if he knew that would be my first request.

"What about going to the gardens?" Levi whispers in my ear on his way to the bag, tossing clothes to Mary and quickly changing into his. I look back at Luke, who shifts uncomfortably, finding now that he has nowhere else to look but at me. He isn't so intense anymore. His grey eyes are empty, and I feel nothing when I look at him. No hate, No love. Nothing.

"Can you take all of us to the garden?" I request, firmly holding my ground, though I'm literally itching to get out of these clothes and into the blue doctor scrubs that hang loosely from Levi's body.

Luke turns away, frowning as he listens to the person who lives in his ear, in the omnipresent ear chip. "Okay," he nods, turning around, waiting for me to change. Levi faces the wall, and Mary sits up in her bed, holding her clothes in her hands, her head hanging down. I strip, keeping my stupid rainbow sports bra on because, at this point, it's the only personal possesion I have left. Levi and I leave the cell following Luke, but Mary's unsteady footsteps don't echo behind us.

"You coming?" Levi stops.

"Sweetheart, I can't see anything anyways, and my body is too stiff to walk around all day." She rubs her necklace between her fingertips, placing her clothes neatly on her pillow.

"Mary," I sigh, walking back over, kneeling in front of her and placing my hands on her bony knees. "We will find you a nice rock or chair to sit on, because even though you can't see, you can still feel the warmth of the fake sun or whatever's in there. Smell the flowers, sweet fruits and savory vegetables. I bet we can sneak a bite of those. Levi and I will support you there and back. I don't want you to miss this, not after twenty some odd years of being locked inside. I want to spend my last day with my new friends," I say gently, injecting persuasion into my vocal cords. I don't care if I have to use the soul ruler parts of me to change her mind. I want her to keep living until she can't.

"Friends," she snorts, though a smile pulls at her lips. "Fine." She shakily puts her hands on mine, using me to pull herself up. "Don't know if you just convinced me because you're dying or if it was the soul rulers," she mumbles, holding both our arms as we hobble along, surprising me when I can hold her up with no problem or fatigue. I almost feel stronger than I did before my blood was taken.

"Both," I smile, imagining Luke rolling his eyes as I watch Levi hold back a laugh.

After we travel down the third hall, Luke stops, pushing a glowing button on a slick black and grey marble wall. It's the only marble wall I've seen in this place. It slides to the side, revealing a sparkling glass elevator with only one glowing button on the inside. We step in, the doors hissing shut behind us. It shoots up, turning and pressing my stomach down.

"You mean this whole time we could have used an elevator and not gone up and down the damn stairs," I huff, watching Levi's face drop, his lips pinching together.

"It only goes to the gardens. Anyway, your cardio needed improvement," Luke smirks, watching Levi squeeze his eyes shut and hold his stomach as he becomes queasy, though there's probably nothing but stomach acid for him to throw up.

"I like the stairs," Levi groans, and Mary slaps the back of his head. "What the hell?" We all stumble as the elevator comes to a stop.

"Do you feel sick anymore?" Mary asks, lacing her hands in front of her.

"No, but we aren't shooting up anymore," Levi argues, rubbing his head. Mary simply shrugs, linking her arm in his.

The elevator door slides open, introducing us to MC's sacred garden. We all are rendered speechless as we step onto the cushioned grass. Even Mary's mouth falls open as the sweet smells float around us, and Luke, who I didn't think appreciated beautiful things, slows to allow his eyes to linger on every inch of the room.

It's not a single floor with neat rows and simple plants like I thought it would be. Instead, it's made up of five floors that have had large holes cut out of them, making this area a five-story room. Nothing is organized. The bottom floor has clumps of sunflowers, wheat and corn. On the ledges are apple, lemon, fig and avocado trees, luxuries we'd never get. Grapevines, berries and things I've never seen before hang over the ledges and climb up the walls. Pink, purple, yellow, orange and black flowers cover almost everything else. Some might have medicinal purposes, though I think most are for show or just for Maddick. Levi points at the hover plate moving from floor to floor, meant to carry workers, but no one's here. It's all for us.

Light pours through the ceiling that appears to be open, or maybe modified like the lab ceiling to look like the sky — because that can't be the real sky. It never looks like that so close to winter. I can't tell what floor we're on. Most of the windows are covered, and the ones that aren't are too high up for me to see out.

"Look," Levi whispers, moving us further into the room, pointing out objects that glide through the air.

"Bees?" I squint at their bodies. From far away, they're hard to follow even if I weren't so mesmerized by everything else in the room.

"Look closer," he presses, smiling at my interest. Birds and bees fly closer, coming to check us out. Their bodies glisten as the sun hits them, and the closer they get, the more mechanical their buzzes and chirps sound.

"Robots?" I gasp. Never in my life have I heard about bug robots. Levi laughs, shutting my open mouth. I move further in now on my own, forgetting everything.

"They use them to pollinate the plants and pick seeds, without the annoyance and the mess of the real ones."

"Do all the buildings have a place like this?" I ask, and for some reason, the urge to cry overpowers me. This is a different world, a peaceful place that doesn't connect to the horrors of this building at all.

"I don't think so. MC often tends to this place himself. I doubt the other two would care whether their gardens were pretty or not." Levi sets Mary on a mossy patch of grass, glaring at Luke, who guards the door, too curious to stay still or to be angry and ignore the beauty of his surroundings.

Levi grabs my hand, and we run through the sunflowers, around the wheat, jumping onto the platform that carries us from floor to floor. We climb to the top of each tree, picking the best fruit, carrying them in our shirts and placing them in front of Mary, who holds each one to her nose, inhaling deeply before taking a bite. We discover the ceiling and the windows are like the lab, designed to act as a greenhouse, keeping everything happy and warm.

We run, jump and climb until Levi's body can't handle it anymore, and we fall into an open space between the sunflowers and wheat, not wanting to shut our eyes and miss a second of this. When Levi catches his breath, he springs back up, running off and reappearing with a multicolour handful of flowers. He moves my ratty hair, fanning it around me and placing the flowers over the knots.

"What are you doing?" I giggle, the noise unnatural to me, yet it makes so much sense here, in this air, in this light.

"Capturing the moment," he laughs, closing one eye. He makes a square with his fingers pointing at me. He snaps his tongue, making it sound like the flash of a camera, then frowns, flopping back down beside me, stealing a flower from my hair and placing it behind his ear.

"Harley, you don't deserve this," he sighs, biting a chunk out of a juicy red apple. The scent is so inviting to my mind but so toxic and nauseating to my stomach.

"Levi, I'd rather it be me than anyone else. You know that," I smile. He goes to defend me, but I stop him. "Today I want to forget — because, right here," I find his hand in the grass, giving it a squeeze, "right now, tomorrow doesn't exist."

"Okay."

Our hands stay locked together for support, to remind each other no one dies alone. I want to get Mary to share this moment with her, but I can hear her talking Luke's ear off, so I decide to let her keep harassing him.

Levi shares what his life was like before he became a prisoner, how he wanted to do the same thing as his mom and study agriculture and farming in school. He tells me about his friends, fighting off Hunters with Uri, his first kiss, his first boyfriend, and how Uri supported him and protected him every single step of the way.

I tell him about my life, how I raised J and did the same for him as Uri did for Levi. I tell him about my mom and Eric and how J got taken. I tell him about Jimmy, his dark and goofy personality, how we spent years pretending not to love each other, only to finally share how we felt days before I was taken — how I am so grateful for having that little time to love him, to feel the love he has for me.

Levi asks about the gang, determining Rey and Johnny to be insane — in the best way. Buckey and Tequila are soul mates because they both steal and are kind of badass. Ace and Finn are his favourites, and Até is a dulled-down version of the three brothers. Every time I say Uri's name, he cries, and I let silent tears slide from my eyes throughout, even when I mention Até.

"I believe deep down in my soul," Levi says, wiping at his face, sitting up, " that we'll be okay." He winks, getting to his feet and smiling down at me, smiling so wide his hollow cheeks seem fuller and his eyes less weary. "I'm going to check on Mary, see if she's killed Luke yet." He disappears into the corn, and I relax my muscles, my mind.

"*Spe*," I think, giving it one last attempt, not believing it could work or that any of this is true. Maybe I'm just an average person with voices in my head.

"Harley, I'm here," Spe says, shutting my eyes with her voice, bringing me into a dark room, where a drawn-out figure stands in front of me. It's nothing but a silhouette with a glowing blue outline painted around it. Spe's hands stretch to my cheeks. I don't move. I let her warmth, her breaths, her life, hold me. *"Harley, my greatest grandchild,"* she speaks, her voice altering to sound like my mom's did before the drugs — fluffy and honey-like. At the thought, the silhouette changes to look like my mom, her wavy brown hair thicker, eyes less yellow and more aware, her skin unflawed, teeth no longer rotting with her smile.

"I thought the soul rulers only had the seven sisters in their souls?" I inquire, stretching my earth-bound hand through the grass to see if Levi has returned, but he hasn't.

"You are the last soul ruler left on earth. When I got older, my father told me about what my mother and my aunts did to keep me and our bloodline alive. I promised myself to never let someone like my grandfather have control over people or have the opportunity to wipe us out ever again. So I promised, if necessary, to give my soul to the last remaining soul ruler, to make sure she could help stop the leaders who wished to destroy the bloodline."

"But why is your grandfather's soul in here too?" I gesture to the darkness around me. I become distracted by the empty darkness, wondering why this space hasn't been filled with something useful.

"He had the same idea, I suppose. To prevent you from succeeding. I fought him to get here, to help you connect to the seven souls and enhance your abilities before tomorrow."

"They're going to kill me," my voice breaks. She pulls me into her arms, smelling of cherries and ice cream as her hair ruffles over my nose.

"Not if you connect to all of us and if JC does what I think he will. Not if you choose to live." She pulls back, cupping my face again. Mary's voice breaks into the darkness for only a second, telling Levi to let me rest. I push it away as fast as it appears. I can't let Hope — Spe go now. *"I know you can't see your own future, but I can tell you that this isn't when it ends,"* she says, somewhat sadly. I don't know whether I should love this news or dread it.

I wish her face weren't my mom's because my heart breaks for her now. I had made peace with the fact that I will die thinking she hated me and she, thinking I hated her, but now it's been dragged up to join all the guilt and regrets I have.

"What do I do?"

"*You must connect a memory to each of the sisters' abilities. This will help you contact them, it will help you control and center yourself,*" she explains, her body fading back to her silhouette form, a faceless ghost — my mom gone again. I panic, reaching for her, but my hand passes through as she becomes mist falling back into darkness.

"Help me," I cry.

"*I can't show you what makes you so special, or which memories make these abilities so powerful to you. I'm only here to remind you of it and to help you see the light when everyone else sees nothing.*" She snaps her fingers, light pouring over the dark until all I see is the redness of my eyelids.

"Please. Please don't leave me," I sob, my voice no longer in my head but in my throat — only the feeling of the earth beneath me.

"Harley, it's okay. Wake up," Levi whispers, jostling me lightly, stroking my hair.

"*Goodbye, my sweet grandchild. My mother, my aunts and I will be here when you realize what gives you life, what gives you power. Do what I say and you will survive, just as I did.*" Spe's voice fades into a gentle buzz, then nothing.

Tension creeps into my windpipe, my arteries, my brain.

"Levi, can you get Mary, please?" I manage to ask. He calls out for her but doesn't leave my side.

Before opening my eyes, I grab Levi's knee, not wanting to face reality in this beautiful, other-worldly garden, but there's no reason to delay. In order to survive, I have to put the perfect memory to power, wisdom, beauty, healing, war, peace and future, all before tomorrow. How the fuck am I supposed to do that while my mind continues to race?

"I'm right here," Mary wheezes from only moving a couple feet. This outing is taking a toll on her body, which is so used to sitting in a cell all day, unable to move more than a couple steps.

"How are you doing?" I ask, opening my eyes, sitting up and taking both their hands.

Don't cry, I scold myself, feeling the tears move to the surface, clinging to my lower eyelids. *Not now.*

"I can't complain, but I'm not here to talk about myself." She rests her hand over mine, patting it like I imagine my grandmother would have if I had met her.

"Spe spoke to me," I whisper, exhaling all the tension from my body. Mary's eyebrows lift, her lips opening slightly, then pinching together, not saying anything. I wish she knew more, could tell me exactly what to think, what to do. "She said in order to get stronger, I have to connect a memory to each of the abilities before tomorrow. I need more time with no interruptions." My words begin to quicken as I force myself to appear calm, only increasing my panic. Mary stops me by picking a flower and holding it under her chin, yellow reflecting onto her skin.

"You see this?" She moves it under mine, then to Levi. "Buttercup. Something so small and simple can be so unique and powerful, even though it's meant to be just another flower among millions." She brings it to her nose, inhaling it, then slips it into her breast pocket.

"I don't understand." I look to Levi for help, but he's as lost as I am.

"I may be blind, but I know there is always a world around me. Even when I feel lost, like I can't get to the one thing I need. I don't panic. I know if I am calm, my mind will have more room to think, instead of filling with stress. Your heart and your mind already hold all the answers — you are already halfway there. We'll get you time, and you will be okay," she reassures me. Every time she opens her mouth, my respect for her grows.

Suddenly, the fake sky begins to cloud over, and it starts to rain, slowly at first, then all at once. The plants shift toward the water, stretching to quench their thirst, and Levi does the same, getting to his feet, raising his arms above his head and opening his mouth wide. I tilt my head back, the cold water pelting my flesh. It pulls me from all my problems as I open my mouth, revelling in the feeling of the rain on my parched tongue. Mud forms under our bodies, squishing between my toes. Levi pulls me up while Mary lies back, stretching out her body like she's going to make a snow angel.

"Come on!" He laughs, leaping from puddle to puddle, splashing me, grabbing my hands, spinning us around.

"I'm getting dizzy," I yell, laughing.

Our hands slip, sending Levi stumbling back. He lands in the biggest puddle, smiling as wide as his lips will allow, showing me the dirt in between his teeth. That's when I feel the first soul connect.

"Pure beauty is formed in the ugliest of situations," Beauty — Pulchritudo whispers, connecting to my mind.

Levi makes every moment bearable, beautiful. Even with the fresh air and these plants, this room wouldn't be this freeing without these two people. I let myself cry with the protection of the rain to hide my tears. The water runs over me, wrapping me in everything that makes me, 'me.' I pull off my shirt, not caring if they see my grimy fucking rainbow sports bra.

"I don't care," I breathe as the water washes away the dirt, shadows and the hate toward my mom, Eric and Até. "I don't care," I smile, a real smile.

Levi copies me, letting the water fall down his too-visible rib cage. He wraps me in his arms, and we hold each other for one last goodbye.

"Okay, that's enough. Let's go, leave the food behind, and we'll get you new clothes," Luke yells from the safety of his covered doorway, looking at the rain as if it might melt him.

We step into the elevator, leaving puddles and muddy footsteps everywhere we go. I wring out my hair, making sure the mess we leave behind is a hassle to clean up. Levi shakes his head like a dog, and Mary slows her pace, giving the water more time to fall from her clothes and us more time out of the life-sucking cell.

"New clothes are on the bed. I'll be back in the morning," Luke grunts, shoving us into the cell and slamming the door, barely taking the time to lock it before quickly running off.

"Okay, kid, you should get to that connection shit before he comes back at dawn." Levi throws pink scrubs at my face, pulling me into a gentle hug, the smell of sweat and dew clinging to him. He looks good in pink; it enhances his eyes.

He pulls himself onto the bunk above Mary, who crawls into her bed, still in her soaking wet clothes. A smile lights up her face as she pulls the blanket over her head.

I settle into my bed, wet hair pressing against my cheeks, "Okay," I breathe, and force my eyes shut until only peaceful darkness fills my mind, and I find the same place Spe brought me.

This time a projector sits in the middle of the room, pointing at a white cloth. Beside the projector is a simple red stool with a carved box on the surface. I instinctively sit down, holding the box in my hands. It's abnormally light, even with blank slides neatly placed inside. I switch the projector on, the golden glow illuminating everything as I slip in the first slide. Nothing happens. I hit every button, even punch the machine but no luck. *"Think,"* I whisper, starting with the oldest sister. *"Imperium."*

Colour flashes across the screen, resolving into faces, and I'm back in The Sticks. The memory streams from my mind into the projector, playing like a movie on the screen. I'm in the musty Warehouse, with hordes of cheering people encircling me. I stand in the fighting ring, adrenaline and rage causing the screaming crowd to become silent to my ears and mind. I turn to see Rey lying unconscious to my left on the dusty cement floor, Jimmy and Uri shielding him from our last three opponents from Amy's gang as Finn tries to wake him. Tequila and I take on Amy ourselves, punching and kicking until only Amy and I remain. My fists are bleeding, my lip cracked, my ribs broken, the first time I realized pain wasn't an issue.

Then Amy's on the ground. Her whole gang is on the ground. My gang is circled around me, Rey held between Uri and Jimmy.

We're younger and less muscular in this place. Jimmy looks fourteen, Rey has chubby cheeks, and Uri still seems awkward around us. This was our first fight as a gang. It was our first win. We didn't stay to celebrate our moving up in the rankings or to bathe in the cheers of victory. We walked out, heads hung.

Winning didn't make me feel powerful. The gang did — their loyalty, strength and the need to protect each other. I felt power in their love, knowing I picked good friends.

The memory ends, and the screen goes back to white, the wall in my mind falling brick by brick. Someone walks into the room, but I don't look. I take another slide out, *"Sapientiae."* Different images flash across the screen until my mind settles on one.

Five Hunters surround me, snarling, grunting, their breath outlined by the frozen night air. Street lights flicker, pasting empty shadows on every surface, not a human there to bail me out. I had just endured a light beating from Eric but I wasn't disoriented enough to settle for a space in my alley on the mouldy couch, but I wasn't careful enough either.

"Scared, little girl?" A Hunter snickers, punching his hand, licking his thin, pale, dehydrated lips.

"No," I say, my voice so hushed that they laugh harder.

The five of them step closer, leaving a sliver of a gap between two of them, underestimating my speed and size. I slip past, sprinting faster than my legs want to allow, my vision growing blurry as I somehow reach The Shed, and fists start to fly.

This memory was from the second time I got jumped, when I sent two Hunters to the hospital. I led all five to the bog behind The Shed, trapping three of them in the muddy quicksand and taking on the other two.

The warrior part of me drove me to kill them, but I stopped myself. I even took the two to the hospital. I don't know what happened to the three.

They were never found, and no Hunters ever entered The Shed beyond that day.

The screen goes blank again, and as it does, two souls connect, Bellum and Sapientiae sharing this memory. I was wise in trapping the Hunters, skillful, intelligent and brave for fighting them alone, knowing I could win.

"About damn time," Bellum grunts, slapping the back of my head. I turn to see four featureless figures guarding my back, their bodies outlined with glowing blue light.

"Well, that's not creepy," I mutter, trying not to jump out of my skin at the sight of them.

"You'll get used to it," Pulchritudo whispers, her breaths ruffling my hair. I can tell she's trying her hardest not to hug me. Is it even possible for her to hug me? I ignore the shivers rolling through my body as I slip another slide into the projector.

"Pax," I whisper, waiting for the screen to change again, but it stays blank, *"Pax,"* I repeat, looking behind me, but they just shrug.

"Try Medicus," Imperium nudges me with her elbow. I feel the connection go right through my arm. I try not to cringe too hard, taking a deep breath and ignoring their stifled laughs.

"Medicus," I whisper. The screen switches to an image of Finn sitting on the table in The Shed. His eyebrows are furrowed in concentration as he stitches up a significantly deep cut on Jimmy's arm. This was the first time I returned to healing, the first time I felt normal and helpful again. The connection to Medicus instantly sticks, and another figure appears behind me.

"I'm easy," Medicus shrugs, jostling her sisters and looking over my injuries as if she could heal them right here. Maybe she can.

"Futurae," I continue, the word leaving my lips like a ghost leaving a body.

The vision of Jimmy with his smile and sparkling eyes, and of J sitting at the riverbank flashes across the screen for only a second before another figure pops up, crossing her arms.

"She's easier," Sapientiae snorts, "*not one for the dramatics.*"

"But her visions — *you know what, never mind...*" I trail off, not wanting to dive into an argument about how unbelievably traumatizing and dramatic the visions she gives me are. I turn back to the screen, one more connection to make.

"Pax," I say, waiting, yet still the screen doesn't change. I try switching the slides. "*Pax!*" I yell twice more before frustration courses through my veins, and I throw the box across the room.

"*That stubborn bitch...*" Bellum grunts, storming out, leaving through the wall. What the hell is the matter with me? Peace has been with me the whole time. Why is she the one I can't connect with?

"*It's not you. You might need more rest,*" Imperium says soothingly, switching off the projector. She crouches beside me, her face mirroring mine, and, for a second, it's as if I am her.

"*I don't need rest, I've slept all night,*" I argue, rubbing my hands across my face, feeling incapable of controlling what's inside me. Incapable of doing anything right.

"Harley."

"No. I need to do this now."

"Harley." Imperium's voice silences me, halting my overpowering desire to keep looking through all the slides 'til I hold the right one. "*You have time. You can't force this. Like Ace said, you — your world knows nothing of what peace is. Your memory of peace is buried under millions of others. It won't surface right away,*" she says, shooing away her sisters. They wave at me, wishing me luck, Pulchritudo blowing me kisses before they walk back through the wall. The white sheet rolls up, and the projector vanishes at the snap of Imperium's fingers, the slides flying back into the box, leaving with everything else.

"But—"

"*No, Pax told me not to push you, so rest,*" she demands but in a way that doesn't feel so threatening.

"Well Pax could help me rest if she just connected—" Imperium cuts me off as she snaps again, and unwillingly my mind falls to sleep, dreams pulling me under, blanketing me.

CHAPTER 31
(JIMMY)

"Ten minutes 'till drop," Jasper radios from the front of our stolen supply truck, where twelve of us sit cramped in the back. The air is saturated with the overpowering scent of burnt rubber, sweat and nerves.

Ryker never told us her contact's name, but whoever it is must be close to the leaders. We've spent four days hammering each nail of information given to us into our minds: how many Hunters will be guarding the torture room on floor thirty and the prison on floor twenty-five, how to avoid each surveillance camera hidden in the halls in case they fail weren't turned off, how many minutes it will take to reach our assigned floors, and the exact time Harley will be led to her — her execution.

"Shall we all be completely honest with ourselves?" Rey bounces with the truck, carelessly smudging the tattoo on his neck. It's meant to act as part of his disguise, along with the blackberry juice dyeing his hair. "Do we really think the Hunters won't be prepared for my beautiful masterpieces," he says, referring to his stupid smoke bombs.

"Would you shut up," Johnny scolds, his voice strained with nerves. His disguise consists of a shaved head, Ryker's orange contacts and a nose piercing he begged to have.

As much as it hurts me to say this, Rey's right. We have nothing but timing and luck on our side. And what are the odds of getting in and out alive — twice? I suppress the thought, focusing on the hope that tomorrow Harley will be in my arms once more.

Finn pats my shoulder reassuringly, his face ashen as he plays with the knives in his pocket. I didn't want him to come; no one did, but he insisted. Finn argued that since he's the medic, he'd be the difference between Harley making it to camp or not, and not a soul dared to argue with that.

He, Tequila and Buckey have berry-dyed hair as well. Both Tequila's eyes have been made the same piercing blue colour using Ryker's contacts. Buckey's face has been made to look beaten to the point of unrecognition, and Finn's freckles are covered by makeup. Platforms put in his shoes elevate him to be almost the same height as Uri.

All of us wear Hunter uniforms and disguises. We don't actually know if the leaders cared enough to remember all our faces or if they kept tabs on any of us, so we figured it's better to be safe than sorry.

"Two of our Hunters will meet us in the supply room," Ace mutters to himself, repeating the plan for the fourteenth time since he got in here. No one tells him to shut up because, in a way, I believe it reassures us. "Cameras will hopefully be shut off for thirty minutes. If not, we keep our heads down and away from corners." He pulls at his fingers, surely counting every turn this truck takes. "We have ten minutes to get to the fifteenth floor before the cameras are shut off. A group of six will head to the torture room, and the other six will head to the prison — Finn will be with Jimmy's group because Harley will most likely be in the torture room, since she is to be ex ..." He trails off, not able to speak the word aloud. All of us have been tip-toeing around the word execution, except Até, but even when she says it, a visible shiver rolls through her body.

"Once we get in, Malick and I will find rides," Ryker radios from the front, her voice even more breathy over the walkie. "Jasper will join the group going to the prison — once you're in, you're on your own." With these words, everyone seems to still, the pressure and risk of this mission sinking its claws into our skin.

"Today's her birthday," Tequila whispers solemnly as she leans into Buckey, her breaths curling through the frozen air, her shoulders shaking as she holds back tears.

"Snap out of it," Uri says abruptly, his voice booming louder in the enclosed space. "You're acting like she's already gone. If any of you were in her situation, she wouldn't let her emotions get in the way, she would fucking fight till they tore her apart." We straighten at his words, at his strength. "I owe her my damn life, and I intend on getting her back, or to die trying." Uri gets to his feet, not looking any of us in the eyes as the truck screeches to a stop. His speech does nothing but dump gasoline on the pit of fire already blazing in my chest.

We stay silent, a collective breath drawn in as a six-code knock pounds against the door. Uri raises his gun, unlatching it on our side and flinging it open. Two Hunters stand before us, both the man and the woman holding an arm out to us, revealing a howling wolf tattoo previously concealed under their sleeves.

"Rita — Mitch," Até nods in greeting as she sticks knives into her black combat boots.

"You have ten minutes to climb the stairs and get to floor fifteen before they cut the surveillance in the halls. It will be turned off till someone notices, which hopefully will be longer than thirty minutes — we'll try to get you as much time as we can," Rita instructs, leading us to the entrance, then disappearing into the shadows with Mitch.

As we climb, all twelve of us work to prevent the sound of our footsteps from bouncing off the stairwell walls, but even the lightest shuffle travels up and around us. No one speaks, and I swear the pounding of my heart can be heard by everyone around me, and the thin sheen of perspiration covering my skin can be seen by all in the dim light.

When I was younger, my mom had a saying she would repeat to herself when fear gathered in her chest. "If you can dance with the demons and sing with the angels the devil will let you live. For you are able to do the one thing he could not."

It seemed to calm her, but no one understood what it meant, and I never got to ask. My grandma said it had something to do with willpower and facing your fears. "If you can meet your demons and still sing of the good in life, your fears will lose their power and no longer possess the ability to drown you." This saying has been playing on repeat ever since we got in the truck and has become louder as we climb the stairs. It's more than fitting because today, my fears intend to suffocate me and laugh as they push my head underwater. We have no room for errors and can allow no hesitations on our way to get Harley. A minute could be the difference between a warm and cold body.

A timer beeps on Uri's watch as we reach the fifteenth floor, signalling it's time to split up. They go through the door to find the stairwell that will take them to the twenty-fifth. We continue up, heading to the seventeenth floor, to find the door that will lead us to the thirtieth.

The most daunting thing about this building is the way the stairs were designed. It's not one continuous staircase going all the way up. They're separated after the eighteenth floor, continuing at the ends of different halls. Some head up, some head down, and some skip two or five floors. It was most likely designed to slow down intruders, rather than for fire exits or anything like that.

The humidity in the air clings to my clothes and restricts my lungs as we move in twos through halls and up stairs. Tequila and I lead, her movements fast and noiseless, the gears in her head turning on overdrive.

The halls we run down are mostly empty. Asteroid said they're mainly used by cleaners or low-level workers. He's been right so far; we've only run into four Hunters who greeted us with respectful nods, accepting us without question.

"Left," Finn whispers, running with the map Asteroid drew up for us. Finn doesn't hold a gun, only medical supplies and his knives, though I made sure Rey had an extra in his pocket just in case.

We sprint down the hall reaching the final flight of stairs we must climb before we are on the same floor as the torture room. I feel sick

— anticipation, fear and nerves fizzing and swelling in my stomach at the thought of seeing Harley, wondering what state I'll find her in.

Tequila opens the door a foot, holding her breath as she cautiously peers around the edge, listening for footsteps, whispers, anything. Suddenly she pulls back, getting out of the way before the door has a chance to slam on her neck. I grab her arm as she stumbles back, her eyes wide with paralyzed fear. Before I can ask what the hell just happened, four Hunters burst from the stairwell, bearing rifles and gas masks.

Without hesitation, Buckey and Johnny open fire, taking out two of the Hunters, injuring the third and the fourth, who mistakenly stumbles in Rey's direction. Rey pounces, somehow getting on the fourth Hunter's back. I swear Rey's fucking laughing as the Hunter lurches, slamming both of them into the wall, trying to rid Rey from his back. Rey's unfazed by the impact as he takes his knife and jams it into the Hunter's throat.

I turn back to the door, letting go of Tequila as the third Hunter grunts, releasing his gun as a bullet buries itself in his shoulder. He twists, somehow dodging the rest. The Hunter locks his eyes on Finn, then lunges towards him. I don't have time to shoot. I spring forward, knocking the Hunter off course, slamming his head into the floor. He punches, hitting my shoulder and jaw, the pain radiating through my bones, only to be dulled by the adrenaline spreading through my muscles. I move to his back, wrapping my legs around his chest and pressing my fingers into his eyes. He screams, clawing at me as blood warms my fingers. I grip his head, and in one aggressive twist, I break his neck, and his screams cut off, his body falling limp.

"I can hear more coming," Tequila hisses, closing the door of the stairs and attaching something to the handle. I can hear them too, not only coming from the stairs but from the way we came. We've been radio silent since we started up the stairs, so even if we wanted to call for backup — even if we could, no one would answer.

"If we go down this hall and take two lefts, there should be another stairwell that leads to the torture room," Finn offers, helping me to my feet and moving us along. As we run, the approaching footsteps grow louder, drowning out my thoughts.

"Now would be a good time to set it off," Rey says, covering his ears. Johnny does the same. Without question and before Tequila warns us, I cover mine too. She pulls something from her pocket and presses a button that triggers a popping noise. Then the hall fills with a series of high-pitch screeches that makes my vision tipsy. The sound only lasts a couple of seconds, but even that short time with my ears plugged is enough to make me stumble a couple times.

I shake my head, turning the corner, correcting my vision just in time to be greeted by five Hunters. For a second, they remain calm, nodding at us before seeing the blood spotting our faces. They run at us, not firing, most likely ordered to take us alive, but that doesn't stop us. We take down two Hunters, their bodies twitching and their faces twisting into an expression I can only describe as inhuman. We miss the rest, everyone still slightly disoriented by the noise.

"Here," Rey yells, heading into a room as the faint sound of footsteps begins to thunder in my ears, the threat stabbing my gut. None of us think to question his decision before filing in after him. We're trapped either way. We may as well have a door between us.

"Help me move this," Buckey says, pushing a large filing cabinet in front of the door, sliding it in place just as the pounding begins. Finn crouches down, covering his ears.

The room is dim, so I can only make out the outline of beakers and a metal table in the middle of the floor. I can tell by the way Rey is looking around, awestruck, that it must be a lab. Johnny smacks him across the head, bringing Rey back to reality.

"What do we do now?" Tequila asks, sliding something into her pocket. Her face is pale, and her sweat is now tinted a berry colour as her red hair begins to show. I toss her my hat, and with a terrified smile, she slides it on.

I crouch down, shaking my head, racking my brain for a simple solution. We can't go out the windows or through the vents, and there's no back door. There's only one way out, and we're running out of time.

I stand, straightening, checking my gun as I move to the door. I can count ten or so voices arguing on the other side, maybe more. I wave Buckey over, gesturing to the filing cabinet.

"Are you crazy, you can't go out there, we're outnumbered." Tequila grabs my arm, pleading with me to think about this.

"Listen," I hiss, pulling my arm away. "Either way we're fucked. I'd rather die than be trapped here and taken in the end — and for every second we waste, the chances of Harley dying and J being left alone increase — if I have to, I'll kill every single Hunter out there, by myself." She looks at me, searching her brain for another solution, only to end up nodding when she finds none. Her understanding gets the rest of the gang to slowly gather around us. "Once we move this, the door will open, and they'll stumble in. I don't think they're allowed to kill us right away, maybe not at all, so we already have the advantage," I explain, watching as they nod.

Buckey and I get in position, everyone else pressing close to the wall, raising their guns and pointing to the place the Hunters will fall. "On three," I whisper, pushing my fingers through my hair before pressing my palms to the cool metal. I watch the gang's terrified faces transform into determination, the weight of their deaths clamping to my head and squeezing. I look to Buckey, who nods. "One...two...three." We move the cabinet aside, watching as the door flies open.

CHAPTER 32

(HARLEY)

When Imperium cautiously releases me from my dream-filled stupor, I'm no longer in the cell. Mary's not lying with her blanket pulled over her face. Levi's not sleeping or watching over me. I'm in my custom-made room, designed just for me, for this day.

The chair I find myself in is slightly rusted and creaky. Wires twist around my ankles and stomach, holding me in place. It's barbed wire; every time I move or breathe, the spikes dig further into my flesh. I don't see why that's needed when my handcuffs are chained to the table. I'm not going anywhere.

I lift my head to find a large camera positioned directly in front of me, the lens cap on, red light blinking. A thick cord runs out the door, moving past Luke, who is stationed in the corner of the room, a purple welt on his forehead and a silver bracelet locked around his wrist. He's not looking at me, but I can see the scratchy redness of his eyes when he glances around the room. He doesn't move when he hears my shifting body. He only taps the side of his ear, listening, whispering to the air.

"Luke?" I whisper, my ears ringing, dizziness flowing around my brain as hot blood drips down my stomach and ankles. Luke keeps his head down, shaking it slightly, warning me to stop, that they're listening, watching.

The handle jiggles, and the door opens to let AC and JC in, both wearing all black, their hair greasy and slicked-back, ready for an audience.

"Happy birthday, Harley," JC smiles, pressing his palms into the table while AC removes the camera lens. AC has a fresh cut on his lower lip, drops of blood falling to his chin. He looks scared, as though he's seen a ghost.

"What's that for?" I groan, my forehead aching as I look at them. I have a concussion, a goose egg somewhere on my head. That's how they got me here without waking me.

They both smile as JC removes a small needle from his pocket, the liquid in it muddy.

"We are using you as an example of what will happen to those who go against us, even the ones made for power," he says, pouring foul-smelling clear liquor down my arm, stinging my irritated skin.

"I did nothing to threaten you — except being born. You started this. I only wanted to save my brother. I didn't even know what I was," I snarl, twisting my hands against the metal.

If they hadn't taken J, I might have gone my whole life without knowing about the rulers. The leaders made things worse for themselves. They brought me here. They put me in the position to learn more, to connect.

"Exactly. If you weren't born, none of this would have had to happen," he smiles, injecting the substance into my veins, causing the light blue lines to turn a darker shade as it mixes with my bloodstream, slithering toward my heart.

"I have a brother and a dad. The bloodline won't end when you kill me," I mumble, wishing I could keep my mouth shut for once.

"Yes, but after the injuries your brother sustained while in our care, it would be a miracle if he can even have kids — and if by some chance he survived your poorly planned rescue, can have kids, and if your dad is still alive, worse comes to worst, we just kill them," AC laughs.

I stiffen, suddenly and sharply as a high-pitch scream slices through my head, sending my vision out of focus. My chest pulls inward. My fingers curl, the muddy liquid swirling through my brain, my lungs, igniting my soul. Then it stops, and all I feel is stiffness.

"What—"

"I call it liquid pain, I created it. It's a more extreme version of what Maddick gave you," JC says, letting the pinprick from the needle pool and dome — it doesn't stop. The blood keeps coming until the surface tension breaks, the red running down to my elbow. I can no longer clot my own blood.

"Where is he?" I interrupt, not quite sure if I wish Maddick were here or if I'm glad he's not.

"Not one for these types of events, never had the stomach for it. He's probably in his stupid garden," JC laughs tensely, moving beside the camera, glancing at the door, waiting for someone, maybe even relieved that his twin isn't here. "Honestly, Harley, I might be so talented that the drug stops the soul rulers from talking to you altogether."

"Fat fucking chance," Bellum screams at him, her voice scratchy and strangled.

"Language," Pulchritudo scolds.

"Shut the—"

I almost can't stifle my laugh, but I manage to keep my face passive.

"The camera..." AC continues, cracking his knuckles, filling the silence with his obnoxious liquid voice. He talks as if water is pouring from his mouth, as if he's drowning in his own saliva. "...will display your execution on the floating billboards throughout the cities and on the screens we have set up in the towns. Your friends in No Man's Land might even be able to see some of it." He removes the lens cap, looking for JC's approving nod.

My heart sinks. It lives in my abdomen now, in an empty pit, filled with venomous spikes. *I not only left them with no explanation, left them alone, but now they have to watch me die. J has to watch me die. Jimmy, the love of my life, has to watch me die. It will kill them.*

"Did you figure out how to use my blood and bone marrow yet?" I ask, choking on the bile and fear dancing on my teeth.

"No, but we have enough samples not to need you anymore."

"If you kill me, your soul will be taken in my place, you do know that, right? I'll still be here threatening your power, and you'll be dead — are you ready for that?" I exclaim, leaning into the barbs, letting the pain fuel me, not hold me back.

"I do, yes." He stands straighter, clasping his hands behind his back. "That's why I'm not participating. Someone else is very excited to be leading this." JC nods toward the door, and when he does, I get the feeling that a part of him, even a part of AC, doesn't want the person to come in. I don't either.

An older man with a salt and pepper beard and greying hair hobbles in, using a cane to balance. He has freckled, wrinkled skin and round red scars scattered over his face, signs of his drug-driven life. His light eyes glare at me, almost changing colour every time he blinks, unable to decide what they want to be. "I think you're familiar with our father, Boris — well, I guess you know him as Bob," JC introduces.

My eyes widen, watching the man move in front of me. His transfermation, standing upright rather than slumped over my kitchen table, hung over from the drug and alcohol-filled parties, has changed his whole appearance.

"Miss me?" he gloats, his voice so deep and off-centre it makes my world spin.

In the many years he's lived in my kitchen, I've never heard him speak or say anything to me at all. I never saw him move, except to watch my fights. I've never seen him as anything but a hopeless addict, not a retired leader. That day when I yelled at my mom, she told me there was so much I didn't understand. She looked over at Bob for a second, terrified, silently warning me of the man who watched me for years. He tested my leadership by making me take on the responsibilities of the Warehouse.

"You bastard," I spit, lurching toward him.

"Don't worry, your mom's fine, maybe a little heartbroken but fine. By the way, that line, 'My mom died when my dad did,'" he mimics my voice, "Now that — that was a good touch." He smiles, "Luke, get me a chair." He snaps his fingers, not looking away from me.

Luke doesn't move. He shifts uncomfortably, staring at the metal on his wrist. Boris doesn't ask again before pressing something that looks like a watch. Luke lurches to the side as his neck muscles strain, fighting the current rolling up his arm into his brain. He stands, sliding his chair over, then jerks back against the wall as another wave of electricity slides him to the ground. This new punishment of Luke must be a result of him trying to help me once he decided he didn't want to watch me die.

"I've watched you for a long time, watched you grow up. You are quite impressive really. The way you fight, like you've been training since you were young. How you get people to listen—"

"Why are you doing this?" I interrupt, pushing my hands into the table, more metal burying itself further into my skin. "We gave you a place to stay. You didn't need one. I shared my rations with you and J, and my mom did too. You didn't need that either. I set a fucking glass of water out for you every time I came home," I yell, abandoning my detached appearance.

"And I respect that, but I didn't care for any of it. I'm a retired leader. My sons are in power. I played you, and you didn't even think to question me. That's the one fault of a soul ruler; they tend to see the beauty before they consider the bad. It's your weakness. So is love," he says, displaying the same small habits as JC: pursing his lips, slowing his words, tilting his head. He probably thinks it makes his appearance more intimidating.

"I swear to every fucking thing in this universe, I'll kill him," Imperium seethes.

"I'm starting to rub off on you," Bellum applauds her.

"I know this is a touchy time, but can we watch our language please?" Pulchritudo whispers.

"Shut the hell up," they all scream.

"So are they talking to you now?" Boris asks, directing my attention back to him. Curiosity fills his face, but all I can focus on is how sick he looks. The whites of his eyes are almost yellow, and his skin is tinted the same. It's most likely liver failure or something along those lines.

"You're dying," I tell him, leaning back, gaining my cool once more. The two brothers move beside their father, but Boris raises a hand, making them step back to the camera. Luke slumps further down.

"Guess who's back?" The high-pitched voice interrupts. His words screech in my head, drilling burr holes into my brain. *"Just here to enjoy the final show."*

"Never mind, let me kill him," Imperium says. I feel her lurching toward him, everyone holding her back, even Bellum. Boris's lips move, but I can't hear him — everyone's too loud.

"Would you all stop talking, for just one fucking second?" I demand, repositioning myself, though I know there's no chance of feeling comfortable.

"Speak up," I groan out loud, rolling my eyes, catching Boris off guard, acting as if his sickness has muffled his words.

"Okay?" He rolls his tongue, "Yes I'm sick, I'm dying. The treatments have stopped helping me, even Stem 47. We have no idea why, but that's the reason I'm here. I'm not scared of death."

"If you kill me, I'll live anyway, your soul will be taken instead of mine," I say again, feeling every bit of doubt and anxiety spike with my voice.

"Maybe or maybe not. See, I was a leader, but I stepped away from power. I was the first to obsess over the soul rulers, my sons got that from me. I'm their father. I don't take orders from them. Besides, I don't want more power. I'm killing you to silence my obsession, the thing that keeps me up every night, and maybe even to hurt your father if he's still out there — you know, I liked him. He was a good kid, I taught him a thing or two before he turned against us," Boris grins, watching me, waiting for me to say something, do something. I don't.

"We're live," JC whispers as the light on the camera changes from red to green. He touches his father's shoulder lightly before stepping aside, but Boris pays no attention to his sons or thanks them. He's too fixated on me.

"You may leave," Boris orders, fiddling with something by his feet. AC glares at his dad, stalking out of the room, but JC lingers a bit longer, looking at me almost jealously before he hurries out.

Boris continues to clatter around with his bag, dropping items on the floor, laughing to himself.

"What are you waiting for?" I bark, continuing to lean forward, feeling the barbs widen the holes in my flesh, nothing healing.

"Would you stop doing that?" Medicus scolds, her voice more strained than the others.

"Let her, it will make this faster," the high-pitched voice chuckles. I wish I could punch him in the face, punch both of these arrogant men.

"Likewise," he screeches back.

"Are you listening?" Boris asks, scooting his chair forward, making sure not to block the camera.

"Honestly, no. I have a lot more dominant voices trying to get my attention," I smirk, forgetting I'm live on the floating billboards. Angry chatter from millions of people seeps through the walls.

"Hear that? They don't like you," he gloats, tilting his head toward the sound. "You know most of them kill for fun, meaning they wouldn't follow you anyways."

"No, they kill to survive. They kill because that's the life you forced them into," I argue, calmer despite his accusation. He's the reason I'm here, the reason my kind are hunted, the reason J was taken and tortured. He's the reason this world is so fucked up.

"They kill because they were born to. If they didn't like it, they'd stop," he counters, his cold leader demeanour crumbling. He's not strong enough. This is his last chance to show off who he used to be. He's not young anymore. He's not powerful.

"No, they were raised to. And those who despise killing innocent people die," I say, pausing, a new idea, a battle plan, folding into my thoughts. "How do you know their hate isn't directed toward you? You became their saviour, the person who gave them new lives. You came up with ways for them to kill each other. Then you neglected them, abandoned them, leaving a worse version of yourself to make things more unliveable, unbearable — they hate you, as much as I do." I make my words bolder. Luke smirks, and Boris narrows his eyes, widening his shoulders and opening his chest.

"You're good at honing in on a person's greatest weakness. So am I." He leans down in his chair, bringing up a wooden paddle, a serrated knife and *my* dagger. "I believe this is yours," he snarls at me, letting the blade glint in the camera. The rubies shimmer in the light, along with the words '*Sacrifice For Our People*' boldly engraved into the freshly polished silver. "Pretty little thing, isn't it?" He presses the tip of the blade to his finger until blood slides down his flesh, dripping onto the floor. Luke starts to slide up the wall slowly, soundlessly, but the fabric of his clothes swishes against the wood. Boris snaps out of his taunting rant and presses his watch. A hand wraps around my heart as Luke groans, trying to yell, but the muscles in his throat are paralyzed. He crumples back down, twitching.

"Stop," I yell, before my common sense tells me not to waste my time on Luke or show Boris that other people's pain hurts me more than it hurts them.

"See? You care too much for people. Even the one who handed you over, the one who was ready to let you die after all you did for him." He flips the paddle into his hand, hitting my face before I can think to try and find a way to protect myself. The connection stings more than anything I've felt before, as if he drenched it in hot sauce that now seeps into my pores. "I could always bring your cell mates up here. That boy and that arrogant smart mouth Mary."

"NO!" I lurch toward him.

"That's what I thought," he says, swinging again, the paddle just missing the meat of my eye, touching my nose, swelling my lips. "I got a lot out of her about the soul rulers — well, as much as I could before something went wrong and she became blind. She never talked to me again after that, or anyone really." He pulls up a small gun, taking his time to load in the bullets.

My jaw clenches until my neck and ears want to explode. I use all my strength not to move, not to fight toward him. It's what he wants. I've encountered many people in my life whose egos and god complexes are bigger than their hearts.

He made Mary blind, I think.

"You think you can scare me," I spit, my lips floppy, the motion uncontrolled as they move with my words. He takes the serrated knife, sliding it from my shoulder to my elbow. I bite my tongue as it bites into my flesh, slicing my muscles and nerves. It hurts more than it should, but it's not agonizing. My vision isn't failing me, and I can still think. The shot JC gave me isn't working the way it was intended. "You think you can hurt me. Eric is my stepdad, my gang is ranked third, and I've been hunted my whole life, like everyone else. I know pain better than you. I can last, and the longer you sit here showboating, the longer I have to get this serum out of my system. Faster with all this bleeding."

"It lasts twenty four hours, even with your metabolism, even with your abilities." He raises his head and winks, then without hesitating, he takes my dagger and drives the blade through my hand until it's buried in the table. Heat, radiation, fire, every type of pain sprints up my arm into my heart, my throat, my chest. "You are weak. How can you be a soul ruler if you can't handle this? If you can't fight back?" he yells, his knuckles colliding with my chin.

I swallow my screams. "You're the weak one," I say, my voice strangled as I try not to move, flinch, breathe. "You're torturing me — killing me because you're scared. Scared that someone other than you and your family will run this place. You know people will turn on you and take their revenge." I take in a sharp breath, feeling hot tears soak my cheeks. "You're terrified that you can't do this one thing for your sons because you've never done anything for them, you've spent so much time obsessing over me. I can see it in their eyes and in yours. They're scared of you. They don't love you. No one ever will, not even if you let them." I hold in every bit of air I can grab, making use of every molecule of oxygen. "Soul ruler or not, I would die for all of my people, and they would die for me. Do you believe your sons would do the same for you?" Cheers from the crowd drift through the wall, mixing with and bringing strength to my words as they linger. Their truthful fingers pull at his hair, crawling into his ears, up his nose, down his throat, peeling his eyelids back until he has no choice but to see that I'm right.

He lunges forward, locking his hands around my neck, squeezing until I have to fight against the wires, the restraints. I don't care that I'm sacrificing my muscles and veins or that I'm moving the knife, making the opening longer.

"They only love you because of what you are," he grunts, pushing, tightening his grip.

I have to breathe. I need to breathe. Even if it's easier not to. I struggle and twist, but his grip is too tight. He waits until I'm blue to release his hands from my neck. My head pounding, eyes bugging, I gasp for air, taking in everything, even the dust that feels like glass in my throat. Involuntary tears sting my face. I want to throw up.

At the edge of my vision, I watch Luke's muscles flex as he fights with himself, trying to stay put. He wants to help, but he can't; no one can. I move my lips to yell at Boris, to ask him to hurry up, but I can't find my voice. It drags and catches on the way to my mouth.

"*I'm tired,*" I tell the sisters, Spe, and even in my head, my voice breaks.

"*I know, Harley, but you have to connect with Pax. You only need to last a little longer, someone will see this, someone will help,*" Imperium encourages, her voice the strongest, fighting with me.

"*I'm so tired,*" I whimper, not sure if I'm in my head or in the room. I feel small and child-like. Almost as if I'm sick, spending the day at home, curled up in Jimmy's bed or held in his arms.

"*I know.*"

"*Even If I keep fighting, if I live, they will keep looking for me, for ways to kill me, and if I get out of here, they'll never stop hunting me.*" My realization momentarily brings silence to all the voices.

"I know, but if you don't keep fighting, you're leaving everyone else to suffer, to continue living in a world where they're scared of walking in the streets and executions are broadcasted for entertainment," Sapientiae says, her voice only a whisper in my quiet brain.

"But I'm just so tired," I repeat because I don't know what else to say.

"Yes, and that's when you figure out how strong you are, what type of person you are meant to be. We don't give up," Imperium says, her words turning into outstretched arms, cradling me.

"Think about Jimmy," Pulchritudo adds.

"And J," Medicus pipes up, briefly leaving her draining, exhausting work of keeping me alive.

"And Ace, Uri, Tequila, Finn, Rey, Johnny, Buckey," Spe continues, showing up for the first time since she told me what to do.

"Think about the friends you've made and the family you've grown up with. You'd be leaving them to live under the rule of the brothers, maybe even Boris now," Bellum says, with only the slightest bit of harshness and anger remaining in her words.

I wait for someone else to try and convince me not to give up. I wait for the high-pitched voice to show me how pointless this all is, but no one says anything. No one uses their abilities to make me feel more capable.

"Okay."

I rub my wrists across the cold metal until thin red lines coil down the chains, pooling on the table. I can no longer smell the rust that dyes my flesh. Only the smell of the iron leaving my body and staining my dry skin consumes the air. My left hand is stiff, the steel knife taking all its feeling, slicing my nerves. I stop fighting the barbed wire, and even if I wanted to fight against it, I couldn't. My flesh is moulded to it now, to the point where I can feel the hot metal in the muscles between my ribs.

I lift my gaze slightly, and when I look into the camera lens for the first time, I don't see my reflection, not the one I saw in the cracked Shed mirror mere weeks ago. I see a girl, my age, my height, exactly like me, yet so alien at the same time. My tears leave lines in the red dripping from my swollen eye, so swollen I'm surprised tears can be squeezed out. The person looking back at me is skinnier, paler, a skeleton with flesh, greasy knotted brown hair and plain brown eyes, her skin pulled tight as if trying to hold her together.

I observe her for a moment, watching as she blinks when I do, as her chest rises and falls at the same pace as mine does. She is me, but she is not, because I am stronger than that. I know that if I am not weak, no one can hurt me. I use all my strength to sit up straighter in defiance, in an effort to show the people forced to watch my last seconds of life, that I never gave up. And if J is watching, if Jimmy is watching, I want them to know I fought till the end, that I fought to get back to them. Hairs stand up on the back of my neck like soldiers as I hear Boris's voice echo in my brain.

"I'll give you three minutes to think about the life you will no longer have," he hisses, his tongue snapping each syllable, his curling smirk returning as I lift my chin.

I think about those I've killed to be here. The two Hunters in Dead Man's Hill, my bullet finding one's chest, my silver pointed knife glinting in the rising sun before finding the other Hunter's neck. The sniper I shot without thinking. Emerson, who is asleep in the ground because she fought for me. The boy with forest green eyes I failed to save, burning in the school. My friends, my gang, my family and countless more who might be dead because of me.

"One minute..." a voice, almost mechanical, utters. Boris stands, checking the clip of his gun, making a show out of emptying the clip until only three bullets remain.

"Let's hope one does the trick," he laughs, though I know he won't make it quick, won't make it pleasant. This has been his dream, his sons' dream to end the bloodline.

He takes another knife from his pocket, burying it in the shoulder of the same arm where my dagger sits in my hand. It's too damaged to feel anything but a pinch, which pulls at my vision, folding it into memories, until I sit at a table in my old house, where the rooms are — were — always filled with light, love and laughter. My mom dances around the kitchen in her yellow silk dress, singing.

The sun will rise
The moon will fall
They share the sky for their love is strong.
The sun has clouds
The moon has stars
Lending company when they are apart.
Though on special days
The sun will dull its rays
Allowing the moon to sit by its side
Their love shining brighter as one
In the darkest of times.

My dad steps into the kitchen, smiling like the moon. He grabs his shining sun, kissing her and spinning her around, causing J and I to stifle giggles. Then he lifts little J above his head, giving him wings and letting him fly like a bird through the clouds and the stars.

"Ten, nine, eight..." the mechanical voice screeches. Boris rips out the knife, his knuckles colliding with my shoulder. I see my friends sitting in a circle, playing cards, punching each other's arms, and body checking the winning person.

"Seven, six, five, four ..."

Jimmy laughs. His sweet, beautiful laugh that gives his eyes the illusion of sparkling ice when soft light hits the surface. I feel the warmth he gives when he encloses me.

I move a finger on my good hand, tapping out 'I love you' in Morse Code, hoping that's the only part Jimmy and J see. With my stare, I beg Jimmy to turn himself and J away from the floating billboards displaying my death.

"Three, two, one," the voice yells.

"Time's up, sweetheart," Boris says, taunting me, smiling so wide it hurts my face. "Do you have any last words?"

I force my vocal cords to let me be heard, "You can kill me, but nothing will silence your obsession, your guilt. It will kill you, and the people who don't believe in this type of life will never bow down to you or your sons," I spit, splattering blood across his face.

He moves so close to me our noses almost touch. I pull away, but he only moves closer. A loud crash makes me jump as Luke breaks the door handle, kicking the door open, leaving, not able to watch anymore, even if it means he'll be electrocuted, but Boris doesn't touch his watch.

"Then let's take this slow so I can kill my guilt before I kill you," he whispers, his breath smelling of blood and dead souls. "What is it you say to your dying?" he drawls, stepping back, holding his gun away from him, toward me. He lowers it, firing, shattering my shin. "May your body lie in the dirt and your soul find hell?" he taunts, shrugging.

I stop the screams from bursting out of my mouth. I hold my lips together, willing them shut, not giving Boris, Jackson or Aron, who have to be watching, the satisfaction of hearing my pain.

Bang, bang, bang!

Gunshots echo from the hallway. Screams of panic and frantically-issued orders draw Boris's attention away from me, his gun dropping further.

"Harley, HARLEY!" Jimmy screams.

Jimmy!

My heart wants to beat again. I try to wake my body up, scream for Medicus to keep me alive for a little longer. I don't care if I die. I just want to see Jimmy, to feel his warmth, to look into his eyes one last time.

Bang. Another one of Boris's bullets catches me by surprise as it connects with my shoulder, ripping through tendons and muscles, hopefully not damaging a major artery. My head jerks up, a small scream escaping, not because of the pain or the pressure of the impact but for help. So Jimmy knows I'm here. I'm right here.

The Hunters guarding the door jerk, falling lifeless to the ground. Jimmy and Tequila burst into the room, muddy and soggy with rain. The others must be in the hall because I can still hear gunshots, fists hitting faces and screaming. So much screaming. Boris uses his last bullet on me, missing my chest, hitting the same spot on my shoulder, and this time, my screams are born from pain. It's burning through my body — I'm on fire.

Finn, Johnny and Rey run through the door, their eyes meeting mine, looking away just as fast. *Am I that hideous?* Rey and Johnny guard the door, and Buckey comes into focus. Finn tries to get to me, but Boris still stands in their way.

"Six against one. Stand down or die," Jimmy yells, wanting to lunge toward me, but Boris pulls out his knives, starting to throw. Jimmy tries to fire, but his gun jams. He throws himself at Boris, preventing the others from just shooting him. Jimmy uses his body as a shield, taking several knives, fighting to make Boris feel the same pain as I do. Fists, elbows and knees hit flesh and bones. Someone cries out, and then I hear nothing.

My world becomes an out-of-control car, spinning on ice as ringing fills my ears. Tequila's hands find me, freeing my body from the chair, cutting the barbed wire away and yelling something, but all I hear is ringing. Hands lift me, testing if I can walk, then placing me on the door that used to belong to the frame once they realize I can't move my legs. They break into a run, bouncing me with every step — hot poison-like liquid pooling around my body, sticky on my fingers.

"Stop," I gasp, feeling more blood sprinkle my lips as I cough. Gently they set me on the floor.

"Hey, kiddo," Jimmy whispers, bending down, stroking my hair, kissing my forehead and wiping my bloody face with his sleeve.

"Kiddo?" I croak, my vision unable to decide whether it would like to be blurry or clear. He smiles, tears falling from his eyes, a bruise forming on his cheek, a gash on his collar bone. I try to check if the knives hit him anywhere else, but I can't lift my head. Rey, Buckey and Johnny guard the table, and Finn works overtime to stop my bleeding, yelling orders at

Tequila, though she doesn't understand what he's asking her to do. This is the first time I've seen him truly distressed while treating a patient.

"I know, sorry. Didn't mean to say it, but you only just made me stop calling you that, I know you don't like it — I'll just stick with beautiful, or baby. No, baby sounds weird. Beautiful, I like beautiful — Harley, I missed you so much," he babbles on, terrified, concerned for my life. I want to stay in this world and watch his glossy sweet blue eyes, but every time Finn does something, a jolt of pain rolls up my body, punching me back into my world of memories.

My dad and mom are speaking now, reading a poem to J and me. We're in my room, J snuggled up in my bed. He's four and I'm nine. A thunderstorm shakes the walls, turning out the lights, the Hunters play games in the dark. The air is filled with thunder, lightning and blood-curdling screams. Our parents sit at the end of my bed, reading the words my dad wrote to ease us into sleep on these nights where we can dream of a peaceful world.

We'll take you up to Lullaby Mountain
Where you both shall be free
Where raindrops heal memories
And fairies live in peace
We'll bathe in the sunlight
And dance with the worms
We can swim in the river till dusk returns.

"Harley, stay with me," Finn's voice breaks into my thoughts. He frantically presses cloth to my wounds, wrapping it around me, fighting to make me stable so they can move me to safety before thousands of Hunters find us. Jimmy traces the curves of my face with his fingertips, tears trickling onto my cheeks, unable to help Finn and not wanting to leave me.

"You're crying," I note, wanting to lift my hand to wipe under his eyes, but one may still have my dagger stabbed in it, and the other won't listen to my brain's commands.

"Harley, you have more important things to worry about," he laughs for a short breath, trying too hard not to break in front of me.

"Worrying about you is the best part of my day," I whisper, my vision softening, pulling me back into the past.

My parents hold both of us now, my mom twirling my hair, smiling as J's eyelids become heavy.

Your fears will unravel
Disappearing with the sun
On Lullaby Mountain, you will always be strong
Our arms will bring safety
From the nightmares that lurk deep down in your heart
On Lullaby Mountain, we will never be apart

"Harley, please don't leave me, please," Jimmy begs. This time I pull myself back to reality, to feel his lips press firmly to mine as he tries to bring life back into me. "I have you now. We'll get out of here," he says into my hair, protecting me with his arms. I return his kiss, but I can't stay. I want to hear my parents' voices one last time.

"*That's dangerous*," Medicus warns, assisting Finn, giving him all her power to save me.

It's okay, I think, unfocusing my eyes.

J is asleep beside me now, softly breathing. My parents look at each other, smiling, all the love in the world belonging to them and no one else.

Your dreams will soar higher
Taller them any tree
Till they mix with the stars
For you always to see.

"*Pax.*" The word forms in my mind like a whisper as she pulls me into her arms, telling me it's okay as our connection finally holds. My body feels funny, tingly almost. Maybe it's too late.

"It's okay, Harley, you're okay," Jimmy's voice breaks as he lightly shakes me. Finn and Medicus both yell for him to stop.

I want to say it'll be okay. My lips move, but my voice doesn't carry any volume. Jimmy brings his ear to my mouth, his floppy, soft hair tickling my nose.

Even messed up, he's beautiful in every possible way. I think that's why we work so well together. We both once had happy families that are now broken, allowing us to love each other, not only in our happiness but in our pain.

"Get ready to move in a minute," Finn calls.

"Work faster," Jimmy spits, snot and tears falling everywhere. I love him.

"It's okay." I finally get the words out, his eyes no longer frantic as they stay locked on mine. This time, I'm the one holding him in place.

"No!" he says, pushing back his hair. Every time pain fills his words, my heart wants to break, my chest strangling everything inside.

"What was the other thing you promised yourself the first time you met me?" I interrupt, moving my words slowly so all of them can reach his ears and distract myself and him from the inevitable. He bites his lip, hiding their quiver.

"I — I promised I would marry you behind the old church, in the very spot we met, surrounded by the roses and everyone we love," he whispers, his voice breaking on his last words.

Finn says something. Rey and Johnny move back to the door, their faces both wet with tears. Tequila remains steady for all of us, Buckey at her side. Warmth rushes through me, along with the will to live — the need to live. I love him. I can't leave him.

"You're right, you would have scared me off," I cough, and he smiles. "I love you," I breathe, feeling something lock around my consciousness. He presses his lips to mine, my body tingling.

"I love you so much," he sobs. Spit stringing from his mouth as he moves his lips from my forehead, his voice blending with my vision again.

"Let's move," Finn yells, his voice further away, at the other end of the hall, the city, the world.

"We're going to move you. We can't stop, it might hurt, but I promise on the sun you will be okay."

"Help the prisoners," I say, remembering Levi and Mary as my mind fuzzes and scrambles.

"The other group went there," he says, keeping one hand on my arm and one hand on the door as they pick me up. *Good,* I think, letting my body relax, allowing the souls that still hold on to take over.

Tequila takes the lead, moving us forward. My blood pools again, but this time no one stops. I don't want them to. I want them to get out, even if I don't make it with them. My eyes feel heavy, sandbags sewn onto my lashes.

Jimmy's lips move, his eyes falling to mine every chance they get, but I can't hear him. My world has fallen quiet, gone to nothing, as white light covers my pupils and relief silences the din from reaching my ears.

"It's okay," I say one last time, letting my eyes close, the last verse of Lullaby Mountain clear in my mind.

So close your eyes
And in your dreams
We'll take you up to Lullaby Mountain
Where you both shall be free.

I curl up beside J, letting his head rest on my arm as I pull him closer. He smells of cinnamon and apples, and as we lie in the protection of each other's arms, I wonder if he was right. I wonder if Lullaby Mountain still waits for me.